UNSPOKEN

**Center Point
Large Print**

UNSPOKEN

ANGELA HUNT

CENTER POINT PUBLISHING
THORNDIKE, MAINE

This Center Point Large Print edition
is published in the year 2005 by arrangement with
WestBow Press, a division of Thomas Nelson Publishers.

Scripture quotations are taken from the Holy Bible, New Living
Translation copyright © 1996. Used by permission of Tyndale
House Publishers, Inc., Wheaton, IL 60189. All rights reserved.

The text of this Large Print edition is unabridged. In other
aspects, this book may vary from the original edition. Printed in
Thailand. Set in 16-point Times New Roman type.

ISBN 1-58547-685-4

Library of Congress Cataloging-in-Publication Data

Hunt, Angela Elwell, 1957-
    Unspoken / Angela Hunt.--Center Point large print ed.
      p. cm.
    ISBN 1-58547-685-4 (lib. bdg. : alk. paper)
      1. Gorilla--Fiction. 2. Animal welfare--Fiction. 3. Human-animal communication--Fiction.
    4. Large type books. I. Title.

PS3558.U46747U57 2005b
813'.54--dc22

                                                                                2005016643

I want to know who I am—
and what it was that made me that way.
—CREDITED TO ANTHROPOLOGIST LOUIS LEAKEY,
in the 1988 film *Gorillas in the Mist*

Ask the animals, and they will teach you.
Ask the birds of the sky, and they will tell you.
Speak to the earth, and it will instruct you.
Let the fish of the sea speak to you.
They all know that the LORD has done this.
For the life of every living thing is in his hand,
and the breath of all humanity.
                    —JOB 12:7–10

1

I am writing this under duress.

My brother the lawyer says *duress* is the wrong word, because it implies threats or illegal coercion, and he hasn't exactly put a gun to my head and forced me to sit at the computer. He has, however, suggested that the act of recording the events of the last few months might help them form a cohesive whole and make sense. I'm not sure they can ever be understood in terms of human reason.

I am certain of one thing—after reading this, my academic colleagues will have a riotous laugh at my expense and consign these pages to the recycle bin. Some will fly to their computers and fire off scathing rebuttals to *Scientific American* and *Anthropology*; others will send snide e-mails to researchers on the other side of the globe, complete with smirky emoticons and flocks of exclamation points. People I have spent years hoping to impress will spread vicious gossip about me for a few weeks, then wipe my work from their conversations with the same disdain with which they wipe their soiled shoes.

Crackpot. Pretender. Glorified zookeeper—they'll call me those names plus a few unprintable variations. They'll accuse me of anthropomorphism, hypocrisy, and religious zealotry. They'll petition the university to deny me the PhD for which I've sacrificed every semblance of a normal life over the last several years.

As I said, I'm writing under duress.

Psychologists claim that the act of dressing events, feelings, and realizations in words can prove therapeutic—perhaps it will. I may be different by the time I complete this memoir . . . I *know* I am greatly changed from the woman I was a few months ago.

All I can ask of you, skeptical reader, is a measure of trust. I would not lie about a story guaranteed to ruin my reputation. I'm a strong believer in objectivity, empirical facts, and pragmatic systems. I've been trained to record demonstrable data, not whim, fancies, or fleeting thoughts. I am, above all, a scientist.

Those are only a few of the reasons why I've resisted the urge to record this story. I'm not sure I can put the experience into words . . .

My brother Rob says I have found my starting point—*words*. Sema, the western lowland gorilla entrusted to my care eight years ago, was fascinated by words. Like Helen Keller, whose intellect caught fire when she connected the water flowing over her right palm with the sign Annie Sullivan was pressing onto her left, Sema fell in love with words the day I taught her to ask for *more* by bringing the fingertips of her hands together. *Do you want more oatmeal? Ask for* more. *Do you want more juice? Sign* more. *Yes, the watermelon is delicious. And you can have* more *if you ask with the sign.*

Critics of animal language studies often claim that primates are merely engaged in mimicry when they speak with whatever means we've taught them, but I saw a spark of comprehension in Sema's button brown eyes that afternoon. She began signing *more* for every desire—more food, more drink, more hugs and kisses.

At the beginning of my study, she was a five-month-old bundle of black fur, an uncoordinated but playful infant. By the time of our first language lesson, she had mastered a teetering version of a knuckle-walk, but she did not walk bipedally unless she could follow in my footsteps and grip the hem of my lab coat. Just like free-living gorilla infants who follow their mothers and hold tight to their rump hairs, Sema tottered behind me and grinned in self-congratulation.

Even after the passing of eight years, she still enjoyed clinging to the back of my lab coat—though by then she did it not out of necessity but affection.

And she continued to love words.

Four months ago, on a cool January afternoon, Sema sat at the computer working on her reading. The program, designed for human preschoolers, flashed a picture on the screen, then offered a series of words. By tapping the appropriate arrow on the keyboard, Sema could match a word to the picture. By clicking the space bar, she could instruct the computer to speak the word she'd highlighted.

When I looked up to check on her, she was grinning at a photo of a golden retriever. The computer offered three word choices: *dog, cat,* or *fish.*

Delighted by the photograph, Sema clapped her hands, content to celebrate the puppy without doing the work. I turned and placed my hand over hers, directing her smooth, thick fingers toward the arrow keys.

"I know you like the puppy," I said, using my no-nonsense voice, "but you can look at pictures when you're done with your work."

She pulled her hand free of mine. *Gorilla finished,* she signed in American Sign Language.

"Oh no, you're not." Laughing, I reestablished the pressure of my hand on hers. "Which word matches the picture?"

As Sema studied me, I knew she was debating the wisdom of defiance. Because gorillas are social animals, an individual's status in the group is of crucial importance. I had 'established my dominance when Sema passed through the equivalent of a human child's "terrible twos." I had been firm but loving, using time-outs, redirection, and playtime deprivation to discipline my charge's willful urges. Sema still occasionally tested me, but not often, and her maturity was a good thing. At five-six, I stood seven inches taller than my girl, but my 120-pound frame could not have withstood a purposeful pounding from a muscular 250-pound gorilla.

After deciding to be a good girl, Sema pressed the proper keys, then grinned at me. *Dog.* The computer's monotone voice filled the trailer. *The dog is sleeping in the sun.*

"You'd like to be sleeping now, wouldn't you?" I gave her shoulder an affectionate squeeze. "I think we're almost finished. Are you ready for your nap?"

Sema opened her mouth in a wide smile that revealed

her pretty pink tongue, and then lifted her hands from the keyboard. *Sema play outside?*

"Oh, sweetie." I pointed toward the window, where raindrops streaked the glass behind the protective chain-link mesh. "You don't want to play in the rain, do you?"

Sema spread her thumbs and pinkie fingers into the *Y* sign and shook both hands. *Play play play.*

I laughed. "Okay, you've worked hard today, but let's play inside. Why don't you get something from your toy box?"

Pleased to be released from the computer, Sema dropped from her stool and knuckle-walked to the big wooden crate that held her toys. I moved to the counter where my notebooks waited—I needed to record her new sentence constructions while they were still fresh in my mind. Dian Fossey, the courageous anthropologist who gave her life to protect the endangered mountain gorillas living near Africa's Virunga volcanoes, had always typed up her research notes at each day's end. Since her brutal murder in 1985, she had become a legend . . . and an inspiration to me and thousands of other researchers who adore gorillas.

I had just reached the bottom of the page when I heard the clang of the mailbox. I opened the trailer door and leaned into the rain long enough to wave at the mailman and pull a stack of damp letters from the box.

Sema looked up when I closed the door. *Letter for Sema?*

I flipped through the envelopes, then shook my head.

"Don't think so. All for Glee."

Sema looked out the window, probably hoping the mailman would return with a treat for her; then she picked up her human baby and stood the doll in an empty plastic basin. She was pretending to give the baby a bath, an activity she had witnessed on television.

Knowing the doll would keep her busy for a while, I glanced through the letters—by some quirk of technology, two were addressed to "Sema Granger" and contained offers for credit cards. Another company offered Sema a free medium pizza with the purchase of a large. I considered giving those letters to my girl, but she'd only shred and eat them. Like most people, she had the good sense to prefer meaningful correspondence.

I paused as a familiar return address caught my eye— The Thousand Oaks Zoo, Clearwater, Florida. For an instant my stomach tightened, then I tossed the letter into a basket on top of the refrigerator. Let it collect dust with the other Thousand Oaks letters.

One other envelope caught my attention. Addressed to me, it had come from the University of South Florida—a friendly reminder that all doctoral candidates had a limited time to complete their dissertations. "According to our records, you have already been granted two extensions. We will therefore expect your dissertation within twelve months of the date on this correspondence . . ."

Twelve months. How was I supposed to postulate, research, and document an earthshaking discovery in only twelve months? To date I had been playing catch-up; Sema and I had yet to cover new ground.

I tossed the letter onto the counter, then pitched the rest of the mail into the trash and returned to my journal. My pen scratched across the blank surface of a new page, automatically inserting the date, then my thoughts slowed. In some dim recess of my mind, a group of neurons not occupied with journal writing wondered if I should open the letter from Thousand Oaks. After all, my former employer still technically owned Sema . . . but I had asked my brother to handle the zoo. When a girl had a crack lawyer at her disposal, she didn't have to worry about letters, no matter how many might collect atop the fridge.

"Give gorilla hot cookies," I wrote. *Sema consistently demonstrates the proper use of adjectives as modifiers.*

I glanced up as someone jiggled the doorknob. Sema looked up too, distracted from her play, and I lifted a restraining finger as I walked to the peephole. "Let me see who it is, sweetie."

"Glee!" Through the door I heard my brother's muf-fled voice. "For heaven's sake, I'm drowning out here."

"Oh, good—guess who's come to visit?" Grinning at Sema, I unlocked the door and threw it open. My brother stood outside, a sheet of dripping newspaper over his head.

"About time," he grumbled, stamping his way into the trailer. He paused to wink at Sema. "Hey, big girl. You got a hug for your Uncle Rob?"

"Wait a minute." I eyed him with suspicion. "Are you healthy?"

"As a horse."

"Anybody in your office sneezing?"

"Not a soul, Glee. You don't think I'd come here bearing cold germs, do you?"

He advanced toward Sema with a lawyer's ingrained confidence, but I couldn't help but worry. Gorillas are notoriously prone to respiratory infections, and because they've not developed our level of resistance, captive animals succumb to human viruses and bacteria even more easily than people do. If I had to go out during cold and flu season, for the next several days I always wore a surgical mask when I worked with my girl.

Rob approached Sema, waited for her to give him an open-mouthed gorilla smile, then knelt at her level. She wrapped her arms around him, nuzzled his cheek with her lips, then pulled away to show him her baby doll.

"That's a nice baby." He grinned. "But where are her clothes?"

"Sema doesn't seem to see the need for clothes," I told him. "Besides, I think those outfits are too tiny for her fingers to manipulate."

When Rob stood, Sema lowered her head and sniffed his coat pocket.

"Uh-oh—are you looking for a treat?"

Sema's eyes lit with anticipation. *Good gorilla. Give candy.*

I interpreted her signs, then leaned against the counter as Rob asked, "Have you really been a good gorilla?"

Good gorilla. Hurry, hurry, hurry.

"All right. Can't keep a pretty gorilla waiting."

Rob pulled a lollipop from his pocket and offered it to my girl.

I winced. "I've told you not to bring her c-a-n-d-y."

"It's sugar free, Sis, so don't worry."

"Worrying is what I do best."

"Tell me something I don't know."

Rob stepped back, leaving Sema to unwrap the lollipop at her leisure. I understood why she loved my brother—to her, he represented fun and games and treats. I, on the other hand, was the disciplinarian, teacher, and the overseer of vitamins, health, and nutrition. In short, a mother.

I leaned against the counter and met my brother's gaze. "What brings you out here on a day like this?"

"I'm glad you asked." He shucked off his raincoat and hung it on a wall peg, then pulled something from his inner suit pocket. I grimaced at the sight of another envelope imprinted with the Thousand Oaks logo.

"Do we have to talk about that now?"

"It's time, Glee." He pulled out pages and unfolded them. "They're ready to take you to court."

"Let 'em." I lifted my chin. "Sema's been with me eight years, and not once during all that time did they ever mention wanting her back."

"She's still the zoo's property."

"I refuse to think of her as property. She's a child, Rob, and she's rightfully mine. I raised her, nursed her, taught her to speak—"

"Did you ever stop to think that your accomplishments might make Sema even more valuable to the zoo? They want her back, Glee, and I don't think you're going to be able to dodge this indefinitely. They're tired of sending letters; their lawyer filed suit last week." The corner of his mouth lifted. "You should know all this."

I rolled my eyes. "Oh, they've probably tried to tell me. I haven't opened a letter from those people since I asked you to step in."

He scowled, his brows knitting together. "Don't be foolish. Ignoring the problem won't make it go away."

"I'm not ignoring it, I'm giving it to you. You're my lawyer, so do your thing and get those people off my back and out of my life."

Rob sank into a chair. "Surrendering her wouldn't be the end of the world, you know. You're always saying she needs gorilla company."

"A mate, sure. A baby would be wonderful. But if I give her back to the zoo, they'll put her in a preexisting gorilla group. She'll be at the bottom of the pecking order, and that won't be good for her."

Rob glanced at the ceiling as if appealing to a higher authority, then closed his eyes. "Are you afraid she's forgotten how to be a gorilla?"

The question was ridiculous, but I swallowed hard before I answered. "Sema knows she's a gorilla. She'd probably do fine if she was habituated to other animals gradually. But she's been the queen bee around here for so long—"

"You mean she's been treated like a person." Rob's voice dropped in volume. "She eats with a spoon from a plate, she uses a computer, she watches TV. You're terrified she won't know how to relate as an animal."

"She *is* a person," I snapped. "If personhood requires will and emotion and personality, then Sema is every bit as much a person as you and—"

"She's not human, Glee. You can quote all the animal experts you like, but you're never going to convince a Florida judge that Sema is human. She's an animal, therefore she's property."

My voice broke as I acknowledged the sad truth. "Sometimes she talks about visiting other gorillas. I know she'd like to. But she would have no idea how to function in a gorilla family."

"Wouldn't instinct kick in?"

I shrugged. "Maybe . . . maybe not. We don't know a lot about how much gorilla behavior is culturally transmitted and how much is instinctive. So there's no certain way to know if she could function within the zoo's gorilla family."

Though we kept our voices low, Sema knew we were talking about her. She pretended to concentrate on her lollipop, but her eyes kept darting from Rob's face to mine.

Correctly interpreting the lull in conversation as an opportunity to join us, she stuck the candy in her mouth and knuckle-walked to my side. Wearing an expression of pure innocence, she crouched at my feet and smiled. *Sema want gorilla,* she signed. *Sema want gorilla baby.*

"Oh, Sema."

Rob's brows lifted. "What'd she say?"

"She wants to have a baby—a real one."

"Okay . . . isn't that a good reason to send her back to the zoo?"

I gave him what I hoped was a withering look. "I thought you were supposed to be on my side."

"I am on your side. And when I took the case, you told me you wanted what was best for Sema. If she really wants a baby, she's going to have to return to the zoo."

"Not necessarily." I picked up a clipboard and flashed it in Rob's direction. "I've been looking at available captive males around the country. I think I might be able to arrange a transfer and get a male out here, perhaps permanently. Of course, we'd have to build an addition to the play yard and install another trailer at the back of the property—"

"And where are you going to get the money to do this?"

Stymied by the question, I averted my eyes. My inheritance had allowed me to go to college and live independently for years, but expenses and the declining value of mutual funds had nearly depleted my accounts. Rob had used his inheritance to put himself through law school and establish a practice. His investment was producing a healthy income; mine had resulted in a master's degree in anthropology and a talking gorilla that might be taken from me.

"I could go public." I spoke the dreaded words in a whisper. "I could publish the results of my work to date and establish a nonprofit organization. That's what Penny Patterson did when the San Francisco Zoo came after Koko."

My brother's eyes flashed with interest. Even if he hadn't had a gorilla niece, he would have been familiar with the story of Dr. Penny Patterson, who began teaching gorilla sign language in 1972. Koko, who'd been born in the San Francisco Zoo, remained the zoo's property throughout the early years of Dr. Patterson's work. When the zoo pressed their claim for ownership, Dr. Patterson founded The Gorilla Foundation and purchased Koko with donated funds.

Trouble was, I didn't have time to establish a non-profit organization, and I was reluctant to let people know about my work. I identified with Dian Fossey, who had resented outsiders because they often spoiled the natural interaction between her and the mountain gorillas. For my part, I knew I'd hate working with curious onlookers, reporters, or academic rivals breathing down my neck.

"What you need is publicity." Rob nodded for emphasis. "You've kept yourself squirreled away too long."

"I don't want publicity—not yet, anyway. I'm close to a breakthrough, but we're not quite there."

"What are you waiting for? Sema is amazing."

"She's not Koko."

Rob blinked at me. "What?"

I pulled the empty lollipop stick from Sema's lips and tossed it in the trash, then gestured toward the toy box. As she lumbered away, I looked back at Rob. "I don't want to reproduce Dr. Patterson's work. If Sema can only do what Koko can do, the reaction to my dissertation will be one collective yawn."

"They can't expect you to cover as much ground. After all, you've only been working with Sema a few years; Koko's been around forever."

"We *are* going to cover more ground—and soon, I hope, because I'm supposed to hand in my paper within twelve months. Sema's making good progress with her reading, but we haven't achieved the goals I'd like to meet. She recognizes words, but sentences . . . well, she hasn't learned that a string of words on a page represents a complete thought. That concept might take a while to master."

Rob settled back in his chair and crossed his legs, resting his ankle on his knee. "You'd better fill me in, Sis. The more material I have to throw at the judge, the better your chance of keeping Magilla Gorilla."

"You really want to hear this?"

"Let me have it."

I shook my head. Despite his affection for Sema, Rob had never shown more than a passing interest in my research; sometimes I thought he considered Sema the world's most exacting pet. His mind didn't wonder about the origin of human life, the mysteries of interspecies communication, and the narrowing gap between humans and the higher primates—no billable hours involved in those thought processes.

Still, if he could convince a judge that my work held unique promise, maybe His Honor would tell the zoo to take a flying leap.

"Okay." I pulled out a chair and sat at the low table. "Koko was a year old when Dr. Patterson began to work with her, but I started signing to Sema when she was only days old. She learned her first sign at seven months. And studies have shown that babies—primate *and* human—absorb the basics of language in those very early stages. Koko is amazing, but Sema has come just as far in half the time—undoubtedly because I spoke to her, read to her, and signed to her when she was still an infant."

Rob pulled a leather-covered notepad from his coat pocket and clicked a silver pen. "And this is important because?"

"Because language is one of the things that has always separated humans from animals. Because animals don't speak a language we can understand, we have assumed they don't feel grief or longing. We've assumed they have little or no memory, can't conceive of the future, or possess self-awareness. There are some people who still think animals don't feel pain! I intend to prove there's not such a great gulf between us."

Rob stopped writing. "You're not trying to teach Sema how to *talk,* are you?"

"Not verbally. Others have tried with chimpanzees and found them unable to pronounce most English sounds—one couple needed six years to teach a chimp four words. But gorillas have their own verbal language—screams of alarm, belches of contentment, grunts of rebuke, high-pitched barks that signify curiosity, aggressive roars, and playful chuckles. In time, as gorilla sign language combines with natural verbal sound and signing mothers teach their offspring, gorillas could develop a hybrid language nearly as complex as our own."

Rob kept making notes, but from the sudden arch of his brow I knew he found my ideas far-fetched.

"The cultural transmission of language isn't as far-out as you think, Rob."

"No?" His voice cracked, then he let out a whoop that made Sema drop her beloved plush bear. "Your honor, I'd like you to meet my sister, Dr. Doolittle—I mean, Dr. Granger. She not only talks to the animals, she's convinced they want to talk to us."

I crossed my arms. "Animals already talk to each other. Dolphins, parrots, whales, and gorillas in the wild know how to communicate. Their methods vary in sophistication, but they have no trouble getting their message across—"

"Spare me—I think I've caught the gist of your argument." He closed his notebook. "Let me play devil's advocate for a minute, will you?"

Reluctantly, I nodded.

"The lawyer for the zoo will make much of the fact that gorillas are social animals. He'll say Sema would be happier living in a gorilla family than with you. How would you respond to that?"

I smiled. "Why, Rob—you've been reading."

He snorted softly. "That's the difference between us, kiddo—I read the mail that crosses my desk. The zoo's lawyer has done a great job of spelling out their arguments."

"Why would they tell you what they're going to say?"

"They want to settle this out of court—they don't need the publicity of a trial. So what's your answer?"

I thought before replying. "Gorillas do establish firm family bonds. But Sema has never lived in her natal group. She was born in captivity, taken almost immediately from a mother who proved incapable of nurturing her, and placed in my care. Sema has emotionally bonded to me. I am her family."

"And how do you know you are able to meet her needs?"

"That's an idiotic question."

"Answer it anyway. I know they'll ask."

I inhaled a deep breath. "All living creatures need safety, security, food, shelter, and affection. I've provided those things for Sema for over eight years."

"And how do you know you're providing the best possible care for this animal?"

I scowled. "Don't call her an animal. She's an individual."

"Not according to the law. She was born to one of the zoo's captive gorillas, so she's an animal belonging to Thousand Oaks."

"Slaveholders used that same argument to condone slavery, you know. Slaves weren't considered human until after—"

"We're not about to take up the cause of civil rights and slavery." The teasing light vanished from Rob's eyes. "If you start harping on unrelated social issues, the judge will consider you a troublemaker. You'll lose Sema before you can blink."

"The issues are not unrelated."

"Maybe not, but until science can prove a gorilla has the right to legal personhood, save your breath and help me win. If you go into the courtroom and try to mount a case for animal rights, you're going to lose." He drew a breath. "So—how do you know you're providing the best possible care for this animal?"

I looked at Sema, who had spread her faded Care Bear comforter over the inflated inner tube on the floor. She sat in the center of the circle, arranging the fabric over the tube in a sort of rimmed nest—a truly instinctive habit observed in all gorilla species.

In a few moments, she'd be napping. Under my direction, her days consisted of a predictable, orderly routine: eat, learn, play, rest, and eat again. As her provider, playmate, teacher, and friend, I had become the focus of her world.

On the other hand . . . she had become the center of my world too.

"I know I'm giving Sema what she needs because she loves me." I blinked away a sudden rush of tears. "I can't lose her, Rob. I don't care what you do, but you have to find a way I can keep her."

My brother leaned forward, his elbows on his knees. "I love you, Glee, and I know how much Sema means to you, but have you considered that maybe it's time to give her up? Honestly, kiddo, sometimes I think you're *too* involved with this animal. You have no social life, you don't date, and you have yet to earn the respect you deserve for your work. Maybe you should let her go."

I shook my head. "You can't understand, but that's okay. I didn't realize how involved I'd become until after I'd been working with her a while." I lowered my voice as Sema hugged her plush bear and curled up in her nest. "I don't miss dating, I've never had much of a social life, and soon I *will* write my dissertation and earn my doctorate. Until then, all I can say is . . . Sema's worth it."

Sighing heavily, Rob stood. "Can I use your kitchen to make a phone call? Let me talk to this other attorney—maybe we can work out a compromise."

"Thanks, big brother." I stepped to his side, then rose on tiptoe and kissed his cheek. I caught a whiff of some expensive cologne and smiled—the only scent clinging to my skin and clothing was eau de gorilla.

"I'll stick around until we know something," he said, speaking in a lower tone because Sema's eyes had closed. "Come on up when you're done and I'll tell you what I've learned."

I took his raincoat from the peg on the wall and handed it to him, then stood back and watched him go.

2

While Sema slept, I turned off the computer, put the flash cards away, and swept the remnants of my girl's morning snack (shredded wheat biscuits and Jell-o) from the table and into the trash can. When the trailer had been cleared of clutter from our enrichment time, I snapped the padlocks on the fridge and the cabinet doors, then stood back to make sure I hadn't forgotten anything.

I'd been trying to forget the threat hanging over our heads, but something in my heart melted when my gaze crossed Sema's sleeping form. At 250 pounds, she bore little resemblance to the bug-eyed ball of fluff that had ridden on my hip as an infant, but our connection had never been stronger. When I scooped her up from the bloodied straw where her mother had abandoned her, Sema weighed four and a half pounds. Wet and shivering, she looked like any pink-skinned, helpless infant, and I fell madly in love.

At the time of Sema's birth I'd been a part-time animal technician at Thousand Oaks Zoo. As a graduate student working toward a degree in anthropology, I'd been heavily influenced by Dian Fossey and Penny Patterson, so I'd jumped at the chance to work with the higher primates. The area of language development fascinated me, and in Sema I saw an opportunity to follow in Dr. Patterson's trailblazing footsteps.

After a week of caring for the abandoned infant, however, ambition became the least of my motivations. In the first few days of Sema's life, her survival was all that mattered. Captive gorillas do not always make good mothers, but inexperienced graduate students are not much more qualified. I broke several rules when I ventured into the gorilla night room and snatched Sema; I broke others when I insisted on caring for the infant myself. Fortunately, the gorilla curator was not eager to undertake the twenty-four-hour care of a newborn, so I became Sema's nanny. I moved a cot into the office area, learned how to bottle feed a gorilla infant, and pestered the zoo veterinarian until we found a formula that suited Sema's finicky stomach. In the back of my mind, I hoped the intense experience would help us bond, but I had no idea how completely our lives would intertwine.

I nursed her, played with her, crooned to her. With Sema nestled in my lap, I read picture books aloud, watching with delight when her round brown eyes began to focus on the brightly colored pages. As she grew older, I signed to her, then manipulated her fingers and showed her how to form the signs I was using. Because gorilla hands are shaped differently than human hands—the thumb is farther away from the fingers—we modified standard American Sign Language, also known as Ameslan, to create signs Sema could use and understand. During her first year, she learned an average of one new sign per month.

Since sign language is not an exact mode of communication, interpreters primarily derive the meaning of basic signs from context. Fluent signers develop their own "shorthand," just as we do in spoken speech, and when teaching Sema, I didn't bother with conjunctions such as *and* or worry about pronouns like *you, I,* or *him* and *her.* Neither did we trouble with tenses, which are designated by time indicators. Because Sema and I spent so much time together, we had little trouble understanding each other.

After a year, I realized I could only do so much while

Sema lived at the zoo. The gorilla curator had kept her out of the general gorilla population, but I knew he'd be unable to justify the expense of maintaining a gorilla that remained inaccessible to the public. He suggested that I arrange a demonstration of Sema's linguistic abilities, and after Alden Johnston, the zoo director, saw how far my girl and I had progressed, he graciously allowed me to transfer Sema to an environment where we could continue our work without interruption.

Mr. Johnston and I sealed the deal with a handshake—I would cover the expense of Sema's training, medical care, and food while the zoo retained ownership. "We have plenty of gorillas," Dr. Johnston told me as Sema toddled behind me and clung to the back of my lab coat. "What we don't have is an abundance of visionary researchers. Take her, my dear, and let us hear from you every few months. We're expecting great things."

With Dr. Johnston's generous encouragement ringing in my ears, I used a chunk of my inheritance to buy a small house on an acre of rural land. I put an empty trailer beside the house, arranged for a contractor to build a gorilla-sized playground complete with swings, elevated platforms, and hanging ropes, and moved Sema into the trailer nestled beneath a hundred-year-old live oak. We covered the windows with mesh fencing, replaced the carpeting with linoleum, and installed an exercise bar in the space that would be Sema's bedroom. Sema and I were both thrilled with the exercise bar—she had been using my body as a jungle gym, and my muscles needed a break.

After settling in, Sema and I began the serious work of teaching, learning, and playing—after all, a wise teacher makes learning fun, and Sema loved to play.

To my great delight, by her third birthday Sema had begun to invent her own signs. One of my proudest moments occurred when she pointed to a bracelet I was wearing and called it an *arm ring*. On another occasion she pointed to my hairbrush and called it a *scratch comb*.

Because Dr. Patterson's Koko loved kittens, I introduced Sema to a friend's cat, only to have her back away and shake her head *nooooo*. My girl, I discovered, preferred dogs and puppies. But she used her innate dislike of felines creatively—once I fed her an olive, only to have her spit it out and tell me she hated those *cat grapes*.

While we learned together, I kept an eye on Dr. Patterson and the much older Koko. Koko took photos for *National Geographic*; she appeared in television documentaries and held online chats with astonished fans. As people watched Koko think, speak, and paint surprisingly realistic paintings, they began to understand how much humans and the higher primates had in common.

In the last decade of the twentieth century, gorillas moved from obscurity into the international spotlight. The film *Gorillas in the Mist*, featuring the story of Dian Fossey's life and work, helped focus the world's attention on the plight of endangered gorilla species. Zoos that had previously displayed gorillas in steel cages spent millions to create habitats that would not only give the animals room to roam but present them with interesting challenges. Best of all, zoos began to exhibit their gorillas in groups. Animals that had spent years battling boredom in solitary confinement found themselves reestablishing contact with others and creating families.

Far from the hot light of gorilla publicity, I taught; Sema learned. Her vocabulary grew; she learned to read simple words and produce vocal speech through a computer. I finished my master's degree and began working for my doctorate.

By the time we entered our eighth year of partnership, I had finished the required coursework for my degree. All that remained was my dissertation, but Sema and I hadn't quite accomplished my objectives.

My grand plan was simple—I wanted to step beyond Dr. Patterson's work and teach Sema to read simple sentences. I dreamed of the day when my girl would be able to pick up a copy of *Green Eggs and Ham* and sign the story to a class of kindergartners.

Sema's ability to read would imply much more than a simple facility with language—reading would demonstrate that gorillas could imagine, assimilate abstract concepts, and even appreciate meter, rhyme, and humor.

When I could demonstrate that gorillas possessed the intellectual and emotional range of human children, I would publish a book that would establish my place in the annals of anthropology. Offers to speak and write and consult would pour in, along with a steady income. Sema would be able to relax; we would grow old together on my one-acre tract.

One day I would retire, knowing that with a little help from Sema and Dr. Seuss, I had forever bridged the gulf between humans and animals.

Satisfied that Sema was sleeping soundly, I flipped the light switch and stepped onto the small wooden porch outside the trailer. The rain had stopped. The exercise area to my right lay under a blanket of quiet; the tire swing stirred in the breeze. Central Florida had proven to be a wonderful place for raising gorillas—given the species' susceptibility to pneumonia and other respiratory infections, the mild climate was perfect. The heat could be stifling, particularly in late summer, but Sema's ancestors came from equatorial Africa. With their shorter body hair, smaller nostrils, and narrower chests, lowland gorillas were better adapted to the sultry climate than Fossey's mountain-dwelling friends.

I left Sema's trailer and strode across the field of ankle-high grass. Rob's BMW looked out of place on my property—one gleaming boy toy among so many gorilla-sized playthings—but my brother had never been shy about flaunting the fruits of his labor.

Thoughts of Rob reminded me of the zoo, the letters from the difficult and extremely unimaginative new director, and the threat of losing Sema. A cloud settled over my brain, as oppressive and dark as the sky overhead. I wanted to rant and rave, but I couldn't yell at Rob. He had warned me that I'd have to face the zoo officials sooner or later . . . I suppose I'd hoped that if I kept tossing their letters aside, they'd eventually give up and leave me alone. Mother always said it took two to tussle, and tussling was the last thing I wanted to do.

A sudden thought quickened my step as I hurried toward the house. Rob was on the phone when I came through the kitchen doorway, but he lifted his pencil in greeting as I wiped my feet on the rug.

"I'll present this to my client." He glanced at a scrawled page in his notebook. "We'll get back to you. Thank you for your time."

He lowered the phone, then drew a deep breath.

"Wait." I slipped into the chair at the head of the table. "Before you tell me what they said, listen to this—why are they so all-fired interested in having Sema back now? I could see why they might want her if they were developing a new habitat or something, but I think the gorilla population at Thousand Oaks has remained steady over the last few years. They've had a couple of deaths, but they've also had new additions. They're not short on animals."

Rob lowered his pencil. "I asked about that. They said Sema is now breeding age, so she needs to be habituated to a gorilla group."

I shook my head. "I don't buy it. They already have two mature females, and both have bred successfully. There is no shortage of western lowland zoo gorillas, so what's their real motivation?"

Rob shrugged. "All I know is what they've said, but I can tell you this—they are determined to see this thing through. Their lawyer filed suit, but he's willing to settle. He seems to think you wouldn't want this to go to trial."

"If it means being allowed to keep Sema, I'd like nothing better."

Rob picked up his pencil and rolled it between his fingers. "Brad Fielding's name came up."

I stared at Rob. "What's Brad Fielding got to do with anything? He's in San Diego."

"Not anymore—he's been working for Thousand Oaks for about six months. He's the new gorilla curator."

I brought my hand to my mouth.

Rob cocked a brow. "Want to tell me the story behind that look, or are you going to keep me in the dark? I know you two used to date."

I snorted. "I don't think you can call what we did *dating*—all we ever did was argue."

"What about?"

"Everything. Fielding's a zoo guy down to the bone. He lives and dies by rules and policies, and I drove him crazy because I couldn't care less about the rules. We did go out a couple of times, but mainly to argue about the animals."

"So . . . do you think they're involving him in this dispute because he's now in charge of the gorillas? Or is there something else I should know?"

I closed my eyes and exhaled a deep breath. "Fielding and I got along pretty well at first, but we had a huge blowup when Sema was born. He was on duty that night; he saw that Amma had given birth. When he came into the office and told me, I freaked. He wanted to leave the baby in the night room, hoping Amma would catch on and start nursing. I wanted to take the baby out right away—every minute we let her lie there, she would grow weaker. I knew that most mothers pick up their infants immediately and start nursing, but Amma was completely uninterested. Since I'd heard reports of mother gorillas eating their young, I didn't think we had any time to waste."

Rob's eyes rested on me, alive with speculation. "So what happened?"

I shrugged. "Fielding had more authority, so I shouldn't have done anything. But when he picked up the phone to call the vet, I slipped out of the office and went into Amma's night room. She was asleep, so I grabbed Sema and ran out. Fielding was furious when he saw me with the baby. If Sema had died, I'd have been fired for sure—I think Fielding wanted to fire me anyway. Lowly part-time techs, you see, weren't supposed to enter the night rooms when the gorillas were inside, and we weren't ever supposed to touch the animals. But I knew I had to do something."

"Good grief, Glee—I knew you were a troublemaker at home, but I had no idea you broke rules at work."

I shook my head. "I knew I was risking my neck and my job, but if you'd seen her, Rob, lying helpless in that straw . . ." I looked away as a lump rose in my throat. "I'd do the same thing again, no matter what Brad Fielding says. No way I could sit there and do nothing."

"Why did they make such a big deal about what you

did—couldn't they return the baby after you checked it out?"

"Not really. A mother who isn't interested in an infant at birth isn't likely to develop an interest after time has passed."

"So . . . Fielding could testify that years ago you broke the zoo's rules and disobeyed his order. Could he do any other damage?"

"If he's honest, he'd have to admit I've always had the animals' best interests at heart. But I don't trust him, especially if he's working for Thousand Oaks again. He could say anything."

Rob glanced at his notes. "What do you know about Kenneth Matthews?"

I gave my brother a black look. "He's been the zoo director for about three years. I don't know him personally, but the fact that he's pressing for custody of Sema proves he's nothing like Dr. Johnston."

"Do you know much about him?"

"Just that he's a retired businessman and a politician. I see his picture in the paper all the time—he's always attending parties to raise money for the zoo's educational and conservation programs."

"That's a good thing, isn't it?"

"Sure, if the money benefits the animals. I don't think raising thousands of dollars for more lemonade stands in the park is terribly commendable."

Rob gave me a *let's-be-reasonable* smile. "I think your prejudices are showing."

"Okay . . . he has done some good things. I haven't

followed the news too closely, but I do know Thousand Oaks has won certification from the American Zoo and Aquarium Association since he took over. AZA approval is a big deal, and it will do a lot to elevate the zoo's status. But I reserve the right not to like the guy."

"Well . . ." Rob shifted his position in his chair. "I've been thinking a lot about this, Sis. These folks from the zoo aren't going to give up on their gorilla—they want her, and they want her as soon as they can get her. But if what you say about Ken Matthews is accurate, perhaps we can offer to buy Sema."

I felt the corner of my mouth twist. "We're not all made of money, Rob. I can't afford to buy her. Besides, I'm afraid they'll ask for more than a reasonable fee. They'll say Sema is worth more because of her linguistic abilities."

"I could lend you the money."

Overwhelmed by the unexpected gesture, I gaped at my brother. "I don't think that's a good idea."

"Why not?"

How could I explain? Cheri, my pencil-thin sister-in-law, loved my brother . . . and his money. You wouldn't have to be psychic to pick up her conviction that I'm insane and Sema's nothing but a smelly ape.

I offered a less hurtful explanation. "Thanks, but no thanks. I can't take a loan from you, because I have no idea when I'll be able to pay it back."

"Call it a gift, then. We could establish that nonprofit foundation you mentioned, and I could write the amount off on my taxes."

From the width of his grin, I strongly suspected he was teasing. Would have served him right if I took him up on his offer, but I couldn't. First, Cheri would never forgive him . . . or me. Second, it wouldn't be fair.

When our parents died in '95, their will directed that the estate be evenly divided between me and Rob. Everything Rob has brought in since then is his, hard-earned and well-deserved.

I gave my brother an indulgent smile. "I'm not going to take your money, Rob, so forget it. You and Cheri probably need every dime to pay off that McMansion you're living in."

He waved away my concern. "We're doing okay. And the house wasn't as expensive as you seem to think it was."

Under other circumstances, I'd have argued the point. Six months ago Cheri persuaded Rob to sell their modest home in an older part of town and move into a gated golf course community. I kept asking Rob when he was going to take up the sport; he kept insisting he was still looking for the perfect pair of plaid pants.

Touched by his concern, I reached for his hand and squeezed it. "You're doing enough representing me pro bono. Let that be your charitable contribution for my cause."

His eyes melted into mine for a moment, then he closed his notebook. "Tell you what. Let me work on this a couple of days, and then I'll get back to you. We'll do our best to hammer out a satisfactory agreement."

He stood, paused at the window to check the weather,

then came around to squeeze my shoulder. "Hang in there, kiddo. I'll be in touch."

I placed my hand over his. "Rob?"

"Yeah?"

"Whatever you do, know this—defeat is not an option. Losing Sema would be like having my heart ripped out."

He bent to place a kiss on the top of my head. "I know, Sis. I know."

3

The next three days passed in a quiet blur. Rob didn't call, but neither did I receive any threatening letters from Thousand Oaks and their lawyer.

Though my heart felt as though it were beating on borrowed time, Sema and I maintained our daily routine. We read, played, and ate together as if nothing in the world were wrong.

I hoped for a miracle, but I couldn't escape my pragmatic nature. One afternoon I buckled Sema into the passenger seat of my four-year-old Honda CRV and considered driving to Mexico. Why not take my girl and run? The state police would put out an Amber Alert if I snatched a child, but no one was likely to alert the authorities because a woman had skipped town with a gorilla.

We settled for a trip to Tampa and back. I told myself we were going because Sema loved looking for dolphins in the bay as we drove over the long Howard Franklin

Bridge. That night, though, I lay in bed and wondered if we'd taken a test drive for our great escape . . .

No. I've heard mothers complain about how hard it is to travel with all the equipment required for babies; traveling with a gorilla is far more involved. Sema would need her nesting material, her toys, her books, and her computer. I would need my journals, my records, and daily access to pounds and pounds of fresh produce . . .

We couldn't run.

On Friday morning, I checked my watch, then turned to Sema: "Do you want to wear your necklace?"

Her eyes brightened. She moved to the cabinet where I kept her leash and tugged at the door. While I put my journal away, she pulled out her leather collar and brought it to me, grinning her pink gorilla grin.

"You're excited, huh? I don't blame you. Looks like it's going to be a beautiful day. But you'll need your sweater, sweetie. It's cold outside."

The forecast called for a high of sixty degrees. While thousands of vacationing Canadians in our coastal county found sixty degrees positively balmy, this was sweater weather for an equatorial gorilla—especially one who lived year-round in a climate-controlled trailer. I couldn't risk Sema catching a cold.

While I fastened her collar, my squirmy girl reached toward the closet again. When I had finished fastening her "necklace," she leaned toward the storage space and pulled her orange sweater from a hanger. She had two sweaters—one orange, one blue, both size extra large—but orange was her favorite color.

She grinned as I helped her slip it on, then she signed *pumpkin.*

I laughed. "Yes, it is the color of a pumpkin."

Give more pumpkin?

For a minute I thought she wanted another sweater, then I realized she was thinking of food. Pumpkin was one of Sema's favorite treats, but they are hard to find in January.

"Sorry, girlie, but they don't sell pumpkins in winter." I lifted the end of her leash, then slipped the loop over my wrist so I could sign as I spoke to her. "We have another treat today. Some people are coming to see you—friends from the college. You'll be a good girl while they visit, won't you?"

Sema tilted her head in a thoughtful pose. *Sema good gorilla. Sema love people.*

"Yes, I know you do. These people are going to talk to me and watch you play. I know they'll think you're beautiful."

Sema pretty gorilla. Sema love people. Sema love Glee.

Sema turned toward me, a purposeful pucker on her mouth. Not one to miss my cue, I bent and touched my lips to hers, then felt the strength of long gorilla arms twining around me.

"I love you, Sema," I whispered close to her ear. "Now let's go outside and play."

Sema was happily looking for edible treats I'd hidden

in her enclosed play yard when seven graduate students arrived. They had been sent by Dr. Eugene Wharton, my anthropology prof at the University of South Florida. I had completed my master's degree under Dr. Wharton's guidance, and occasionally he asked me to hold lectures for promising young researchers.

Two of these students, Dr. Wharton had told me on the phone, were planning to spend the summer working at the Karisoke Research Center, a remote African outpost established by Dian Fossey. They would be studying and interacting with mountain gorillas, so they needed to learn as much as possible before trekking into the jungle.

I ignored a twinge of jealousy as the students grabbed folding lawn chairs and gathered around me in a semicircle. I would love to visit Karisoke myself . . . one day. But like most women with children, I'd had to make tough choices.

Living with Sema was better than a thousand trips to Africa.

When the students had settled, I gestured toward my girl and launched into my standard lecture. "Sema is a western lowland gorilla, subspecies *gorilla gorilla gorilla*. She was born at the Thousand Oaks Zoo to a first-time mother who had no idea what to do with an infant. When I looked into the night room where her mother had given birth, I found Sema lying motionless while her mother slept—after having eaten the afterbirth. Afraid the mother might try to eat the infant, I stepped in, scooped up the baby, and wrapped her in a towel . . . and that's when Sema and I first met."

I clasped my hands and studied my guests. Most of them wore the half-bored expressions of young intellectuals woodenly fulfilling a course requirement, so I couldn't tell if they'd come out of genuine interest or because Dr. Wharton threatened them with failure if they didn't show up.

I turned toward the play yard, where Sema had balanced on the plastic roof of her Little Tykes playhouse. "She's really lovely, don't you think? That sweater is her color."

Seven faces swiveled toward the enclosure. Aware that she now had an attentive audience, Sema clapped, then grabbed a hanging rope and sailed from the playhouse to a platform mounted on the wire wall, an acrobatic black-and-orange blur. When one of the girls applauded, Sema grinned, then dropped to the ground and knuckle-walked over to her playhouse. There she sat on the grass and picked up a bedraggled picture book.

I propped my elbow on my blue-jeaned knee and continued with the condensed version of our shared history. "You may think I'm overly sentimental, but I sensed a special connection with the infant the moment I lifted her into my arms. I suggested we name her Sema—the name means *to speak* in Kiswahili."

One of the students—a thin girl with spiky red hair—leaned forward. "What was your position at the time? I mean, what did you do at the zoo?"

"I was a graduate student at the university"—I smiled

to acknowledge the link between us—"working part-time at the gorilla pavilion. I spent a lot of time off the clock, though, after Sema arrived. Newborn mammals are demanding no matter what their species."

The three women twittered at this while the faces of their male companions registered varying degrees of indifference. Why should these guys worry about the care of infants? If they were anything like the young men I knew in school, they were more concerned about eventually becoming big names than exploring and overcoming the elements that separate us from others in the animal kingdom.

"She's awfully *big*," one of the guys said. He crinkled his nose as he gestured to the trailer. "How can you live with her in there? Isn't she . . . you know, unpleasantly aromatic?"

I forced a laugh. "Gorillas do have a unique scent—sort of a musty, sweet smell, like rhubarb pie. After a while, you either grow to like it or you scarcely notice it. After all, I'm sure we smell strange to gorillas. And the trailer is Sema's home. Though I spend a lot of time with her, I live in a house." I considered pointing to my home under the oaks, then thought the better of it. I liked my privacy, and if Dr. Wharton had described me as some kind of brilliant and successful researcher, the sight of my one-bedroom cottage might disappoint a student who dreamed of fame and fortune.

My suspicions about my former professor were partially confirmed when the redhead looked up from a sheet of typewritten notes. "Dr. Wharton says your research is unique among those who focus on primates. We watched a video of Dr. Patterson working with Koko, but Dr. Wharton says your project is different."

"Of course, because Sema is a different individual." I braced my hands on my knees. "I owe a lot to Dr. Patterson and Koko, just as they owe a lot to those who taught sign language to chimpanzees. Koko and Sema have certain things in common—both were born in a zoo, and both had to be taken from their mothers. Sema was much younger, though, and that's the primary difference between them. I had always hoped to be able to teach a gorilla to speak, but I didn't think we'd begin until Sema was much older. But one night I was rocking Sema in the room we used as a nursery because she was fidgety and wouldn't sleep. So I tucked her into the crook of my arm, pulled a picture book out of my bag, and read her a bedtime story. I figured if the ritual calmed human babies, why wouldn't it calm a gorilla?"

An eager look flashed in the girl's eyes. "Did it work?"

"It didn't put her to sleep, but at some level she began to assimilate words. I had read about researchers at the Georgia State University Language Research Center who tried to teach Matata, a bonobo, a language consisting of printed symbols. Kanzi, Matata's foster baby, was allowed to remain with his mother, but he appeared completely uninterested in the lessons. When Matata failed to learn, the researchers returned her to the field station. Once his mother had gone, however, Kanzi surprised the team—even though he had appeared to be completely bored during their enrichment sessions, he had learned everything the researchers tried to teach Matata. His younger brain was more receptive to language learning. The younger the subject, the more successful the effort—that's one of the primary tenets in my theory of psycholinguistics."

The redhead looked up, her pencil poised over her notepad. "Could you define that, please? Psycho-whatever?"

"Psycholinguistics is the field of human language development. The subject's age is the primary difference between my work and Dr. Patterson's. I began reading to Sema weeks after her birth; Koko was a year old before Dr. Patterson began to teach her."

The redhead scribbled madly; the other two girls watched Sema. One of the guys nodded with his eyes closed as if he'd missed his nap; two of the others whispered to each other.

Didn't they understand what I was trying to accomplish?

I stood and placed my hands on my hips. "Too many people assume a huge gulf exists between man and the animals," I told them, looking pointedly around the half-circle. "For too long man has been considered the center of the universe, the crowning glory of some deity's creation. Nothing could be further from the truth. Humans are advanced animals, and the gap between mankind and the higher primates narrows every day. Gorillas feel every emotion humans feel. They use tools. They establish and maintain strong family bonds. They mourn when a beloved friend dies. They understand time and space; they retain memories for years. Silverbacks, the guardians of family groups, lay down their lives to defend other group members— in fact, sometimes I wonder if gorillas are *more* advanced than some human beings."

"You *can't* believe," a bearded young man interrupted, "that apes are as intelligent as people."

"I didn't say that," I folded my arms, "but neither are they mindless, soulless creatures put on earth solely for our use and pleasure. Sema has proven that they are teachable, but they also have much to teach us. But before we can make progress on this front, we have to protect them. Far too many gorillas are being killed for sport and for bush meat. Civil war in Africa has decimated the mountain gorilla populations in Rwanda, Zaire, and Uganda. The lowland gorillas' natural habitat is constantly threatened by the encroachment of farmers and cattlemen, and their numbers have declined 70 percent since 1994 because of war in Africa. These are intelligent, peaceful animals, and only time will tell if they can survive their contact with humankind."

The bearded student turned his attention to Sema. "You'd almost think," he said, "she's *reading* that book."

I glanced over at my girl. She had spread a copy of *Blueberries for Sal* on the grass and was signing as she studied the pictures. I couldn't see her hands clearly, but I caught a glimpse of the words *give more berries*.

"She may be retelling the story or reading the words

she knows," I explained. "Or she may be talking to her-self—"

"Whoa," the bearded guy interrupted. "She doesn't *talk*. She waves her hands around, but unless I'm mistaken, no one has actually taught a monkey to *speak*."

Struggling to suppress my rising irritation, I forced a smile. "She's *not* a monkey. And she may not speak with words *you* can understand, but Sema communicates exceptionally well. And she is most definitely engaged in that story."

"Wait a minute." A thin student pushed his glasses up the bridge of his nose. "Are you saying you can teach a gorilla to read? That's impossible."

"Is it?" I lifted a brow. "Sema has already learned how to recognize several written words; we're now working on stringing words together in sentences. She has a working vocabulary of over a thousand signs and understands more than twice as many spoken words. She initiates conversations, uses complete sentences, understands abstract concepts, and routinely scores between seventy and ninety-five on IQ tests. One hundred is considered normal for a human."

"But . . . *reading?*" The red-haired girl shook her head. "That's incredible."

"Not really. Researchers have taught chimpanzees that numerals represent particular amounts of candy. In trial after trial, chimps have learned to choose the larger number and win the larger reward. If chimps can associate numerals with numbers and gorillas can associate words with objects, why can't we teach them that connected words represent complete ideas?"

One of the young men tossed me a look of pure disbelief.

"I know it sounds a little crazy," I assured him. "But fifty years ago most anthropologists would have insisted that animals could never possess anything akin to human language. Yet by learning sign language as well as spoken and printed English, Sema has already become bilingual."

"Does she speak gorilla?" The redhead's eyes sparkled as she watched my girl. "You know—hoots and belches and the like."

I didn't know this student at all, but I was beginning to like her. "That's a great question. Since Sema has never actually lived with gorillas, she is less vocal than most. I've read about gorilla language in Fossey's book—I'm sure you all have—and Sema rarely makes those natural sounds. She signs instead."

I glanced up at the sky, where a scarf of cloud had blown off the sun and left us squinting in the light. I closed my eyes and searched for some profound parting words.

"I think those of you who are going to Africa will have a wonderful time," I told them. "Just remember that these animals are individuals, as unique as we are. We are close kin. In fact"—I gestured to Sema—"did you know humans and gorillas share the same blood types? Our mouths also have the same number of teeth and our bodies the same number of hairs per square inch, though, of course, gorilla hair is longer and

48

coarser. Ninety-eight percent of our DNA is identical to theirs. Why shouldn't we share the same abilities?"

When I looked back, the skeptical student had lit a cigarette. "Are you saying"—he paused to draw on his cancer stick—"your gorilla could read and understand my anthropology book?"

As twin plumes of smoke drifted from his nostrils, I reached out and plucked the cigarette from his hand, then ground it out with a defiant twist of my sneaker. Television had acquainted my gorilla with enough unhealthy habits; I didn't need these students to remind her of one.

With the offending item ground into the dirt, I pasted on a smile. "I'm not sure the average American on the street could understand your anthropology text. Sema is an eight-year-old gorilla with the mental capability of a seven-year-old human child. Though she has reached reproductive maturity, in terms of learning and cognition she is still a youngster." A half-smile curled on my mouth as I scanned the group. "I like to think we're all still children in many respects. None of us is ever really finished with learning, are we?"

The red-haired girl asked a few other basic questions—what did Sema eat, where did she sleep, did she have a favorite toy?—then I glanced at my watch. "If you'll excuse us now, it's time for Sema's lunch. Thank you for coming, and please give my regards to Dr. Wharton."

The students stood and drifted away, but the redhead came toward me, a glow on her fair complexion. She had to be in her early twenties, but she could have easily passed for fifteen.

"Thank you." She extended her hand. "I've been dying to get out here to meet the famous Sema. I'm Claire Hartwell, and I work in the gorilla pavilion at Thousand Oaks."

The name *Thousand Oaks* sent a small gnat of worry buzzing in my brain, but I batted it away and shook the girl's hand. Since she was only a student, she probably knew nothing of my troubles with the zoo's administration.

I made an effort to be pleasant. "You're an animal technician?"

"Yes—that's what you used to do, right? I spend most of my time preparing food for the g's, but every once in a while I get to help with other things. I think gorillas are fascinating—I could work with them forever."

I glanced past her to the mesh wall of the play yard, where the others had advanced to get a better look at my girl. Playing to her audience, Sema had climbed to the rope netting at the top of the enclosure and was somersaulting over the net with no regard for the twenty-foot drop below.

"Show-off," I whispered.

Claire followed my gaze and watched Sema for a moment, then turned back to me. "It was really nice of you to let us come out here. I'm envious of the relationship you and Sema share. At the zoo, you know, we work under a hands-off policy. We watch the g's and take care of them, but we hardly ever get to interact with them, you know?"

I nodded, only half listening as I watched to be sure none of the other students got stupid and decided to stick a hand through the mesh. They were safe as long as Sema was performing her acrobatics, but she could drop to the ground in a heartbeat, and she had no appreciation of her own strength.

"Well . . . thanks again, Ms. Granger. I really appreciate your time."

Claire's voice snapped me back to reality. I'd seen this kind of wide-eyed enthusiasm before, but at least hers was *informed* enthusiasm.

"You're welcome. By the way"—I gave her a thin smile—"how do you like working with Brad Fielding?"

"Brad? You know Brad?"

I nodded. "We worked together before he left for San Diego."

Her smile broadened. "Isn't he the best? Sometimes I think he knows everything about gorillas. And he loves the g's. Really loves 'em."

If he loved gorillas so much, why did he get so mad at me for rescuing Sema? I swallowed the bitter words that rose to my tongue and substituted a smooth reply: "I'm sure he does."

I stepped toward the gate leading into the play yard, effectively ending the conversation. I waited there, biding my time, until the last student got into his vehicle.

When our visitors had gone, I opened the gate and stepped inside. "Sema? Ready for your lunch?"

Sema slipped through one of the holes in the rope net overhead, then crawled hand over hand as if she were crossing a set of monkey bars. When her toes dangled in front of my face, she dropped to the ground, grinning. *People visit more?*

"Not today, sweetie. We're going to have a snack and let you take a nap."

First play ball? She tilted her head and smiled at me, knowing full well I found that look irresistible.

"Okay—but only for a minute."

I jogged across the play yard and found her rubber kick ball, then tossed it underhand. Sema caught it easily, then threw it past me. "You stinker!" I ran for it. "You're trying to wear me out!"

Sometimes I wondered which of us had been the trainer and which the trainee.

When I turned to find her again, Sema was panting in her silent gorilla laugh, her pink mouth and tongue bright in the darkness of her face. *You dirty stink nut,* she signed. *You crazy woman!*

I held the ball, pursing my lips as I beheld the creature I had molded from infancy. I never meant to teach her how to insult me, but, like a human child, Sema has picked up attitudes I never meant to impart.

We played a quick, breathless game of dodgeball. Sema hid behind her playhouse as I sent the ball flying over her head. She retrieved it and launched it into the air. Together we watched it sail nearly to the wire-covered roof, then it arched and landed with a splash in the wading pool five feet to my right. I jumped, but too late, and Sema applauded when water splashed my jeans.

"Sema!" I exaggerated my look of horror. "Did you mean to get me wet?"

Sema make fun. Hurry hurry more play. Throw ball.

"This is fun for you, maybe. Not so much fun for me, especially when it's cold."

"Want me to bring you a towel?"

The unexpected sound of a male voice sent a chill up my spine. I whirled around, expecting to find that one of the grad students had returned, but the man standing outside the enclosure was no student.

Brad Fielding.

For an instant my brain stuttered. Fielding, in the flesh, looking better than he had when we parted so many years ago. He wore his brown hair shorter now, complimenting the spikes of a cowlick that rose at the edge of his forehead in a disobedient spray. His trim physique had not changed much, but though I knew he stood only four inches taller than I, somehow he seemed bigger . . . and far more imposing.

A flash of irritation heated my face. "What are you doing here?"

"I came to see you—and the gorilla, of course." His brown eyes shifted to Sema, who had straightened at the sound of anger in my voice. "How is she?"

"She's fine—and it's time for her lunch."

His mouth tipped in a wry smile. "You make her wear a *sweater?*"

"I don't force her; she likes it. Besides, I don't want her catching cold. And now I'd appreciate it if you'd move away so I can take her inside."

Fielding lifted his hands in a *no harm, no foul* gesture, then stepped back. Not far enough, though, for Sema could still see him.

"It's all right," I told her, signing as I spoke. "He is—" I hesitated. He wasn't a friend, not at the moment. But I'd never had a reason to teach Sema the word *enemy*.

"Would you please move farther back?" I spoke in a voice as cool as the January breeze. "Out of sight would be best. She may not cooperate if she's distracted."

Without replying, Fielding turned on his heel and slid his hands into his pockets. He walked toward the driveway, whistling as if he hadn't a care in the world.

"Come, Sema." I lifted her collar from the box by the gate and fastened it around her neck. "Let's go inside. Would you like some apple juice? After you have your snack, maybe we can read a book."

Sema like juice. Sema like man visit.

"Do you, now?" I grimaced a smile that probably didn't fool her. "You are a nice gorilla, you know that? Come inside and let's get your juice. You can drink it while I get your lunch from the fridge."

Sema and I crossed the short distance from the gate to the trailer, then she climbed the porch steps and bounded inside. I followed and locked the door, then slipped the padlock from the refrigerator to pull out a juice box.

She slipped out of her sweater as I jabbed the short straw through the foil opening. "Here, sweetie."

While she slurped her juice, I pulled her lunch tray

from the fridge and set it on the low table. The arrangement of alfalfa sprouts, carrots, oranges, and green beans sprinkled with cooked hamburger even appealed to me.

Sema set down her juice box and picked up a peeled orange, then bit it as she would an apple.

"Good girl. When you're done, which book would you like to read?"

Pumpkin Patch.

Her signs were sloppy on account of the orange in her hand, but I understood. "*Polly's Pumpkin Patch*? Let me get it."

Sema ate her lunch while I riffled through our library. By the time I found the book she wanted, she had gone into her room and made herself comfortable in her nest.

She grinned when I came through the doorway. *Play tickle?*

I held up the book. "I thought we were going to read."

Hurry, hurry, play tickle.

Sighing, I dropped the paperback and lifted my hands. Wriggling my fingers like some mad tickler gone amok, I whispered the sounds Dian Fossey had used to charm both human and gorilla infants: "Oouchy-gouchy-goo-zoooom!"

On cue, Sema stiffened and lay back, bracing herself for my scrambling fingers. I scurried them over her belly and wriggled them into the wells of her underarms while she convulsed in silent laughter.

While she caught her breath, I offered the book again. "Don't you want me to read about the pumpkin patch?"

Sema took the book, then dropped it into her lap. *Sema look book. Glee find man.*

Not for the first time, I marveled at her stubborn memory. She hadn't forgotten about Brad Fielding.

I gave her a careful smile. "You don't have to worry about him, girlie. I'll find the man while you read your book. And I'll be back when you wake up from your nap, okay?"

Sema didn't answer, but opened her book and studied the first page with an artificially bright interest.

Steeling myself for what was bound to be an unpleasant encounter, I opened the door and stepped outside.

4

I found Fielding standing by his car, one hand in his jacket pocket, the other pressed against the rough bark of an oak tree. "This is a lovely specimen," he called as I approached. "We'd love to have more mature trees like this for the primate habitat."

"You can't have my oak . . . and you can't have my gorilla."

His brown eyes flashed a warning. "She's not your gorilla, Glee. Sema is the registered property of the Thousand Oaks Zoo."

I took a deep breath and flexed my fingers until the urge to throttle him had passed. "That remains to be seen, Fielding. I'm not sure you can actually own a thinking individual. Sema is as cognizant as any child

56

and a great deal more self-determining than many inca-pacitated human adults—"

"I didn't come here to argue philosophy, Glee. I came out of goodwill."

"Goodwill?" I spat the words back at him. "Unless you've come to say I can keep Sema here and continue my work, I fail to see what kind of goodwill you could possibly offer."

He sighed heavily, then leaned against his car with his hands behind his back. "I'm not your enemy; I'd like to be your friend. After all, I think we both want what's best for Sema."

"How would you know what's best for her? You haven't seen her in eight years. You don't know her personality; you don't know what she can do—"

"I've read your quarterly reports—they're impressive. You've done some amazing work."

I took no pleasure in the compliment because I have never trusted praise from an enemy.

"Sema is mature now," he continued, "and you and I both know mature females have strong maternal instincts. She's going to want a baby, and there's no way she can be a mother as long as you keep her separated from other gorillas."

I had no rebuttal for that argument. Sema *did* talk about having a baby, and lately she had begun to carry her dolls even more frequently than she carried her favorite plush bear. She played with all kinds of dolls, human and gorilla and ursine, but I'd caught her trying to nurse her gorilla dolls . . .

"I could find a silverback," I argued in a weak voice.

"You know that's a long shot. Gorillas breed best in extended family groups. You'd need at least another male and another female, and you're not equipped to care for that many animals."

"I'll find a way." I lifted my chin and glared at him with every ounce of determination in my body. "Sema and I have overcome obstacles before; we'll overcome them again. But you're not taking her from me. She's not ready to be introduced to a gorilla group, and frankly, I'm not sure how successful her habituation would be. She knows people better than gorillas."

He looked at me for a long moment without speaking, then straightened and took a step forward. "Listen, I know we didn't part on the best of terms—"

I lifted my hand, cutting him off. "Ancient history. Totally irrelevant."

"I want to clear the air; I don't want the past to cause problems between us. I think this can work out for everyone. I want to respect your work and do what's best for Sema. And I think we can accomplish both those goals by having Sema live at the zoo."

I shrugged. "I disagree. So I suppose I'll see you in court."

"That won't be fun for either of us."

"Doesn't matter. I'm not giving up without a fight."

He stood there, examining my face with considerable absorption, then pulled his hands from his pockets and opened the car door. I strode toward the house, but the sound of his voice stopped me in my tracks.

"If you change your mind, call the zoo and ask for my office, okay?"

Maybe the remark was innocent. Maybe he didn't intend to remind me of his exalted position as gorilla curator—*he had an office!*—but his words rankled nonetheless.

After Fielding left, I hurried to the house, paced for a few minutes in the living room, then grabbed my purse and headed to my car. The interior smelled faintly of gorilla—a stack of Sema's blankets filled the back, waiting for their spin in one of the local Laundromat's commercial washers—but to me the scent was comforting, a reminder of someone I loved.

I shoved the car in reverse and peeled out over the pebbled drive, heading toward Indian Rocks Beach. Sema would sleep for at least another hour, and if she woke before I returned, she'd amuse herself with the books and toys in her room.

After twenty minutes of dodging tourist traffic on Gulf Boulevard, I pulled into the fourteen-unit motel owned by my grandmother, Irene Posey. Paint had weathered out of the fading letters of the sign advertising "Posey's Pink Palace," but the neon No Vacancy sign could be read from fifty yards away.

Unabashedly old, weather-beaten, and comfortable, Posey's Pink Palace sprawled like a drunken floozy between two high-rise condominiums clad in discreet beige stucco. The previous resident-owners (who had called the place "The Pink Shell Motel") had added units whenever and however they pleased, so the overall effect was a haphazard jumble of architecture and shades of Pepto-Bismol.

I parked on the wispy strip of grass that served as an overflow parking lot, then traipsed over the walkway to the ground-floor apartment where Nana lived. Herman the parrot squawked at my approach—"Hey, cutie!"

"You flirt," I told him, moving toward the door marked *Manager*. "You say that to all the girls."

No one stood behind the tall counter in the office, so I pressed the bell that rang in Nana's apartment. Except for the housekeeper who came in each morning to wash linens and clean rooms, my grandmother ran this place alone, serving as manager, reservations clerk, hostess, and concierge. Rob and I often urged her to hire someone to give her a break from the place, but she insisted that as long as she could work, she wanted to work.

I think she enjoyed feeling needed.

A moment later Nana breezed through a swinging door, her face flushed. "Glee! What a nice surprise!"

My mother's mother is not the stout, gray-haired, sixtyish granny depicted in most Norman Rockwell paintings. Irene Posey probably passed sixty a few years back—she would never tell me her age—but no one could deny she had retained a full measure of beauty and grace. Blessed with a model's slim build, she dressed like a college girl and moved with the energy of a woman half her age. She wore her white hair in a stylish layered cut and wouldn't think of leaving her apartment without a minimum of blush and properly applied mascara.

I've caught Nana scrubbing toilets in the apartments on her hands and knees, but even then she managed to look like she just stepped out of a magazine ad. During the off-season, in fact, Nana frequently worked as a catalog model for Dillard's and Burdines. On many a Sunday morning, I have opened my newspaper to find her smiling at me from a black-and-white ad for ladies' sportswear.

She stepped out from behind the counter and wrapped me in a hug. "What brings you out here, child?"

"Not much."

She didn't relax her grip, but steadily focused on me, her eyes as blue as the sweater tied around her shoulders. "You think you can fool your grandmother? Something's bothering you, I can tell."

My gaze drifted from her bright eyes to the ceiling. "Well . . . maybe."

"Is Rob all right?"

"He's fine, last I heard."

"Then it's Sema. How is she?"

"She's good. But it looks like—"

I choked on my words as the bell above the door jangled. A man came in, bringing the scent of the sea with him. He wore red swim trunks, a sleeveless white tee shirt, and leather sandals with black socks. His fair skin was already as pink as Nana's shirt, and I knew he'd be wanting tea bags for his bath before the night was over.

The sunburned tourist removed his bicycle cap,

exposing a painfully pink pate. "Mrs. Posey," he said, speaking in a charming British accent, "the wife and I were wondering if you could recommend a lovely restaurant?"

I suppressed a grin. European travelers gravitated to the Gulf beaches, and they seemed to prefer establishments with a personal touch. Posey's Pink Palace was one of the few remaining owner-operated motels on Florida's west coast.

Nana smiled at her guest. "You can get a quiet dinner at the Hungry Fisherman. Go left out of the parking lot and drive north for about two miles. The food is great and the price reasonable."

"Thanks." The man nodded at me, then shuffled away. I heard Herman call, "Hel-*lo,* baby!" before the door closed.

I met Nana's gaze. "He's going to need tea bags."

"The British have trouble imagining any use for tea outside a teacup." She winked at me. "Don't worry, I've stocked their medicine cabinet with Solarcaine. And now I want you to come inside and tell me what's on your mind. I can fix you a cup of hot chocolate, and I just pulled a pan of cookies out of the oven . . ."

For some reason, cocoa and cookies sounded wonderful.

"Thanks, Nana." Like a little girl, I let her take my hand.

In between bites of the most heavenly oatmeal raisin cookies on the planet, I sat on the sofa and told Nana

62

about the letters I'd been receiving from Thousand Oaks. "Rob is handling things for me," I finished, "but sometimes I think he'd rather I hand Sema over and be done with my research. He seems to feel I need a social life more than I need my doctorate."

"I know you don't want to hear this, hon, but I think he might be right—for now, anyway." Nana's eyes narrowed. "We both worry about you taking care of Sema all by yourself."

I stiffened. "I don't do all the work myself. My vet sends over an assistant if I need help."

Nana lifted her mug and smiled at me over the rim. "You work too hard, Glee. When is the last time you went out to a movie with friends?"

I didn't even attempt to remember. "I don't miss movies. When I need to relax, I go into my room and watch old films on TV. Or Sema and I watch movies together—Disney videos, mostly."

"I wasn't concerned that you're missing movies— I'm concerned that you're missing *friends*. Aren't you even a little tired of planning your schedule around a gorilla?"

I sighed heavily and kicked off my shoes, then pulled my legs beneath me. I knew I could safely ignore Nana's question—this was one of those occasions when she felt she had to say certain things because she was the Responsible Adult.

But I was an adult now, too. And if I wanted to stir things up, I could ask her why she wasted her energy running this rundown motel when she could be living the life of a glamorous widow in a swanky retirement village . . .

I didn't have the energy to argue with her. I'd come to her apartment because something in these jumbled rooms made me feel better.

From the radio on the bookcase, strains of soft music poured into the living room. Some soulful singer sang, "Lord, what a variety of things you have made! The earth is full of your creatures . . ."

I looked toward the window as the song continued: "Here is the ocean, vast and wide, teeming with life of every kind, animals both great and small."

Mr. Mugs, Nana's elderly Chinese pug, chose that moment to prop his two front feet on the sofa and smile at me.

"Hey, Mugs." I scratched him between the ears. "Where's your pal Charlie?"

"Those two." Nana rolled her eyes. "I wouldn't be surprised if Mugsy has found a way to lock Charlie in the closet. The other day I heard screaming and found the poor cat shut up in a bathroom cabinet. Apparently Mugsy opened the door and bumped it shut after Charlie climbed in."

An instant later, Charlie, the tabby cat who adopted Nana two years ago, bounded into the room and leaped onto the back of the sofa. Too heavy to lift more than his forepaws off the floor, Mr. Mugs growled softly as his nemesis draped himself over the top of the cushions and dangled a paw over Nana's shoulder.

Mr. Mugs's frustration erupted in an abrupt bark, to

which Charlie responded by blinking. Once.

I couldn't help laughing. These two castoffs (Mr. Mugs had come to Nana from the Pinellas County Pug Rescue) pretended to despise each other, but more than once Nana and I had come back from shopping to find dog and cat side by side at the window, their eyes intently searching the sidewalk for their best human friend.

Nana was a rescuer. This hand-me-down motel had sheltered many guests (and their pets) over the years, and this cozy apartment had protected me and Rob after our parents died. They perished, in fact, on this beach—on a hot July afternoon of my fifteenth summer, they went for a swim by the fishing pier. They'd been swimming there dozens of times before, but on that day a treacherous riptide caught their tired bodies and carried them out to sea.

Rob had been eighteen that year; he buried his grief in frenzied preparation for college. I had no outlet for my grief, so I shared it with Nana. I moved into this apartment and as we mourned together, I discovered how much we had in common. Nana and I were both independent, we thrived on hard work, and we loved animals. I had always been a little intimidated by my grandmother's striking good looks, but one day as I watched her don leather gloves to rescue a trapped pelican from a cast-off fishing net, I realized that truly beautiful women did not sit on a shelf like gilded china. Truly beautiful women—*useful* women—were more like the simple glazed stoneware that serviced Nana's kitchen table.

After she had freed the bird, Nana smiled at me with sand sprinkled over her arms and blood streaming from a nip above her brow. In that defining moment, I decided the popular girls at school were flakes; the girls who mimicked movie stars and television celebrities were fools.

I wanted Nana's kind of hands-on beauty more than anything in the world.

The memory brought a lump to my throat, so I tickled Mr. Mugs's chin. "You can't chide me too harshly about my love for Sema," I said, my voice thick. "Look at you. I know how much these guys mean to you."

Nana smiled a silent *touché*.

I pulled Mr. Mugs into my lap and leaned back into the sofa cushions. "I guess we both have the animal lover's gene. Maybe it skips a generation."

"Your mother loved animals, too." Nana's voice went soft with memory. "But your father's hardware store kept her busy. Between you, Rob, your dad, and the store, she had her plate full."

I chucked Mr. Mugs under the chin, then wrapped my hands around my cup. "Did she have pets as a kid?"

Nana's smile deepened into laughter. "Oh, lots. Once she brought home two chicks that had hatched in the incubator at her elementary school. In the eighth grade she wrote some scientist and told him she was interested in gerbils; before I knew it, we had received a box of twelve in the mail. Six males, six females—you can imagine the result. I think our family personally populated Pinellas County with the wee beasties."

I smiled as a memory—a safe one—brushed my face like a breeze. I must have been about ten when I found a baby bird on the ground, probably a nestling that had fallen out of a tree. Crying because I didn't know what to do, I carried the baby to Mom, who put it in a shoe box. The bird sanctuary had already closed for the day, but she helped me situate the box under a lamp so the mostly featherless creature could stay warm until morning. We took the helpless little thing to the sanctuary on the way to school the next day, and I remembered feeling cheated because we couldn't care for it ourselves.

Nana was right . . . Mom had loved her animals and her children the best she could. Dad's hardware store never quite reached a level of prosperity, so when she wasn't with us, Mom was at the store working on Dad's books, counting boxes, or weighing nails.

But she had always taken the time to help with the stray animals I brought home.

"A righteous man regards the life of his beast," Nana whispered, idly stroking Charlie.

I looked up, half-convinced she had been reading my mind, but she was gazing into Charlie's eyes and running her nails through the glossy fur at the back of his neck. A new song played on the radio, something surprisingly funky for a religious station.

Piety was another constant with Nana—a trait I had definitely not inherited. Mom and Dad raised us to be churchgoers, but I lost interest in God about the time I entered middle school. My parents forced me and Rob to attend Sunday services, but we sat in the back pew with our arms crossed, our minds steeled to resistance, our faces fixed in matching pouts.

After the funeral, my feelings about God shifted from bored indifference to hot resentment. Nana tried to persuade me to go to church, but I railed against her, screaming that it wasn't fair for Rob to be allowed to skip church at college while I had to go.

As much as I loved my grandmother, I couldn't accept her devotion to a God she proclaimed as loving, kind, and all-powerful. If God had been all-powerful, why hadn't he turned the tide that carried my parents away? If he was kind, why hadn't he blessed my father instead of forcing him to sweat for every dollar he earned? If he was such a master designer, why'd he create an ocean of equal parts beauty and treachery?

Nana tried to explain—I remember her defining the word *sovereignty,* the conviction that everything happens according to God's will—but in the end she quietly retreated, though she opened my bedroom door every Sunday morning while she cooked the best breakfast of the week. Hoping the scents of sizzling bacon, buttery eggs, and cinnamon coffee cake would lure me from bed, she sang as she worked in the kitchen, old hymns about trusting and obeying and following . . .

Not once did I rise to the bait. When she left for church each Sunday morning, the food was cold, the invitation unanswered. By the time I graduated from college, Nana's entreaties, along with memories of a few awkward first dates and the embarrassments of adjusting to a menstrual cycle, had become part of a history I did not want to recall.

I looked up, my face burning with the memory of how much grief I'd caused her. "Know what, Nana?"

"What, dear?"

"I love you."

She met my gaze, her eyes bright with speculation, her smile half-sly. "Feeling a little sentimental today, are you?"

"I suppose I am." I rose from my chair and walked to her side, then bent to press a kiss to her cheek. "Gotta run—Sema will be awake soon. Thanks for the cookies."

"You're welcome, sweetheart. Come anytime . . . because I can always use an excuse to bake a few goodies."

5

On Monday morning I gave Sema her breakfast, dressed in a white blouse and black skirt, and called my vet to see if they could spare an animal tech for gorilla-sitting. They promised to send Ethan, a burly young man Sema knew and liked. By the time he arrived, I was as tightly wound as a fiddler's string.

"Read her some books; let her play with her toys; take her out in the yard if I'm gone more than an hour." I tapped his arm as I sidled past him on the porch. "Make sure she wears her sweater and collar if you go outside.

I should be back in an hour, maybe two—if it's going to be later, you'll have to give Sema her lunch tray; it's on the shelf in the fridge."

Ethan gripped the doorknob and grinned. "No problem. Sema and I always have fun together."

"Okay, then, see you later—I've gotta run!"

I gave him a quick wave and hurried toward my car. Rob had called the night before to tell me about a hastily called meeting in the judge's chambers—an unusual move, he said, but one that might be promising.

"I've been talking to their lawyer," he told me. "And I think we've found a way to settle this situation. Meet me on the courthouse steps at 9:30 tomorrow morning."

He didn't answer when I pressed for details, but told me to be prompt. So at 9:29 I roared into the downtown parking lot, fumbled with change for the meter, then ran for the courthouse in a pair of leather pumps, the dressiest shoes I owned.

Rob came striding down the steps, the sun gleaming off his light-brown hair. He wore a tailored shirt beneath a tan suit that emphasized his athletic build. Looking at him—the image of a successful lawyer—I felt unspeakably grateful he had chosen to study law instead of veterinary science.

"Hi." He slipped an arm around my shoulder and squeezed. "Was it hard to get away?"

I struggled to catch my breath. "It's always hard, and nearly impossible with only a few hours' notice."

He glanced at his watch. "You're right on time. Come on, this way to the judge's chambers."

He charged up the steps, leaving me to scamper behind him. "Are we going to trial?" I called, lengthening my stride to match his pace. "What is this, a preliminary meeting?"

"You'll see." Though he smiled, something in his voice set my teeth on edge.

We passed through a security checkpoint where I suffered the humiliation of having a stranger paw through my purse. I tried not to watch as a man in latex gloves pulled a packet of baby wipes, a banana, and a container of peeled carrots from my bag.

Rob's eyes widened as the guard pulled out Sema's plastic sippy cup. "Good grief, Glee, do you always carry the contents of a small kitchen in your purse?"

"I do when I'm in a rush."

I followed him through the metal detector, wondering why he seemed ill at ease. He hadn't told me much about this meeting . . . did all lawyers keep their clients in suspense?

"Don't play games with me, Rob."

My brother turned and gave me a look of wide-eyed innocence. "What do you mean?"

"If I were a regular client, you'd tell me everything. So lay it out for me now."

He reclaimed his briefcase from a guard and held it with both hands as I waited for my purse. "We'll be meeting with Judge Oliphant, Ken Matthews, and Tom Kremkau, counsel for Thousand Oaks."

I took my bag from a uniformed woman who slid it toward me. "And the purpose of this meeting?"

"I told you—they want to avoid a trial. *We* want to avoid a trial. This pretrial settlement conference is good news for everyone, so relax."

I hooked my purse on my shoulder, then followed Rob down a tiled hall, up a flight of scuffed steps, and down another corridor. We paused before an oak door labeled "Chambers of the Honorable Geoffrey Oliphant."

Rob met my gaze and smiled, then opened the door and took charge with quiet assurance. Leading the way, he approached a young man at a small desk—a law clerk, I presumed. "Robert Granger, counsel for Ms. Glee Granger," he said, producing his card. "And this is my client. We have a meeting with Judge Oliphant."

The clerk accepted his card, glanced at it, then smiled at me. "His Honor is still on the bench," he said, rising. "Mr. Kremkau and his clients have already arrived, so you're welcome to go on in."

Rob nudged the small of my back, propelling me into a book-lined office dominated by a massive desk and high windows. Incoming shafts of morning light blinded me for a moment, but after adjusting my position I saw my adversaries seated in front of the desk—a slender man with dark hair and a briefcase on his lap, almost certainly the lawyer, and Ken Matthews, the director of Thousand Oaks Zoo. Brad Fielding sat next to Matthews. He nodded when our eyes met.

I looked away. Rob hadn't mentioned that Fielding would be present, though his presence made sense. After all, I doubted that Matthews knew the first thing about gorillas, and Fielding was the exhibit curator.

All three men stood as I approached. Ever polite, Rob walked over and shook each man's hand; I nodded to acknowledge them and sank into a leather chair opposite Ken Matthews. Rob was welcome to charm the opposition—that was his job, not mine.

My brother sat beside me as Mr. Kremkau made an offhand remark about the chilly weather. I ignored him, leaving Rob to handle the chitchat. I was wishing I'd brought a book to read when Fielding lifted his hand and waved to catch my attention. "How's Sema this morning?"

Aware that the others were listening, I smoothed my hands on my skirt. "She's fine."

"This cold snap bothering her at all?"

"Not really—she keeps her sweater on when we go outside, and her trailer is heated." Then, not to put too fine a point on my protective care, I added: "You've seen that she's in excellent health."

Matthews, whom I knew more by reputation than acquaintance, folded his hands. By the look of his white hair and lined face, I'd place him in his mid-sixties, but I could see no evidence of weakness in either his face or form. He was as meticulously groomed and self-possessed as a TV talk show host, and his dark suit looked more expensive than Rob's.

He inclined his head toward me, the barest token of respect. "Ms. Granger, it's a pleasure to meet you. I've heard many wonderful things about your work."

So . . . he was going to be charming, too. I was sure

his pleasant approach meant something: we were playing some game, but I didn't know the rules and didn't care to learn them.

"Thanks." I gave him a tight smile, noticing that he didn't mention my quarterly reports I'd filed on Sema's progress ever since taking her from the zoo; I had never shirked a single custodial responsibility. Fielding had read my papers, but apparently Matthews hadn't taken the time.

He's probably been too busy raising money for more souvenir stands.

I looked up as a cleverly disguised paneled door opened and yet another man entered the room. The Honorable Geoffrey Oliphant, I assumed, walked to the massive chair behind the desk, his unzipped black robe flowing over gray slacks and a white dress shirt.

"Sorry to keep you all waiting," he turned his back to us as he slipped out of his robe, "but I had to handle a motion, and you know how lawyers can talk."

Polite laughter fluttered around the room and the men rose as if they were being controlled by an invisible puppeteer. After a moment's hesitation, I followed their example.

With only the barest smile at the corner of his mouth, the judge turned and clasped the back of his leather chair. "Good morning. Have a seat, please; this is not a formal hearing."

After introductions had been made, Oliphant took his seat. "All right," he crossed his legs—which, I noticed, were as hefty as a silverback's—"we're here to talk settlement. We all want to avoid a trial, of course, especially since a public hearing would give our community a black eye."

Rob leaned forward. "Your Honor, I fail to see how my client's work could possibly affect the community—"

Oliphant's brows lowered in a rush. "Thousand Oaks is largely supported by state and county tax dollars, so yes, I think it's fair to say our citizens might be a little disturbed to hear their zoo was forced to pay thousands in legal costs to reclaim property from an overzealous former employee intent upon domesticating a wild animal."

My brother stiffened. "That's a prejudicial comment, Your Honor, and completely untrue. The gorilla under dispute is not a pet. My client is a scientist, a pioneer in the field of psycholinguistics. And for the last eight years she has pursued her work at entirely her own expense."

Oliphant folded his hands and leaned back in his chair. "How, exactly, is your client a pioneer? I had my clerk look into the matter, and he has yet to find a single paper or article published by Ms. Granger."

"The project is complicated and highly involved," Rob countered. "My client is waiting until she has finished gathering the required data. She does plan to publish a groundbreaking study within the next twelve months."

My brother spoke with more confidence than I felt, but I kept my expression under control. I would agree to almost anything to keep Sema. Since I had to publish my dissertation in twelve months, I'd compile the data on Sema's reading progress and extrapolate credible conclusions. At best, the report would be a tease for gorilla experts the world over—I wouldn't reveal *everything* I intended to undertake, but I could make a respectable effort.

I found myself wishing the judge could read my thoughts as easily as Sema could read my body language. I caught his eye and gave him a careful smile. *If you could get these zoo people off my back, there's no limit to what Sema and I might accomplish.*

The judge looked away, his mouth twisting as Rob continued to make my case.

I glanced at Ken Matthews, who was nonchalantly studying the white tips of his neatly trimmed nails, then my thoughts came to an abrupt halt. Why was the judge making the zoo's case? Why didn't Matthews look even a little bit tense?

In one startling instant I realized what Rob must have known the moment the judge entered the room— Matthews and Oliphant were pals. Oh, maybe they weren't golf buddies or brother Elks, but they both relied on the public's goodwill; both men were paid by tax dollars. They wanted to make the zoo's lawsuit go away . . . and they could get their wish if they'd only let me keep Sema.

Rob talked; the judge countered. Kremkau said something; Rob's neck flushed above his collar.

Why, this meeting had probably been Matthews's

idea . . . or maybe Oliphant's. In either case, they both stood to win if we settled before the lawsuit went to trial.

The judge pressed his hands to his desk. "Ms. Granger," he turned the heat of his gaze on me, "you have in your possession an animal owned by the Thousand Oaks Zoo, correct?"

Somehow I found my voice. "I've had her for eight years, Your Honor. I took custody of her with the full blessing of Alden Johnston, the former zoo director."

He lifted his hand, cutting me off. "A simple yes or no will do, thank you. Now"—he turned to Matthews—"Mr. Matthews, the zoo would like that gorilla returned, correct?"

"Absolutely." Kremkau, the lawyer, spoke for Matthews. "The animal is now mature. It needs to be habituated so the zoo can continue its highly successful primate breeding program."

Oliphant cast the lawyer a warning look. "As I said, a simple yes or no will do."

He turned to Rob. "Mr. Granger, on what grounds does your client believe she has a right to keep this animal?"

"Possession is nine-tenths of the law, Your Honor," Rob said. "Ms. Granger has spent years teaching and caring for this gorilla. She has conducted unique research in the field of interspecies communication and hopes to soon publish her results. And while this gorilla is no pet, she has bonded to Ms. Granger. The animal speaks; she reads; she communicates in two languages.

To interrupt Ms. Granger's work now would be a travesty of justice *and* science."

The judge swiveled toward the opposition. "In theory, Mr. Kremkau, does your client have any objection to Ms. Granger continuing her work with this animal?"

"How can the gorilla be bred," Kremkau sputtered, "if she is not part of the gorilla community? My client contends that gorillas are social animals and cannot happily exist apart from a gorilla group."

"My client is this animal's family," Rob argued. "Sema depends on Ms. Granger for food, companionship, and affection. I have seen them together, Your Honor, and their relationship is . . . well, it's extraordinary."

Brad Fielding leaned across the chasm between the two groups of chairs. "Perhaps that dependence is not such a good thing." He shifted his attention to me. "I can't help but wonder if Sema knows she's a gorilla."

My adrenaline level spiked. "That's preposterous."

"Not all gorilla behaviors are instinctive," Fielding continued, speaking now to the judge. "Female gorillas who do not watch other mothers do not learn how to care for their infants. Gorillas learn how to eat, mate, and groom each other by watching others in their group. Sema has learned amazing things about how to be human—what she's lacked is the opportunity to learn how to be a gorilla."

The judge leaned back and closed his eyes for a moment, then focused on me. "Do you agree, Ms. Granger, that habituation would benefit the gorilla under discussion?"

"I definitely do not. Tearing Sema from the only home she's ever known would be the most traumatic event of her life."

Oliphant shook his head in admonishment. "You didn't answer my question. Would she benefit from exposure to other gorillas?"

I found myself staring at Fielding as my brain floundered for an answer that wouldn't dash my dreams. The answer to Oliphant's question was obvious to anyone who had studied primates—gorillas are extremely social creatures and desperately need the company of their own kind—but Sema seemed to be an exception. She spent nearly every minute of her waking hours with me, so she had never lacked for company or conversation.

I struggled to keep my voice steady. "Sema has never given me any reason to think she wants to live in the zoo. I am her companion. We are together all day, every day."

The judge propped his chin in his hand and smiled. "How is that possible? Even the most devoted caretaker needs some time for herself."

"Gorillas sleep between ten to fourteen hours at night," I answered, "and they rest every afternoon after feeding. I've learned to adjust my schedule so I'm with Sema when she's awake. I do other things during her naptime."

"Surely," Oliphant said, "you would appreciate having someone to share the burden so you can have more time to call your own."

I lifted my chin. "When I need an extra pair of hands, my vet sends an animal technician who works by the hour."

"Still, the daily workload must be incredible."

"Your Honor," Rob interrupted, "I fail to see the relevance of all this. My client has given this animal exemplary attention for eight years. Quality of care is not at issue."

The judge lifted a brow. "I didn't mean to imply Ms. Granger is not an adequate caretaker—as a mediator, I'm hoping to impress the advantages of an alternate solution upón your client."

In that moment, I knew we would lose. The Honorable Geoffrey Oliphant favored Thousand Oaks, so if we went to trial, we'd have one strike against us from the beginning.

My eyes flicked at the zoo director, who was studying his hands and smiling to himself. "Let's cut to the chase," I told the judge, catching sight of my brother's alarmed expression from the corner of my eye. "And let's speak in plain English, please."

Oliphant actually smiled. "Why don't we look at the zoo's proposal."

I sat in stunned silence as briefcases opened on both sides of the room. Kremkau passed papers to Matthews and Fielding; Rob handed a single printed page to me.

I glanced at the heading—*Presettlement Proposal, January 10, 2005.* Lines for signatures appeared at the bottom, while a list of stipulations filled the center of the page.

"What you see before you"—Oliphant picked up his copy of the proposal—"is the zoo's suggested solution to this quandary. We are open to your thoughts, of course, but I think I'm safe in saying that none of us wants a protracted case. Extensive publicity would not be good for the zoo or Ms. Granger. The Thousand Oaks proposal is, I believe, quite generous."

I looked at my brother, who wouldn't meet my gaze. "Rob"—my voice had gone taut as rage seared my cheeks—"we need to talk. Now."

Oliphant nodded to Rob. "Take a minute."

Moving on legs that felt wooden, I stood and moved out into the anteroom, then whirled to face my brother. "You knew about this proposal?"

Rob carefully closed the door behind him, then spoke in a lowered voice. "Of course, Glee, I told you I'd been talking to Kremkau."

"Why didn't you talk to *me?*"

"Come on, Glee, I've done nothing *but* talk to you."

"Not about this, you didn't. You sold me out. You brought me here and hoped I'd be too intimidated to say anything."

Behind me, someone coughed. "Excuse me. I'll let you have some privacy." I turned in time to see the law clerk gather his papers and duck into the hall.

Rob waited until the door closed, then rounded on me. "I didn't think you'd be intimidated—and I knew you'd fight for the issues that are really important to you." The line of his mouth clamped tight and his throat bobbed as he swallowed. "Good grief, Glee, can't you understand that you can't win as long as you insist on keeping property that isn't yours? You won't try to raise the money to buy Sema; you won't let me lend you the funds. All right, fine, but that means you're going to have to share your gorilla. Matthews wanted to cut you out of the picture entirely, but I convinced him he needs you to care for Sema. According to the terms of the proposal, you'll be able to continue your work indefinitely. You'll even draw a salary and full benefits. You'll just have to conduct your work at the zoo."

Something in me began to tremble. "What—what if we reject this proposal and go to trial?"

"You could lose Sema entirely. If the trial garners a lot of negative publicity, you could earn a reputation among your colleagues as a troublemaker . . . how would you feel if you could never work with gorillas again?"

Unable to bear the hot light of his eyes, I turned to stare at a painting—a mediocre Florida landscape, complete with alligators, egrets, and pink flamingos. Hotel art at its finest.

"You should have told me," I whispered.

"You would only have argued."

I shrugged and looked over my shoulder. "Maybe. But I wouldn't have embarrassed you in front of all those people in there."

"Glee." His cheek curved as he smiled. "On at least two occasions I have driven around town with a gregarious gorilla in my passenger seat. How could anything *you* do possibly embarrass me?"

Despite my intention to maintain self-control, my chin wobbled and my eyes filled with tears. I dashed the wetness away, then accepted the handkerchief Rob pulled from his pocket.

"Ready to go back in?"

I sniffed and patted my lower lashes dry, then nodded. "Let's go."

6

We walked into a silence so thick I could hear the swish of my skirt with each step.

"Thank you," Rob sank into his chair. "We're ready to proceed."

Oliphant picked up his copy of the proposal. "As you can see," the judge explained, "Ms. Granger will be required to return the gorilla called Sema to the zoo within seven days—provided, of course, the animal is healthy and free of communicable disease. Once the gorilla arrives at the zoo, it will be kept in a separate holding facility until it can be gradually and carefully habituated to the existing gorilla population. At that point the animal will join the other gorillas' daily routine, with the following exceptions: Ms. Granger will be allowed to continue her work with the gorilla for one two-hour session each day. Ms. Granger will also be reinstated as an employee of Thousand Oaks Zoo, where she will work under Mr. Fielding, gorilla curator. Ms. Granger will be allowed input concerning Sema's care, conditioning, and breeding. In addition, she will conduct daily performances for the public so others may learn about the animal's unique abilities."

"Absolutely not!" I glared at Fielding, my breath burning in my throat. "Sema is not a circus act!"

"No," Matthews responded, speaking in the tone he might have used with a three-year-old, "she is a zoo animal. We put animals in zoos so people can observe them. If this animal is as unique as you say, we have every right—even the responsibility—to let the public see her."

Ignoring his boss, Fielding leaned toward me. "I know you care desperately about saving the world's remaining gorillas, Glee. As long as people think of the g's as big, hairy apes, there's no connection, no real concern. But if they see Sema and realize how human she is, they'll change their opinions. Sema could be a huge voice for gorilla conservation. You could end every demonstration with a plea for donations to the groups who are trying to enforce the ban on poaching and the bushmeat trade."

I looked away, disgusted by the mention of money. I'd never doubted Fielding's honest concern for gorillas—in this area, at least, his stubbornness was a virtue. But what I'd read of Matthews had convinced me he was far more concerned with enlarging his role as head of the local animal kingdom than sending money to the impoverished Africans who patrolled the gorilla preserves.

Rob dropped his copy of the proposal onto his brief-case. "So far I fail to see any good reason why my client should acquiesce to all these stipulations."

"I'll tell you why." Kremkau's voice filled with quiet menace. "Because we are ready to sue on the grounds of wrongful possession. We'll have no problem proving the animal belongs to Thousand Oaks, and we'll have no problem demonstrating that in the past your client has willfully and callously disobeyed the instructions of her superiors at the zoo. From the beginning, she has placed her desire to conduct research before the zoo's interests, and she has insisted on fabricating humanlike responses from a creature that is and always will be only an animal."

I opened my mouth to argue, but Matthews cut me off. "The media would have a field day with this." His eyes gleamed above an expression that would not qualify as a smile in any creature's expressive lexicon. "I think our best interests lie in compromise. Ms. Granger—you may continue your work with Sema. But she will live at the zoo, where she was born and where she belongs."

I brought my hand to my lips and resisted the urge to look at Rob. I wanted to dig in and fight, but I knew I'd lose. I could only conceive of one sure way to win—if I held a press conference and demonstrated Sema's unique abilities, I could make a public case for keeping her in her present situation. But if I did that, I'd be playing into Matthews's hands. I'd be doing what he wanted to do, and I would not put my girl on display like a circus freak.

As an individual, Sema deserved better.

Aware that every man in the room was waiting for my response, I squeezed my brother's arm. "I won't put her on display," I looked directly at Matthews, "and I want a month to help her adjust to the idea of moving. I'll need to teach her about the other animals and help her understand what's going to happen."

Matthews nodded. "You can have the month. But since public education is one of our primary purposes, you *will* conduct public demonstrations. We can postpone these, however, until the animal has adjusted to her new surroundings."

"Give her a year," I countered. "And I'll need your promise she won't have to perform if she's sick, upset, pregnant, or nursing an infant."

Matthews's watery blue eyes gleamed above his glasses. "We'll consider it. But after the agreed-upon interval, she'll perform every afternoon in the gorilla pavilion."

I lifted my hand. "Every *Saturday* afternoon—and only if I'm available to interpret for her. Though I realize I'll be working for Fielding, I want to remain in charge of Sema's welfare."

Fielding shifted as if he would object, but Matthews spoke first. "Agreed. If you two have a disagreement about Sema, you may have the final word. In all other circumstances, you will defer to Mr. Fielding."

Rob looked at me, apology in his eyes.

"The proposal contains other provisions." Kremkau glanced at the paper in his hand. "Salary stipulations, a guarantee of job security, benefits—all are spelled out, and all, I believe, are quite generous."

Rob nodded. "We might want to tweak an item or two, but everything looks good."

"Well." The judge tapped a rhythm on the edge of his desk. "I do believe we have reached an agreement. Mr. Kremkau, why don't you write up a draft of the revised agreement and send it to Mr. Granger's office. I'd like to have a signed copy of the settlement in my office by next Friday."

Just like that, the battle was over. The judge stood and moved to shake Matthews's hand; Rob took my arm and led me toward the door.

"I am sorry," he murmured as he reached for the knob. "You're right, I should have given you the details—"

"Glee?"

I turned at the sound of Fielding's voice. He stood behind me, looking strangely out of place in his khaki uniform. The ghost of a smile touched his mouth with ruefulness. "Look, I hope there are no hard feelings. I'm looking forward to having you on our team."

He had to be lying. What employer would want a reluctant woman, especially one with whom he shared an unpleasant past, on his staff? He didn't want me in his life any more than I wanted him, but within days a legally binding document would decree that we had to work together.

For a moment I couldn't speak, then I winced. "I wish I could say I was looking forward to joining you, but I can't. This has been the worst day of my life . . .

and you've been a huge part of it."

Grateful for the stalwart support of my brother, I took his arm and left Brad Fielding with his cohorts.

7

Quiet cloaked the trailer when I returned, the silence broken only by the gentle sound of Sema's deep breathing. Ethan sat on a stool by the table, a paperback novel in his hand. "She's been great," he whispered when I came in. "We played; we read a couple of books; then she ate lunch. She's been sleeping about an hour."

He grinned as I searched for my wallet in the depths of my shoulder bag. "She was signing away while I was reading to her. I picked up a little of what she was saying, but I think she got impatient. She kept pointing to me, then she'd hold her nose and do this—"

I looked up to see Ethan close his fist, then brush his thumb twice against his upper teeth.

Even through the pain of bitter disappointment, Sema could make me smile. "She was calling you a *stinky nut*."

Ethan grunted. "That rascal. I *thought* she was insulting me."

"Relax. She likes you. You should hear what she's called me over the years."

I pressed a wad of bills in Ethan's palm, then opened the door. "Thanks. You were a lifesaver."

"Anytime."

As his footsteps echoed over the wooden stairs, I closed the door and realized even this dark cloud had a silver lining. If Sema lived at the zoo, I'd never again have to pay a gorilla-sitter.

She was still sleeping when I pulled my stool over to the counter, but I heard her stir when I clicked on a desk lamp. I held my breath and waited, but no other sound came from her room.

I bent over my daily journal and scribbled the date at the top of a clean page, but my vision blurred as tears filled my eyes. How could I tell Sema she would have to leave the only home she could remember? Though I had resisted the coming change with all my might, I couldn't let her glimpse my anger or fear. Sema always picked up on my moods, and if I were edgy, she'd be upset, too.

An upset gorilla was not easy to handle. Even the most amiable animal could be dangerous if provoked into a temper. Long ago I had covered the trailer's windows with chain link fencing and replaced the doors with gates. Sema packed a wallop of a punch even in play.

I lifted my gaze to the ceiling and blinked until my vision cleared, then scrawled my thoughts across the top of the page: *I will have to convince Sema that this transition will be a Good Thing, I have to prepare her and tell her she'll love living at the zoo.*

As a performing monkey?

I swallowed hard, tamping my anger. In that moment I could have choked Ken Matthews with pleasure.

I heard more sounds from Sema's room, followed by the chink of the latch on her gate. Ethan wouldn't have locked it, knowing I'd be returning soon.

I felt her enter the room, but kept writing until I heard the sound of her panting breaths.

"Hey, sweet Sema." I turned and gave her a broad smile. "How are you feeling?"

She tilted her head, considering, then touched the thumb of her spread hand to her chest in the sign for *fine*.

"That's good. Did you play with your dolls today?"

Play Bear. Play man stinky nut.

"You should be careful, sweetie. You might hurt Ethan's feelings if you call him a stinky nut."

Shame stinky gorilla.

Sema shook her head, then knuckle-walked toward me. I smiled as I watched her come, then felt my heart melt when she sat on the floor by my stool and signed *Kiss please kiss.*

"Aw, did you miss me?" I slipped off my stool and knelt, then wrapped my arms around her neck and gave her a kiss. She returned my embrace, kissing me on my lips and both cheeks, then she released me. *Sema thirsty.*

"Are you? Okay—do you want apple juice or orange juice?"

Sema grinned. *Apple drink.*

I opened the fridge and pulled out the appropriate juice box, then inserted the straw. When I turned, Sema had climbed onto the revolving stool by the counter.

Sema spin.

"Oh, you want to play, do you? I thought you wanted a drink."

Hurry hurry spin.

"Oh, all right." Laughing, I set the juice box on the counter, then placed my arms around Sema's shoulders and gave her a whirl. She spun on the stool, her eyes wide, her mouth slack in openmouthed delight. When the stool slowed to a stop, Sema didn't hesitate: *Sema spin more!*

I turned my girl until my arms ached, then I told her no more. "Too much spinning will make you sick. Time for your drink, okay?"

Sema gave me her hand as she slid to the floor.

I laughed. "Are you dizzy? How do you feel?"

Fine happy.

"Good. Here's your drink."

She took her juice and drained the container in one long pull. When the box was empty, she shook it, then tossed it toward the trash can in the corner. This time, it went in.

"Good for you!" I pointed to the computer, humming faintly in the corner. "Would you like to see something special? I have some big news, Sema."

New toy?

"New . . . friends. Gorilla friends. I think you'll want to meet them."

Sema didn't always want to work, but that day I didn't have to bribe her to sit at the computer. She hurried to her special low stool that enabled her to reach the computer keyboard on our low table. With the wireless mouse in my hand, I opened Internet Explorer, then navigated to the Thousand Oaks site. From the list of exhibits on the left side of the screen, I chose the gorilla pavilion. Instantly, the computer monitor filled with the photos of the resident group—five healthy animals of differing ages.

As always when presented with images of her own species, Sema was transfixed.

I left my keyboard and moved to her side. "See this handsome guy?" I pointed to the photo of the imposing silverback. "That's Dakarai. He's a good gorilla, very nice. Strong, too."

Sema tapped the screen. *What name?*

"Dakarai," I said, thinking aloud. "We need a sign for him, don't we? Okay—how about this?" I made the sign for D, reached up to touch the brim of an imaginary baseball cap, then thumped my chest with alternating fists. I'd combined the signs for *D, man,* and *gorilla,* but after a little practice the grouping would mean only one thing to Sema: *Dakarai.*

I repeated the sign. "Can you sign his name?"

Sema's gestures were a little less emphatic, but she studied the silverback's picture as she signed, so I knew she made the connection.

"Dakarai," I signed his name again, "is thirty-two years old—older than Glee! He is the strong leader of the gorillas at the zoo. He has lived in many zoos, but now he lives . . . well, he lives somewhere special."

Enchanted by the silverback's photo, Sema leaned

forward and kissed the image on the screen, then signed his name. *Dakarai.*

"You are one smart girl."

I used the arrow key to scroll down to the next photo. If Dakarai had been Sema's father, I might have stood a good chance of keeping her, because zookeepers are reluctant to breed fathers and daughters. Incestuous breeding does not take place in the wild, and inbreeding is not good for zoo populations. But though Sema was born at Thousand Oaks, both her mother and her father had passed away.

The next photo featured Aisha, a twelve-year-old female, and her son, Rafiki, a two-year-old male who would soon be weaned.

"Look, Sema." I pointed to their images. "This gorilla has a baby! Would you like to know their names?"

Name gorilla baby?

"The mother gorilla is Aisha"—in keeping with our previous pattern, I made the sign for *A,* followed by signs for *woman* and *gorilla*—"and the baby is Rafiki. Let me help you with those signs."

We had to improvise on the *R*—Sema's short thumb couldn't quite reach her bent fingertips—but with a few attempts she managed to make signs I could interpret.

Rafiki baby? Sema have baby?

"Rafiki is Aisha's baby. One day you may have a baby of your own."

I scrolled down to the next picture—a blackback, an immature male whose pelage had not yet begun to turn silver. "That is Mosi," I explained, creating a sign for the handsome youngster. "And this"—I pointed to another photo—"is Kamili, another female. These words tell us she will soon have a baby—would you like to see it?"

Sema see baby? Give baby drink?

I laughed. "We'll see, sweetie. Maybe you can see all these gorillas. Would you like that?"

Sema like gorillas. Sema visit gorillas? Sema ride in car?

"Not today, but maybe soon." I reached out and tenderly traced the dark outline of her cheek. "In a few days, maybe we can visit the gorillas. Until then, I'm going to print out their pictures so you can look at them every day and practice their names. We'll hang them on the wall in your room, okay? Would you like that?"

Sema like big gorillas. Sema like Dakarai and Rafiki. Sema like car visit.

She looked away as the wind rattled the window, then, distracted, she ambled toward her toy box. I smiled, content to let her go, but her enthusiasm left me feeling a little disappointed. If Brad Fielding or his boss had observed Sema's excitement, they'd tell me my concerns about a difficult transition were completely unrealistic.

Yet I'd done exactly what a mother sending her child off to kindergarten would do—prepare her youngster for a new and possibly frightening experience by painting it in the most attractive light possible.

But I wasn't sending Sema to an innocent place like kindergarten—what Matthews and Fielding required of me felt more like sending her to prison.

8

On Saturday night, after putting Sema to bed and making sure the trailer was locked tight, I climbed into my Honda and headed over to Nana's. Saturday night dinner at my grandmother's apartment had been a tradition since Rob and I left home, though our grown-up responsibilities sometimes kept us from regular attendance. Rob's wife, Cheri, never complained about going to Nana's in my presence, but I think even Mr. Mugs could tell she wasn't thrilled about spending a weekend night in an aging cinder-block motel when she could have been ensconced in her box at the Tampa Bay Performing Arts Center. Over the last year, Rob and Cheri's attendance had dropped from four times a month to once or twice . . . if we were lucky.

As for me, I went whenever possible, for what working woman would pass up a home-cooked meal? When Sema was younger, I often took her with me. Though my girl loved visiting and Nana loved Sema, my grandmother's furniture could only withstand so much gorilla enthusiasm. Once Sema and Mr. Mugs played chase through the apartment—while the pug hid under the bed, Sema leaped up and dangled from Nana's picture molding until it gave way and splintered on Sema's head.

As she picked up the shattered pieces of wood, Nana had tactfully suggested that all future visits between Mugsy and Sema be held in the gorilla trailer. I had to agree.

The weekend following our pretrial settlement, I drove toward the beach and grimly wondered if Rob would show up. We'd spoken on the phone earlier when he called to tell me to expect a copy of the final agreement, and our conversation had been pleasant enough. But when we were around Nana, we had a tendency to slip back into our contentious sibling roles. I didn't want to spend the evening reliving my teenage years.

I pulled off Gulf Boulevard and parked in the grass, then pocketed my keys and strode toward the apartment. Herman let out a whistle at my approach. "Hey, cutie!"

"Hey, Hermie. What's for supper?"

"Hey, cutie!"

"That's nice." I opened the office door, then slipped behind the reception desk and tiptoed through the doorway that led to the kitchen. I found Nana at the stove, about to pour a bowl of cubed potatoes into boiling water.

"Hey." I gave her shoulder a squeeze and filched a potato from the bowl. "Can I help?"

She made a face as I bit into the white cube. "You're eating that *raw?*"

I shrugged. "Sema does."

Nana poured the potatoes into a pot, then set the empty bowl on the counter. "I was sure you'd outgrown that habit by now."

I swallowed the last bite and leaned against the counter. "What can I do to help?"

"Nothing, hon. There's a ham in the oven, rolls in the breadbasket, and a cherry pie somewhere around here.

96

Except for the potatoes, we're all set."

I glanced at the table, set for four. "Are Rob and Cheri coming?"

"As far as I know." A faint line appeared between her brows as she stirred the boiling pot. "How are things between you and your brother?"

So she'd heard. "What did he tell you?"

"About the settlement? Not much."

"Well, I don't hate him or anything, if that's what you mean." I slid down the counter, where something lay beneath a crisp cotton dish towel. I lifted the edge and found the cherry pie.

I was about to pinch off a bite of the crust when Nana threw a pot holder at me. "Don't nibble at my dessert!"

"Sorry." When Mr. Mugs barked an alarm, I looked up to see Rob enter the kitchen.

"Hey, ladies." He paused to kiss Nana's cheek, then grinned at me. "Still speaking to me, kiddo?"

"Do I have a choice?"

"I guess you don't—unless you want to have a really quiet supper."

I glanced behind him. "Where's Cheri?"

"She had a women's shindig in Tampa. It's just me tonight."

Nana squeezed his arm. "I'm glad you came. Now, move out of my way so I can get the ham out of the oven."

The corner of my mouth twisted as I looked at my brother. Despite everything that had happened, I was glad to see him.

• • •

After dinner, we pushed our empty plates in one direction and our chairs in the other, giving our bellies room to expand. Nana sat at the head of the table, tempting us with more pie, but Rob and I both insisted we'd had enough.

"Then why don't you two go on out to the porch?" Nana suggested. "I'll bring mugs and the coffeepot."

"Don't you want us to help you clean up?"

"The dishes will wait. The magic of the moment might not."

Grinning, I followed Rob onto the wooden plank porch that opened to the gulf. Night had settled like a velvet blanket over the beach, and somewhere behind us, a nearly full moon had streaked the sand with silver. I wrapped one of Nana's soft lap blankets around my shoulders and settled into one of the oak rocking chairs. The only sounds were the creak of my brother's rocker, the gentle sound of breakers, and the occasional murmur of human voices from passersby.

"I'm glad," Rob called from the next chair, "you're still speaking to me."

I smiled up at the silver pepper of the stars. "I'll always speak to you, Rob. I might also *yell* at you on occasion, but I guess you know that."

"Yeah . . . the silent treatment's more Cheri's style than yours."

That comment piqued my curiosity. I shifted to study his face, which had grown pensive. "Having trouble at home?"

He shrugged. "Nothing major. It's just . . . sometimes she's so *needy*. She expects me to read her mind and know what she wants even before she wants it. She's not like you. You don't seem to need anybody, but Cheri . . ." He released a hollow laugh. "She's not like you. She's definitely high maintenance."

And I wasn't? I made a face, not sure if I'd been complimented or insulted.

Rob jumped up as Nana bumped the screen door with her hip and stepped out with a tray of mugs and a steaming pot. A few minutes later we were all three sipping coffee and rocking to the rhythm of the waves, our faces turned toward the moonlit sea.

It should have been a perfect moment, but my thoughts kept returning to Rob's comment. Not *need* anybody? Where did Rob get that idea about me? I needed people; I had all kinds of needs. If I didn't need family and friends, why on earth did I drive out here every Saturday night?

"Praise him, sun and moon, praise him, all you twinkling stars." From her chair, Nana quoted words I'd heard a hundred times before.

Let every created thing give praise to the LORD,
for he issued his command, and they came into being.
He established them forever and forever.
His orders will never be revoked.

From my rocker, I looked over and caught Rob's eye. We were used to Nana's SPOs—spontaneous poetic outbursts. She'd been erupting in psalms and various verses for as long as I'd known her. Sometimes she'd be overcome by rhythm and rhyme in the middle of her housework; sometimes a quiet moment like this would pull the poetry out of her.

In any case, we knew it was useless to interrupt. If we tried to carry on a conversation beneath her recitation, she'd only raise her voice in an effort to hear herself above our muttering. Clearly, she didn't care if we listened . . . during her poetic praises, she'd told us, she spoke to God.

I let my head fall to the back of the rocker, content to sit and listen to Nana's poem. She had a lovely speaking voice, expressive and clear—developed, I assumed, during the years she taught high school English.

> "Praise the LORD from the earth,
> you creatures of the ocean depths,
> fire and hail, snow and storm,
> wind and weather that obey him,
> mountains and all hills,
> fruit trees and all cedars . . ."

Her voice wrapped around me like a comforting arm, at once powerful and gentle. Nana and I had reached a truce about God—I didn't complain about her spontaneous psalms and she no longer nagged me about going to church. But on nights like this, I loved hearing her mellifluous voice. It flowed like a stream, connecting me to events in my childhood, to my parents, to nights when my entire family had gathered on this porch to grill hot dogs and hamburgers after a day of sand and salt and fun. Like tired windup toys, we would sink onto railings and chairs and watch the stars come out as Nana's words ran together in a velvet flow.

> ". . . wild animals and all livestock,
> reptiles and birds,
> kings of the earth and all people,
> rulers and judges of the earth,
> young men and maidens,
> old men and children.
> Let them *all* praise the name of the LORD."

I waited until I was sure she had finished, then lazily lifted my hand to flag Rob's attention. "Did you ever think about that?"

"About what?"

"About reptiles and birds . . . you know, talking. Whoever wrote that bit realized animals communicate with each other. Imagine finding interspecies communication in the Bible."

Nana chuckled. "Animals communicate with God, too. And Scripture contains at least two stories where they spoke directly to humans."

I knew she wanted me to ask for details, but I decided to let the opportunity pass. No sense in getting into an argument after the sweetness of cherry pie.

I was driving home from Nana's when an answer hit me

like a slug in the chest—Ken Matthews obviously wanted a performing gorilla, but he'd won his case because he kept insisting that gorillas needed to bond with a social group. So Sema would *have* to be accepted by the gorilla group at Thousand Oaks or . . . Matthews would have to return her to me.

What if her habituation failed?

The bond between me and Sema couldn't be stronger. In many ways she was like a child, accustomed to having the human world revolve around her. The process of successfully introducing her to a gorilla family would be infinitely more challenging than habituating an ordinary zoo gorilla.

If Sema didn't thrive with the others—if I could make sure she *wouldn't* thrive—I could take my girl home again.

Goose bumps rose on my arms as I gripped the steering wheel. What could be simpler? I could make all the outward efforts for her adjustment—I'd have to be sure she knew how to cope well enough that she wouldn't be injured by the other animals—but if she wasn't adjusting after a few days, I could plead her case with Fielding and even call in some other primate experts. A few respected voices from influential institutions would force Matthews's hand. After admitting I'd been fair enough to give Sema an opportunity to join a social group, he'd have no choice but to allow me to take her home.

In the coming month, I could tell Sema we'd be leaving home for a little while, but we'd be coming back. And while the prospect of meeting new gorillas had excited her, once she realized they didn't speak her language or play her games, she might grow tired of them.

I didn't like the idea of manipulating her emotions, but on several occasions even Dian Fossey had to choose between two evils in order to protect her gorillas. Then again, maybe I wouldn't have to manipulate anything. Sema might grow weary of the grand gorilla experiment without any help from me. After all, as a zoo animal she wouldn't be allowed to go for rides in the car, run free in an open field, wear her sweater in bad weather, or eat the occasional box of Jujubes . . .

Given a little time, I could persuade Sema to pine for home. To convince Matthews, however, I'd need Brad Fielding's support. He would have to back me up when I noted Sema's inability to adapt. I'd need him in my corner if I was going to convince Ken Matthews that she needed to live with me.

The thought of fostering a friendship with by-the-rules-Fielding was about as appetizing as ketchup on a cookie, but if I had to do it for Sema's sake, I would.

9

The day of Sema's transfer arrived with rain and oppressive clouds. I awakened abruptly, sat up in the gloom, and tried to remember why I'd been dreading this day.

A cold shiver spread over me as my memory focused.

I'd been avoiding thoughts of Sema's transfer, trying to see it as only a temporary detour and a brief inconvenience, but the cold darkness of the rainy morning filled me with the dullness of despair. I wanted nothing more than to curl up beneath my blankets and wish the world away. I might have done just that, but someone rang my doorbell.

My heavy eyes widened at the sound. Some ever-optimistic part of me, fed by Nana's stories of miracles and divine provision, sparked my lethargic blood with hope. Maybe Rob stood outside to tell me the exchange had been called off—no, he would call. But something odd had happened, because no normal person went around ringing doorbells at 7:00 AM.

Grabbing my robe from the foot of the bed, I pulled it over my cotton pajamas and hurried to the door. I flicked on the porch light and peered through the peephole. Brad Fielding stood on my stoop, a white paper bag in one hand and a Styrofoam cup in the other.

I pressed my palm to the back of the door and held a breath. *Fielding?* Maybe Matthews had changed his mind and found another female gorilla. Or maybe something had come up and they didn't want to move Sema today. The rain might be a problem, or one of the other animals might be sick—

Not caring that I still looked like a woman who'd just been pulled from bed, I opened the door. "What? What's happened?"

"Good morning to you, too." With an artificially bright smile, he held up the cup. "I thought you might like some coffee. And doughnuts—they're Krispy Kremes."

Momentarily speechless, I stared at him. Why was he bringing my favorite doughnuts at this ungodly hour?

He waved his peace offering before my eyes. "Coffee? Doughnuts? Hello? Anybody awake in there?"

I pushed my bangs out of my eyes. "Is everything all right? The transfer's still on?"

He nodded.

I turned away as the heaviness in my chest reasserted itself. "Come on in. I'll meet you in the kitchen, but I need fifteen minutes."

By the time I'd had a quick shower and pulled on jeans and a sweater, I felt a little more awake, but I was still puzzled by Fielding's appearance. I ran a brush through my hair, wondering if he paid sunrise visits to other zoo employees. If he was trying to win me over . . . I nodded at my reflection, remembering my recent resolution. If he was trying to win me over, I should let him. I would need him as my ally.

Steeling my resolve, I headed toward the kitchen. I found him sitting at the table, a doughnut in his hand, a glass of water on the table. He was reading my morning paper.

I arched a brow at the sight of the glass from my cupboard. "Glad to see you made yourself at home."

"I don't drink coffee." His gaze lifted to meet mine. "I remembered you do."

He remembered? "Yeah. Thanks."

"By the way," he returned his gaze to the newspaper, "nice place you've got here. Real cozy."

I sank into an empty chair and popped the plastic top off the foam cup, trying to remember when Fielding and I had split up. Our last official date took place shortly before Sema was born, so I'd been living in my crowded apartment near the beach. An eternity ago.

After adding sugar and cream to the cup, I took a sip. The coffee was good . . . and appreciated, but I wasn't quite ready to tell him so. With all that had happened between us, Fielding would question my motives if I became too friendly too fast.

"So"—I set the cup on the table—"do you always go out for coffee before sunrise?"

He lowered the paper, then folded it into a neat rectangle. "I thought you might need some help getting Sema ready for the trip. I brought the tranquilizer gun."

My latent suspicions flared into alarm. "I'm not using the tranq on her. It's not necessary."

"Glee." He spoke in a patient, superior tone. "Zoo regulations require all incoming animals to be tranquilized during transport. For their safety as well as ours."

I met the reproach in his eyes without flinching. "Sema knows how to ride in a car. And I'm the only one who'll be handling her, so there's no risk."

He shook his head. "Regulations require two or more handlers—"

"Forget your regulations for once, will you? Sema is an exception; she has to be. She'd be traumatized if I shot her with a dart, and she'd be harder to move as dead weight. If she wears her collar, I can walk her into the facility without any problem."

Fielding looked at me for a long moment, then brought his finger to his lips. Obviously, he wanted to tell me off, but was forcing himself to remain quiet.

"There's no way you're going near Sema with any kind of gun," I continued, taking advantage of his silence. "She's never seen one, and I don't want her to even know what they are." Despite my irritation, I couldn't stop a shudder. Whenever guns were mentioned, I couldn't help but think of the poachers in Africa who killed gorillas for sport and meat, mercenaries who slaughtered entire family groups and sold adult heads and hands to wide-eyed tourists.

I reached out and pressed my fingertips to Fielding's arm. "Please. I promise it'll be okay. Just let me know where and when to bring her—clear the area if you like, and I'll walk Sema in with no fuss at all."

He lowered his hand. "Will you at least consider giving her some kind of sedative? Valium, maybe? I could have Dr. Parker prescribe something."

I shook my head, but couldn't stop a smile. Fielding was proving to be more agreeable than I had anticipated. "She's going to be confused; I don't want her woozy, too."

"Call me when you're ready to come in." He pulled a business card from his shirt pocket and slid it across the table. "My cell number's at the bottom."

I lifted the card. "I'll call right before we leave."

He crossed his arms and leaned back in his chair. "I

need to run over a couple of other things, then I'll get out of your hair."

"What else?"

"Well, the rules. You've been doing your own thing for a long time, Glee, but now you're going to have to be a team player. That means you'll have to allow the staff to have complete access to Sema."

"Gorilla pavilion employees, you mean. There's no way Sema is going to be gawked at by every Tom, Dick, and Harry who works at Thousand Oaks—"

He waved my objection away. "Of course I meant gorilla personnel. That's me, Claire, and, if necessary, Dr. Parker and his veterinary crew."

I bit the inside of my lip, then nodded. I knew Dr. John Parker; he was a good vet and a busy one, so he wasn't likely to be nosing around and getting in my way.

"There's more." Fielding caught my gaze and held it. "You'll be expected to work with the other gorillas, too. We're a team; we all do a little of everything, so don't be surprised if you find yourself on the schedule for some jobs that may seem a little beneath your dignity."

I flashed him a steely smile. "I doubt you could ask me to do anything I haven't done before. I can handle my share of the workload."

"Good. Just one more thing."

"Yeah?"

"Your uniform."

I shook my head. "No way. I always work in jeans and my lab jacket. Sema is less distracted when I wear consistent clothing."

"Then Sema can get used to your lab jacket over your uniform. Thousand Oaks requires all employees to wear khaki pants and the company shirt—I have one in the car for you." He tilted his head, taking my measure. "You're a medium, right?"

I felt like telling him what he could do with his stupid uniform, but Nana always said one could win more friends with cookies than criticism.

I stood and let my fingertips fall to the table. "Any other rules you need to enforce? Because if you're finished, I have a lot to do this morning."

"One more thing." Fielding stood too, his chair scraping the linoleum. "I want you to properly introduce me to Sema so she'll know me when she arrives."

I made Fielding wait until I'd prepared Sema's breakfast. When I'd finished loading the tray with mixed greens and fruit, I reluctantly led him from the house to Sema's trailer. The sky had stopped drizzling, but lingering raindrops sprinkled over us as we walked beneath the sprawling oaks.

I batted at my bangs, trying to dislodge a few water droplets.

"By the way," Fielding said. "I like your hair that way. Short and shaggy suits you."

"Um . . . thanks. I think." Not certain that I wanted to encourage any further personal observations, I quickened my step and led the way up the stairs that led to the trailer.

"Sema's probably still asleep," I said, jangling the

keys in the lock. "I usually wake her up when I come in."

The atmosphere inside the trailer was heavy with early-morning quiet. I set the breakfast tray on the table, then tiptoed across the room to unhook the latch on the gate to Sema's room. She lay curled up in her Care Bear nest, her hand resting on her cheek, her stuffed bear sandwiched into the crook of her arm.

As Fielding waited in the doorway, I sank to the floor beside my girl. "Hey, sweetie," I whispered, trying to ignore the pressure of Fielding's eyes on my back. "Are you ready to get up?"

Sema's eyelids fluttered, then lifted. Seeing me, her black lips spread in a broad smile, then her eyes closed again. *Sema sleep.*

"I know you're awake. I saw your smile. Besides, you can't sign in your sleep."

Her eyes opened; her grin deepened.

"Today's a big day, girlie." I reached out and ran my finger down the furry length of her arm. "Today we get to visit the other gorillas."

Her eyelids flew open. *Hurry hurry visit.*

"Don't you want to eat first?"

I could almost see her mind shift gears. Always eager for food, Sema pushed herself into a sitting position, then looked toward the doorway.

Her eyes widened when she saw Fielding. *What man?*

"Sema," I deliberately slid to the side so our guest could observe this exchange, "that is *Fielding.*"

"Hang on a minute." A note of impatience lined his voice. "You may think of me as Fielding, but I'm pretty sure I'm on a first-name basis with all the other g's."

I cast him a quick, irritated glance, then shrugged. "Have it your way." I turned to face Sema. "His name is Brad. You sign it like this." For the sake of simplicity, I combined the sign for *B,* an upraised flat hand, with the sign used to indicate a person, a downward movement of both hands with palms facing each other.

Sema understood immediately. When she signed *B-person* and grinned at Fielding, I hoped he had the good sense to recognize his name.

"Brad takes care of the gorillas we're going to visit," I told her, signing as I spoke. "He knows Mosi and Kamili and Rafiki and Aisha and Dakarai."

"She knows their names already?"

"Sure." I pointed to the photographs taped to Sema's walls. "She's been signing to the pictures for weeks now."

"Wow." Fielding stepped into the room and crouched behind me. "Will she talk to me?"

"If you talk to her. Otherwise, she might only talk *about* you." I rested my arms on my bent knees, wanting Fielding to see how special Sema was. Only when he realized how much she could understand—and how much more she could learn—would he realize that confining her in a zoo was nothing short of criminal.

Fielding clasped his hands together. "Hi, Sema. How goes every little thing?"

Sema tilted her head and blinked, clearly puzzled. I laughed. "She's fairly literal and doesn't always understand slang," I told him. "Ask her how she's feeling. I ask her that every morning, and I'm always amazed at the range of her responses."

Fielding nodded, then turned back to Sema. "Hi." He spoke as stiffly as a middle school boy practicing his lines for the school play. "How are you feeling today?"

Sema grinned and shook her head, then signed a response. "Fine," I said, interpreting. "Sema happy to visit gorillas. Sema loves gorillas. Sema loves stinky gorillas."

Fielding quirked a brow. "What's that about?"

I shrugged. "I'm not sure, but she usually uses the word *stinky* when she's feeling mischievous."

"Oh." Moving slowly, Fielding reached forward and gingerly touched Sema's arm. "You be good, okay? I'll see you later."

Mesmerized by the items in Fielding's shirt pocket, Sema stretched out her long fingers and daintily withdrew a felt-tip pen. "You have to watch her," I warned. "She'll rob you blind if you're not careful."

"That's okay. I have others." Fielding watched, smiling, as Sema pulled off the cap and situated his pen between her dark fingers. With the air of a distracted poet searching for a notebook, she held the pen high and looked around her nest.

Leaving her to her entertainment, I wrapped my arms around my knees and turned to Fielding. "It'll take me some time to get the car packed. I'm bringing her flash cards, her favorite books, her bedding, and her portable toilet. Has the observation room been cleaned and prepared?"

Grinning at Sema, he inclined his head. "Done."

"I'll be bringing some of her favorite snacks, too. I know you'll want her to eat what the other g's eat, but you'll need to let Sema be an exception for a while. She's used to having her juice boxes after enrichment sessions, for instance, and sometimes I give her treats as an incentive. I'll keep track of all those things, but you can't expect me to record every little bite in the diet log."

Still watching my girl, Fielding's face split into a grin. "Do you often encourage her to do *that?*"

I turned as Sema reached up and made three bold marks on the plasterboard.

"Sema!" My voice rang with rebuke. "You know you're not supposed to write on the wall!"

Thoroughly busted, Sema reacted with a human defense mechanism—she popped the inky tip of the pen into her mouth, then withdrew it, looking for all the world like Marlene Dietrich taking a drag on a long cigarette.

Beside me, Fielding chortled.

I rose to my knees. "Sema! What do you think you are doing?"

While her right hand held the pen, with her left she made a *V* with two fingers and tapped them to her lips. *Smoking.*

Fielding looked at me with laughter in his eyes. "No need to translate that one."

I blew at my bangs in exasperation. "She picks these things up from TV. I try to shelter her, but sometimes I'm not quick enough."

He shook his head. "I hope you're documenting these kinds of things. I think she's just demonstrated that animals can tell fibs."

"I hope you don't think I taught her to do that."

A thoughtful look entered his eyes. "I've never had kids, but I don't think you have to teach children how to lie. That kind of thing comes naturally."

The remark about having kids opened the curtain on a memory I thought I'd closed off forever. Fielding had just come out of a live-in relationship when we dated eight years ago. Rumor had it that he'd asked his girlfriend to marry him because she was expecting a baby, but then suddenly she wasn't pregnant and the stress of whatever happened—I didn't ask—caused them to break up. Fielding moved out, and back then I'd been so fascinated by him that I'd happily put his ex-girlfriend out of my mind.

I hoped he wasn't thinking I might be interested in him again. I leaned over and straightened Sema's blanket, hoping to appear nonchalant. "You ready for breakfast, girlie?"

Eat now?

"Sure. Why don't you go potty while I get your tray?"

Fielding stood and moved out of the way while Sema knuckle-walked to her toilet. His grin widened when she sat to relieve herself.

"I'd double your salary if you could teach the others

to do that," he said as I stood and moved to the doorway. "Cleaning the night rooms can get nasty."

I left the bedroom and moved into the kitchen. "That's why I taught Sema to use the toilet," I called. "I got tired of changing diapers."

"Too bad you don't care for cleaning up." Fielding's voice simmered with mirth. "Because as the newest employee at the pavilion, that's going to be one of your jobs."

At some moments even a grown woman can be tempted to stick out her tongue and behave like a five-year-old. That was one of those moments, but as I lifted the plastic wrap from Sema's tray, I reminded myself that I was a professional. A scientist. And as of that morning, a salaried employee of Thousand Oaks Zoo.

I couldn't help it. With my back to Brad Fielding, I stuck my finger down my throat in the nearly universal sign for *gag me*.

After that, I felt 100 percent better.

10

We pulled into the zoo's main parking lot at quarter past ten. Sema rode in the passenger seat beside me, her girth spilling over the bucket seat. My girl always loved the car, and this ride held extra appeal for her. As we drove through the familiar streets near our home, I told her we would visit the gorillas for a little while. Though she didn't seem the least bit worried, I assured her that soon she'd be sleeping in her old room again. "For a few nights, though, you're going to have a new room in a new place."

As I pulled up to the security checkpoint, Sema leaned forward and strained against the shoulder belt. She pointed to the soda machine next to the guard shack. *Hurry juice drink.*

"Not now, sweetie. We have to visit the gorillas. They have a nice big home with trees and ropes and toys."

I rolled down my tinted window as the security guard approached. The young man waved, then crouched to peer at my passenger.

"We're supposed to meet Brad Fielding at the entrance to the Gorilla Pavilion." I flashed the parking pass Fielding had given me. "He's expecting us."

The poor guy didn't know what to do. "Um . . . all visitors have to sign in."

"Fine." I waited until he handed me a clipboard, then signed my name across a dotted line. Without hesitation, I passed the pen and clipboard to Sema, who scrawled a wavy line across the sign-in sheet.

I maintained perfect composure as I handed the clipboard back to the dumbfounded guard. "Thanks."

Brimming with enthusiasm, Sema clapped her hands and feet as we drove toward the tall enclosure that served as home to the zoo's gorilla population.

I let my gaze rove over the scenery as we passed several African-themed pavilions. The last few years had brought many changes, some of them good, many of them instigated by Ken Matthews. Though I knew several of the habitats had been improved, the place seemed slicker now, more artificial. With Disney World only ninety minutes away, other tourist attractions keenly felt the pressure to compete. Why use real grass in the habitats when artificial turf kept its emerald color year-round? Why install a water fountain every fifty yards when you could sell flamingo-colored snow cones for five bucks each?

I hated to see Thousand Oaks become too commercial—it had been around in my mother's day, and something in me wanted it to remain a community attraction. It had begun as a petting zoo on farm land donated to the city of Clearwater in 1935. Pinellas County, which was largely rural in those days, teemed with native wildlife, so the petting zoo expanded to include sanctuaries for birds, bobcats, armadillos, opossums, deer, gators, and wild boars. As the collection grew, so did the property. When in 1976 an eccentric local millionaire donated his menagerie of two tigers, a retired circus elephant, an aging gorilla, a lion, and more than two dozen peacocks, Clearwater's petting zoo officially became Thousand Oaks, complete with its own board of directors. The zoo achieved respectability when a team from the AZA granted certification, but Tampa's Busch Gardens, only twenty miles away and far more visible on tourists' radar, gave our zoo tough competition.

I glanced at Sema, who seemed completely absorbed in the sights outside her window. Though I knew she wouldn't understand, I felt compelled to explain a little of what I was feeling. "I was only a year old when the board took control of this place," I told her. "Nana has pictures of my mother swinging me at the playground."

Sema turned, her attention pricked by the word *swing*. *Sema play?*

"Not today, sweetie, and probably not while you're visiting the zoo. But when you come home again, we'll play on the swing in your play yard, okay?" *If* we went home again.

A discreet sign on this employees-only road told me to head left for the gorilla pavilion. After I took the left fork in the road, I spotted Fielding by a green gate painted to blend with the forest mural on the side of the building.

Sema recognized him at once. *That Brad!*

"I see him." I nosed the car into the closest parking space, then killed the engine and looked at my girl. "Ready?"

Fine visit good. Sema love gorillas.

"I know you do, honey."

I turned at the crunching sound of shoes on gravel. Fielding stood outside my door and peered through my open window. "Did you tranquilize her?"

"No. She's okay."

Fielding closed his eyes, then blew out his cheeks and met my gaze. "All right, bring her out, but keep a hold of her leash. I don't want anything to spook her."

"She'll be fine." I unbuckled my seat belt, then got out of the car and walked around to Sema's side. Eager to begin her adventure, she pulled on the door handle as I approached.

"Okay, girlie." To satisfy Fielding, I grabbed the leather handle of the leash. Sema had been trained to wear a collar and leash as an unpredictable youngster; now she wore the collar out of habit. She could easily pull me off my feet if she wanted to, but on most occasions she was content to walk by my side.

I helped her out of the car, then held out my hand. Instead of taking it, she stepped back and grabbed at the hem of my lab coat—the unthinking reflex of an uncertain gorilla youngster.

My girl talked big, but she was feeling small. Her vulnerability tore at my heart, but I bit my lip and told myself this transfer was only temporary.

I blinked back hot tears and met Fielding's gaze. "You can lead the way," I said, hoping he wouldn't interpret the quaver in my voice as fear.

I wasn't afraid, not at that moment. I was reluctant. Loving Sema as I did, I was not yet ready to share her.

11

The grand gorilla pavilion at Thousand Oaks had been completed in 1997, two years before I first came to work at the zoo. The designers had done their homework. Hailed as one of the most natural zoo environments in America, the habitat in which the gorillas spent most of their day offered trees, rocks, grasses, and fallen branches for the animals to manipulate. Because the most prevalent problem for captive gorillas is simple boredom, each morning the gorilla keepers hid bunches of edible greens called *browse* throughout the habit in order to encourage the animals' exploration.

When Sema and I arrived, however, I was more interested in the indoor areas. Walking in the chilly shade of an overcast sky, we followed Fielding to a pair of double doors. While we waited for him to swipe his card key through the scanner, I looked up and saw a security camera trained on us. I was fairly certain the camera hadn't been there eight years before, but everyone was more security conscious these days.

When the door clicked, Fielding pulled it open. "After you, ladies."

Sema looked at me with a question in the crinkled caverns of her eyes. *Gorillas here?*

"They're in the play yard now, sweetie. But let's look at your new room."

When we stepped into the long hall I nearly choked on the mingled scents of straw and gorillas. Sema's nostrils flared as she sniffed and asked again: *Gorillas here?*

"Be patient, girlie. You might see some of them in a few minutes."

Fielding pointed to the first doorway on the left. "I thought we could keep Sema in the observation room until her habituation period is over," he said. "Later we can move her down the hall with the others."

I nodded. Each animal slept in his or her own night room, but those rooms were interconnected. Chain link gates had been installed in case any of the animals needed to be separated, but the g's used the gates more often as swings than doors.

I took Sema's hand and led her into the observation room. A reinforced one-way mirror had been installed along the western wall of this space; the mirror looked into a secluded grotto in the habitat not visible from the public viewing area. In her observations of free-living mountain gorillas, Dian Fossey had discovered that animals needed time to be alone, so this small area was the zoo's attempt to give the g's a measure of privacy while they were inside the habitat. If an animal retreated to this cave often, the gorilla staff and the vet could watch for signs of sickness or boredom through the one-way mirror.

Out of respect for a gorilla's strength, the tempered glass mirror had been covered with a layer of chain link mesh on both sides.

I had to agree with Fielding's choice of accommodations. This room was at the opposite end of the building and far from the other gorillas' night rooms. Sema would be able to catch an occasional glimpse of the other animals, but they couldn't see her. She'd be able to talk to me about them before she had to meet them face-to-face.

Sema knuckle-walked farther into the room and looked around, then picked up a handful of the straw covering the floor. She sniffed it, nibbled at a dry stalk, then spat it out. An offended look filled her eyes when she turned to me. *Stinky grass?*

I caught Fielding's eye. "As you probably noticed, we

don't use straw in her room at home. I brought her bedding, though; it's in the car."

Brad slipped his hands into his pockets. "We'll get it later. Come on; I'll give you the rest of the tour."

I glanced back at Sema, who was peering through the wide window. "Has the place changed much?"

"Not since you were here last, but bring Sema. Let's let her get familiar with her surroundings."

I smiled and held my hand toward Sema, pleased that Fielding was not treating her like an ordinary animal. Any other new arrival would be bedded down and left to acclimate, but Sema deserved to be escorted by the gorilla curator.

"Right across the hall, you'll remember"—Fielding pointed to a door on our right—"is the kitchen."

The food preparation area lay behind a reinforced steel door, and little had changed here. A huge refrigerator stood against the wall; boxes of organically grown produce waited on the counter. Off to the side, a small kitchen dinette served as a place where the human inhabitants of the gorilla pavilion could snatch a bite to eat.

Sema walked over to one of the boxes and peered through a ventilation hole. *Give apple?*

"Not now, sweetie. Maybe later."

She shook her head, frustrated that I'd misunderstood. *Give gorilla apple?*

"Oh, you mean the other gorillas? They'll have apples later. Maybe for lunch." I reached out to take her hand, but she wasn't finished. *Sema give apples?*

"Not today. Maybe later."

I caught her hand and we continued our tour. The open hallway that led to the habitat lay across from the kitchen and just past the observation room. The area around the sectional roll-up door smelled strongly of gorillas, and Sema's hand tightened around mine. If we had stopped, I know she would have again asked to see the g's, but Fielding kept us moving.

"Here's the office." He tapped on another painted steel door and lifted a brow. "Will she want to see that?"

"Might as well show her everything."

Brad turned the knob and held the door open with his shoulder. A quick glance assured me nothing much had changed—the computers were new, maybe, and the security monitors hung from the ceiling now instead of cluttering a table. But the three oak desks looked antique.

"This is the office," I signed to Sema. "This is where Glee and Brad will work while you are with the other gorillas."

Sema knuckle-walked over to a desk, then picked up a framed photo of a baby gorilla. She studied it a moment, then puckered up and pressed a kiss to the glass.

Beside me, Fielding laughed. "I see she's fond of Rafiki."

"Is that his picture?"

Fielding nodded. "Claire sent me a copy when he was born. Aisha came from San Diego, you know, so I knew her there. When Matthews called and offered me this job, I couldn't believe I'd be lucky enough to work with Aisha again."

I looked away, not wanting him to read the surprise in my eyes. I'd forgotten that Rafiki's mother transferred from the San Diego Zoo before Fielding did . . . and the news that he had established a relationship with her gave me hope. He had to understand the emotions that bound me and Sema.

My girl climbed into Fielding's desk chair, then grinned at me. *Hurry hurry spin.*

Groaning, I shook my head. "She loves swiveling chairs. If I spin her, we'll be here another ten minutes."

He laughed. "I've got time."

"Really? I don't remember you being this laid-back, Fielding."

"Oh yeah? Well, time changes things. And people."

More impressed than I wanted to admit, I went to Sema, put my arms on her shoulders, and gave her a spin. The chair spun lazily, squeaking as it rotated, and Sema shook her head. *Hurry more hurry.*

"This chair doesn't want to hurry."

Stinky chair.

"Let me give it a try." Brad straightened and moved toward Sema, then spun the chair with considerable more force than I'd been able to muster. While Sema dropped her jaw in panting laughter, I looked around the office. A row of wide windows enabled us to see into each of the night rooms. A window in the south wall looked into the passageway that led to the habitat, but there was no window into the observation room where Sema would be living for the next few days.

A flicker of apprehension rippled up my spine. "I won't be able to see Sema from here." I struggled to keep my voice light. "I'd like to be able to see her."

Fielding stepped away from the spinning chair. "Maybe not having a window is a good thing."

"How so?"

"Well . . . if she can look in here and see these swivel chairs, what are the odds she'll settle down and go to sleep?"

For an instant I thought he was serious, then I saw the twinkle in his eye.

I touched the tip of my index finger to my tongue, then made an imaginary mark in the air. "Score one for you, Fielding."

"You didn't keep her in constant sight at the trailer, did you?"

"Well . . . nearly."

"She'll be fine, Glee. You worry too much." He nodded toward the hall. "Want to put her away for a minute? I want to show you the night areas."

Not wanting to argue, I extended my hand. "Come on, girlie, let's walk back to your room and see what Glee has in her purse."

After settling Sema with a coloring book and crayon, Brad and I left her alone and walked down the long hallway that led to the connected night rooms—four on the left, one on the right. I couldn't help but smile as I looked into the rooms—if I were an eight-year-old gorilla, any one of these would be the bedroom of my dreams. High platforms had been mounted to the walls and filled with sweet oat straw for nesting. Fire hoses dangled from the twelve-foot ceiling and canted to opposite walls, creating the illusion of huge woven webs. To create a tropical ambiance, some enterprising (though not terribly talented) artist had covered the walls with pictures of trees, vines, snakes, and tropical flowers.

I gestured to a particularly disproportioned image of either an elephant or a rhinoceros. "This, um, art is new."

Fielding snorted. "Matthews's granddaughter painted these rooms a couple of months ago. You should have seen the g's reactions—we had to bribe them with baked apples to get them to go into their rooms. I watched the monitoring videos the next morning and saw that Dakarai stayed awake all that first night to make sure the frightful creatures on the wall didn't bother his family."

I pressed my hand to my chest, touched by the story. I loved Sema and wouldn't trade her for the world, but there's something wonderful about a silverback. In the wild, a silverback will defend his females, lovingly play with his children, and patiently wait for sick or injured family members to keep up as the group forages for food. A devoted silverback will give his life in defense of his group members—in fact, that's why so many gorillas die when poachers set out to capture an infant for zoo collections. The mother, the silverback, even older siblings and other females will pound and bite anyone who threatens one of the group's young.

I took another look at the night rooms, then counted gorillas on my fingertips. "All these rooms are in use?"

"All but the exam room—but remember, Rafiki is still sleeping with his mother. By the time he's ready to sleep alone, we'll probably be ready to transfer Mosi to another zoo."

He didn't need to explain. A gorilla family can only have one dominant silverback, so maturing blackbacks were often transferred until they meshed with a group where they could achieve dominance and establish a family of their own.

I followed Fielding into the last space, the room used for medical examinations. This room looked much like the others, but it had a scale built into the floor, and a steel door separated it from the other night rooms. If an animal needed to be quarantined, it would be kept in this space, but a reinforced window in the steel door allowed the animals to see each other.

"Well, except for the habitat, that's the grand tour." Fielding leaned against the wall. "I know you probably don't need a refresher course in operations, so why don't you give me your car keys and I'll go get Sema's things."

Surprised by his thoughtfulness, I pulled my keys from my pocket and dropped them into his palm. After I followed him into the hall, I stopped in my tracks, surprised to see Sema looking around as if she owned the place. She seemed oblivious to us as she ambled along the passage, tapping at the windows, pressing her palms against the walls, audibly sniffing the rich scents of gorillas and straw.

I glanced at Fielding. "We didn't lock the door."

He gave me a lopsided grin. "Remind me never to underestimate her."

Sema caught my eye. *Gorillas live here?*

I gestured toward the end of the hallway. "The gorillas sleep down there, sweetie. You're going to sleep in the room with the big window. Want to look at it again?"

She took my hand; together we walked down the corridor. By the time we had settled down with the coloring book, Fielding came in with Sema's inner tube, blankets, and worn Care Bear comforter. He dropped her bedding onto the floor, then stepped back and propped his hands on his hips. "She doesn't travel light, does she?"

I shrugged. "What female does?"

Sema got up and pulled the inner tube into the corner, then dropped into the center, her arms propped on one side, her legs hanging over the other. *Gorillas?* She signed again. *Where gorillas?*

I was growing weary of the question. "The other gorillas are out in their play yard." I pointed to the one-way mirror. "You might be able to see them if you look through this window. You can't meet them today because we have to make friends slowly. But you'll meet some new people. You've already met Brad."

Slowly, Sema signed his name.

I looked at my new boss. "Did you catch that? She's talking about you."

Brad gave me a lazy smile. "I see I'm going to have to learn a few signs just to keep up around here."

"So I finally get to welcome Sema!"

I flinched as a female voice cut into the conversation. Fielding and I both turned as a red-haired girl moved through the doorway. The girl wore the employees' requisite khaki pants and matching shirt, but her bright blue sneakers were definitely not regulation.

"Glee Granger, meet Claire Hartwell." Fielding gestured to the young woman. "Claire's been at Thousand Oaks for three years now. She's studying veterinary medicine at USF."

"And she's taking Dr. Wharton's anthropology class. We've met." The memory of our first meeting brought a wry smile to my face. "Claire came out to the trailer with a group of students."

Claire blushed. "Wow, you remembered."

I laughed. "You asked good questions. That made an impression on me."

"I'm so glad you'll be working with us," Claire said, extending her hand. I lifted my hand to meet hers, but she stepped forward and offered a handshake to Sema before I could protest.

Utterly charmed, Sema accepted Claire's hand as if it were a gift, sniffed delicately at the fingertips, then dropped it and clapped.

I took a deep breath to calm the leaping pulse beneath my ribs. "That wasn't a good idea. She could have broken your fingers without even trying."

Claire grinned away my rebuke. "I knew she wouldn't."

"And you could hurt her," I continued. "If your hands are dirty, you could pass along all sorts of bacteria and viruses—"

"I just washed my hands . . . with antibacterial soap." Claire squatted before Sema. "You don't have to worry; I know how to handle the animals."

I cast Fielding a *help-me-out-here* look, but he only shrugged. "Claire's good, Glee, and she knows her stuff. You don't have to worry about anything if Claire's around."

"All the same," I lowered my voice, "I don't want just anybody in here with Sema, do you understand? She's not used to this situation, and I don't know how she's going to react to new stimuli—"

I halted as a buzzer shattered the stillness of the hallway. Claire and Fielding looked at each other, then Claire said, "I'll get it."

I waited until she left the room. "Was that the door?"

"Yeah."

"Who buzzes?"

"Delivery people and zoo staff who forget their key cards."

"I thought we were the only three employees at this pavilion."

"We are, but there are custodians and security people and Dr. Parker, the vet . . . and Matthews, of course."

I snorted. "He's the last person I want to see today."

The words had no sooner left my lips than Ken Matthews appeared in the doorway, a sheen of perspiration on his silver brow.

"There she is!" He bent forward and peered at Sema like a man inspecting the grill of his expensive new car. "How is she settling in?"

For an instant I feared he'd walk forward and try to touch Sema as Claire had done, but the man wisely kept his distance. Sema had always been able to sense my feelings, though, and when I tensed at the sound of Matthews's voice, her smile disappeared. As the director peered at her, she peered back, her eyes narrowing into dark slits.

"We just got here," I managed to say before Fielding stepped between Sema and Matthews.

"They're doing fine, sir." He extended his arm in an attempt to herd the newcomer out of the room. "Why don't we leave Glee and Sema alone so they can get used to her new room?"

Fielding walked forward, but Matthews stepped to the side, to better stare at Sema. "I have a reporter waiting outside." He regarded my girl with a bland half smile. "I thought it'd be good to get a couple of shots of the animal for tomorrow's paper. We want to take every opportunity to stimulate public interest."

I glared at the zoo director, but Fielding shot me a warning look. "Sema won't be available for viewing for quite some time," he pointed out. "Maybe it's not a good idea to arouse public interest just yet. I think we should wait at least a week after we know she's successfully habituated. Arousing public interest now—well, that'll put us under pressure we don't need."

As ticked as I was with Matthews, I had to admire Fielding's approach. He was absolutely right, of course—the last thing we needed were legions of mommies and daddies clamoring to have their children meet the famous talking gorilla. Once they learned Sema lived on the premises, they'd start asking for her, and once they started asking, Matthews's patience would only last so long.

Fortunately, Fielding's calm persuasion overpowered the director's eagerness. After a final glance at Sema, Matthews backed away, but not without a parting jab.

"Ms. Granger"—peering over Fielding's outstretched arm, he lifted a brow in my direction—"you seem to have forgotten that Thousand Oaks employees are to be in uniform whenever they are working on zoo property. That rule includes you."

I showed my teeth in a forced grin that, if I were a gorilla, would send the young ones scrambling for the treetops.

But I didn't say a word. If my plan to reclaim Sema was to succeed, I needed to have these people—including Matthews—on my side.

12

I didn't think Sema would remain awake long after our arrival. Her anticipation, combined with the stimulus of so many new sights and sounds, resulted in an exhaustion that lured her into sleep not long after Matthews and Claire left her new room.

While she napped, I ventured into the office. Fielding's desk stood against the windowed wall; two other desks occupied the opposite side of the room. Claire had obviously made herself at home at one, for a framed picture of a young man stood in the corner while a zoology textbook lay open above the kneehole. The third desk—a sorry specimen that lacked a solid veneer, a lock, and a chair of any sort—was littered with clipboards and notebooks.

Fielding came whistling into the room, then paused when he saw me. "Is your girl all settled in?"

I nodded. "She's napping, so I thought I'd have a look around the office. I guess I'll need to get organized."

Fielding followed my gaze to the cluttered desk, then hurried forward, a blush coloring his cheek. "Sorry about the mess. Let me move this junk out of your way."

I suppressed a smile as he lifted an ungainly stack of notebooks, then shoved them onto the top of a filing cabinet. "I didn't know how much stuff you'd bring over today," he said, gathering up the clipboards. "Moving Sema was enough of a challenge."

"It'll take me a while to figure out what I need to transfer. I tried to pack light, just in case—" I bit my lip. "Never mind. You don't need to worry, I won't bring all that stuff you saw in the trailer. Just a few logs and journals and a few of Sema's toys. I'm going to store most of my materials at home."

133

I crossed my arms and smiled at the empty spot before the desk. "Any chance of finding me a chair? Preferably one that doesn't spin."

"Doesn't spin—oh, yeah." He grinned. "I'll put in a requisition, but in the meantime, I think I can rustle up a chair somewhere. Let's see what we can find."

With nothing else to do, I followed him into the kitchen, where he pulled a chair from the dinette set. The padded red leatherette seat was ripped in several spots, but of the four chairs it was in the best condition.

He offered it with a smile of chagrin. "I'll get that requisition out today."

"It's okay, Fielding." I reached for the chair, but he held on to it.

"Of course, you know you can use anything in here— the microwave, fridge, coffeemaker—and the bathroom's through that little door in the corner."

I wanted to tell him nothing had changed in the eight years I'd been away, but maybe he was rambling just to fill the empty silence. So I decided to talk about something useful. "I often use treats in Sema's enrichment sessions, so I'll need a place to store her food and juice boxes."

"Help yourself to a cupboard. You might want to mark her stuff, though, so Claire doesn't help herself." He grinned. "She's partial to juice boxes, too."

I chuckled and stepped forward to take the chair. "That doesn't surprise me."

"I was thinking"—Fielding lowered the chair to the floor—"we should probably move Sema into the exam room sometime next week. Or we could put her in the area Dakarai's using now—that way she could see the other g's through the fencing, but she won't have access to them if we keep the gate closed."

My nerves tensed as Sema's move suddenly shifted from the indefinite future to *next week*. "You think we should move her so soon? You don't have to let Matthews pressure you. We need to give Sema time, see how she adapts."

His mouth curled in a one-sided smile. "I think she'll adapt with no trouble, but I'm completely open to your input. You can call the shots, but don't stall the project out of stubbornness."

I drew a quick breath. "As if I—"

"Come on, Glee, I know you're not happy about this. I've got to give you credit for coming and being pleasant, but you and I know you don't change your mind easily."

"Fielding," I whispered, my eyes moving into his, "do you remember how you felt when you and your girlfriend—what was her name?"

Something that looked almost like bitterness entered his face. "Who—you mean Felicia?"

"Yeah. Do you remember how you felt when you two lost that baby?"

The black pupils of his eyes narrowed and trained on me like gun barrels. "Why would you ask about that?"

"Because that's how I'll feel if I lose Sema. You got upset even though you never even saw that fetus. Now imagine how you'd feel if you'd loved that child for eight years and *then* lost it."

He didn't speak for a long moment. When he did, a silken thread of warning lined his voice. "You are way out of bounds, Glee. A gorilla is not a baby."

I lifted my chin. "I don't see much difference."

His gaze rested on me, remote and black as the ocean depths. "Then there's something seriously wrong with your perspective."

Unnerved by the intense shift in his demeanor, I faltered in the silence and wondered if I should apologize or leave him alone . . .

He lifted his clenched fist and methodically unfolded the fingers to scratch his chin. When he spoke again, his voice had returned to its usual pleasant tone. "The sooner Sema is habituated, the sooner Matthews will be happy. When Matthews is off my back, I'll be happy, too. Happy people make for a happy zoo, or have you forgotten that?"

"I haven't forgotten."

"Good."

He drew a deep breath, then exhaled slowly and glanced at his watch. "If there's nothing else you need, I ought to go. I have to run some samples over to Dr. Parker's office."

I lifted the sorry-looking chair and backed away. "I'm good. Thanks."

And as I walked toward the office, I couldn't help feeling that I had trespassed on memories he didn't like to revisit. The situation with Felicia had happened years ago; the entire episode was practically ancient history.

I'd been wrong to bring it up. Stupid, really.

I glanced over my shoulder. "I appreciate your help, Fielding."

I hoped he'd turn and see the sincerity on my face, but he merely lifted his hand in an absent wave and moved toward the exit.

As Sema slept, I decided to explore the outdoor areas of the pavilion. A high wall enclosed the interior of the zoo and concealed employee parking lots and staff entrances. The side of the wall facing the employee areas had been painted beige; the interior side had been adorned with a camouflaging mural of jungle trees and vines.

I slipped through a disguised doorway in the wall, then strode down a concrete sidewalk that led to the viewing area for the gorilla habitat, the pride and joy of Thousand Oaks Zoo. The public area outside the actual habitat had been designed to resemble a jungle outpost. A thatched roof covered a small area with stone benches for extended observation. An artist had painted fake chalkboards with the names and birthdates of the gorillas. High in the eaves of the roof, two video monitors allowed visitors to observe any g's in the grassy area and in the secluded cave outside the observation room.

The habitat itself was a spacious quarter acre with man-made hills, shrubbery, sprawling oaks, and two caves where the animals could retreat. The first cave led the animals to a Plexiglas wall where they could get up close and personal with zoo visitors. The smaller cave took them to the one-way mirror where they could study an image of themselves while people in the observation room studied them.

Unfortunately for Sema, who'd grown accustomed to man-made toys in her play yard, the habitat offered no Little Tykes playhouses or rubber balls, but plenty of logs, branches, and other natural materials for gorilla games.

The north end of the habitat featured a grassy meadow standing open to the sun and sky. Only a moat and a waist-high wall on the spectator's side separated the animals from the public. The ten-foot-deep moat curved around the edge of the habitat in a gentle semicircle, then the dark water disappeared beneath a stone bridge where more dedicated observers could stand and watch the gorillas while eating Congo Cotton Candy or sipping Simba Smoothies.

The sun had just passed its zenith when I sank to a bench in the shade of the grotto. Several of the gorillas crouched in the large cave, and despite my reluctant acceptance of the situation, I felt a warm glow flow through me as I observed the small gorilla group. Because I'd come to know these individuals through their biographies on the zoo's Web page, I felt as though I were meeting pen pals for the first time.

The silverback, Dakarai, sat closest to the glass, his broad back more muscular than any heavyweight wrestler's. He had turned to glance in my direction when I sat down, but now he sat with his back to me, his attention focused on his family. At Dakarai's right, ten-year-old Mosi played with a chain of Spanish moss. The young gorilla kept looking up at Dakarai, his expression evoking a strange sense of déjà vu. After a moment, I remembered—Mosi's guarded glances reminded me of the TV commercial featuring an adoring boy who gazes reverently at his favorite football player and finally finds the courage to offer the man a Coke.

Smiling, I searched my memory for details about these two. According to information posted on the Web site, Dakarai had been born in the wild, captured by poachers as a four-year-old (and undoubtedly orphaned in the process), and sold to a European zoo. There he lived mainly in solitary confinement until the Thousand Oaks Association purchased him and Mosi in 2001. Since then Dakarai had lived here in peace and contentment, the quiet leader of a prosperous gorilla family.

His son, Mosi, on the other hand, had been born in captivity and reared by humans. Mosi's mother proved unable to care for her baby, so zookeepers nursed the infant while allowing him to maintain contact with the group. His human connections proved important when his mother died from respiratory infection a year after his birth.

My gaze wandered over the other gorillas. The female sitting across from Dakarai had to be Aisha, the dominant female or, in human terms, the "first wife." At twelve, Aisha had successfully borne and nursed two-year-old Rafiki. One of the lucky ones, Aisha had been born in the San Diego Zoo and reared by an attentive mother. Because she had benefited from and witnessed exemplary maternal care, she had proven to be a wonderful mother for Rafiki.

How appropriate that her Swahili name meant *she is life.*

I looked up as Dakarai's second female, the pregnant Kamili, knuckle-walked into the grotto, probably seeking shade from the afternoon sun. She leaned toward Dakarai, then drew back and settled in a spot near the cave's entrance.

I found myself feeling sorry for her. Kamili's inferior social position seemed to result in anxiety, especially when she sat in close proximity to Dakarai and Aisha. My suspicions were confirmed when Aisha hooted at Kamili, then ambled over to Dakarai, sat beside him, and began running her long fingers through his fur, a grooming ritual noted among great apes throughout the world. Almost anyone could have picked up her nonverbal message: *he's my man, so keep your distance.*

Not one to be upstaged, Kamili reached for Rafiki, pulled the baby onto her lap, and began grooming the youngster. I half-expected Aisha to rise up and snatch her child from Kamili's grip, but she kept grooming the silverback.

I studied Kamili, looking for special signs of pregnancy within her round gorilla belly. At ten years old, she was pregnant for the first time. Because she'd been born in captivity and raised by humans, we would have to be vigilant when it came time for her baby to be born.

I blinked at a sudden realization—according to the material I'd read, Kamili was due in early April. I was hoping to be home with Sema by then, but if Matthews insisted that we make occasional visits to the zoo—a compromise I'd be willing to consider—we might well be here when the blessed event occurred.

Reluctantly, I shoved the thrilling thought aside. I couldn't allow myself to become attached to these animals. If our attempt at habituation failed, Sema and I might be home within four weeks. We'd miss meeting Kamili's baby, but a gorilla birth would allow Ken Matthews to focus on something other than a talking gorilla.

I lifted my head as Rafiki escaped Kamili's grip and executed a series of somersaults across the floor, finally crashing into his father's strong arm. Dakarai looked down at his son, then lifted the grinning baby with one hand and cradled him in the bend of his arm.

The scientific researcher in me melted into a puddle of sentiment. Silverbacks have been known to kill men, wild beasts, and even infants fathered by rival males, but they are generally the gentlest of fathers.

I blinked away a sudden smattering of tears. I had to focus my thoughts. I'd come out here to study this group in order to see how Sema should approach them. If my plan failed and she were fully habituated, she would enter this group with a lower social rank than Aisha. Depending upon the animals' personalities, she might even rank lower than Kamili.

How would she handle such a demotion? Though she'd been born in captivity, she'd never known anything but lavish human attention and near-constant stimulation. I had been her social group, teacher, mother, and friend. She had been the center of a human's universe, so how would she react if these gorillas ignored or mistreated her?

Until that moment, I had hoped I could convince Fielding that Sema couldn't be habituated while secretly believing she *could* join this group. But as I watched Dakarai with his children and his females, I couldn't help but wonder if these gorillas would know what to make of her.

I rested my elbow on my knee and parked my chin in my hand. Sema tended to pout when she didn't get her way; in her early years she had thrown temper tantrums worthy of a spoiled starlet. We'd worked through most of those childish behaviors, but if Sema tried to reason with these gorillas as she reasoned with me, Dakarai might react with fierce resistance.

For my beloved girl's sake, I decided to scour the trailer for *Natural Wildlife* videos of free-living gorilla behavior. Over the next few days, Sema and I would watch these videos together. I'd spent eight years teaching her how to relate to humans—the least I could do now was spend a few days teaching her how to relate to her own species.

I'd be walking a fine line for the next several days. I wanted Sema to be safe when she interacted with the other g's, but I didn't want her to adjust completely. If she did, I'd never be able to take her home again.

Fielding's left brow shot up when he saw me walk into the office with my overnight case and a sleeping bag. "May I ask what you're doing?"

I dropped my burdens by the side of my sorry-looking desk. "What does it look like? I'm preparing for a slumber party."

"That's not a good idea, Glee. You said you'd follow the rules."

I took a deep breath and adjusted my smile. "Since when are pajama parties against the rules?"

He crossed his arms. "I've been trying to cut you some slack because I know this situation is . . . unusual. But what good do you think you're going to accomplish by spending the night? Sema has to make a break from you sooner or later."

"Then she can make it later. She might have a hard time adjusting to all this. I want to be here if she does."

"Glee." Fielding's voice flattened. "The other animals come in, adjust, and manage to cope perfectly well."

"Sema's not just another animal."

"Sometimes I wonder if you forget she *is* an animal."

I met his gaze, careful to keep my voice low so Sema wouldn't overhear. "What is an animal, Fielding? Something with fur? Some creature with the misfortune of not being born *homo sapiens*? Animals have emotions, too, and Sema has them in high definition and surround sound. She won't understand if I take off and leave her."

"You might be surprised—she's a big girl."

"She's a big baby and you know it."

"I know she doesn't need to be mollycoddled."

I inhaled a deep breath. "Listen to yourself. I know you've spent the night with sick gorillas. You've stayed awake to see a mother safely through labor. I know you, Fielding, and I know you wouldn't think twice about sticking around if one of the other g's needed you. Sema may not be sick, but she needs me, so I'm spending the night. So go about your business and forget I'm here. I promise I won't go through your desk or burn the place down while you're out."

Though his brow remained as low as a Neanderthal's, Fielding unfolded his arms. "You can stay—but only for one night and you can't sleep in her room. That's strictly against zoo policy."

I turned and moved toward the door. "Like I care about policy."

"There's a cot," Fielding called over the creak of his chair. "It's in the storage closet. You can set it up in the hallway outside the observation room."

A little amazed at how easily he had acquiesced, I smiled as I entered the kitchen. A moment later Fielding peered around the edge of the door and gave me a warning look. "Don't say anything to anyone about this. And if you wait a minute, I think I can find you a pillow."

After Sema's dinner, I commenced our regular evening routine: one storybook followed by tooth brushing and a light application of baby oil on the soft portions of her face and the smooth areas of her chest. These tender rituals had bound us since Sema's infancy, and I didn't want to disturb them.

By eight o'clock, my girl and I lay awake in the steady glow of her Jungle Book nightlight. Even in a sealed building, the night around us had filled with the noises of all sorts of creatures—the chuff of lions, the trumpeting of elephants, the call of roosting birds. From closer at hand, we heard the rustling sounds of the other gorillas as they settled into their night nests.

Ignoring the cot Fielding had set up in the hallway, I stretched out in my sleeping bag on the straw-covered floor. Sema sat in her inner tube-comforter nest, her chin resting on her chest, her eyes round as she listened. Every few minutes she would ask *What noise?* and I'd try to identify the sound we'd heard.

She broke into a grin when we heard the wail of a siren on the highway. *Hurry hurry truck?*

"That's right, sweetie. The same hurry trucks we heard at home."

After an hour of playing "what's that sound?" Sema curled up on her Care Bear comforter and drifted into a doze. Knowing she would sleep for the next several hours, I crawled out of my sleeping bag, pulled a few bits of straw from my hair, and crept through the complex. Though I was as emotionally drained as I'd ever been, my body would not shut down before 11:00 PM.

After getting a cup of water from the cooler in the kitchen, I walked down the long hallway and looked through gates into the other night rooms. Silence had settled over this end of the building, broken only by an occasional rumbling belch, an innocent vocalization Dian Fossey had interpreted as *I'm here*.

The gorillas were shadowy sleeping forms inside their darkened rooms, but I felt a thin blade of foreboding slice into my heart when I looked into one room and saw a pair of glowing eyes watching from above.

Dakarai.

The silverback did not yet know me; no wonder he was alert and on guard. Obeying a primitive instinct, I ducked my head and took a half-step back, reflexively signing *sorry* as I retreated.

As I walked back to the office, I wondered if my presence could have an effect on the other gorillas. I didn't plan to be around long, but if I became a permanent part of their lives, might my occasional signing make an impression? Would the other animals pick up new words? The older animals might not, but Rafiki was young, bright, and adaptable.

I stepped into the office and stood in the glow of a solitary desk lamp. With nothing else to do, I sipped my water and watched the bank of digital cameras mounted on the walls. Six monitored the habitat; six others monitored the night rooms. The equipment operated at all times, Fielding had explained, and motion-activated sensors would record anything that moved throughout the night.

The improved security impressed me. When I worked here in before-Sema days, the setup had been far more primitive. One night a man had purposely remained in the zoo after closing, then he crawled over a railing and dropped into the lions' habitat, waiting for sunrise and an opportunity to "wrestle the king of beasts." Fortunately, a motion detector picked up the man's movements and activated a video camera, which malfunctioned after a few minutes. The next morning, the blinking red light caught the lion curator's attention; blind luck revealed the trespasser sleeping under a tree. Instead of wrestling a pride of lions, the man tangled with a pair of security guards who successfully removed him before the animals were released.

The memory drew me to Fielding's desk, where I realized the man was still as tidy as a cat. While piles of unorganized clutter littered my desk, his files accordioned in a neat stack, his pens waited at attention in a leather pencil cup. Several books, including Fossey's *Gorillas in the Mist*, stood erect between two wooden bookends. His books, I noted with a frisson of horror, had been ordered by height—the tallest hardcover on the left, the shortest paperback on the right.

Only one photo occupied Fielding's desk—the framed five-by-seven Sema had kissed. I picked it up for closer examination. Rafiki must have been no more than two months old when the photographer snapped the photo. The little gorilla looked like a downy ball of fluff with bugging golden brown eyes.

I smiled at the picture and tenderly traced the outline of the infant's round head. In time that head would elongate and grow into a splendid sagittal crest like his father's; in fourteen or fifteen years Rafiki would be ready to lead his own family group. If Dakarai still reigned at Thousand Oaks, Fielding would transfer Rafiki to another zoo.

Despite the irritation that rose from within me every time I spoke to Fielding, I couldn't help but smile as I set the picture back on his desk. The man had no sports paraphernalia on his desk, no girlie calendar in view, no portrait of a girlfriend.

Only baby Rafiki.

Clearly, the man had his priorities in order.

13

A bright light pried at my eyelids. Groaning, I rolled over in the straw, then glanced at my wristwatch: 5:30 AM. The early shift had arrived.

A moment later I heard Claire's sneakers squeak over the tiled floor in the hallway. I turned back toward the offending light in time to see the girl slap her hand across her mouth. "Oh! I'm so sorry, Glee! I didn't know you were here."

"It's okay." I pushed myself up, then raked hair from my eyes and peered up at Claire. "Time to eat, is it?"

"Time to prepare breakfast 'n browse," she whispered, tiptoeing into the kitchen. "Go back to sleep if you want. It takes me a good hour to get everything together."

"I'll help you," I said, struggling to pull my legs free of my sleeping bag. "Just let me splash some water on my face."

After taking a few minutes to freshen up in the restroom, I pulled on clean underwear, jeans, and a fresh T-shirt, then slipped into my dingy lab coat. When I stepped out into the kitchen, Claire had already covered the dinette table with plastic bowls the size of industrial garbage can lids. She slid a plate of baked apples from the microwave as I dropped my overnight case into an empty chair.

I leaned against the wall, watching as she slipped vitamin pills into the center of each soft apple, then tossed an apple into each bowl. "Do you feed them the same thing every morning?"

"Pretty much—but what we give them, of course, depends on what's in season. The local grocer leaves boxes of produce by the door every morning at five; we try to feed the animals and get the browse into the habitat before eight. Once the g's are awake, the first thing they want is food."

She grinned at me beneath her spiky bangs and I grimaced back at her. "Do you mind if I take what I need for Sema's breakfast?"

"Help yourself."

I grabbed one of the bowls from beneath the counter and picked through the boxes of organic fruits and vegetables. Along with different kinds of leafy greens, I found several of Sema's favorite foods—apples, oranges, cantaloupe, assorted peppers, string beans, corn, and brussels sprouts.

I had to admit, the zoo had good grub.

I picked up a cantaloupe and weighed it in my palm.

"Do you slice fruit like this?"

Claire smiled. "Sometimes I'll cut them in half, but not always. Dakarai likes to smash melons against the wall and eat the broken bits."

"Sounds messy."

"It is."

I felt a blush burn my cheek as I set the cantaloupe in Sema's bowl. I usually sliced my girl's foods; sometimes I inserted juicy cantaloupe segments between slices of soft bread. I didn't dare admit this to Claire—no sense in telling her how thoroughly I had spoiled my girl. But my overindulgences might work in our favor if Sema didn't like the change in feeding routine. If we were going to make a case for maladjustment, no issue would be too trivial to consider.

I added greens, apples, and a mixture of brightly colored peppers to the bowl, then sprinkled the mixture with a handful of chickpeas. Sema ate between ten and twelve pounds of produce a day, along with several snacks, three juice boxes, and at least half a hamburger.

I glanced over my shoulder at Claire, who hummed as she doled veggies into the plastic bowls. "You're awfully chipper for this awful hour."

She stopped humming as the tip of her nose went pink. "Sorry."

"You don't have to apologize—I'm just not a morning person. I've always been grateful that Sema likes to sleep until eight or so."

Claire scooped up an armload of corn on the cob. "I can't help it—I like getting up early because I love watching the sunrise. I grew up in Cocoa Beach, and the sight of the sun coming up over the ocean—wow. Just thinking of it can take my breath away."

From lowered lids, I shot a quick glance at my companion. Was she kidding?

"It's so spiritual," she went on, dealing ears of corn into the bowls. "Even the sky itself seems to celebrate the glory of mother earth. It's like every sunrise is a celebration, every night a benediction." She shrugged slightly as a smile lit her face. "You may think I'm crazy, but I don't think I'll ever get used to it. I see the glory of nature in almost everything, especially the animals, but nothing paints as simple a picture as a sunrise."

I looked toward the door, half-expecting Fielding or a team from *Candid Camera* to come barreling through the doorway. When seconds passed and nothing happened, I shook my head and went back to filling Sema's bowl.

"That's nice. You sound like my grandmother. She's religious too."

"Religious?" Claire sucked at the inside of her cheeks for a minute, her narrow eyebrows working. "I don't think of myself as religious anymore. I used to go to church three times a week, but I got fed up with being stuffy and conventional. The earth is so much more alive, you know?"

"You're not religious? Then how would you describe yourself?"

She tilted her head, her gaze roving the ceiling tiles as

if the answer were printed above our heads. "I think I'd say I'm . . . spiritual. In tune with the spirits of the earth and sky. That's why I love the gorillas—I yearn to hear the songs of the gorilla nation; I want to experience the ties that bind us together."

I felt a smile creep over my face. Claire might be young and a little flaky, but at least she understood the link between humans and animals. "Believe it or not, I understand."

I watched as she stacked the first three bowls, then lifted them with both hands. "Do you need help?"

She peered at me around the sloping edge of a bowl. "You can get the door for me; after that I'll be fine. We slide the bowls through the spaces at the bottom of the doors. While the g's are eating, I'll hit the stairs and get started on the browse."

"I don't remember seeing stairs."

"They're on the outside of the building—and not much more than scaffolding, really. We toss bundles of browse through openings in the covered part of the habitat," Claire answered. "With a little practice, you'll be able to land browse in the tree branches and high on the rocks—and that's good for the g's. You know—gotta keep them interested and active."

I nodded. The harder the animals had to work for their snacks, the better off they'd be. Sema, on the other hand, had spent her life pursuing rewards through more intellectual pursuits. Though I had occasionally scattered browse in her play yard, she was not going to like having to climb trees and race the others to win a fistful of celery.

Another reason why she might hate living here.

I felt a little like dancing as I lifted her bowl and carried it to her room.

After Sema had eaten her breakfast, I took the empty bowl back to the kitchen, then paused in the doorway to the office. Fielding had come in while I fed Sema. He sat at his desk, a clipboard in his hand and a frown on his face.

"Hi," I called, purposely trying to maintain a pleasant tone. "Didn't hear you come in."

He looked up. "Morning. How did you two make out last night?"

"Fine, once we got used to all the strange noises." I pulled away, about to return to Sema, but Fielding cocked a finger at me. "Got a minute? Now that you and Sema have settled in, I think we need to go over the work schedule."

I forced a smile. I knew this was coming—and while I didn't mind working around the clock for Sema, I wasn't thrilled about being distracted by a schedule that would have me cleaning up after five other animals too. But such was the price I'd have to pay until Sema and I could go home again.

I grabbed the tattered dinette chair from my desk and slid it toward Fielding's. "No time like the present."

He waited until I sat down, then cleared his throat. "First, I want to assure you that we appreciate your work with Sema. We want you to continue, but that will involve only a couple of hours per day, right?"

"Technically, that's true, but even when we play, we're signing and communicating. It's not like I have hours of free time in a day. When she naps, I'm usually recording my notes about her progress or entering data into my computer. When she's playing with her toys, I still have to clean up after her, prepare her foods, sanitize her sleeping area—"

"And that's where we'll help. Claire and I have been handling the food prep and cleaning for five gorillas, so adding one more isn't that big a deal."

I stiffened as his implication became clear. *Caring for one gorilla is child's play; we've been handling five.*

Fielding glanced at a letter on his desk, then eyed me with a calculating expression. "I know you've been accustomed to calling your own shots, but now we need you to be a team player. For the next week or two, I'd like you to conduct your sessions with Sema in the mornings and reserve her afternoons for activities that will aid her in habituation. We'll begin today by allowing her to visit the other night areas, to smell the others' scents and begin to identify them. If all goes well, by the end of the week we'll move her into the exam room—the other g's will be able to see her through the window, but we'll keep them separated. When we're sure she'll be safely received, we'll introduce her in the habitat. We'll try the first meeting on a Sunday morning because we can better monitor the situation if the zoo is closed."

I nodded slowly. Fielding's plan sounded reasonable,

but I needed to let him know of my doubts. I wanted him to see the problems as I saw them, so if that meant teaching him to see the glass as half-empty rather than half-full, so be it.

"I think you should know," I lowered my gaze, "that I've had some real doubts about whether this will work at all."

"You said Sema was doing well."

"She's fine *now*—in her private room and with me close by. But how would you feel if you were suddenly ripped from your home and dropped into a culture where no one spoke your language? Even if you knew the people and were familiar with their scents, not being able to communicate might drive you a little crazy."

Fielding leaned back and crossed his arms. "We've habituated gorillas before. Even animals from pathetic circumstances."

"But no one's ever habituated a talking gorilla to a captive group. Sure, Sema's excited now about being with the other g's, but how is she going to feel a month from now? She may regress; she may withdraw; who knows?"

"That"—Fielding leaned forward—"is why you're here. To make sure the transition goes well. You'll still have your daily time with her; you can keep her skills sharp."

I crossed my arms and shrugged. "Whatever."

He lifted the clipboard. "We'll see what happens," he said, "but in the meantime, you need to start keeping regular hours. Claire has been handling the early shift alone—I want to cut her back to three days a week and let you handle four. She needs time to study and you need time with Sema, right?"

I narrowed my eyes. Rising before sunup has never been my idea of the best way to start the day, but if I had to prepare breakfast for six gorillas and deliver browse through trapdoors in the rooftop . . .

"Good grief." The words slipped from my tongue. "I'll have to start in the middle of the night until I get the hang of it."

Fielding laughed. "The produce doesn't arrive until five. And you'll get the hang of it in no time. It's not rocket science."

I sighed heavily. "Okay."

"Whoever doesn't prepare breakfast 'n browse has to clean the night rooms," Fielding continued. "Old straw swept out, clean straw put down, any and all dung tagged and bagged."

"Wait." Tagged and bagged dung was a new routine since my days at the zoo pre-Sema. "I don't know these g's. How am I supposed to know which droppings belong to which animal?"

"Claire and I will help you at first, but in time you'll learn to recognize the way the g's build their night nests." Fielding skimmed the chart on his clipboard, then dropped it to his desk. "They have distinctive styles. Just bag the droppings, tag them with the name, and remove the soiled straw."

Chuckling, I lowered my head into my hand.

"What's so funny?"

"Nothing," I shook my head. "I suppose I thought—I mean, it was so easy to potty train Sema."

Fielding snorted. "Right. Like I'm going to teach our gorillas to use a porta-potty."

I exhaled a deep breath. "Okay, I tag and bag the dung. Then what? Send it to the lab?"

"Only every other day," Fielding said. "There's no need for an exam if the animals aren't sick. The minute one of them exhibits any kind of symptom, however, we rush all the stool samples to Dr. Parker's office."

"Got it."

"Also," Fielding continued, "Claire and I expect you to work us into your routine with Sema. She's your project—we respect that—but she's also the zoo's property. Mr. Matthews wants all of us to be able to handle her—that means we'll all need to communicate with her at least in a basic way."

Something in me rebelled at the idea. "Hold on a minute, Fielding. That wasn't part of the deal."

The corner of his mouth dipped in a frown. "Trust me, learning sign language is the last thing on my priority list. But Matthews has a point—what if you come down with the flu? Break your leg? Take a job in Timbuktu? If something happens to you, we'll be responsible for Sema. So it's not only right that you teach us: it's prudent."

I took a wincing little breath. By-the-rules Brad, a man who once made my heart beat at double speed, had become a card-carrying member of the Anal-Retentive Administrators' Association.

"Prudent," I repeated, my voice like chilled steel. "Good grief, Fielding, when'd you become such a pain in the rear?"

Wearing the weary and patient expression with which a father might regard a teenage daughter, he looked at me. "We also share the lecture duties." He pulled a sheet of paper from a drawer, then slid it toward me. "You know the drill—give the standard speech for special groups; answer questions. And keep an eye on the monitors in case we get people throwing trash into the moat. We don't often have trouble, but you know kids . . ."

I glanced at the paper. *Welcome to the Gorilla Pavilion, home of Thousand Oaks's lowland gorilla population. As you look at our animals, you'll notice that the faces of gorillas are different from one another, just like humans. Gorillas and humans have many things in common, but they differ, too. A man's arms are equal in length to his legs, but a gorilla's arms are a foot longer than his legs. The big toe on a gorilla's foot is more like a thumb on a human hand, enabling the gorilla to grab things with its feet . . .*

The paper went on, describing the gorillas' large stomach, family structure, and temperament. The material was standard stuff, yet comprehensive, simplified so even an elementary school student could understand.

"Any problem with that?"

I glanced up. "Did you write this?"

Fielding nodded.

"It's pretty good."

"Thanks. That leaves one last thing." He pitched a

pair of rubber gloves into my lap. "The newest employee has to empty the trash cans every Monday, Wednesday, and Friday. Sorry, but it's tradition."

I tossed the gloves back. "I don't think I am the newest employee. I worked here before, remember?"

He pushed the gloves to the edge of the desk. "Sorry, but Claire's been here three years—and that gives her more seniority even if we count your previous employment. You're definitely at the low end of the totem pole."

I gathered up the gloves, shot him the most withering look I could generate, then headed off to talk to Sema. As I stalked through the hall, I realized that both my gorilla and I occupied the lowest position of our social groups. Sema might not mind, but I definitely did.

14

As Sema enjoyed her afternoon nap, I donned the rubber gloves and walked toward the empty night areas. The zoo's gorilla group had been outside for hours, but the musty, sweet scent of gorilla still lingered in the air at this end of the building.

After undoing the latch on the first gate, I stepped into the room and studied the night nest in the straw. The compact rimmed oval occupied the corner of the room—where, I imagined, the animal had felt safe surrounded by two solid walls.

A soft voice interrupted my musings. "Have you figured them out?" Claire stepped into the room behind me. "Can you match the nest to the gorilla?"

I bit my lip, then stepped closer to the nest. The dung inside was well formed, solid, and sizable, indicating a healthy adult specimen. "Um . . . Aisha?"

Claire laughed. "Actually, Mosi slept in this room last night. You'll always be able to identify his room because he likes to sleep in the corner. The biggest nest always belongs to Aisha and Rafiki—the baby still sleeps with her, and probably will for at least another year. Aisha's nests are always a little flattened in one corner because Rafiki can be rambunctious early in the morning."

I pulled a ziplock bag from my pocket, turned it inside out, then used it to scoop up the droppings in the straw.

Claire grinned. "I can tell you've done that before."

I snorted softly. "Even potty trained gorillas make mistakes."

I turned the bag right-side out and zipped it, then pulled a felt-tip marker from my other pocket and labeled the specimen with Mosi's name.

"Up here," Claire stepped into the adjoining room and pointed to one of the iron platforms hanging on the wall, "is Dakarai's nest. See how the edges are less built up than the others? Sometimes I think he only makes a token effort. He uses just enough straw to cushion his behind, then he's set."

I placed one hand on my hip and studied the platform over my head. "Wonder why he likes to sleep up there?"

Claire shrugged. "Because he's the sentinel, I suppose. The guard."

"That makes sense. Though if an intruder were approaching from the hallway, Mosi would see him first."

"Yeah, but Dakarai would *sense* him." She arched her auburn brows into twin triangles. "Never underestimate the power of the silverback. He's one amazing guy."

As we moved into the next room, Claire slipped her hands into her pockets. "What kind of nest does Sema build?"

I laughed. "The Care Bear kind. I never wanted to mess with straw in the trailer, so she makes a nest with blankets tossed over an inner tube. She likes to sleep next to this old Care Bear comforter I found at a yard sale."

"Really? I don't think a comforter would last in here. The other g's like to rip things up."

"That would break Sema's heart. Maybe . . . maybe habituation isn't such a good idea."

Claire looked at me with a startled expression, then shrugged. "I'm sure it'll work out. We'll just have to keep straw in Sema's room and let her get used to it. If we take away the Care Bear blanket tonight or tomorrow—"

"Not yet." I pulled another plastic bag from my pocket. "I'm not rushing her toward something that might not work at all."

Claire helped me clean the rooms, demonstrating the

best ways to knock straw from a raised platform, scrape old straw up with a pitchfork, and run a disinfectant-soaked mop over the textured concrete floor. When we had brought several bales of straw into the area and scattered the fresh material throughout the rooms, I thanked her and went to wash my hands.

She had left the building by the time I came out of the bathroom. Grateful for an opportunity to spend time alone with my girl, I worked quietly until Sema woke from her nap. Then I offered her a box of juice and told her I had something to show her.

She glanced toward the TV and VCR I had set up while she slept. *See movie?*

"In a few minutes, maybe. But not now."

See gorillas? Play with gorillas?

"Not yet, sweetie. But I'd like to show you where the gorillas sleep."

With her hand firmly in mine, I led Sema into the first night room. Her jaw dropped as she took in the painted pictures, the iron platforms, the fire hoses stretched from wall to wall.

As attractive as those sights were, they didn't satisfy her. She pulled her hand free of my grasp. *Where gorillas? When gorillas visit?*

"The gorillas are outside. They aren't ready to meet you, but I thought you might want to look at the room where they sleep. See how they use straw for a nest?"

Despite her obvious disappointment, Sema walked through the rooms, peering around corners and looking up through the platforms' fretwork as if an animal

162

might be hiding just out of sight. She knuckle-walked through the layer of straw Claire and I had put down, occasionally picking up a handful and sniffing it. At one point she sat back and knuckle-beat her chest, spreading the hollow *pok-pok-pok* sound throughout the rooms, then she scampered back to my side.

Gorillas sleep here?

"Yes, Sema, every night."

Sema sleep here?

"Not tonight, sweetie. Perhaps soon you can sleep in there."

I pointed to the empty exam room, but Sema shook her head. *Stinky Glee. Sema sleep here, here, with gorillas. Hurry hurry sleep here now.*

"Not now," I repeated. "But come with me and I'll show you a movie. Would you like to watch gorillas on TV?"

See gorillas!

Taking my enthusiastic charge by the hand, I led her back to her room. While she napped, I had rifled through Fielding's video collection and found a *Natural Wildlife* DVD of free-living gorillas interacting in the jungle.

As I slipped the DVD into the player, I glanced over my shoulder. Sema had climbed into her blanket-covered inner tube and nestled her plush bear in her arm. She looked like a middle school girl settling in for videos and snacks at a slumber party.

Maybe she *was* more human than gorilla . . . and while I didn't want her to settle here, I didn't want her to be injured or traumatized when she was allowed to interact with the other g's. I'd studied this video when I first began working with gorillas, and I knew it contained footage of animals demonstrating proper submissive behavior.

I hoped Sema would watch and learn.

15

For the next three days, I wrestled with an undeniable reality. Each morning I woke in Sema's room, convinced I'd be able to slip away at five o'clock like every other full-time zoo employee, but at four thirty I'd look at my girl and see loneliness in the deep wrinkled wells of her eyes.

I couldn't leave her. If I left, she'd be completely alone.

And so I got up every morning, helped Claire prepare breakfast 'n browse, and staved off Sema's persistent questions about the other animals.

After breakfast, I tried to help Sema concentrate on her reading, but like a child counting the days until Christmas, she didn't want to think about anything but the other gorillas. She ended most of our arguments by calling me a stinky nut and facing the wall in a silent pout.

Films proved to be our salvation. Sema watched the free-living gorillas with fascination—and fortunately, Fielding had a vast DVD collection.

One afternoon Claire stepped into our room. "We had

to show films to Kamili," she said, a shy smile lighting her face. "She was raised by humans, remember? When she came into heat, she desperately wanted Dakarai's attention, but she couldn't figure out how to approach him. So one day we brought her into her night room, set up a TV outside the window, and left one of these DVDs playing. A month later, we confirmed her pregnancy."

At that point I wasn't overly concerned about Sema's reproductive knowledge, but I wanted to be sure she understood the group's social structure. As she watched the film, I sat beside her and provided a running narration in spoken English and sign language.

"See that silverback? Isn't he handsome? Dakarai is the silverback here," I told her. "He is the leader and he protects the others. He does not know you, so when you meet him, he may scream; he may beat his chest; he may rush toward you. If he does, don't run away. Just lie down on your belly and be still."

Sema's round eyes drank in the images, but I wasn't sure how much she understood. On the off chance she was thinking of herself as some kind of a human hybrid, I found footage of an angry male charging Sigourney Weaver from the movie *Gorillas in the Mist*. Sema watched the charging silverback, then turned to me.

Gorilla angry? Gorilla run?

"Yes," I told her, "but keep watching. If you stand still like that woman, the gorilla will calm down and be good. Then Sema and the gorilla can be friends."

I left the DVD playing and stepped out to get a juice box from the kitchen. The search took longer than I had planned—Claire had moved our juice boxes to another cupboard—and when I returned, the film had advanced to the scene where native poachers murdered Dian Fossey's favorite gorilla friend, Digit. Sema's eyes had gone wide and her hands lay silent in her lap.

Silently berating myself for my stupidity, I hurried to punch the power button, then lowered my head as the screen went black. I've always been careful to shield Sema from unpleasantness, so how could I have forgotten the tragic events of this film?

Maybe I could change the subject and distract her. Brightening my voice, I pasted on a smile and turned. "Look what I have, sweetie. Apple juice, your favorite. I even punched the straw for you."

Sema didn't look at the juice box, but gestured in frantic, sloppy signs: *Men hurt gorilla. Why?*

I sank to her blanket as cold reality swept over me in a choking wave. I had tried to teach Sema about life's most important concepts, but I had failed to teach her about death.

Where gorilla? Where Glee's friend gorilla?

I hesitated, blinking in confusion, then I realized what she meant. She had transposed the movie characters and real life; in her mind, I was Dian Fossey, she was Digit.

"Oh, sweetie. The gorilla died." Carefully, I made the open-palmed sign for *die*. "He's gone."

Where gorilla?

166

I shook my head. "He's nowhere, sweetheart. When you die, you go away."

Sema didn't answer, but hung her head and stared at the floor. Respecting her silence and her sorrow, I gave her a hug, then left the juice box on the straw and stepped outside.

Sema usually drifted right off after lunch, but that afternoon she sat in her nest and cried for nearly thirty minutes before finally falling asleep. Her sad hooting echoed down the hall and lifted the hair at the back of my neck—I'd never heard her express such sorrow, though Penny Patterson had written that Koko mourned in a similar fashion when her favorite kitten died.

Desperate to help my girl, I went in search of Fielding and found him at his desk. "May I ask how we're doing on the time line for Sema's habituation?"

He shot me a frown. "I thought you were in no hurry."

"I'm not, but Sema is. She's driving me crazy with wanting to see the others. She's—well, I think a little more exposure will be good for her. She's ready."

Fielding took a deep breath, then checked his calendar. "We could move her into the night area this week and try the first face-to-face contact this Sunday—which means we should move her into the exam room Friday or Saturday. If we don't feel confident about proceeding, we don't have to."

"Okay." I pressed my lips together and stood. "I'm going to run home to pick up a few things. I'll be back in about an hour."

Fielding looked at me with a smile in his eyes. "You mean you still have stuff at your house? I thought you'd moved all your earthly possessions into Sema's room."

"Very funny. You're a regular laugh riot, Fielding."

"I'm only half-joking. You need to break the connection, Glee. You can't expect her to bond to the other animals if she's still tied to you."

"I'm working on it. She's here, isn't she?"

"Yeah, but you haven't let her spend a single night alone. I don't know what you're afraid of—"

"I'm not afraid of anything."

"Aren't you?"

The question hung between us, but I wasn't about to answer. I was afraid of hurting Sema, having my work amount to nothing, watching my girl suffer—but Fielding didn't need to know my fears.

"An hour." I rapped on his desk. "I'll be back."

The house smelled stale and musty when I walked through the door. I hit the switch for the fan, then noticed the telephone answering machine blinking in a steady rhythm. I dropped the mail onto the kitchen counter, jabbed the play button on the machine, and moved to the refrigerator to pluck a Diet Coke from the shelf. My grandmother's voice filled the kitchen as I popped the lid.

"Hi, Glee. Listen, I know you're really busy right now, but we missed you at dinner Saturday night. Rob and Cheri came, can you believe it? So don't let us down this Saturday. We want to know how you and

168

Sema are adjusting. Call me if you can. Love you!"

I gulped at my soft drink, closed my eyes against a sudden onslaught of carbonated bubbles, then sighed as a telephone solicitor tried his best to convince me that I needed to subscribe to the *Wall Street Journal*. As if I had extra money to invest!

I moved to my room, turned on the small television on the dresser, and listened to the local news and weather channel as I fumbled through a drawer for clean lingerie. I desperately needed a shower—several days of paper towel baths in the small employee restroom had taken a toll. My hair, which was supposed to be worn in a carefree, fluffy style, looked far more flat than fluffy.

After stepping into the bathroom, I stripped off my filthy khakis and detestable tan shirt. I would wear one of my old T-shirts back to work; I had neither the time nor the inclination to do laundry. If Matthews saw me out of uniform—well, he wouldn't, because I'd be wearing my lab coat.

I was about to step into the shower when a phrase from the television grabbed my attention. "Ken Matthews," a helmet-haired anchor declared, "director of Thousand Oaks Zoo, announced a stunning new attraction at a press conference today. From the jungle-themed dining hall outside the gorilla pavilion, Matthews announced that Sema, the world's second female talking gorilla, had recently returned to the zoo and was in the process of being introduced to her new gorilla family."

I gripped the shower curtain, alarm needling through my veins. What in the world was Matthews thinking? How could he go public with this news now?

I yanked my robe from the back of the door and threw it over my shoulders as I padded into the bedroom. The camera panned a crowd at the zoo—no mistaking those painted walls or that vendor-studded sidewalk—and settled on Matthews, white hair perfectly in place, gold-rimmed glasses glinting in the sunlight. Wearing a light blue dress shirt, red suspenders, and a red tie, he stood outside the gorilla pavilion with Dakarai and his family in the background. As the camera zoomed in, a microphone picked up his voice: ". . . and we look forward to the thousands who will come for an opportunity to have a conversation with a genuine talking gorilla."

I dug my nails into my scalp as the camera cut back to the newscaster. He smirked at his female partner. "By the way, Marie, do you know how to talk to a fish?"

"No, Don." She flashed a bleached smile at the camera. "How do you talk to a fish?"

"You drop him a line."

I closed my eyes, waiting until the urge to leap back into my filthy clothes had passed. Every particle of my being wanted to fly to the zoo and confront Matthews about this latest idiocy, but what good would it do? The zoo owned Sema. The zoo director had every right to invite people to see her.

I would be completely unable to prevent Sema from becoming a tourist attraction unless I could convince Fielding that Sema could not adjust to life in the habitat.

First, though, I needed to speak to Fielding and warn him about his boss's foolhardy action. And since I wanted Fielding on my side of this debate, I should go to him smelling of something other than gorilla.

An hour later, still steaming, I pulled into my parking spot behind the gorilla pavilion. My temper had spiked when I first heard the news; now a dozen indignant questions kept my anger at a slow boil. What gave Matthews the right to schedule a press conference without first speaking to me? Had he discussed this with Fielding? If so, had Fielding kept the news from me? He might have, because he knew I'd be furious, but how dare he!

I slammed the car door and covered the distance between my car and the employees' entrance with long strides. My hands trembled as I fumbled for my key card, but I finally found the card at the bottom of my purse and zipped it through the lock.

The sound of Claire's laughter echoed in the hall as I came through the doorway. From the shadows on the floor I could tell she stood in Sema's room, her hands flying as she signed and spoke aloud: "You want me to scratch you?"

What was going on? Was the entire *world* conspiring against me today?

I took two quick steps, then hesitated as I watched the interplay of shadowy figures. Sema was talking to Claire. She often talked to other people through me, signing her thoughts while I interpreted. This was something new, something important.

Transfixed despite my anger, I leaned against the wall and remained out of sight.

"Oooohhh." Claire laughed. "I get it now. You want to be *tickled!* Come over here, then, and I'll tickle you."

I stepped forward in time to see Sema knuckle-walk toward Claire, her mouth open in a pink grin.

I couldn't allow this. "Claire, do you *want* to get hurt?"

She whirled, a flush brightening her face. "What?"

"I thought we had a policy of not touching the animals."

"Sure, but Sema's—"

"She is not a pet, Claire, and she's very strong. She could hurt you without intending to."

Claire stiffened. Though her blush betrayed her embarrassment, her eyes revealed her anger. "Sorry. I didn't mean to threaten your dangerous gorilla."

I leaned against the door frame and studied Sema, who was observing our exchange with interest. Because her moods vacillated with mine, I needed to restore peace . . . as smoothly as possible.

I pushed a smile across my lips. "Sorry for nearly taking your head off." I kept my voice low. "By the way, where'd you learn to sign?"

Claire gaped at me, probably wondering if I'd developed multiple personalities in the last hour.

"Church," she finally answered. "I used to interpret services."

"You're pretty good. But Sema doesn't understand

straight American Sign Language. Some of her signs are a little different."

Some of the frostiness left Claire's eyes. "I noticed that. I also noticed that you've invented unique signs. I didn't know the sign for *tickle*." The beginnings of a smile tipped the corners of her mouth. "That word never came up in a Sunday sermon."

I laughed. "I can imagine. Sema taps her underarm when she wants to be tickled." I remained silent a moment, waiting for Sema to realize that I was not angry with Claire. "How long have you two been talking?"

A wall sprang up behind Claire's eyes. "I don't know. A few minutes."

I smiled again. "I'm not mad, Claire, just concerned—and curious. I don't think Sema has ever directly conversed with anyone but me, so I'd like to know how the situation developed."

The girl leaned against the wall. "It was no big deal, really. I was walking by and saw Sema was awake. I opened the door and casually signed, 'Hi, Sema,' and she responded with the sign for *C-person*." She shrugged. "I figured that's what you had taught her to call me, so I asked how she was feeling. She signed *fine*, so I asked if she wanted anything, and she started tapping her underarm. She had her mouth open, like she was laughing. That's when I figured out that she wanted me to tickle her."

I nodded, absorbing the information in a pleasant haze of disbelief. How amazing. Sema had behaved as naturally as any individual being greeted by another. She had not only responded appropriately and logically, but she had demonstrated her ability to recall a name and place it with the proper person . . . I had to record every detail.

"Thanks, Claire." I gave her a genuine smile. "This is a red-letter day."

Claire snorted softly and sidled toward the door. "If you say so." Moving out of the room, she raised her hand. "Bye, Sema. Catch you later."

Sema leaned sideways, watching Claire walk away, then righted herself and looked at me. *Claire gone?*

"She's going to work." I slipped my lab coat over my nonregulation T-shirt. "And I've got to go talk to Brad. Would you like some juice before I go?"

Good juice. Apple juice. Hurry hurry want apple juice.

I laughed. "I get it; you're thirsty. I'll be right back."

Leaving a happy gorilla girl slurping from a sippy cup and watching *The Wizard of Oz*, I went in search of Fielding. I found him outside, sweating in the sun as he and another khaki-clad employee unloaded baled straw from the back of a pickup truck.

Fielding grinned when he saw me. "What's the problem now, Glee?"

"Did I say there was a problem?"

"You're wearing that look."

I pressed my lips together, purposely waiting in the shade until they had finished and the driver pulled

174

away. When Fielding and I were alone, I stepped forward and crossed my arms. "Why does Matthews think he can schedule a press conference about Sema without talking to me first?"

Fielding pulled a handkerchief from his pocket and mopped his brow. "If you'll recall," he spoke in an even and measured tone, "Sema belongs to Thousand Oaks Zoo. Despite the agreement the lawyers hammered out, I don't think Matthews is required to consult you about any of his decisions."

For an instant my head buzzed with angry words, then one question shot to my lips: "Did you know?"

"As a matter of fact"—his gaze rose to meet mine—"I did, but only about five minutes before Matthew stepped out to speak to the reporters. I wanted to warn you, but you'd already left the pavilion."

"What was Matthews thinking? We're trying to accomplish something on a slow and steady course, so why did he go public with the news now?"

"He didn't announce a date," Fielding pointed out, "and he knows our first priority is getting Sema safely habituated. After that's accomplished, why not give the public a chance to meet her? A few minutes of social interaction shouldn't interfere with your work—it might even prove interesting. How many other signing gorillas are regularly exposed to the public?"

"None, and with good reason. We can't let people come up to her. She could be exposed to all kinds of illnesses—"

"Matthews can't be planning on face-to-face interaction," Fielding interrupted. "Whatever he does, it'll be safe. Maybe we can rig something up with cameras or closed-circuit TV—she could interact with people from the safety of the observation room." He mopped his face one more time, then grinned at me. "Why wouldn't that work?"

Because I'm not planning on being here. I had to bite the inside of my lip to keep from screaming the words. If my plan succeeded, Sema wouldn't adjust to habituation and Fielding would agree she'd be better off at home.

This conversation might have been a mistake. I'd come on like an adversary and I desperately needed him as a partner.

"Fielding," I injected a worried note into my voice, "what if Sema doesn't adjust? I've been trying to help her—you have to admit that—but I'm not sure this is going to work. She may be fascinated with the others for a while, but you were right: she *is* used to being the center of attention. I'm afraid she will fail to thrive after a while . . . and we may realize she is better off living in human society."

Fielding stuffed his handkerchief back into his pocket and gave me a wry smile. "I think she'll do fine. And I think the move will be good for both of you. Sure, Sema's going to have to learn how to be a gorilla. She's going to have to learn that the universe doesn't revolve around her, but isn't that part of growing up? Kids do it. Sema can do it too."

"But she's not a kid—"

"Did you ever stop to think, Glee, that maybe this move will be a good thing for you, too? I mean, think about it—can you name another thirty-year-old woman who has focused her entire life on the well-being of an animal?"

For an instant I was speechless, then names sprang to mind: "Dian Fossey. Jane Goodall."

"Fossey? She cared for a species, not a single animal. Some folks say she cared more for gorillas than for people, and look what all that caring got her—a machete through the skull. Goodall, on the other hand, cares for chimpanzees, but she also has a husband and family. She learned how to balance her work and her life."

I stared at him, unable to believe what I was hearing. "You think my life is out of balance? How would you know, and why on earth should you care?"

Fielding stepped back into a sliver of shade, then leaned against the wall. "We used to be friends," he said, his brown eyes lit with a golden glow. "And friends look out for one another. If we're not friends anymore, well, maybe I should keep my mouth shut. It's your call, Glee. If you want me to keep quiet, all you have to do is say so."

I couldn't find words to answer. This conversation had not proceeded the way I wanted it to; he had wandered into topics I never meant to discuss.

So I responded the way any self-respecting researcher would—I lifted my chin and met his gaze head-on.

"We might still be friends," I answered, "if you hadn't

been so intent on leaving Sema alone the night she was born."

A sudden spasm of regret knit his brows. "Will you never forget that night? I'm sorry. You were right and I was wrong. But that was eight years ago. We've both learned a lot since then."

"Yeah, we have."

I looked down and nudged a clump of grass with my sneaker. He'd never apologized before, but an apology couldn't restore the closeness we had once shared. We had learned about each other. I knew he would always be by-the-book-Brad and he knew I would always be a boat rocker. How could two people of such differing perspectives be good friends?

We could work together . . . but no more than that. We were just too different.

"When you're ready to talk about our work," I avoided his eyes, "I'll be with Sema."

Wrapped in as much dignity as I could muster, I turned and walked away.

16

Sema and I were watching the Wicked Witch of the West screech her way into a puddle when Fielding leaned into the observation room. "Just got a call from Matthews's secretary," he said, his face locked in neutral. "He wants to meet with us."

Turning so Sema couldn't see my expression, I looked at Fielding and frowned. "When?"

"Now. I told her to give us a few minutes and we'd be right over."

I rolled my eyes, but something told me it'd be useless to protest. I had no idea what Matthews had up his sleeve, but this might be the time to tell him about my concerns. I could hint that Sema might not adjust, that she'd make better progress and be happier in her trailer . . . and maybe Fielding would support me.

I told Sema I'd be back in a few minutes, then stood and closed the door. Fielding followed me down the hall and together we stepped out into the bright sunshine.

With a gentle tap in the small of my back, he steered me onto the sidewalk that led to the executive offices.

I fell into step beside him. "Do you know what this is about?"

He shrugged. "You saw the press conference, so you probably know more than I do."

"You're Matthews's gorilla guy."

Fielding gave me a wintry smile. "Lay off, Glee. I'm not the enemy."

I was about to meet his remark with sarcasm, then thought better of it. Fielding was right—at this moment, Matthews was the enemy. I needed to focus on him.

My skin contracted into gooseflesh the moment we entered the director's air-conditioned office. I ran my hands over my arms and shivered. "Good grief. Is he raising penguins in here?"

A sweater-clad secretary gave me a wan smile. "Ms. Granger," she said, standing. "Glad you could make it.

Let me tell him you and Mr. Fielding have arrived."

She walked away, leaving us to shiver in the frigid atmosphere. Avoiding Fielding's eyes, I looked around the room. Aside from the wild animal prints on the walls and the Arctic temperature, nothing in this space reminded me of animals—no musty smells inhabited the carpet; no straw littered the floor; no chain-link fencing protected the windows. And though I had inspected the secretary from head to toe, I hadn't spied even a spot of khaki.

I looked up as she opened a paneled wood door. "Come this way, please."

She ushered us into a large wood-accented room dominated by a desk that must have weighed two tons. Animal prints adorned these walls, too, and a zebra-skin rug lay at an angle on the floor—an odd choice for a man reportedly concerned with the conservation of the world's wildlife.

"Welcome Brad, Glee," Matthews said, standing. He gestured to two guest chairs before the massive desk. "Have a seat, please. I've been eager to talk to you about the latest developments with our extraordinary gorilla."

I was tempted to play dumb—after all, I might have missed the press conference entirely if I hadn't gone home and turned on the television. But apparently Matthews assumed Fielding would fill me in on the details.

The zoo director sank back into his chair. "The news about Sema was well received at the media event this afternoon." He grinned at us above his folded hands. "Privately, I had a couple of people assure me that this could be the biggest thing to hit our field since the giant pandas arrived at the National Zoo in Washington."

Fielding spared me the trouble of asking for clarification. "I'm sorry, sir, but I missed the conference, and I'm a little confused. The newspaper reported that Sema would return to the zoo when we settled the lawsuit. So why all the excitement today?"

Matthews's feathery brows shot up to his hairline. "Because today we announced our plans to build a new complex for our talking gorilla." He leaned back in his chair and swiveled to face me. "I've been talking to some of the leading experts, and they're almost unanimous in their opinion that Sema will never be properly habituated. Her background's too different, she's too set in her ways to learn new behaviors, and she's been imprinted with human patterns rather than primate."

Prickles of alarm nipped at the backs of my knees. What experts had he been talking to? Realizing that the situation was slipping out of my control, I gave him a forced smile and a tense nod of agreement. "That's been my contention all along, Mr. Matthews. That's why I think it'd be better—"

"To build a special exhibit for the talking gorilla." He finished my sentence and tapped the desk for emphasis. "It'll be expensive, but the increase in attendance should pay for the project in less than a year. And you don't need to worry about a thing, Glee—the gorilla will have her own play yard and a private night room in

181

the back. I have an architect already working on the plans."

I glanced at Fielding, whose face had gone bright with color. "Mr. Matthews, I'm not sure—"

"Best of all," the director said, ignoring me, "the new facility will house a replica of an old-fashioned school-room. We'll build a gorilla-sized desk and put a chalk-board on the back wall, complete with those old phonics charts that used to hang in every American classroom. Zoo visitors will look in through a one-way mirror so they can watch you work without interrupting your sessions."

Stunned by sheer disbelief, I couldn't speak.

Apparently taking my silence for gratitude, Matthews continued. "No need to thank me. I know you're con-cerned about continuing your research, so we'll arrange the schedule around your routine. We wouldn't want you to stop training the animal."

"Training?" The word came out hoarse, forced through my tight throat. "You train a dog, a seal, a race horse. Training implies punishment and reward for pre-determined behaviors. I have never *trained* Sema to do anything but use the toilet—everything else she's learned has come from *teaching*."

Matthews gave Fielding a *what's-her-problem* look, then shrugged. "Only a question of semantics, and it really doesn't matter. Just continue your project and we'll all be happy. The research has been your focus all along, hasn't it?"

I stared at him as my grand plan cracked and crumbled. What was *wrong* with this man? Yes, I cared about my research, but I cared most about Sema! I had nearly worn myself out warning him that she wouldn't thrive in a gorilla group, and now he was behaving as though he'd believed my contention all along. But now, of course, he wanted to control the situation and he wanted the zoo to profit from my hard work.

"This plan is stupid and cruel." The words slipped from my lips before I had time to consider a more diplomatic reaction. "You'll be condemning Sema to a life of loneliness."

"I'm afraid Glee has a point," Fielding added. "We owe this animal a chance to bond with a family. Primates are social creatures, Mr. Matthews; they need each other. Sure, Sema's background is unique, but she's still a gorilla. I think it'd be grossly unfair to place her in a solitary habitat."

Uncertain how to proceed, I looked from Matthews to Fielding. I had wanted to use Matthews's argument to defeat Fielding's habituation plan, but if I stressed Sema's uniqueness now, I would consign her to a fate far worse than life with a gorilla family.

"Sema would be miserable," I met Matthews's gaze, "if you made her live alone. To keep her in a separate pavilion and expect her to entertain an unseen audience . . . it's the worst thing I could ever imagine for her."

Matthews's eyes gleamed. "You kept her alone at your place."

"Not really. I was with her nearly every waking moment. I can't be that close to her if you put her in a separate pavilion, because you've given me other responsibilities, and I refuse to live at this zoo. You can't ask me to live in a cage any more than you can keep Sema in solitary confinement. She's more than an animal, Mr. Matthews; she's a unique individual who deserves an opportunity to live the life for which she's best suited."

When Matthews's eyes glazed over, I suspected he was remembering similar comments offered by activists who spoke at nearly every meeting of the American Zoo and Aquarium Association. Most animal devotees are vehement in their beliefs, and they range from hard-core members of PETA, who protest any sort of animal experimentation or captivity, to anthropologists who believe animals should possess the same legal rights as human beings.

Even though I agreed with many of those positions, I couldn't let him lump me in with rabble-rousers who frequently caused trouble for zoo directors.

"You see, Mr. Matthews," I forced a smile, "the great apes are not so different from us. Over a hundred years ago, Thomas Huxley said apes belong in the same family as *Homo sapiens*. Now we know their genomes are similar to ours, and it's entirely proper to refer to the great apes as fellow hominids. Not only are our genetics similar, but apes have complex emotional and social lives. Sema is living proof that they feel, they think, they can communicate. Sema is special, and she needs to be treated with respect."

Matthews studied me for a moment, then picked up a

carved paperweight and idly thumped it on the desk. "Let's see how the habituation progresses." He peered over his glasses at Fielding. "If there's any difficulty, let me know at once. We'll remove Sema from the gorilla population, put her back in a separate living area, and see how she adjusts to a schedule of public exhibitions. If she manages and Dr. Parker finds no evidence of trauma, we'll proceed to build a separate pavilion."

He hadn't listened to a word I said, but one thought had crystallized in my mind: until an hour ago, I had wanted our habituation attempt to fail for *my* sake. Now, I desperately needed it to succeed . . . for Sema's.

According to the terms of our settlement, the zoo couldn't fire me for twelve months after Sema's transfer. After that period, however, what would prevent Matthews from dismissing me? I'd be powerless to stop him, especially since I'd made no secret of my disagreement with his policies.

And Fielding was right—what if something happened to me? Sema would be kept alone in her pavilion, fed in the mornings and evenings, trotted out to perform for the crowds with an interpreter like Claire, and led back into her room. They wouldn't treat her as the special personality she was—no one but me seemed to appreciate her uniqueness as an individual.

Without another word, I rose from my chair in one fluid motion and left Matthews's frigid office.

After returning from Matthews's office, I stepped into Sema's room, handed her an apple and a box of orange

185

juice, then crouched to look her in the eye. "I'm going home," I told her, signing as I spoke. "I need to sleep in my bed, OK?"

I desperately needed a night to cocoon in safety. As much as I loved Sema and wanted to comfort her during this transition, at that moment she was better adjusted and more at peace than I.

Sema bit into the apple and chewed, watching me with a somber expression. Then she set the apple on her blanket. *Claire play with Sema?*

"No, sweetie, Claire has already gone home."

Brad play with Sema?

"Brad's here now, but he'll be going home soon."

She gaped at me as if I'd just asked her to explain algebra. *Sema go home?*

My eyes burned with frustrated tears. "Afraid not, sweetie. You need to stay here."

Her mouth opened in a half smile. *Gorillas stay with Sema?*

I nodded, grateful I could give her at least one positive answer. "Yes, the gorillas will be down the hall. Remember the rooms we visited the other day? That's where they'll be."

Sema considered a moment, then gave me a big smile. *Sema sleep with gorillas! Hurry, hurry, visit gorillas.*

"Not tonight, girlie. You need to sleep in this room. Maybe later this week you can visit the gorillas. We'll talk about it tomorrow, okay? But now I'm going to put a movie in the VCR and let you watch television."

She looked down at the floor, then picked up her apple.

The sight of her sad acceptance hurt worse than her pitiful questions. "Sema, can I have a hug?"

After a moment's hesitation, she wrapped her arms around me.

"Thank you, sweetheart. I'll miss you while I'm gone."

She gave me a kiss before pulling away, then went back to eating her apple. I stood and pulled the movie I'd chosen from my purse. I'd selected a *Natural Wildlife* video on African animals because I thought Sema ought to be acquainted with the different creatures living at the zoo . . . and because the DVD would run for two hours. By the time the film ended, Sema would be drowsy and ready for sleep.

I punched the play button, waited to be sure the DVD loaded properly, then backed away and squeezed Sema's shoulder. Still munching on the apple, she watched the opening credits.

I had done everything a responsible caretaker should do; my charge would be safe and content until morning.

Why, then, was I feeling suffocated by guilt?

17

I had just stepped out of a steaming bubble bath when I heard a knock at the door. Muttering under my breath, I peeked out the bathroom window and saw a black Toyota 4-Runner in the drive—Fielding's vehicle.

What was he doing here? Spurred by the thought that something might have happened to Sema, I pulled on my robe and threw a towel over my dripping hair, then hurried to the door. "What's wrong?"

Fielding held up a white paper bag as if it were a charm to ward off evil spirits. "I've got chips, salsa, tacos, and a six-pack of Diet Coke. Can we talk?"

My anxiety melted into irritation. I wanted to shoo him away, but the smell of food triggered a hunger pang that twisted my stomach. For lunch I'd had nothing but an apple and some celery, and it'd been ages since I had really good tacos.

I opened the door wider. "I figured you for a beer man."

"Used to be." He stepped past me and entered my small foyer. "Used to be a lot of things. These days it's diet soda or water for me." He glanced at my robe, then grinned. "Nice outfit. Much better than the uniform."

"Shut up." I closed the door and gestured toward my cluttered kitchen. "Make yourself at home while I get dressed. You'll find the glasses—never mind, you already know where they are."

After locking myself in my bedroom, I pulled on a pair of jeans, then paused before the closet. Which should I choose, a soft sweater or a sweatshirt? I had no reason to impress Fielding, but no man who spent his days in a primate palace could prefer looking at a woman in utilitarian fleece.

I pulled a soft pink sweater from a shelf and slipped it over my head, then towel dried and combed my hair.

After a quick zip of lipstick and a smear of mascara, I thought I might look presentable.

Fielding was sitting at my kitchen bar, glass in hand, when I padded into the room in bare feet. The air smelled of fried foods and Mexican spices.

"Chips, salsa, and tacos?" I frowned at the takeout he'd spread on a paper plate. "That's not what I'd call a balanced dinner."

He shrugged. "I didn't want to order too much—I wasn't sure you'd let me in."

"If I hadn't been starving, you wouldn't have made it through the door. Hang on, maybe I can whip up a salad."

I busied myself at the counter, washing a slightly wilted head of lettuce, chopping tomatoes, and trying not to wonder why he'd come. We were coworkers and we did have a history, so either of those things might account for this visit . . . or maybe he'd come to talk about Matthews's latest harebrained idea.

His reasons didn't matter. I was so desperate for answers I was willing to hear anything he had to say.

"You know," he called, "I looked in your fridge."

I chopped the nub off the head of lettuce, then twisted out the stem. "Isn't that a little like going through someone's medicine cabinet?"

"You even eat like a gorilla. Fruits and veggies—you're disgustingly vegetarian."

I laughed. "I learned to eat like that because of Sema. After a while, it became easier for me to eat her food than shop for two species. But I do share fast-food burgers with her now and then—even pizza every once in a while. And she *loves* those portable pudding cups."

"You've ruined her, you know. If she shares what she knows with the other g's, we'll have the only gorilla group in the country demanding to eat pudding with a spoon."

"That's the point, isn't it?" I glanced over my shoulder at him while I tore the lettuce. "When Sema has a baby, I'm hoping to see signs of cultural transmission. I think Sema will teach her babies to sign, to read, yes, even to use a spoon. Free-living gorillas teach their offspring how to interact, forage for food, and care for the elders."

"The jury's still out," he said, picking up a tortilla chip, "on how much of that behavior is learned and how much is instinctive."

"I think most of it is learned—and other species also demonstrate cultural transference. Did you know that bottlenose dolphins eat by swimming rapidly through schools of fish? Well, there's a group of bottlenose dolphins off the coast of western Australia that teach their young to protect themselves by spearing soft sea sponges with their long noses before they go charging into a school of fish. That behavior hasn't been recorded with other dolphin groups, and the reason is cultural. If dolphins can teach their young to wear sponges, why can't Sema teach her children everything she knows?"

Fielding propped his elbow on the bar, then rested his head on his hand. "Ease up, Glee. It's been a long day.

You don't have to make your case with me."

Sighing, I turned toward the sink and stared at my reflection in the window. I don't know why we always seemed to end up in an argument. And he was right—it *had* been a long day, though at the end of it we had both been on the same side.

I dropped the lettuce into a bowl, tossed in a handful of chopped tomatoes, then sprinkled the lot with grated Parmesan cheese. Simple, but it'd have to do. After plucking a bottle of Italian dressing from the fridge, I grabbed two plates from the cupboard and set them on the counter.

I slid onto the stool next to Fielding. "So—did you come here to enjoy my company or do you have something on your mind?"

His mouth shifted just enough to bristle the whiskers on his cheek, then he reached for the salad tongs. "Let's eat first, and then talk. I can't argue on an empty stomach."

We filled our plates and ate in an almost-companionable silence. I found myself looking around my kitchen and wondering what he thought of the place. I'd never been exceptionally domestic, but I knew where everything was, and the place was clean. The curtains didn't match the dish towels, though, and my steps had completely worn away the pattern on the floor mat in front of the sink.

When we had devoured the meager feast on the table, Fielding pushed his plate away and crossed his arms. "Glee," his eyes narrowed in concentration, "sometimes I wish I knew sign language. I wouldn't be at all surprised to see you telling Sema this move was only temporary and you're taking her home after she's played with a few gorilla friends."

I swallowed hard, my cheeks stinging as though they'd been slapped. "Why would I do such a thing?"

"Because you love that animal . . . and because you're the most stubborn woman I've ever met. But I've got to warn you—if you don't prepare Sema to the best of your ability, she's going to be hurt. She'll either be abused when the other animals test her to establish dominance, or she'll wither away from loneliness in solitary confinement. Because that's where Matthews wants her. You heard him yourself. He wants the talking gorilla as a headliner for his new pavilion."

Too weary to continue with my pretense, I dropped my chin into my palm. "Honestly, before today I was hoping I could take Sema home again, but I have been trying to keep her safe. We've watched videos; I've told her what to do if she's challenged and I think she'll remember. Because if her habituation fails now—well, I don't want her living alone. That would kill her."

"For once, we're in agreement."

I smiled at the sight of warmth in his eyes. "Truth is, Fielding, I don't worry so much about her meeting the other g's—I worry about her living with them."

"What do you mean?"

Torn by conflicting emotions, I hesitated. "I'm afraid she'll be bored when the newness wears off. I'm afraid she'll regress and forget everything we've learned.

Mostly, I'm afraid she'll bond to them . . . and not have anything left for me."

Fielding raised his eyes to my face in an oddly keen look. "At last the truth comes out," he said, his voice warmer than it had been all evening. "You're like a mother who doesn't want her little girl to grow up."

I shook my head. "That's not it."

"Sure it is. Whether you admit it or not, you see Sema as your child. You don't want to lose her." He lowered his gaze, then picked up his glass and swirled the last of the soft drink inside. "I think any parent could understand that feeling."

My thoughts took an abrupt turn toward the ancient past, to the week when "Mr. Dependable" Fielding missed two days of work, then returned, surly and uncommunicative. Later I'd learned that he'd asked his pregnant girlfriend to marry him, but she didn't want to be married . . . or have a baby.

"Sometimes," I said, my voice shakier than I would have liked, "life takes a turn for the unexpected."

He nodded without speaking.

"I honestly wasn't sure Sema could adjust," I admitted, trying to draw the conversation back to the present, "but I was hoping she wouldn't. I wanted to bring her home."

"Trust me, kiddo, that isn't going to happen. Not as long as Ken Matthews is running the show."

"I hate him."

Brad laughed, his smile sloughing off the shadows on his face. "And that's the Glee we all know and love—

the one who's not afraid to say what she's thinking."

Startled by his use of the word *love,* I looked away. "I haven't heard you speaking your mind in front of the big boss."

"Then you haven't been listening. And you're only mad at Matthews because of Sema. Actually, you ought to give the man a lot of credit. He's brought the zoo into the twenty-first century, increased attendance, and he was responsible for our AZA accreditation. I don't know if you're aware that he actually saved Thousand Oaks—the place was near bankruptcy when he took over. This year we'll show a profit. And don't forget"—his grin widened—"Matthews had the good sense to hire me."

I stared at him, unable to stop a smile from spreading over my lips. "I can't believe I missed all those signs of sainthood."

Brad grinned and swirled his glass again. "You can see a lot of things, if you look. Take this problem with Sema—there's an answer; we just have to look for it."

"You actually think we can find a way out of Matthews's grand new gorilla pavilion?"

I heard the faint rasp of evening stubble as Fielding rubbed a hand across his face. "I don't know how, exactly, but it'll help if you try being a team player. Try working with us instead of against us."

I laughed to cover my annoyance. "I've been shoveling straw, scooping poop, and emptying garbage cans. What more do you want me to do?"

"I want you to trust us. Sometimes I get the impression that you see me and Claire as the enemy. For heaven's sake, Claire's practically a kid, but you were awfully hard on her today."

For a moment I couldn't imagine what he meant, then I remembered. "You're talking about when I found her in Sema's room."

"Of course. You really upset her."

"You think she didn't upset *me?* You're the one who's always harping about limited physical contact with the animals—"

"Sema's different and you know it. Besides, from what Claire told me, she wasn't *touching* Sema; she was talking to her."

I crossed my arms, silently admitting he was right.

Fielding shifted on his stool, turning toward me. "It's that mother thing again—sometimes you act jealous and overprotective. You want your baby all to yourself, but that's not how it works on a team."

"That's how it works in research," I countered. "Sema needs a controlled environment."

"Well, you're not going to get a perfectly controlled situation at the zoo, so you might as well factor in certain unavoidable variables. And if you want our support, you're going to have to let us give it—to you, and to Sema."

"And what do I get in return?"

"You get my promise that I'll do everything I can to keep Sema with the other g's. I happen to think she'll do well with the others . . . just like I think you could be a valuable member of our team. But I need you to widen your horizons and think of more than a single gorilla."

Biting my lip, I looked at him. Agreeing with him now meant I might not ever bring Sema home . . . but having her live with the other gorillas would be far better than a solitary life behind a one-way mirror.

Choosing between two evils was easier when I considered the humans attached to each option. Matthews might be a good businessman, but he cared little for the animals beyond their potential to increase the zoo's earnings. Fielding, on the other hand, kept a picture of baby Rafiki on his desk.

"All right," I told him. "I'll do my best."

18

Even the most skeptical critic of animal language studies has to admit that nonhuman creatures can grasp some elements of the English language—a family dog, for instance, can learn to recognize his name, basic commands, and commonly used words like *outside* or *walk*. I've seen Nana's pug nearly turn himself inside out at the mention of a *cookie,* and even Charlie the tabby cat seems to understand what's happening when Nana tells her pets good-bye.

Most people tend to agree with the *Far Side* cartoon that illustrates a man offering his dog, Spot, a detailed explanation while all the dog hears is *blah blah blah, Spot, blah, blah, blah.*

My research, however, has proven that Sema not only

196

understands the words for most common things and activities; she also has a firm grasp on many abstract concepts. Over the course of our project, she has learned the meaning of words like *imagine, pretend, think,* and *remember*.

When my alarm rang at 5:00 AM on Wednesday morning, I awoke in a cloud of contentment—an emotion that had been in short supply since Sema transferred to Thousand Oaks. I shut off the alarm clock, then rolled over and pillowed my head on my hand, a little amazed at the feeling that enveloped me. Fielding and I hadn't found any definitive answers to my dilemma last night, nor had we fallen madly in love. But we had come to an understanding and established a new basis for our friendship—a friendship that felt more stable and mature than the relationship we'd experienced before Sema's birth.

I resolved to teach Sema the meaning of *contentment* as soon as I had a chance.

I slipped out of bed and dressed quickly, then ran my fingers through my hair and glanced in the mirror—I looked okay. Good enough for gorillas and a couple of friends.

After driving to work, I filled the gorillas' breakfast bowls, then delivered them to the night rooms. I waited until I heard sounds of Sema stirring before opening her door. "Hey, sweetie," I called, feeling more hopeful than I had in a month. "How are you today?"

Nine times out of ten Sema responded to my usual greeting with either *fine* or *sleepy*. On that morning, however, she regarded me with a woebegone expression and moved the open fingers of both hands over her face.

Sad.

My cheerfulness shriveled to a lump of anxiety. "Sad? Sweetie, what's wrong? What made you sad?"

She looked at the television's black screen. *Movie stinky.*

"What happened? Did the machine break?"

The power button on the DVD blinked at me; I pressed *play* and immediately the opening screen appeared. Apparently the problem didn't lie in the machine.

I sank to the floor and sat cross-legged next to my girl. "Was the movie bad?"

She lifted her hands, hesitating, then her gaze darted toward the screen. *Bad men, stinky bad.*

I groaned inwardly, wishing I'd taken the time to preview the movie before leaving it with Sema. But what could she have seen in a *Natural Wildlife* production? This wasn't *When Animals Attack* or one of those other voyeuristic productions . . .

Sema's eyes narrowed as they often did when she was thinking hard, then she brought her flat hand to her nose and moved it through the air in the vague shape of an *S.* I remembered the sign: *elephant.* Because we didn't see elephants every day, it wasn't a word we used often.

Apparently she'd seen elephants last night.

"Oh, sweet girl." I rose to my knees and waddled toward the television, where the remote lay atop the

VCR. Taking it and moving back to Sema, I pressed *play*, then *fast forward*.

Sitting together, Sema and I watched a progression of jerky images—gazelles, lions, a tiger, a group of bonobos. None of the segments contained violent images, nothing that should have upset my girl.

Then I saw the first elephant. Beside me, Sema swung her head from side to side in a wide arc. "It's okay, sweetie," I soothed her. "Let me watch so I can help you understand."

I pressed *play* and the images slowed to the normal speed. I saw a group of elephants gathered by a watering hole. Several were older females with calves; nothing violent marred the scene.

Then a sudden shot shattered the elephants' calm. One of the females charged toward two men who appeared in the distant brush; a moment later she fell to her knees in midcharge. Her calf, screaming in fear, ran after her; then dropped to the ground, a spray of dirt rising from the impact of his fall. He did not rise again.

Beside me, Sema whimpered and lifted her hands to cover her eyes. A narrator's resonant baritone cut through the confusion on-screen.

"After the first several shots, the entire group begins to run," he said as the camera focused on the fleeing animals. "The mothers push their young forward. Tina, who had been near Torn Ear when the fatal shot was fired, sustains an injury of her own. The others know she is hurt; they can smell the bloody discharge dripping from her mouth."

Tears stung my eyes as the camera zoomed in on the wounded youngster.

"Tina's mother, Teresia, keeps dropping back to run with her daughter, occasionally reaching over to touch the younger animal with her trunk. But at last Tina's strength gives out. The others in the group stop as well. By this time, blood pours from Tina's mouth and her sides heave with every breath. She slips from her feet and tumbles to the ground, dying with a single shudder."

Like Sema, I wanted to avert my eyes from the television. Mercifully, the cameraman kept his lens focused on the group of elephants huddled around their wounded relative.

"At this point, Teresia and Trista panic," the narrator continued, "Notice how they work their tusks under Tina's back and beneath her head. At one point they succeed in lifting her into a sitting position, but her body, of course, cannot remain upright. Watch Tallulah—see how she tries to stuff a mouthful of grass into Tina's mouth? She is desperately trying to evoke signs of life where life no longer exists."

I held my breath as I watched the bigger elephant try to force-feed the dead animal. They reminded me of a scene depicted in Fossey's book—a female gorilla had died during the night, and at sunrise the silverback had mercilessly beaten the body. I had read of other gorilla groups in which ailing animals were "picked on" by the others. Could what looked like cruel behaviors actually be well-intentioned?

I thought the elephant scene could get no worse, but

then Teresia, Tina's mother, knelt down and worked her tusks under the dead elephant's shoulder. Pushing with all her strength, she began to lift, and when she was finally able to stand, the weight of the dead youngster snapped Teresia's ivory tusk only a few inches from her lip. I flinched at the loud pop of breaking bone. The narrator didn't need to comment; anyone could see the ragged bit of remaining tusk within a bloody sheath.

Tears had begun to sting my eyes when the elephants ran; now they welled up and overflowed, running down my cheeks. Sema turned her back to the screen and picked up one of her gorilla dolls, which she rocked in her arms.

"The elephants know they cannot defeat death," the narrator intoned, "but they do not leave. They stand beside Tina's body for hours, gently caressing it with their trunks and feet. She has fallen on rocky soil, but the others scrape up trunkfuls of earth and scatter it over the carcass. Trista, Tia, and the others break branches from the surrounding shrubbery and place the limbs on Tina's body. By nightfall, their burial is complete. Slowly they move away, lingering at a distance until Teresia, who had maintained a vigil over her daughter, slowly lumbers off to join them."

I pressed the stop button, then powered the machine off. Beside me, Sema leaned against me, her face to the wall, her chin resting on her chest in the universal body language of sorrow.

Elephant, she signed again, *elephant die. Sad, bad sad.*

I nodded, not trusting myself to speak, as the memory of my own losses passed through me like an unwelcome chill. I closed my eyes as images flashed on the backs of my eyelids—sheet-covered bodies on the beach, the strobic glow of the ambulance's red lights, twin sprays of lilies on matching coffins at the front of the church.

I was trying to prove that humans and animals could use language to bridge the gulf between us, but grief was a far more pervasive link.

Wordlessly, I slipped my arms around Sema's warm bulk. Locked in her embrace, I wept for myself and my animal friends half a world away.

19

I never got around to teaching Sema the word *contentment* that day. She'd already learned *die* from watching *Gorillas in the Mist*; the elephant footage had reinforced that sad concept. I would have liked to shelter her from any further examples of the word, but life had other plans.

Sema and I were in the office together after lunch—I was trying to record the emotions she'd displayed after watching the elephant movie; she sat pouting in Fielding's squeaky chair because I'd refused to spin her. Claire was working at the computer, probably surfing the Web for gorilla news, while our fearless leader was off doing whatever fearless leaders do when they're not motivating the troops.

Claire broke the silence with a startled, "Oh!" then picked up the remote and powered on the television. I looked up, annoyed by the interruption, but the feeling faded when she tuned to *Animal Planet*. "Just got an e-mail from the Gorilla Symposium," she told me. "Something happened to one of the g's at the Dallas Zoo this morning. *Animal Planet*'s airing a report at one."

I glanced at the clock—12:58, so we were just in time. I turned to Sema, who was kissing the photo of baby Rafiki. "Sweetie," I said, "want to go get one of your toys from your room? Maybe one of your dolls would like to spin."

Sema's eyes narrowed as she considered my request (and probably the motivation behind it), then she slipped off the chair and knuckle-walked out of the office.

"Prevention," I told Claire. "She got really upset this morning after watching a video about elephant poachers. If this report is bad news, I don't want her to see it."

We both looked up as the special came on. We saw a picture of a handsome young blackback, then an overhead shot of a zoo pathway and a blanket-covered body.

Claire groaned. "Oh, no."

The camera cut to a khaki-clad *Animal Planet* reporter who explained the story. Jabari, a thirteen-year-old gorilla at the Dallas Zoo, had come from Toronto nine years earlier. At first friendly and affectionate, the young male had grown more skittish as he matured. But earlier that morning the 350-pound animal managed to slip out of a supposedly escape-proof enclosure and wander the zoo for forty-nine minutes. During that time he attacked three people, including a mother and her small child. While zoo personnel scrambled to contain him, the Dallas police arrived and shot the gorilla, killing him instantly.

I glanced toward the hallway, where Sema had not yet appeared.

"Zoo officials have no idea how Jabari got out of his pen," the reporter said. "Four doors stand between the gorillas and the outside world. Rock climbers have tested the twelve- to sixteen-foot-high walls to be sure no animal could climb them. Electrified wires guard the top of the enclosure, and trees in the habitat have been trimmed so no branches extend over the public areas. Jabari's means of escape is a mystery, but his motivation less so. The young male was maturing, and rivalry within his gorilla family may have caused him to flee."

Claire scooted her rolling chair out from behind her desk and moved closer to the television. "This is awful," she said, her voice soft with disbelief. "How could he escape from a habitat like that?"

I shook my head. "Gorillas are intelligent, and they've lots of free time to figure things out. We may never know how he did it, but sometimes animals escape. That's an unavoidable truth."

The camera cut to an older man wearing glasses and a weary expression. A caption across the bottom of the screen identified him as Gary Allan, gorilla curator of the Dallas Zoo.

"We knew something was going on with Jabari," he said, shaking his head. "Yesterday and the day before he refused to leave the outdoor habitat when it was time for the animals to go to their night areas. If only we'd had more time to figure out what was happening with him."

The scene abruptly shifted to a woman behind a desk: Haven Dewhurst, a gorilla advocate. "Gorillas are nothing but big couch potatoes. As long as they're given food and something to do, they like to stay put. So something had to be going on in Jabari's head, and with an adolescent male . . . well, it could have been anything from rivalry to simple boredom. But this individual had reached the time when young males typically leave their natal group and go off in search of females to call their own, so perhaps that's what he was doing . . ."

I tensed as the top of Sema's dark head came into view at the bottom of the office window. "Claire, would you mind turning that off? Sema's coming."

Claire pushed her chair back and reached across her desk for the remote, but it slipped away from her fingertips and clattered onto the floor. Muttering beneath her breath, Claire slid off her chair and bent to look for it.

I gave Sema a big smile and deliberately ignored the television. "Hi, sweetie. Oh, that's a nice doll. Would you like to spin her in Brad's chair?"

I thought I had spoken in a normal voice, but something in my eyes must have conveyed my unease. Sema looked at me, then scanned the room, ending with a glance at the TV screen, which had returned to the shot of a blanket-draped body on the asphalt.

A dark gorilla hand protruded from the blanket.

Claire found the remote and snapped the power off, but not before Sema turned to me, her eyes alive with troubled question. *Gorilla sleep?*

I swallowed hard and wrapped my arms around myself. "A gorilla died, sweetie, but not here. All our gorillas are safe and happy."

Sema cast another glance at the television, then lowered her chin to her chest and sank to the floor. *Gorillas fine?*

"They're all fine. And in a few days, you'll meet them. Now—would you like me to spin your baby in the chair? Or would you like me to give you a spin?"

Sema had never turned down an opportunity for a whirling ride, but when I stood and extended my hands to help her up, she handed me her baby doll.

Acting with more flamboyance than an Oscar winner, I placed the doll in the chair and spun it, squealing in pretend delight while my heart broke for my girl.

How could I assure her that such things would never happen at Thousand Oaks? How could I assure myself?

I couldn't. Terrible things happened to good people and good gorillas, and we were powerless to do anything about it.

20

Sema frequently evidenced signs of advanced intelligence, even intuition. I saw it in the way she read my frame of mind. The older she grew, the harder it was for me to disguise my moods and to fool her.

I tested her intellect every year by administering an IQ test, even though I knew the results would be skewed because intelligence tests are designed for humans. For instance, one test I administered asked where you should go if it began to rain—to (1) a house, (2) a lake, (3) a tree, or (4) a park. Sema would have answered *trailer* if that option had been given; since it wasn't, she answered *tree*. According to the rules of the test, I had to rule her answer incorrect, though any gorilla in her right mind would run to a tree if the skies opened up.

In her new room at Thousand Oaks, Sema watched the videos I provided and listened intently as I talked about the other animals and reinforced my lessons with their pictures. When I was relatively certain she knew how to recognize (and hopefully, re-create) a submissive gorilla posture, I told Fielding we were ready to meet the other animals face-to-face. On Friday afternoon at four, I walked Sema to the night room usually used for medical exams. A steel door separated this room from the others, but the other g's would be able to see her through a window—and she would be able to see them.

With Claire's help, I carried the most important elements of Sema's gear to the exam room: her inner tube, her Care Bear comforter, and her favorite plush bear. She would sleep here, we all agreed, for the next two nights. If all went well, she would be allowed to enter the habitat on Sunday morning. If all went well, I'd gradually begin to remove the "civilized" elements from her night room until she became comfortable sleeping in a straw nest like the other g's.

When Sema had investigated every corner of the room and seemed content to settle, I gave her an apple, closed the outer door, and moved into the office where I could keep an eye on her from the wide windows.

Outside the building, I knew the signs of activity were fading. The guests had gone home; the other animals had eaten their last meal of the day. Our gorillas would be anxiously awaiting the mechanical clank of the roll-up door that would let them return to their night rooms and a bowl of fresh fruit.

On my signal, Fielding pushed the button that operated the door. As was his custom, Dakarai entered first, protectively leading his group. His gaze crossed Fielding's and moved down the hall, but he halted in midstep when he saw Sema through the exam room window. For an instant he seemed bewildered, then he rose to his full six-foot height, thumped his chest, and charged at the door, halting only millimeters from the reinforced glass.

Even though I had expected some kind of display, I had to grip the windowsill and steel myself to ignore a strong impulse to rush to Sema's aid. With his canines flashing, Dakarai would have provoked terror in even the lions a few pavilions away.

I peeked at Sema, half-afraid of what I'd see. Her eyes had gone wide as the silverback charged, then she dropped facedown to the floor, her eyes averted, her arms curled beneath her.

"Good girl!"

To this day, I don't know if instinct or training prompted her response. But when she dropped, Dakarai stopped roaring. For a long moment the silverback's labored breathing was the only sound in the habitat. Then, as if nothing were amiss, he glanced over his shoulder to check on the rest of his group, then ambled into his night room.

The other gorillas, startled by the silverback's alarm, entered the hallway cautiously. They, too, glanced into Sema's area, but they followed their guardian's example. Each of them entered a pen and began to nibble at their fruit, but I couldn't help noticing that the females occasionally lifted their heads to glance in Sema's direction. Aisha, who happened to choose the room immediately adjacent to the exam area, walked right up to Sema's door and breathed on the glass. She peered through the steam her breath had made and seemed particularly interested in the Care Bear comforter.

When the g's had finished their fruit and constructed their night nests, silence blanketed the area. Fielding dimmed all but the security lights and motioned toward the door. Certain that Sema would pass the night without harm, I followed him out into the hall.

The strong ammonialike scent of Dakarai's fear odor lingered here, and I thrilled to breathe it in. Dian Fossey often wrote about this pungent scent, but in the relative calm of a zoo atmosphere, I rarely encountered it.

Fielding slipped a hand into his pocket as I tapped on Sema's door and signed *good night*. "Looks like they settled pretty quickly."

"Yes—things almost went *too* smoothly."

He smiled. "Don't borrow trouble, Glee. Nothing can hurt her in there."

"Nothing can hurt her physically—but I can't help but wonder what she's thinking. What if Dakarai's charge was more than she expected? She may not even want to look at him again."

"She's a gorilla, Glee. At some instinctive level, she has to understand his reasons for behaving as he did. Besides—" his grin broadened, "once she figures out she's female and he's the g's main man, she'll look at him. Trust me."

I snorted softly. "You men are impossible, you know that? Talk about cocky."

"I call it like it is, sweetheart."

We walked through the exit without speaking, then stepped out into crisp, cool air. The sky had gone dark in the east, but furling ribbons of orange and red and purple streaked the western horizon.

The sight reminded me of Nana, who was probably quoting sunset psalms on her front porch.

Fielding pulled out his keys. "So, do you think we're

on schedule for Sunday? If so, I'll come in early and give you a hand with the breakfast 'n browse."

I grimaced at the thought of turning Sema out among the others after what I'd just witnessed, but I couldn't think of a practical reason to postpone her introduction to the habitat. I had stalled her introduction as long as I could, and I didn't dare wait any longer. If she became comfortable in the group and I documented her progress, Matthews wouldn't be able to claim her habituation had failed.

I nodded at Fielding. "I think we'll be okay. Sema might have a few tussles with the other females, but the time is as right as it will ever be."

"Sounds good." Fielding unlocked his door, then opened it and looked at me. "Something else on your mind?"

"Yeah." I crossed my arms and glanced at the western horizon. "My grandmother makes this big dinner every Saturday night. My brother and his wife are always invited, but they hardly ever come. I need to go because I missed last weekend, and . . . well, I was wondering if you'd like to come, too. We could discuss the g's, if you'd like. Nana would love to hear about them."

A smile ruffled his mouth. "Is your grandmother a good cook?"

"Pretty good. But more than that, she's a real animal nut. I think you two would hit it off."

"I don't know." Fielding slid into his seat. "I'm not sure I'm ready to be fixed up with somebody named Nana. Don't you think she might be a little old for me?"

I slugged his arm as he fit his key into the ignition. "I'll give you the address tomorrow. If you come, though, I expect you to be on your best behavior."

"Good behavior is for work." His eyes gleamed dark and dangerous in the dim light. "After hours, all bets are off."

I dismissed his comment with a wave of my hand, but as I unlocked my door, I couldn't help but wonder. He had been kidding . . . hadn't he?

21

Something in me was relieved to see that Rob's BMW wasn't in the Posey's Pink Palace parking lot on Saturday night. I had a lot to tell Nana, and the selfish side of me didn't want to share her with my brother.

Fielding and I endured a round of Herman's cat-calls, then entered Nana's apartment by way of the office. Her kitchen smelled of bread and meat sauce when we entered, and she stood by the stove, a cardigan tied around her shoulders and white Reeboks on her feet.

"Glee, darling!" Holding her sauce-spattered hands aloft, she gave me a kiss on the cheek, then grinned at my escort. "And who is this?"

"A beach bum." I tossed her a dish towel so she could clean up. "Otherwise known as Brad Fielding, my boss at the zoo. I wouldn't have invited him, but he looked pitiful and hungry."

Fielding thrust out his hand. "Nice to meet you, Mrs. Posey."

Nana laughed as she ignored his outstretched arm and drew him into a light embrace. "Call me Irene, Brad. I've been trying to get Glee to call me by my given name for years, but she's stuck on Nana."

The words reminded me of a commercial jingle, so I sidled over to the sink and began to sing: "I am stuck on Nana . . . 'cause Nana's stuck on me."

"Don't get that song playing in my head; I'll never get it out." Playfully, she swatted my hands away from the dirty dishes, then turned me around and pushed me toward the dining room. "Go on in there and keep my guests company. Grab some napkins on the way, will you? I forgot to set them on the table."

I stopped cold. "Who's out there?"

"A nice British couple, Mr. and Mrs. Willingford, and their little boy, Everett. They're staying here, but they lost all their money last night while they were eating at one of the beach restaurants. Someone lifted Mr. Willingford's wallet out of his coat as it hung on the chair. Isn't that terrible?"

"Didn't they have traveler's checks?"

"Sweetheart, not everybody relies on American Express. They didn't have traveler's checks, and their credit card is maxed out. So I figured the least I could do was demonstrate a little Christian hospitality and fix them a nice dinner."

Fielding said nothing as Nana herded us toward the dining room, but I gave him a pointed look when we stopped by the buffet to search for napkins. "See what I mean?" I whispered. "She's nice. *Too* nice, if you ask me."

"I think the word is *hospitable*." Fielding winked at me. "Too bad you didn't inherit more of her genes."

They say there's a lot of truth in teasing, but I was feeling too optimistic about the future to worry about Fielding's snide remarks. I grabbed a stack of linen napkins from the buffet drawer and led the way into the dining room, braced to greet Mr. and Mrs. Whoeverford. We exchanged introductions, then Fielding and I took our seats.

The couple's nine-year-old son had apparently formed an insoluble bond with Mr. Mugs—the pug perched in the boy's lap, and not even the father's direct command could convince the boy to push the dog away. When Nana entered with a tray of steaming lasagna, however, the power of her uplifted brow caused the dog to lower his head and slink away in shamed silence.

"Amazing," Mr. Willingford said, watching as the boy bent to look for the pug. "I've never met a woman with such brilliant control over animals."

"Animals are easy," Nana answered, taking her place at the head of the table. "It's people who can be difficult." She smiled around the table, then held out her hands and nodded at me. "Time for grace."

I took her hand and Fielding's, then bowed my head out of habit and respect. As she prayed, I couldn't resist a peek at Fielding. He had lowered his head too, but like me, he peered around the table as the words of her prayer flowed over us. When our gazes met, he squeezed my fingers and grinned.

Through the salad and main course, we talked about the best tourist attractions on Florida's Gulf coast, the audacity of thieves who would steal a man's wallet in broad daylight, and the rising cost of gasoline. When Nana announced it was time for dessert, the Willingfords pushed themselves away from the table and declared they couldn't eat another bite. Mrs. Willingford offered to stay and help clean up, but Nana declined her offer.

"You go on up to your room and relax," she said, leading the couple toward the door. "After all, you're on holiday. My granddaughter and I will clean this up in no time."

She turned to look at Everett, who hadn't said five words during the meal. "Would you like Mr. Mugs to come up and play with you for a while?"

The boy's bright smile practically jumped through his lips. "Could he?"

"Mugsy?" Nana called. The pug pranced to the door, his nails clicking on the tile. "Mugs, would you like to play with Everett?"

As if he were accustomed to social invitations, the pug walked to Everett, then sat, tilted his head, and offered the boy a perfect canine grin.

Everett sank to the floor and wrapped the dog in a hug. "He's the best pup ever!"

Nana nodded. "Just send him home when you go to bed—unless you want him to sleep over. Then you'd better let me know so I won't worry."

The Willingfords thanked her effusively, then trooped out of the apartment, Mugsy trotting behind them.

When they had gone, Nana sank into her chair, fanning her face with her hand. Though her posture spoke of weariness, her eyes remained sharp and focused.

"Let's wait on dessert." She trained her bright eyes on Fielding. "Let's talk about your work while our dinner settles. All night I've been dying to hear about Sema's progress, but it seemed rude to talk about gorilla matters in front of the Willingfords."

I thought she'd never ask. "Sema's doing well," I said, looking at Fielding. "Last night we put her in the exam room and let the other animals have a look at her for the first time. Dakarai charged straight at her, screaming loud enough to wake the dead, and poor Sema dropped like a stone."

"The best thing she could have done," Fielding added. "Her submissive response satisfied Dakarai. I don't think the old boy will mind another female groveling at his feet."

Nana's face brightened. "Spoken just like a man."

I picked up a crust of bread and scraped it through a layer of sauce on my plate. "This morning the other g's walked right by Sema's room without making any fuss at all. Aisha gave her an odd look, but I think she's more curious about Sema's toys than Sema herself."

"So when does our girl actually enter the troop?"

"That's *group*, Nana, not *troop*. The big event happens tomorrow morning, if all continues to go well." I

216

gave her a nervous smile. "I never thought I'd say this, but I'm hoping she'll fit right in. If she doesn't, Mr. Matthews wants to build a separate exhibit for Sema and keep her there alone. He wants her to perform for the public—can you imagine? Sema would die of loneliness in a situation like that, and I—well, I couldn't do it. So he'd fire me, and that'd leave Sema to perform with one of those Vanna White wannabes who cares more about looking good than caring for the animals."

"Then we'll pray that won't happen." Nana shifted in her chair and pressed her fingertips to her temple. "Don't you think it was brilliant of God to give animals the same social needs as humans? I'm always amazed at how they mirror our design. They love; they argue; they need each other just as we do. They depend on our mercy just as we depend upon God's."

I picked up my iced-tea glass and shot Fielding a *watch your step* look above the rim.

He cleared his throat. "That's an interesting perspective," he said, his tone polite and diplomatic, "but most zoologists and biologists believe all social systems evolved out of necessity. Over the ages animals and humans learned that more can be accomplished through teamwork than individual effort."

Nana gave him a rueful smile with a great deal of confidence behind it. "Surely you haven't swallowed all that poppycock about man descending from apes?"

"Not apes," Fielding said, "but it's clear humans and primates descended from some common ancestor."

The corners of Nana's eyes crinkled. "With all due

respect, Brad, that's sheer tomfoolery—but I'm not going to debate evolution over my dinner table. It's an old argument, and something tells me you're not going to accept anything an old lady tells you. So let's ignore the mythological science and look at the provable facts, shall we?"

"Provable facts?"

"About mankind and animals. Anyone with a lick of sense can look at the universe and see that pattern and purpose exist in every aspect of the universe—in the stars, in the smallest microscopic life, in the astounding design of our bodies. Simple logic dictates that if life has been designed, we owe our existence to a Designer. And who would that be?"

Brad looked at me as if expecting help, but I shook my head and grinned.

"Um . . . I don't know," he finally said, shrugging.

Nana didn't miss a beat. "Why, God is the designer, of course. The God who formed the earth and everything on it, the God who has spoken to us through his Word. Knowing that he designed us with intellect and curiosity, his Spirit moved upon men of old, who wrote the very words of God, words that answer every question we absolutely need to know."

"That's fine, Mrs. Posey, but—"

"Call me Irene, please. Now, regarding the animals, God tells us we were created to have dominion over them. As he loves and oversees us, we are to love and oversee the animal kingdom. In our fallen state, however, we're not the most responsible overseers."

I couldn't help rolling my eyes. Unfortunately, Nana noticed my reaction. "Why do you resist the obvious, Glee?"

I dropped my elbow to the table. "Nana, if you only knew how many animals have been used, abused, and tortured because people think they are so superior—"

"Probably about as many men, women, and children who have been violated by those whose hearts are dark. Dominion does not give anyone license to abuse God's creation. Parents are supposed to have dominion over their children, for instance, but that doesn't mean we are free to wound them. We are to love, train, and teach them. I think we're supposed to treat animals with similar respect and humane kindness."

"I notice you have a personal fondness for animals, Mrs. Posey," Fielding said, undoubtedly in an effort to change the subject. "Was that your parrot I saw when we came in?"

Nana smiled, revealing the dimple in her right cheek. "Herman? Yes, he's been with me nearly twenty years. I also have Mr. Mugs, whom you've met, and Charlie, a tabby cat who usually makes himself scarce when company comes to visit. Do you have pets, Brad?"

Fielding snorted softly. "Not at the moment. But I had four when I was in high school—Eenie, Meanie, Miney, and Mo."

Nana lifted a brow, a question in her eyes.

"Pigs," he said, laughing.

My mouth dropped open. "You raised *pigs?*"

"Hard to believe, isn't it? They started out as my 4-H

project, but then I got attached to them. It really is true, you know—pigs *are* as smart as dogs." He lifted his glass. "I kept them until I had to go to college, then I sold them to a farmer in Hillsborough County. They probably ended up at the slaughterhouse, but at least I didn't have to take them myself."

"You treated them with kindness while they were yours." Nana's eyes twinkled. "I believe God provided us with animals for food and clothing, but we must always treat them humanely. Too many farmers today keep their animals in small pens with barely enough room to turn around. That, in my opinion, is one of the worst forms of cruelty."

While I tried to imagine the man beside me as a kid in love with a passel of porkers, Nana pressed her point. "You see," she kept her eyes trained on Fielding, "in the beginning God created a perfect world, one without death or decay. Oh, he knew what would happen to his creation, never doubt that, but he also knew he would one day redeem the earth and restore the innocence that would be lost."

I leaned back in my chair, taking pleasure in Fielding's puzzled expression. Nana had found a fellow animal lover, and she wasn't about to let him go until he had received a full dose of her theology. I'd heard it all several times before, and while I often thought Nana was overzealous in matters of religion, I couldn't fault her for loving animals. I loved them, too, but for entirely different reasons.

"I can't prove this"—Nana lowered her gaze as she

traced an outline on the lace tablecloth—"but I suspect animals could talk in the days of earth's perfection. Eve didn't seem at all surprised when the serpent spoke to her in the garden. The Bible is filled with verses about how everything in creation praises the Creator—this could be unspoken praise, of course, or perhaps it's a language beyond the range of human hearing. The Bible also tells us of a donkey who spoke—in human words—to his master."

"Gee," Fielding's eyes blazed into mine with an exaggerated expression of alarm, "perhaps I should have Matthews build a pavilion for talking donkeys."

He was being sarcastic, but Nana didn't take offense. "The donkey's speech was a miracle," she said, shrugging, "but maybe the donkey wasn't surprised when he was able to talk. In any case, when Glee began her work with Sema, I knew that little gorilla would be able to communicate. Not because of that other woman's success, but because the desire to communicate exists in all living things."

"Interesting," Fielding murmured.

Missing the questioning look that passed between me and Fielding, Nana gazed at the windowsill where Charlie had curled up in an elongated patch of sunlight. "They say," she continued, her voice soft, "that if some cataclysmic event were to wipe out every human except infants, those babies would grow up not knowing how to talk. The potential for speech would exist, but not the ability, because we learn from hearing each other. So who taught those first people how to speak?"

Fielding tilted his head. "I suppose language evolved over time."

"Adam learned from God," Nana said, her voice firm. "He named all the animals. And someday, when animals repopulate heaven and the new earth, they'll speak again. The Bible says there are four beasts around the throne of God right now saying, 'Holy, holy, holy is the Lord God Almighty—the one who always was, who is, and who is still to come.' Even the fish of the sea know how to praise God. We can't understand their song, but one day we will. One day we'll discover that we've been wrong about a lot of things."

Figuring that Fielding could use a break, I stood. "How about dessert, Nana? Whatever you have, I'm sure it's good."

She waved my offer away. "It's just cake and ice cream. You sit here and relax; I'll get it."

I waited until she left the room, then I sat and leaned across the table. "I should have warned you. My grandmother's views are a little extreme. And she's definitely not shy about sharing them."

He laughed. "It's okay. My grandmother was a Bible-thumper, too." Though he spoke in a casual tone, a shadow crossed his face. "She was talking about seeing Jesus five minutes before she died."

I hesitated. "Has she . . . been gone long?"

"More than ten years." He met my gaze, then cracked a smile. "You know what? I still miss her. She had strong opinions, but you always knew where you stood with Grandma. You can't say that about many people."

His words echoed in my ears until I watched Nana carry a tray of cake and ice cream into the dining room. In that moment I realized that while she might be opinionated, outspoken, and more than a little eccentric, she had been my anchor in every storm.

If anything happened to her . . . I'd be completely adrift.

22

My stomach had pretzeled into a knot when I entered the gorilla pavilion before sunrise on Sunday morning. Claire had the morning off, but I found her opening boxes of produce in the kitchen.

I dropped my purse on the table and stepped forward to give her a hand.

"You nervous?" she asked.

I groaned. "Barely slept last night. When I did finally doze off, I dreamed that Sema got into a fight with Aisha and Kamili. Aisha was biting Sema's neck while Kamili jumped up and down on her belly and Dakarai stood there thumping his chest—"

Claire laughed. "I think Dakarai's going to love her. He takes good care of his ladies." She pulled a bunch of celery from a box, then idly removed a wilted stalk at the base. "I wonder how Sema slept last night. She knows today's the big day, doesn't she?"

"It's all she's talked about for days. If things don't work out, she's going to be terribly disappointed."

Claire stepped to the sink and turned the faucet. "I

checked on her when I came in—she was sleeping like a baby. All the g's are dead to the world."

I sighed in relief. I'd been reluctant to look through the exam room window because I was afraid I'd see Sema pacing or clutching her bear.

I slid a bag of apples toward the sink. "You didn't have to come in, you know. You could have slept late and enjoyed your day off."

"Are you kidding?" A smile flashed across Claire's pale face. "I wouldn't miss this for anything. It's history in the making."

"I hope so."

And as I lifted the lid on a box of peppers, I realized how desperately I wanted—and needed—this habituation to succeed. Though I hated to admit it, over the last few days I had quietly buried my dream of bringing Sema home again. The only thing that mattered now was keeping her from a life in solitary confinement, an existence more suited to an unthinking and unfeeling android than a social creature like my gorilla girl.

Claire and I worked in a companionable silence, scrubbing and dividing produce among the g's bowls. When we had finished, I wiped my damp hands on a towel. "Thanks for the help—and you don't have to keep working, you know. You could go in the office and take it easy for a while."

"If I'd wanted to take it easy, I'd have stayed in bed." Claire picked up a bowl, set it on two others, then lifted all three into her arms. "Come on—let's feed the g's. The two of us can scatter the browse a lot more quickly than one of us working alone, then it'll be nearly time for—well, you know."

I did know, but apprehension kept my enthusiasm at bay. I stacked the remaining bowls and followed Claire; together we slid them beneath the doors of the night rooms. Rafiki was the only animal moving around, but soon the soft belches he made while eating (*happy rumbles,* Claire called them) would awaken his mother. One by one, the g's would wake up and eat, then they'd be ready to move into the habitat . . . and meet Sema.

Back in the kitchen, Claire and I set about creating bundles of leafy browse. When we had finished, each of us took an armload, then she headed toward the stairs that led to the catwalk over the habitat shelter while I stepped through the narrow emergency door that opened to the gorilla's quarter-acre.

I tried to see the outdoor area with fresh eyes, imagining how Sema would experience it in only a few hours. For ten days my poor girl had been cooped up indoors. Though her accommodations had been pleasant, she loved being outside.

Beyond the curved roof of the sheltered area, the sun was coming up in streaks and slashes. The cool breath of a spring night still filled the habitat, but soon the sun would warm the air until it shimmered with heat. The pathway beneath my sneakers, which had been worn firm by the soles of gorilla feet, curved about the base of a live oak like those at my home. High above the ground I could see sections where the g's had removed patches of bark, but at eye level the tree's outer covering was healthy and whole.

I tossed bundles of browse into shrubbery, hid several in the crevices of rocks, and dropped a few in the private grotto that opened into the observation room. I placed a couple of bundles along the banks of the small stream (Sema would love that!) but refrained from putting any near the steep bank of the moat designed to separate zoo visitors and the animals. The gorillas, Fielding had assured me, had a healthy respect for deep water. They didn't mind splashing in the shallows of the creek, but they tended to avoid the black water of the moat.

I stood in a slanting beam of filtered sunlight and lifted my face to the sky. Sema could love it here—no, she *would* love it. She would love climbing on the rocks, exploring the tunnels in the grotto, and splashing in the creek. She might even enjoy sitting on the grassy hill and watching the zoo visitors. Most of all, she would love being with the other g's—as long as they accepted her.

Above me, I heard laughter. "You look like you're praying or something," Claire called, tossing a bundle of browse through one of the trapdoors.

I squinted up at her as the greens landed with a soft plop at my feet. "Maybe I was."

Nana would be pleased.

Claire and I found Fielding at his desk when we entered the office. I glanced pointedly at the clock, then grinned at Claire. "This *is* a red-letter day. Look who made it in before nine."

226

"Morning, team." He smiled, but his eyes remained serious. "Everything set for the big event?"

I perched on the edge of my sorry-looking chair. "Ready as we'll ever be, I guess."

"Then let's turn the g's out. Glee, you can tell Sema we'll let her join them as soon as they've settled."

Together we walked down the hall to the night area. I slipped inside Sema's room as Claire and Fielding opened the doors of the rooms down the hall.

I gave my favorite girl a broad smile. "Morning, sweetie. How do you feel today?"

Sema dropped her jaw in a panting gorilla grin. *Fine. Visit gorillas now?*

"In a few minutes, I think. Did you get enough to eat?"

She glanced at her bowl, picked clean except for a few pieces of shredded lettuce and some yellow peppers. I should have warned Claire that Sema hates yellow peppers. She calls them *cat bananas.*

"I see you ate almost everything."

Hate stinky cat bananas.

"I know, sweetie. You'll be eating the same foods as the other gorillas from now on, so don't be surprised if you find a few cat bananas in your bowl. You don't have to eat them."

Find apples in tree?

"Maybe. There are all kinds of treats in the trees. You're going to have fun looking for browse with the other gorillas."

Sema and I both turned to look through the window

as the creaking of the roll-up door echoed through the hall. Summoned by the sound, the other gorillas knuckle-walked down the hall and headed toward the habitat. Dakarai moved in the lead, protectively clearing the way, while Rafiki danced behind him, anxious to get outside and play. Aisha followed her son, wearing a concerned expression, and Kamili lumbered behind Aisha, her pregnant belly bulging like a water droplet on the verge of surrendering to gravity. Mosi brought up the rear, pausing to glance into Sema's room as if to ask, *Why aren't you coming?*

"I think," I whispered, "he wants you to come out and play."

Hurry hurry visit.

"Let's wait a minute, sweetheart. The other gorillas need a little time to check things out."

Too anxious to sit calmly, Sema climbed out of her nest, paced along one wall, then picked up her favorite bear and hugged it as though she would force the stuffing through the seams. When the poor toy could not alleviate her frustration, she threw it across the room.

I glanced at my watch. In a few minutes Sema would be pounding on the window, so the sooner we could satisfy her urge to merge, the better off we'd all be.

"Glee?" Fielding opened the door. "You can either take her to the entrance or watch from the public seats. Your choice."

I wavered. Part of me wanted to escort her to the threshold like a parent walking her new kindergartner

228

to the school bus, but Sema didn't need encouragement to take her first step. I needed to watch from the habitat, where I could read the reactions of every animal.

"I'll go to the seats." I gave Fielding a quick smile, then turned to Sema. "Okay, honey, I'm going out front so I can see you when you meet the others. Brad is going to take you outside, okay?"

Wear necklace?

"No, you don't need to wear your necklace today. You'll be free."

She tilted her head slightly, then scampered toward the door.

"Whoa," Fielding called, laughing. "Let's give Glee time to get outside, shall we?"

I slipped through the doorway and down the hall, letting the exterior door slam behind me. By the time I reached the public viewing area, the other g's had scattered throughout the habitat, most of them intently looking for browse. Dakarai looked up when he saw me, but after a moment's scrutiny he lowered his head and continued his search.

I flushed with warmth—after only a few days, he had accepted me. Would he accept Sema as easily?

When the roll-up door began to groan and creak, Dakarai tensed and looked up the hill. Watching his profile, I noted his intent brown eyes and the look of concentration on his face. When the wind blew, I could smell the intense fear odor permeating the air, warning the group that something out of the ordinary was taking place.

Aisha gathered Rafiki into her arms, Kamili crept closer to Mosi. The painted door stopped moving and then, like a starlet making her debut, Sema thrust her head into the opening and blinked in the sunlight.

Dakarai rose to a standing position, his hands tense and waiting. I held my breath, certain he would either roar or charge, delaying my girl's debut for a few more days, but after an interval woven of eternity, the silverback beat his chest, sending the *pukka-pukka-pukka* sound of the gorilla nation through the habitat.

Sema knuckle-walked down the trail and paused to sniff at a hibiscus bloom. Dakarai fell to all fours and drove toward her, the straight line of his strong back sending a message of determination and protectiveness.

I bit my thumbnail and wished Fielding were with me. I needed someone who knew Dakarai to tell me what he might be thinking. At that moment, I needed more reassurance than Sema did.

Apparently oblivious to the masculine threat in the greenery down the hill, Sema plucked the hibiscus flower and nibbled at a petal. That might have been the trespass Dakarai was waiting for, because he roared and rushed forward with a swiftness that belied his 450-pound frame. At the sound of Dakarai's bellow, Aisha tossed Rafiki onto her back and climbed into a tree.

I stared, my heart pounding in my throat, as the silverback charged toward my darling Sema. She had frozen when he roared; now she gaped at him as if amazed that anyone could be so rude. He had charged her before, but this was new territory to be defended, and now she had access to the members of his group.

"Sema," I whispered, "come on, remember the videos. What should you do?"

Just when I was afraid she would turn and scurry back inside the building, Sema dropped to the ground and curled her arms in a submissive posture. Dakarai halted on the trail, then advanced cautiously and sniffed Sema's head, hands, and rear.

I held my breath, afraid to move until Dakarai rose to his feet and thumped his chest. And as the *pukka-pukka-pukka* sound echoed among the carefully engineered rocks and caves, I knew Sema would be safe from the silverback. True to his gender, Dakarai wanted a large harem.

As long as she didn't try to usurp one of the other females, Sema should be fine.

I exhaled slowly as Dakarai ambled away. Sema rolled over and blinked at the sky, then got up and wandered off to inspect another cluster of shrubs. Down at the creek, Aisha let Rafiki climb from her back while Kamili nibbled daintily at an ear of corn.

For twenty minutes the gorillas roved throughout the habitat, investigating crannies and searching for browse and other edible treats. None of the other females approached Sema, so I began to hope they would accept her without making a fuss.

I felt a shadow fall over me as Fielding sat on my bench, then leaned forward with his elbows on his knees. "So far, so good." He gestured toward the silverback. "Dakarai's keeping an eye on her. Have you noticed?"

I followed his pointing finger. The silverback had moved to the highest point on the boulders, looking for all the world like a king surveying his kingdom. He faced west, toward the benches where we sat, but his eyes kept darting toward the north where Sema foraged in the bushes below.

Fielding nudged me with his elbow. "You've done a good job, Glee. This is one of the smoothest transitions I've ever witnessed."

I murmured my thanks, then pointed to Sema. Dakarai was not the only gorilla checking things out. Despite her apparent nonchalance, Sema kept glancing toward me, probably seeking reassurance. The first few times I caught her eye I thought I was imagining things; then she sat up and began to sign.

Stinky Dakarai loud. She tilted her head, looking at me, then added, *Gorillas play ball?*

I laughed and Fielding begged for a translation. I told him what she'd said, then shook my head. "I don't think I'll answer. After all, I won't always be around for her to talk to, and I want her to become accustomed to the absence of visual communication in the habitat." I shrugged. "Besides, I think she wants assurance more than a ball game."

Fielding nodded to Rafiki, who had slipped away from his mother and was approaching Sema with no sign of fear. "Check that out—I think your girl has an admirer."

To my amazement, Rafiki walked to Sema's back and tugged on her rump hairs. When she turned to grin at him, he climbed up her back and wrapped his arms around her neck.

An hour later, Sema lay stretched out on a rock, sunbathing. Rafiki played on the mound of her belly and Dakarai seemed to have accepted the addition to his kingdom. Aisha kept a careful eye on her son, but she'd made no move to challenge his new playmate.

I began to relax. I had feared Sema would threaten the others because she was bright and beautiful and bilingual, but apparently I had assigned human jealousies to gorilla motives. At eight, Sema was younger than Mosi, Aisha, and Kamili, so they might not see her as a threat at all.

I had just begun to think about going inside to eat lunch when Rafiki scampered off to join his mother. Relieved of her babysitting responsibilities, Sema pushed herself up, then knuckle-walked toward me and paused in the shade of an oak tree. Catching my eye, she flashed a pink smile.

Sema loves gorillas!

23

I had thought I knew my girl inside and out, but over the next month, Sema displayed personality characteristics I never knew she possessed. With Rafiki she became a devoted babysitter; with Kamili she behaved as an adoring little sister. She remained at a respectful distance from Aisha, and more than once I caught her tossing twigs at Mosi in a coy little game.

And Dakarai? I think she almost worshipped the silverback. She never approached him directly, but followed him with the others. On many occasions I caught her looking for him, and once when they had both settled into the grotto, I watched her study him with a reverential light pouring from her eyes.

This observation, of course, sounds like pure anthropomorphism, but these impressions can be supported with facts. Sema talked about the others in her enrichment sessions, and every day I heard that she loved Rafiki, liked to play with Mosi, and liked to help Kamili. When she spoke of Dakarai, however, she usually hung her head and assured me that he was strong and big. *Like a bear,* she assured me, giving him the ultimate compliment.

During that first month of her habituation, we settled into a routine. After breakfast in her room, Sema watched the other gorillas troop off into the habitat while she remained behind. For two hours we played together in the observation room, our classroom. For Sema, instruction came in the form of word games on the computer, or we watched videos that reinforced the new words she had learned. After a midmorning snack, my gregarious girl was ready to join the others; by eleven or so, I was ready to let her.

After Sema had loped into the habitat to search for browse and greet the others, I would grab my lunch from the kitchen and walk out to the sheltered observation area. Seated on one of the benches, I would nibble on a sandwich and make notes in my journal or on my laptop, recording Sema's actions, encounters, and any attempts to communicate with the others in sign language. By watching her play in the habitat, I realized again why gorillas and sign language were a natural fit—gestures came naturally to them. Dakarai was not above shaking his fist at zoo visitors who tossed tasteless—and therefore worthless—paper into the habitat. Mosi made a raspberry at one young boy who taunted him, and Aisha once stood at the Plexiglas wall separating the grotto from my bench in the visitors' area and pressed a kiss to the clear divider. Not until I leaned forward and returned her kiss did she withdraw, her goal clearly having been met.

One glorious March afternoon, I sat on the bench with my lunch by my side. Dakarai came to the clear divider and looked at me, then pointedly stared at my brown paper bag. Unsure of what he wanted, I lifted it.

He extended his arm as if to say *hand it over*.

"Sorry, bud," I told him, "but I can't." As if to prove my point, I rapped on the divider with my knuckles. "No can do."

Still he stared. Not certain what else he could want, I withdrew the components of my paltry lunch: an uneaten sandwich half, a bag of peanut butter crackers, a bunch of green grapes, a juice box.

His gaze left the paper bag and transferred to my face. Again he gestured: *give it to me*. Again I shook my head: "I can't." To emphasize my point, I held the bag upside down and shook it, then pressed it flat against the glass, demonstrating that the bag was empty and I couldn't get it to him. He peered at me, his intelligent eyes searching mine, and for a breathless moment I forgot he was a gorilla.

Then he shook his head, fluttered his lips in a raspberry, and stalked away toward Mosi. I watched him go, convinced he would soon tell Mosi that I was the stupidest human he had ever encountered.

I think it's fair to say I fell in love with all the gorillas during that changeable month. I came to know them as individuals every bit as unique as Sema and nearly as expressive even without human language.

Aisha, whom I'd begun to think of as "Super Mom," tended to cling to her active son, who rejected his mother's overprotectiveness by attempting leaps and jumps a more careful gorilla would have avoided. Aisha groomed Rafiki—an activity initiated by mothers and terminated by offspring—as often as he would let her, and demonstrated her strong maternal instincts by letting him suckle—an activity usually initiated by infants and terminated by mothers—at an age when she should have been weaning him.

Kamili, whose name meant *perfection,* wore her impending motherhood like a cloak. She would sit for hours in a shifting patch of sunlight, her eyes soft and dreamy, her mouth slightly open as she watched zoo visitors. A gorilla's belly is no small thing even when it does not contain a new life, and I often thought she looked like a dark fairy hiding behind a furry black boulder.

Dakarai, ever the gentleman, seemed to sense

Kamili's time was near. He would often settle close to her, running his fingers through her fur and grooming her with solicitous devotion.

Mosi seemed to spend most of his time observing Dakarai. As a silverback-in-training, he was learning behaviors that would serve him well when the zoo transferred him to a group of his own. I appreciated Fielding's wisdom in allowing Mosi to remain with Dakarai at this age—because the younger male had been born in a zoo and raised by humans, he sorely needed to learn from gorilla role models.

I observed many things during my afternoons in the visitors' area, but the realization that struck me most often was how little my fellow human beings knew about this gentle and noble species. From overhearing comments made by children and adults alike, I learned that most people think of gorillas either as bloodthirsty, snarling beasts or comical humanoids that walk with a drunken swagger.

And few of the zoo visitors had the patience to sit and learn. Often they would swoop in from another pavilion, sit on the benches long enough to spy one or two of the g's, then hop up and hurry away, eager to display their ignorance at yet another exhibit. Not many guests took the time to read the chalkboards that offered basic information about the lowland species, and whenever Fielding or Claire or I stepped out to deliver our short lecture about *gorilla gorilla gorilla,* even fewer listened.

Yet I could have watched the g's for hours . . . and I

found incredible pleasure in talking to Sema about her new friends. In some ways she seemed like a foreign exchange student who had enrolled at a new school and was infatuated with her classmates. Her communication with them was limited (I quickly came to believe she would always feel closer to me than to any of the animals), but she admired them tremendously.

One morning, however, she told me Aisha had a *stinky mouth*. At first I thought she meant to insult the older female, then a second thought made me pause. Illness can manifest itself through halitosis, so if Aisha had encountered an infection . . .

I told Fielding to send Aisha's most recent stool sample and a nasal swab to the vet's office. The result arrived within hours—Aisha had developed a sinus infection, but Sema's comment had enabled us to catch it before she evidenced the more obvious symptoms and could have infected the others. We slipped an antibiotic-loaded baked apple into her breakfast bowl over the next several mornings and Sema never mentioned Aisha's *stinky mouth* again.

Three weeks after Sema's introduction to the habitat, Fielding met me outside the grotto and asked what he should tell Matthews about Sema's progress.

I folded my arms on my laptop and gave him a relieved smile. "Tell him Sema is fine, she is still making progress in her language studies, and she loves being part of the group. So he can keep his plans for a solitary confinement cell. If he needs to know more, I can tell him what to do with those plans—"

"I get the picture," Fielding said, laughing. "I'll tell him Sema's fine."

I never thought I'd believe that taking Sema away from a gorilla group would be a mistake. She had been so easily accepted that we had high hopes for a successful breeding within a year or so. When she was ready, she would approach Dakarai, and neither Fielding nor I could see any reason why the stately silverback would refuse her attentions.

I knew Sema was thinking about an infant of her own. One afternoon after playing with Rafiki, she found me sitting behind the Plexiglas. *Sema have baby?*

Someday, I signed back. *You will know when.*

The distant sound of sirens crept into our conversation. Sema had heard them before, but she hesitated as they grew louder and closer, agitating the other gorillas.

She caught my eye. *Why hurry truck?*

The increasing shrillness of the sirens unnerved me, too. The emergency vehicle sounded as if it were heading straight toward us.

I don't know, I told her. *Someone is in trouble. People in the hurry truck will help.*

Sema squeezed her eyes tight as if her eyelids could block the awful wail, but her hands kept moving: *Nasty stinky cat cry.*

"Mandi McConnell," Fielding told me and Claire later as he leaned into Sema's night room. "A twenty-one-year-old intern in the jungle cat pavilion. She was giving her family a behind-the-scenes tour when she tossed some food into the white tiger's cage. He went for her arm instead and ripped it off at the elbow."

I grimaced, imagining the horrible accident. "Is she going to be okay?"

"She's in serious condition, but she'll live. The question is whether or not the surgeons will be able to reattach the arm. Dr. Parker anesthetized the tiger long enough for them to retrieve it, but it had already . . . well, it suffered a lot of damage."

I couldn't help visualizing broken bones, torn skin, ripped cartilage . . . And people thought *gorillas* were violent? How little they knew!

I glanced at Claire, who had gone paler than usual. "That's why I didn't want to work with the big cats," she said, looking at me. "They're unpredictable. You think they're calm and content, but you never know what's going on behind their eyes. Gorillas are more transparent."

I shook my head, then deliberately pushed the disturbing thoughts out of my mind. Sema and the other g's had just come in. They were eating, but we still had to collect their dinner bowls and get them settled for the night. I had to follow Sema's usual bedtime routine and read her a story.

I pulled *Caps for Sale* from my tote bag. "What do you think, sweetie?" I flashed the book's cover. "You like this story, don't you?"

Too late, I realized that Sema had heard—and understood—our conversation. She had stopped eating. Her nostrils had gone wide with fear, the hair on her neck

240

bristled, and the odor of fear had begun to permeate the room.

Nasty cat. Sema hate stinky cats. Glee make stinky cat go away.

"Oh, sweetie." I dropped the book and sank to my knees, wrapping my arms around my girl. Over her shoulder, I saw Dakarai shift his position in the next room in order to watch us through the window in the door. "That nasty cat is not going to hurt you."

I pulled back as her hands flew in a flurry of emotion: *Bad cat. Bad animal. Sema good gorilla, Dakarai good gorilla, Rafiki good gorilla.*

"You *are* a good gorilla, Sema, a good animal. But animals aren't bad; this was an accident. The tiger probably thought he was eating food—"

"I agree with Sema." From the doorway, Claire added her two cents, signing as she spoke. "I think some animals are bad just as some people. God didn't make them bad; they choose to be. They ignore cosmic harmony"—she stopped signing and shrugged—"in favor of creating disruption."

My sympathy shifted to irritation. I could understand that Claire was upset and not thinking clearly, but she had no business talking about such nonsense in front of my girl. Sema was like a child, an impressionable, bright, and sensitive youngster.

When I looked up at Sema, her expression confirmed my fears.

What God? Sema imitated the sign Claire had just used.

I choked back an oath as I shifted to glare at my young coworker. "I know you meant no harm," I whispered, "but you can't use new signs at will. I keep strict records of Sema's vocabulary and word usage, so I can't have her using signs I didn't teach her."

Fresh misery colored Claire's face. "Sorry."

"Worst of all, now I have to try and answer her impossible question." I sank to the straw. "Some people," I told Sema, signing as I spoke, "think God is the spirit who created everything. But he's not a friend like me—you can't touch him."

Sema blinked, then turned to Claire. *Nasty cats bad. Good night nasty cats.*

Sighing, I stood and went to get her toothbrush. Sema's thoughts were still focused on the tiger, so apparently my halfhearted explanation of God hadn't made much of an impression.

For that at least, I was grateful. I could deal more easily with real terrors than mythical ones.

24

True to the proverb, March came in like a lion and went out like a lamb. The first day of April dawned clear and bright, and as I carried Sema's breakfast into the exam room, I hoped she had put all unpleasant thoughts aside.

Last night she had asked for her Care Bear before I turned out the light. She had been sleeping without her comforter, inner tube, or her plush bear, but our careless talk of tigers and accidents had triggered her need for the familiar.

She stirred at the creak of the door and opened her eyes as I knelt in the straw by her nest. "Good morning, sweetie," I whispered, not wanting to wake the other g's. "How are you this morning?"

Sema yawned, then smacked her chest in a one-word answer: *Fine.*

"Good." I sank to the floor in a cross-legged position, then plucked a juicy section of pineapple from the mound of fruits and veggies in her bowl. "Look what I have—something delicious."

I had hoped a good night's rest would banish her fears; I had further hoped that the sight of her favorite food would help her focus on something pleasant.

Any other day Sema would have gobbled the pineapple. That morning she lifted the chunk from my fingers, held it aloft for a moment, then slowly nibbled at the edge.

"It's good, isn't it? Nice and sweet?"

She dropped the fruit into her mouth and chewed. *Good. More?*

I laughed. "Yes, there's more. If you eat all your breakfast, I'll see if I can get more pineapple after we finish our work." I left her to eat while I hurried back to the kitchen to fetch the other animals' bowls.

Some scientists, even those who ought to know better, would find it hard to believe that an animal could recall a disturbing incident from the previous day. My research had demonstrated, however, that Sema possessed a long and detailed memory.

She might not mention the tiger today, but I was certain she would bring up the topic again.

After lunch, I sat outside with my laptop. Since Sema had adjusted to life in the habitat, I had been trying to adjust to the idea of publishing my dissertation. At dinner last weekend, Rob and Nana had given me an idea—instead of submitting a study on Sema's progress as a talking/reading gorilla, I would focus my dissertation on what could be learned from the successful habituation of a human-oriented communicative lowland gorilla.

Dr. Patterson and Koko had paved the way for talking gorillas, but Sema had demonstrated that signing primates could successfully interact with their own species—and even prove to be a valuable asset in an established group. As an example I would cite the story of when Sema told me about Aisha's bad breath, which led to the early diagnosis and treatment of a potentially serious infection. I would add other anecdotal information as I observed the animals, and I would supplement these stories with data regarding Sema's language and how it changed after she began to interact with the other g's. I hoped—desperately—that I would be able to record an instance of Sema teaching a sign to one of the others, thereby commencing the cultural transmission of gestural language.

I had been dreading my dissertation, but by the beginning of April I looked forward to the challenge of exploring a situation no one else had investigated. If all went well, I would be able to record Sema's feelings about mating and approaching Dakarai. As my work continued past my dissertation, I would be able to reveal an intelligent animal's thoughts and emotions regarding pregnancy, childbirth, and the nurture of her young. As Sema became more comfortable and experienced within the group, she might be able to explain why gorillas behaved in ways that have mystified researchers for years.

Nana always said God never closed a door without opening a window, and I was beginning to believe her. My fear of surrendering Sema to the zoo had blinded me to the opportunities to be found within these walls. My dread of working with Fielding had kept me from realizing how he maintained a balance between those who would overzealously protect the institution and those who would free the animals in a misguided attempt to protect them.

I looked up from my laptop as something moved in my peripheral vision. On a flat rock by the stream, Sema was signing to Rafiki. *Wet cold water.*

I tapped out the words, the time, and the situation, recording them in my computer journal. I couldn't expect cultural transmission to begin immediately, but Rafiki was the best candidate to learn sign language. He was bright and quick, but best of all, he was young . . .

Movement in the grotto distracted me. Aisha had moved toward the Plexiglas and was looking intently in my direction, probably wanting my attention. Turning from Sema and Rafiki, I slid down the bench until I sat directly across from the leading female.

"Hello," I said, ignoring the approach of a noisy crowd of school-age children. "What's up?"

Aisha stared at me—her eyes could have been saying anything from *don't you know?* to *I can't believe you're so dense.* After a moment, I shrugged. "I'm sorry, I don't understand."

She lifted her gaze, seeming to measure the height of the clear wall between us, then she held up her hand. At first I couldn't understand the significance of the gesture, then I saw that one of her fingers was swollen.

"Oh, sweetie." I leaned across the space between us and pressed my palm against the glass, directly across from hers. "Should I call Dr. Parker?"

After a final look at me—and this time I could not mistake the disdain in her eyes—she reached for a branch one of the other g's had dragged into the grotto. Carefully favoring her swollen finger, she ran her hands over the branch, then broke off one of the protruding twigs. Turning sideways—and obviously no longer looking to me for help—she nibbled at the tip of the twig, then poked at her swollen fingertip with the pointed end.

My breath caught in my lungs. While the use of tools has long been associated with gorillas and chimpanzees, I wasn't sure anyone had ever watched a gorilla use a needle-sharp twig to remove a splinter.

I watched wordlessly as Aisha worked the twig over the thick skin of her dark fingertip, pushing the sharp point in one direction and then another. The group of children descended upon the observation grotto, but they were more concerned with scratching their armpits and making chimpanzee noises than observing the minor miracle occurring before their eyes. Most of them, in fact, had moved toward the stone railing across from the moat by the time Aisha dropped the twig and used her fingernail to extract a splinter nearly as long as my thumbnail.

I grinned at her, impressed beyond words. Dian Fossey had written of mountain gorillas that fed their ailing companions and groomed wounds to prevent infection, but I had never seen this kind of medical self-treatment.

I lowered my head and typed the details in my journal. Farther along the trail to my left, the children were yelling at the g's, but I was too intent upon my notes to feel annoyed.

4/01. Aisha uses sharpened twig to remove splinter from third finger. Possible mute appeal for help before attempting the procedure, displaying of affected digit through observation wall . . .

A noisy splash and hoarse shouting from the visitors' railing sliced through my thoughts. My first reaction was irritation—had those kids thrown a trash barrel into the moat?—then three words found their way to my brain: "Can they swim?"

Who was in the water?

My body seemed to move independently of my mind.

While my thoughts staggered in confusion, my hands shoved my laptop off my lap and my legs sprinted toward the line of spectators along the railing. I was surprised to see several adults mingling with the kids. They were all looking into the black water, its silken surface marked by ripples.

I scanned the grassy bank across from us. Rafiki squatted in the grass, his fingers in his mouth, his eyes trained on the moat. Aisha moved toward him from the shrubs, her mouth open in a scream of alarm. Mosi and Kamili stood motionless on the rocks, while Dakarai charged toward the moat, his back straight, the hair at his neck as taut as his posture.

Again I examined the habitat, searching the treetops, the hiding places beneath the shrugs, the crevices in the rocks. Sema hadn't been in the grotto with Aisha, so unless she was hiding in the private cave at the back of the enclosure—

I reached the crowd and looked toward a blonde woman with a toddler in her arms. "Did you see what happened?"

She nodded, her eyes wide. "The little one was running toward the water's edge while this other one chased him. Then suddenly the big one caught him, tossed him up on the grass, and tumbled into the moat. He went under and didn't come up."

Not waiting to hear more, I spun on my heel and raced toward the employees' exit. Fear spurred my heart—fear and the certainty that Sema lay at the bottom of the moat. She and Rafiki must have been playing tag; Rafiki ran too near the water and Sema tried to save him—

How long could a gorilla survive without oxygen?

Gulping back a sob, I pushed past a woman and her baby stroller, then fumbled with the keypad at the camouflaged door in the wall. I needed help. Someone would have to get the animals out of the habitat while I went in; someone would have to help me find Sema and bring her up. We would have to hurry, hurry, because my life was lying at the bottom of that black ditch, my life, my heart, my love . . .

When the door finally yielded, I flew through the opening, screaming Fielding's name with every step.

25

Biochemistry is not my field, but I've heard that medical researchers have identified certain drugs that can erase a person's traumatic memories. While the topic of their research is provocative, I'm not sure it's necessary. Human nature has its own defense mechanism— as the blood rushes to supply our hearts and lungs and limbs, portions of our brains are abandoned, leaving us with sporadically firing synapses that preserve only the faintest snapshots of distressing events.

I remember running toward the office and seeing Fielding and Claire by the roll-up door. It was already rising, and the sound of its creaking would summon the gorillas as surely as any bell ever rung by Pavlov. I remember thinking that zoo regulations required me to wait until the animals had been removed before I entered the habitat, but who could obey rules at a time like this?

Without speaking to Fielding or Claire, I ducked beneath the door and sprinted over the trail, running past Kamili and Mosi, startling Dakarai.

I remember inhaling the scent of fear—but it might have come from me instead of the gorillas.

I remember scanning the crowd for the blonde woman; she had worn a blue shirt and red shorts. When for a terrifying instant I couldn't find her, I remember hoping someone else had jumped in and pulled Sema out. But who would do such a thing?

When I found the woman, got my bearings, and looked into the dark depths of the moat, I froze in empty-bellied terror—water had killed my parents. Would it now claim Sema *and* me? Unwilling to follow the thought, I leaped feetfirst into the moat a few feet downstream of the blonde woman's position. The water was cold, but not cold enough to cause discomfort. I remember wishing I'd kicked my shoes off so I could feel for Sema with my bare feet.

Then Fielding appeared in the water, his jaw set as he came up, wet-faced, and dove again. I inhaled quickly and ducked beneath the surface, but the water itself seemed to resist my efforts to go deeper. I would need to dive, but it had been so long since I'd been swimming that I couldn't remember how . . .

I had no awareness of passing time. I remember sputtering and spitting and thinking the water tasted greasy, then Fielding appeared with black fur in his grip. A pair of security guards had appeared at the visitors' railing, their khaki uniforms reassuringly sober in a field of tourist colors, and I heard a calm voice echoing over the loudspeaker—*all Thousand Oaks guests must move immediately to the nearest exit. This is not a drill. Please, for your own safety, all Thousand Oaks guests must move immediately to the nearest exit.*

The people at the railing didn't budge until the security guards urged them forward. I shivered and gasped and treaded water and again wondered how long a gorilla could survive without oxygen.

I found myself hoping Claire would think to call an ambulance, then realized she would have to call Dr. Parker. Gorillas did not ride in ambulances; local rescue squads did not respond to animal emergencies.

"Glee!" Fielding's authoritative voice snapped me out of my daze. "We'll never lift her out of here; we'll have to swim through the tunnels with her. Can you help me?"

I wanted to shout that I hadn't been swimming in years, but I shook my head and swam toward him. Turning in the water, I looped my arm around Sema's shoulder and began a slow sidestroke in time with Fielding, dragging my beloved girl through a drainage tunnel that passed under a bridge and echoed with the unidentified scratching sounds of nightmares.

I don't know how long we swam—time ceased to exist, and for a long while I thought I might slip beneath the water and disappear myself. But daylight eventually appeared at the end of the tunnel, and we flowed with the stream into the grassland habitat, home to the zoo's deer and tropical birds. No visitors lined the distant path, and I was grateful for privacy as Fielding and I dragged Sema onto the bank.

I collapsed at her side, my limbs like rubber. My girl didn't move or breathe, and her stillness stirred vague and shadowy memories of the darkest day of my childhood. Grief rose and crested within me, but before it could crash, Fielding hunched over Sema and compressed her chest with his hands. He opened her mouth, blew air into her lungs, and pumped her chest again. He moved with mechanical precision, pumping, breathing, listening—

While I wept.

Dr. Parker and an assistant drove up in a Jeep. The vet waited until Fielding completed a set of compressions, then he knelt at Sema's side.

"We'll intubate," he said, his kindly blue eyes meeting mine. "We'll take over from here."

His assistant placed his hands on my arms and lifted me out of the way; Fielding gripped my shoulders and held me up. I stumbled a few feet backward, then stood on the grass of the Thousand Oaks savanna while Parker worked on my darling Sema.

I remember watching the way his hair moved as he bent forward, several of the silver strands dancing apart from the others as if they had minds of their own . . .

The vet nodded. After he called for Fielding and the man who'd driven the Jeep, the four men maneuvered

Sema onto a stretcher, then slid the stretcher into the vehicle.

My last clear memory of that afternoon is watching them ride away with my girl motionless in the back of the Jeep, the vet's assistant pumping oxygen into her lungs by means of a rubber bulb.

After a quick trip home to change clothes, I visited Sema at Parker's office. She lay on an inflatable mattress in a large cage while a heart monitor beeped softly in the background. A pair of electrodes had been taped to her smooth chest, and a plastic tube ran across her face with protrusions reaching into her nostrils.

"Extra-large tubing," Parker said, following me into the pen. "Gorillas are hard to fit."

The vet pushed at the bridge of his glasses when I turned, then gave me a smile as thin as barley soup. "She's breathing on her own. That's good."

"So she'll be okay?"

"She won't be out of the woods for a while. In a case of drowning, water enters the airways and fills the lungs. Fresh water contains less salt than blood, so the blood chemistry changes and cardiac arrest occurs, but the CPR you and Fielding administered effectively restarted her heart."

"Fielding did it," I whispered. "He saved her."

Strands of thinning silver hair spilled onto Parker's forehead as he shrugged. "For the moment, yes. But water damages the inner surfaces of the lungs, collapsing the alveoli, so it may be difficult for the animal to breathe. In addition, we run the risk of infection . . . and we can't ignore the possibility of brain damage as a result of stroke. The cardiac arrest caused a lack of blood and oxygen to the brain, and human brain death can occur after only six minutes of oxygen deprivation. There are mitigating factors, however—the relatively cool temperature of the water may have given her more time and . . . well, she's not human." His gaze warmed slightly. "I understand she is unique. We are doing all we can to save her."

"When can she"—my voice wobbled—"when can she come back to the pavilion? I think she'd be more comfortable in familiar surroundings."

Parker patted my shoulder. "We'll see how she's doing in the morning. I want to keep her here and on oxygen tonight."

"Can I stay with her?"

Parker's hand settled upon my back. "I want you to go home and rest. I can't have you collapsing on us. If you want her to get well, you're going to need your strength."

"But I've never left her alone in a strange place—"

"No argument, young lady. Go home. You can come back in the morning."

Feeling numb and weary, I followed the winding sidewalks until I reached the gorilla exhibit. I wanted to sit in Sema's room and weep alone, but when I entered the hall, I saw light streaming from the exam room doorway.

I crept forward, shivering as the air-conditioning

touched my skin. When I peered around the door frame, I saw Claire curled up in the straw, her face covered by her hands, her sobs broken and hoarse.

So . . . I wasn't the only one who'd been shaken by the events of the day. Even Claire, our resident earth mother, couldn't believe we'd nearly lost one of our own.

Without speaking, I turned and walked woodenly toward the door, stopping briefly by the observation room to pluck Sema's favorite plush bear from the toy box. I'd go home. Sleep. And come back in the morning.

Maybe by then I'd be able to comprehend all that had happened.

26

I drove to Parker's office at seven o'clock on Saturday morning, half-expecting to find the door locked and no one on duty. My opinion of the vet rose a thousand percent when I found him at his desk, bleary-eyed, smiling, and smelling faintly of coffee.

"Go on in." He jerked his thumb toward Sema's pen. "I think you'll find our patient awake."

When I saw Sema sitting up and wrapped in a blanket, I thought I might burst from a sudden swell of happiness. "Sweetie!"

I hugged and kissed my girl, then pressed her plush bear into her arms. "How are you feeling?"

I had braced myself for nonresponsiveness, but Sema

lifted her open hand and tapped her thumb to her chest: *Fine*.

"That's so *good!*" I sank to the ground beside her, then reached out and wrapped my fingers around the callused skin of her foot. I had almost lost this precious creature, lost her forever.

"Dr. Parker," I called, not willing to take my eyes from my girl, "Can I take Sema back to the pavilion today?"

In answer, I heard the shuffling of steps on the tile floor. The vet didn't speak, and when I glanced up, I found him leaning against the cage, his eyes narrow behind his glasses.

"She can go back if"—he lifted a warning finger—"you agree to meet the following stipulations."

"Anything."

"First, she needs to stay away from the other animals, at least until the danger of infection is past."

"Done. We'll move her back into the observation room. Most of her toys are there, anyway."

"Second—I want temperature readings taken and recorded at two-hour intervals. If the slightest fever sets in, call me immediately."

"No problem."

"Third, anyone who enters her room wears an antibacterial mask. That includes you. Fourth, you call me at any sign of respiratory distress—coughing, sneezing, even a runny nose."

"I'll do whatever you say."

The vet looked at Sema again. "I'll stop by to see her

256

every morning and night. She may recover with no physical repercussions, but . . ."

I shuddered at the thread of warning in his voice. "What?"

"As I said, I'm not sure she hasn't suffered some brain damage. Take it easy with her for the next few days. She's experienced an emotional shock as well as physical trauma."

I squeezed Sema's foot, then rose on tiptoe and gave Parker a hug. My action seemed to surprise him, but he was smiling when I pulled away.

"I can't thank you enough. Not only for staying all night with Sema, but for seeing her as more than an animal."

A furious blush glowed on his cheekbones, but a wry smile twisted his mouth. "I'm going home to catch a couple hours' sleep. If you need me, call the office; the service will page me."

"Okay." I moved to Sema's side, then lifted my hand as another thought struck. "What about her diet?"

"Let her eat whatever she wants. Her appetite may be diminished at first, but it'll recover as she does."

I looked down, where Sema had lifted her hands. *Hurry hurry, eat apple?*

"I'm not worried, Dr. Parker." I flashed him a grin. "I think Sema's already on the road back to health."

While Sema settled in her inner tube/Care Bear comforter nest in the observation room, I peeked through the office window. Fielding slumped at his desk, his head resting on his folded arms. Apparently Parker wasn't the only zoo employee to pass a sleepless night.

I let myself into the office, careful to catch the door before it clicked and announced my presence. After tiptoeing to Fielding's desk, I dropped my hand on his shoulder and squeezed gently.

He lifted his head, then rubbed the back of his hand across his eyes. "What time is it?"

"Nearly eight. And guess what? Sema is in the observation room, picking through her bowl. She's a little subdued, but she's signing. I think she's going to be okay."

The grim line of his mouth relaxed. "Glee, that's good. Really good."

"I thought so too. Parker sent a list of instructions, but I'll take care of everything over the weekend and fill you and Claire in before Monday."

I sank to the edge of his desk, then closed my eyes. "I couldn't have saved her without you, Brad. I couldn't have found her in the water, couldn't have carried her out of the moat, couldn't have done CPR—"

"It's amazing what you can do when you have to." His mouth twisted in a slow grin. "Do you realize what you've just implied?"

I gazed at him, my mind blank. "Um . . . that I could never be a lifeguard?"

"No." He rolled his chair closer, resting one hand on my khaki-covered knee. "You said you couldn't have done those things without me . . . so, for the first time since I've known you, you've admitted that you could use some help." His eyes searched mine. "I never thought I'd see this day."

I held up my hand, laughing off his remark. "Oh, no. Don't go reading anything into what I might say today. I'm under stress, and I know I don't need a cocky gorilla guy complicating my life."

But he stood and moved closer, then held my chin and kissed away my protests.

I sat perfectly still. *This* had never been part of my plan. I had a gorilla to nurse, a dissertation to write, a future to plan . . . the last thing I needed was a romantic relationship with an irritating man.

But his lips tasted sweet on mine, and the man had risked his neck and broken a dozen rules for my gorilla. I couldn't think of a better way to express my appreciation than kissing him back.

27

Over the weekend, Sema and I lazed around the pavilion as though we were on vacation. She slept atop her Care Bear comforter in the observation room; I sat in the corner, my greedy eyes content simply to watch her.

My coworkers seemed to understand my need to conduct this vigil. I made a halfhearted effort to keep up with my regular duties, but both Fielding and Claire came in early and stayed late to take up the slack.

When Sema was awake, I spent most of my time tempting her with food. She ate, though not nearly as much as usual, and bore the aggravation of my taking her temperature with good grace. Fortunately, along with training her to use a portable toilet and pick up her toys, I had also taught her how to hold a thermometer under her tongue.

Though she appeared healthy in all respects, Sema did not mention the accident . . . and that bothered me. I kept expecting her to talk about the incident, to explain how she had managed to fall into the moat, but she acted as though nothing had happened.

While she napped Monday morning, I spent an hour searching the Internet for information on trauma-induced memory loss. If human brains could block out distressing events, why couldn't gorillas'?

Something else nagged at me—when awake, Sema would answer if I asked a question, but she did not initiate conversations on her own. Something in her personality had altered, and I couldn't put my finger on the difference. She seemed strangely passive and distracted. Her gaze would drift along the ceiling or focus on a corner of the room or window as though she were looking at nothing and listening to the wind.

After feeding her a light lunch on Monday afternoon, I turned off a videotape of *Mister Rogers' Neighborhood* and sat next to Sema's nest. Peering intently at her, I caught a breath through my antibacterial mask and hoped my smile would show in my eyes. "How do you feel, sweetie?"

Sema tilted her head and hesitated before responding. *No know.*

"You don't know how you feel? Or you don't know how to say it?"

No sign.

My pulse quickened as I reached for my notebook. This was progress; she wanted to talk and she needed the proper tools. I would help her sort through her emotions and properly identify them. Most important, I would enable her to accept her trauma and move past it.

I opened my notebook on my lap and pulled the pencil from behind my ear. "I'll help you find the sign. Let's see . . . do you feel sad?"

She lifted her fist in the knocking-on-the-door sign that meant *yes*.

I made a note in my journal. "So you feel sad. Do you also feel happy?"

Yes.

"That's okay, sometimes people feel happy and sad at the same time. They can feel *relieved* that a bad thing didn't happen. Do you feel"—I thought of the moat's deep black water—"afraid?"

Sema shook her head.

"Really?" I hesitated. I had to be careful lest I put words in her mouth. Teaching the vocabulary of concepts was a tricky process because I had to make sure I didn't subconsciously encourage her to accept the options I offered. Sema had always been independent enough to refuse inappropriate notions, but I could influence the process by offering the wrong words.

Yet after all she'd been through, how could she not

feel afraid? Maybe she needed something stronger, a word like *terrified*.

Fielding's voice cut into my musings. "How are the Granger girls today?"

A little amazed at the rush of pleasure his voice brought me, I turned from Sema and met his gaze. "We're pretty good. A little confused, perhaps."

"Oh?"

He pulled the mask away from his face long enough to give my girl a broad smile. "How are you feeling, cutie?"

Happy sad.

Fielding lifted a brow. "What's that, ambivalence?"

"If so, this is something new. Sema is usually 100 percent sure of her opinions."

Like a parent conversing in front of an observant child, Fielding lowered his voice. "Maybe it's a post-traumatic stress reaction."

"I'd be relieved if you're right," I whispered, "but I'm still worried about brain damage. She was deprived of oxygen for well over six minutes. In a human her size, that lapse would almost certainly result in damage to the pyramidal cortical cells—they deal with higher functions, like communication and thinking."

"Whoa." Fielding lifted his hand, cutting me off. "You've been reading."

"Yeah—on the Internet, mostly. I wanted to know what we're facing."

We fell silent as we turned to watch Sema. She sat calmly, her hands in her lap, her brown eyes darting from me to Fielding. I was about to ask what she was thinking, but the words died on my tongue when she lifted her head and focused on the open doorway. I tilted my head and tried to follow her gaze, but I couldn't see anything unusual in the area behind Fielding.

My girl opened her mouth in a pink smile, then lifted her hands in applause.

"What?" Fielding turned and squinted at the hallway. "What is she seeing?"

"I don't know." I scooted forward to change perspective, imagining that she'd been entertained by dust motes dancing in a stream of fluorescent light. No matter how I looked, I couldn't see anything.

"Sema." I waved to snag her attention. "Why are you clapping?"

Pretty man.

I shot Fielding a twisted smile. "Don't let this go to your head, but I think she's just decided you're beautiful."

He snorted. "Don't think I'm not flattered, but she's not looking at me. She's looking beyond me."

"There's no other man around."

"I still think you're mistaken—ask her."

Determined to prove him wrong, I leaned toward my girl, who was smiling at empty space.

"Sema?" She glanced at me, obviously reluctant to tear her eyes from whatever had caught her attention. "Sema, is Brad the pretty man?"

She shook her head. *Shiny man pretty. Brad stinky nut.*

I swallowed hard, torn between laughter and panic. "I know Brad is a stinky nut. But who is the shiny man?" I paused, searching my memory for anyone she might have seen on television, a box that might be described as *shiny*. "Are you talking about Mr. Rogers?"

Again, she shook her head. *Shiny man say Sema happy good gorilla.*

Fielding watched the flurry of signs, then stepped closer to me. "Would you mind interpreting?"

"She's not making sense." Again I peered into the empty doorway. "I think she's hallucinating."

"That's impossible . . . isn't it?"

"Why would it be? Neurologically impaired people can experience false visions, smells, even memories . . . who can say what's happening in her brain?"

Sema chuckled, then began signing . . . to the air. "Sema?"

Ignoring me, she tapped her fist against her mouth, a sign I didn't recognize. "Sema, I don't understand. What are you saying?"

"She said it's a secret."

Fielding turned at the sound of Claire's voice. We'd been so intent on watching Sema that we hadn't heard the girl's soft tread in the hallway. I pressed my hand to my chest in relief—Sema must have been signing to Claire.

"Oh, it's you." I gave her a reproachful look. "I thought I told you not to teach her new signs."

Claire looked up as she tied on her antibacterial mask. "I didn't teach her anything; she was signing when I

264

came around the corner. I thought she was talking to you."

I looked at Fielding. "I told you—something's wrong."

He leaned against the wall. "I think you're paranoid."

Claire moved farther into the room. "So—what's the big secret?"

"What do you mean?"

"That's what Sema was signing—something about a secret."

I swallowed to bring my heart down from my throat. I could understand why Sema might be seeing things, but I couldn't begin to comprehend how she could learn to sign a word neither Claire nor I had taught her. Unless . . . could she have made the sign by mistake? She probably had no idea what it meant.

I turned to my girl. Without signing, I asked, "Sema, do you have a secret?"

She looked at me, her eyes widening, and made the sign again. *Secret, yes.*

I forced a smile into my voice. "Do you know what a secret is?"

Hidden story.

I froze, my heart pounding hard enough to be heard across the room. In the past, Sema had invented new signs and compound words like *hurry truck* for an ambulance, but never had she used an established sign I'd never taught her.

I glanced at Claire. Could *she* be lying?

My young coworker crouched on the floor and leaned

toward Sema; I made no move to stop her. "Sema—who told you the secret?"

Sema chuckled again. *Man.*

"What man? Brad?"

Shiny man. Shiny man in Sema's room. Happy shiny man loves good gorillas.

Despite Fielding's assurances that Sema was playing with us, I continued to fret over the changes in her. Brad didn't know her like I did; he couldn't see the subtle differences in her behavior. She was still the fun-loving, funny gorilla girl she'd been before the accident, but she had never made a game of staring into space and talking to people who didn't exist.

I had other important matters to consider as well. Sema had begun to show signs of perineal swelling—she was entering estrus, which meant that from now on she would be interested in the dominant male for two to five days per month. Could we allow her to mate if she had experienced brain damage? At that point I wasn't certain she could be a good mother.

I also worried about how she'd relate to the others when we reintroduced her to the habitat. Gorilla families function according to certain social protocols. Sema had begun to master gorilla etiquette before the accident; would her current flaky behavior cause problems with the others?

After giving the matter much thought, I decided Sema needed an MRI before we could even consider allowing her to rejoin the others. A neurological scan could pinpoint any damaged areas in the brain and reveal the extent of the impairment.

I went in search of Fielding. Our relationship had warmed since Sema's accident, but I couldn't think of the night we kissed without also thinking of the movie *Speed*. At the end of the film, the Sandra Bullock character kisses the Keanu Reeves character and says something about how relationships formed under stress never work out.

So I wasn't exactly holding my breath and thinking of Fielding as my Prince Charming.

I found him raking old straw out of the night rooms and told him what I'd decided. He propped both hands on the handle of his rake as his eyes went dark with amusement. "You're kidding, right?"

"No."

"Well," he returned to his work, "I suppose we could arrange it with Parker. He'll probably give us a hard time about the expense, but given Sema's unique situation—"

"We can't go to Parker."

Fielding stopped raking and squinched his face into a question mark. "Would you mind telling me why not?"

"Because Parker would insist on anesthetizing, transporting, and restraining her. Do you have any idea how frightening anesthesia is for a gorilla? Not to mention the risk of the drugs. Sema wouldn't understand, and she wouldn't like feeling out of control."

"Parker let you drive Sema back to the pavilion the other day, didn't he?"

"Yeah, but he knew I wasn't taking her off the property. Plus, she was groggy with drugs."

"So . . . what did you have in mind?"

I took a step closer and lowered my voice. "You and I will take her in my car. She's a good traveler. If I prepared her, she could walk into any MRI clinic in this county and behave like a model patient."

"Are you crazy? She'd go ballistic in one of those tubes. Shoot, I'd go nuts if I had to spend any length of time in one of those things."

"They're not all tubes, Fielding. They have open MRI towers now, and I found one in Clearwater. We could take her after dark, slip the technician an extra fifty bucks, have the scan, and be back here in less than an hour. She'll behave for me. I know she will."

Fielding's mouth spread into a thin-lipped smile. "We could get in major trouble for this. Taking an animal out of the habitat, seeking a medical procedure without Parker's approval, transporting an unsedated animal— it's against every rule in the book."

"Running through a habitat still populated by animals is against the rules, too, but you did it the other day."

He studied me with only a wary twitch of his eye to indicate he was considering my request, then he lowered his head and continued raking with quick, jabbing strokes.

"After dark," he said, keeping his head down. "And see if you can find an old coat or something for Sema to wear. I don't want the security guard calling Matthews on us before we get ten feet away from the gate."

28

We found the open off-site MRI clinic on Bay Drive. Fielding went in to talk to the technician on duty while I waited in the Honda's backseat with Sema.

I glanced out the window, but I could see only one other car in the parking lot. The Village Inn next door was doing a brisk business, but none of those hungry customers seemed interested in the medical clinic's patients.

"This is going to be fun," I said, reaching up to adjust the antibacterial mask over Sema's nose and mouth. Because I couldn't protect her from every germ in a strange place, I decided to slip a mask on my girl. Accustomed to seeing us in the gauzy masks, she enjoyed wearing one—but she usually tucked hers under her chin instead of over her nose.

After a nerve-racking fifteen minutes, Fielding came out and opened the car door.

"Let's go, sweetie." I handed him the end of Sema's leash and hoped she wouldn't zone out and stop to talk to the halogen lights above the parking lot.

Sema ambled toward Fielding like a beauty queen about to meet an adoring chapter of her fan club. He held the front door open for us; the young man at the desk dropped his jaw as we entered. "You didn't say the patient was a monkey."

I glanced around to be sure we were alone, then gave him a firm smile. "She's a gorilla, not a monkey."

The attendant drew a deep breath, then gave us a crooked smile. "Wow. This is majorly irregular."

"Listen." Fielding stepped forward to peer at the man's name tag. "You have our money, Troy. All you have to do is operate the machine; you don't have to file an insurance claim or call the Associated Press."

"But there's paperwork. I've gotta put something on the form and the films."

"Your patient's name is Sema Granger." Fielding pulled a clipboard from the attendant's grip and began to print in block letters. "We'll take care of everything; you just get behind the controls, okay?"

"Okay." The technician gazed at Sema for a moment, then grinned at me. "Why not? Might be a gas. But he's not going to bite or go crazy on us, is he?"

I wasn't sure how anyone could look at Sema's goofy masked mug and imagine she might attack, but not everyone understood gorillas.

"*She'll* be fine," I said. "Just tell us where to take her and we'll be out of here in a few minutes."

"Cool." The technician glanced at the glass entry doors. "But you guys are going out the back, okay? I don't want you running into my next patient."

"That's fine."

We waited as Troy strolled out from behind the desk, then we followed him into a large room dominated by a beige MRI tower.

"You'll have to remove all jewelry and metal from your pockets." Troy held out a plastic bin. "I hope she doesn't have any metal plates or teeth or anything."

I resisted the temptation to roll my eyes as I unfastened Sema's collar. "She's perfect."

Troy paused. "Um, tell me again what part of the body we're scanning?"

I dropped Sema's collar and leash into the bin. "The brain."

"Gotcha." Troy set the bin aside and picked up a molded piece of plastic. "We'll have to slide her head into this crevice . . . if it'll fit."

Ignoring him, I focused on Sema. She had taken a seat on the floor and was looking around with mild interest. "Are you tired, sweet girl?"

Sleep now?

"You can take a little nap. Can you climb up on this table for me?"

A frown entered her eyes. *Get bear?*

"Not now, Sema, I was thinking maybe you could sit on this table and we could play oouchy-gouchy-goo-zooom. We need you to lie down here for a few minutes and keep still."

When Sema looked at the MRI table, I wondered if I'd overestimated her ability to obey. Even in a compliant state of mind, she might object to stretching out on a strange surface.

I held my breath as she rose and knuckle-walked to the table, then reached out to touch it. *Cold.*

"It'll get warm, sweetie, in a minute. Don't you want to play the tickle game?"

She had to be dead tired. Fielding and I had purposely waited until ten to sneak her out of the zoo, so she should be more than ready to rest.

"Sema." I gave her a broad smile as I slid a plastic chair toward the table. "Can you please climb up here?"

Chuffing slightly, she climbed from the chair to the table, then sat on the edge, her feet dangling. I held up my hands and wriggled my fingers. "Oouchy-gouchy-goo-zoooom!"

Smiling, she stretched out on her back, her body tensing in preparation for the tickling to come.

Grinning, I scratched her belly and her ribs, then trailed my fingers up to her armpits. She laughed silently, her shoulders shaking with each panting chuckle.

"What a good girl you are! Now, Sema, I need you to let this nice young man put this hat on your head. Can you do that for me?"

She tipped her chin back to look at Troy. Tense as a cat, the young man gingerly slid the plastic brace over the crown of Sema's skull. The device, while not a perfect fit, was snug enough to hold her head in a fixed position. The rest of her body, though, remained free—and everything depended on her willingness to understand and obey.

"Okay, sweetie." I moved so she could see me without shifting. "The machine is going to purr for a while, and I'm going to wait outside. When the machine is done, we'll go home and you can sleep with your bear."

Maybe she understood; maybe she didn't. But she closed her eyes, so Troy, Fielding, and I stepped out of the room and moved into the booth adjacent to the MRI chamber. Troy fiddled with dials while I stepped closer to Fielding.

"You paid already?"

He grunted softly. "Had to write a check. I figured cash up front would be the most persuasive factor in our . . . unusual request."

"How much?"

A grin crossed his face. "A lot less than if an insurer had covered it. Do you know they charge $3800 if billed through insurance?"

"How much, Fielding?"

He shrugged. "Only seven-fifty for cash patients."

I stared as a thought bulldozed its way into my mind. "You *will* be reimbursed, won't you?"

"Probably. Parker won't like us going behind his back, and Matthews may have a coronary, but I'll make the best case I can."

"If you aren't reimbursed, let me know. I can't have you spending that kind of money on my gorilla—"

"The zoo's gorilla, Glee. Besides, it's only money. I'm glad I had it."

He leaned away from me and studied the instrument panel across from Troy, so I knew he was trying to change the subject. I also knew the odds of him ever seeing a check for reimbursement were slim— Matthews would be ticked that we took Sema out without permission, and he'd be furious we didn't consult Parker about the MRI.

I glanced out the window, where I could see that

Sema remained almost motionless beneath the huge scanner. One of her hands twitched and her belly rose and fell in a regular rhythm, but I supposed those things didn't matter.

After a moment, Troy leaned back and locked his hands behind his head. "What a trip. You can go get your ape off the table. I'll wait here, if you don't mind."

As eager as I was to see the scan, I was more anxious to get Sema back to a friendlier environment. Leaving Fielding with Troy, I hurried into the next room where Sema snored softly on the table.

I touched her shoulder and felt her startle. "Hey, sweetie. Did you have a little nap?"

Sema sleep?

"Yes, you did. Are you ready to go find your bear?"

I slid the restraining brace away from her skull, then took her hand. She dropped to the floor and I fastened her collar around her neck, then we walked into the room where Fielding and Troy were studying the scan against a light box. From where I stood, the dark film seemed covered in a series of psychedelic ovals . . . each of which, I realized, represented a different slice of Sema's brain.

Troy snapped the light off. "Where would you like me to send this?"

Fielding pulled the film out of the clip. "We'll take it with us. Just give me a folder or something and we'll be out of your hair."

I half-expected Troy to protest, but he only shrugged and handed Fielding a manila envelope.

No one spoke on the way back to the zoo. Fielding concentrated on driving less-traveled roads where we were unlikely to attract attention. I stared out the window as the lights of the city flashed in neon greens, reds, and golds. Sema remained silent and sleepy, her hands resting lightly on her bent knees, my trench coat over her shoulders.

After arriving at the pavilion, I led her back to her room and watched her curl up in her Care Bear nest. After giving her a quick hug and kiss, I closed the door and met Fielding in the office.

He pulled the MRI film from the envelope and mounted it on our own light box. In the past, both of us had studied X-rays of congenital hip conditions and broken bones; neither of us knew anything about stroke.

Glaring at the film, he folded his arms. "We're going to have to hand this over to Parker. I don't know enough to make even an educated guess, but there are a couple of things that stand out to me." He pointed to one of the ovals, where one section of the brain appeared notice-ably different from the opposite side. "I think spheres of the brain are usually symmetrical, but you can see that a large portion of this area is lighter than the same area on the left. And in this shot"—his finger slid to the next oval and tapped a suspicious blur—"this section is darker. I'm not sure what that means, but I suspect we're looking at damaged tissue."

"But you don't know for sure." I pushed the words past the lump in my throat. "Parker may have a dif-ferent opinion."

"Sure, he might. Or he might say there is damage, but it's to some obscure region. After all, you haven't noticed many changes in Sema. She still signs; she still talks to you."

She talks to empty air, too.

The unspoken words hung in the space between us. I didn't dare verbalize them because I knew Fielding was trying to be optimistic. He wanted to encourage me . . . and I needed to let him.

"Your work hasn't been in vain, Glee." His voice vibrated with intensity. "I know what you're thinking, but you don't know the extent of the damage, and you can't allow yourself to think your work has been wasted. You can continue and Sema can adjust. People recover from strokes and heart attacks—their bodies learn how to compensate for the damaged parts."

"Still"—I felt the sting of tears behind the smile I gave him—"I'll never know how far she could have progressed."

Fielding gripped my arm. "She's talking, Glee. You successfully habituated a talking gorilla with an established group. That's incredible!"

"But she's talking nonsense! She's staring into space and signing about things that make no sense. And I'm not sure we can put her back with the others. What if she ends up in the moat again?"

"She won't. And I'm not certain her little quirks are permanent. She may be experiencing some kind of trauma over the near drowning. After all, she's endured a lot in the last few weeks. The habituation, the change in housing, the drowning, the move back into a solitary room—"

"So how am I supposed to know what to do?" The words flew from my lips in a question I knew Fielding couldn't answer.

His hand gentled on my arm. "It's going to take time. Let Parker look at the film. Let Sema settle back into a routine; let's go through the habituation process again, as carefully as before. We have all the time in the world. It's too soon to know . . . what might develop from all this."

That last phrase resonated with hidden meaning, but I was too tired to consider it further. Instead I let my head fall to his shoulder and relaxed in his embrace. Gently we rocked back and forth to the rhythm of our breathing. His hand swept to the back of my neck and I heard the beating of his heart.

Steeling myself against the tide that threatened to carry me away, I murmured a hoarse thank-you, then pulled myself free of his grip and walked off to check on my sleeping gorilla.

29

I held up a flash card printed with the word *apple*. "And what is this, Sema?"

Sema transferred her gaze from the card to the basket of fruit between us.

"That's right, it's one of those. Can you tell me which one?"

Chuffing softly, she plucked the apple from the basket.

"Good girl! You're right, it's an apple." A little disappointed that she'd *shown* me instead of *telling* me, I twisted the knuckle of my right forefinger at my cheek to reinforce the flash card with the sign.

Sema eat?

"Sure, sweetie, help yourself. And while you're eating, look at this—we're going to learn something new."

A week had passed since the accident, and I had almost convinced myself that Sema had returned to normal. She had performed beautifully all morning, recognizing printed words for various objects and activities. I was beginning to think Fielding was right— even though Parker confirmed that the MRI films revealed some areas of damaged brain tissue, those areas seemed to have little to do with speech, memory, or reasoning.

Fielding and I had given Parker the MRI film in the privacy of our office. He'd been aghast when he learned we took Sema out of the zoo, but he also admitted that sedation would have been risky, given the state of her vulnerable lungs. Still, we sat like abashed school children while he scolded us about the dangers of taking Sema into a public building crawling with who-knew-what-sorts of bacteria and viruses . . .

In the end, though, he agreed not to tell Matthews about our unauthorized field trip. "I won't lie for you," the vet said, his eyes lingering on me with what looked like paternal concern, "but since Matthews rarely asks for details about specific animals, I doubt the question will come up."

Shortly after talking to Parker, another thought occurred—Brad and I *had* to reintroduce Sema to the group. If we kept her out of the habitat, Matthews would commence with his plans to house her in a separate facility. I'd been hoping the accident would put an end to Matthews's scheme to put her on public display; then I realized he could use the accident against us.

I held up a new flash card as she bit into the apple and chewed. "Know how I'm always teaching you new words, girlie? Well, this is the word for *word*." I set the card on the floor between us, then tapped the thumb and forefinger of my *G* hand shape against the extended index finger of my left hand. "You know what a *word* is. It's a sign, a sound, or a group of letters on a card."

Sema took another bite of the apple, then set it on the floor and mimicked my sign.

"That's right!" I moved the flash card closer to her. "We learn new *words* every day."

"Excuse me, Glee?" Claire stepped around the corner, a stethoscope around her neck. "Brad wanted me to listen to Sema's breathing."

I nodded. "Come on in."

Sema stopped chewing as Claire placed the stethoscope on her ears, then blew on the silver disk. "Let me warm it up for you, kiddo. Even under all that fur, this thing can be cold, huh?"

My girl grunted softly as Claire crouched and

applied the stethoscope to Sema's back. Fielding hadn't pushed me to prepare her to join the others, and I hadn't wanted to hurry her. Her health, while improved, was not as vigorous as it had been. Privately, I worried that she was still at risk. Some infections took time to develop.

Claire stood, a frown settling between her auburn brows. "I heard a little crackle in her left lung. I'll call Dr. Parker and ask him to stop by."

My eyes caught and held Sema's. "Sweetie, how do you feel?"

She popped the last of the apple in her mouth. *Fine.*

"As you can see, she says she feels okay." I met Claire's gaze. "But go ahead and call Parker. Sema can be pretty stoic, and we don't want anything to get out of hand."

"I'll call him now."

As Claire left, I studied the floor, not wanting Sema to see any shadows in my eyes. Over the years, I'd seen animals fade quickly—the gorilla behaving normally in the morning could be dehydrated and deathly ill by sunset. Animals who lacked speech couldn't tell their keepers when they felt sick, and zookeepers often missed early symptoms of listlessness and fatigue.

My girl, on the other hand, could communicate. So if she wasn't feeling well, she would tell me . . . wouldn't she?

When I looked up, Sema's gaze had moved beyond the room and out into the hallway.

"Hey." I waved my hand before her wide eyes, trying

to reclaim her attention. "Claire had to go to the office, so let's get back to work."

She didn't even blink, but her hands rose to sign: *Sema good gorilla Sema loves God thanks.*

I felt my throat tighten when I recognized the word *God.* Sometimes I could strangle Claire for teaching Sema a word I didn't need in her vocabulary—odd words had a tendency to appear when Sema was feeling temperamental or distracted. Ethan, her favorite babysitter, had once taught her the only word he knew in sign language, and it happened to be an expletive. After Sema saw how I reacted to it, for weeks she used it whenever I asked her to pick up her toys or stop shredding her picture books.

Was this a fit of temper . . . or something else?

I leaned forward, trying to peer around the corner. No one stood in the hall. I knew Claire and Fielding were in the office. The alarm on the exterior door hadn't beeped, so no one else had come in.

Was my girl hallucinating? I made a mental note to research hallucinations during Sema's nap time, then tried another approach. "Sema? Look at me, sweetie, and tell me what you see."

She glanced at me long enough to sign *shiny man,* then returned her attention to the empty hallway.

"Shiny man," I repeated, my voice flat. I pulled out my notebook and yanked the pen free of the spiral binding—I needed to investigate case studies of patients who hallucinated after stroke. Perhaps this was a common occurrence, a condition routinely treated with a specific drug. Surely something could prevent Sema from seeing things that didn't exist.

"Sema," I punched an authoritative tone into my voice, "listen to me. We need to work a few more minutes, then you can have some apple juice. Would you like that?"

Ignoring me, Sema clapped and grinned at the apparition in the hallway.

"Remember this?" I held up the flash card again. "When I teach you a new sign, what am I teaching you?"

Something—perhaps my movement—drew her attention. She studied the card in my hand, then signed *word*.

"Good girl!" I was about to drop the card and hug her, but she kept signing. *Word made world. Word loves Sema word made gorillas people apples bears word loves bears word loves shiny man helper.*

Stifling a groan, I brought my hand to my face and stared at my girl through splayed fingers. Sema rarely signed in a continuous stream; only when she was excited or nervous did she string several words together. Yet these signs made no sense at all.

Maybe she was overusing our word-of-the-day just to spite me—like the time she'd delighted in punctuating every thought with Ethan's sign-language expletive.

I lowered my lashes and exhaled slowly, then opened one eye in a cautious squint, like a cop viewing a bomb about to blow.

Sema remained focused on the hall, her head tilted

and her mouth open in a pink smile. *Kamili's baby,* she signed to the air. *Help Kamili's baby.*

Silently I stood and walked to the doorway, deliberately placing myself between Sema and her illusionary visitor.

"Fielding," I called, my voice cracking. "Can you come here? I think Sema's really sick."

Fielding examined Sema, who had fallen silent by the time he arrived, then looked at me and gestured toward the hallway.

"Just a minute," I mouthed. Because Sema's eyes were heavy, I gave her a juice box and her plush bear, then slipped another Mr. Rogers video into the VCR. One look at her half-closed eyes told me she would sleep . . . and I was beginning to think sleep was the best medicine for her.

After closing the door to the observation room, Fielding slipped an arm around my shoulders and led me toward the office. "Tell me again why you're so upset. She seems fine except for that little crackle, and Parker's coming over after lunch."

I met his gaze over the top of my reading glasses. "She's lost her grip on reality."

He snorted a laugh until he realized I wasn't kidding, then he rubbed a finger hard over his lip. "Perhaps you'd better explain that one."

We entered the office and I took a moment to gather my thoughts as I sank into a chair across from Fielding's desk. "She's been signing nonsense. I taught her to read the word *word*—a difficult concept, but one I knew she could grasp because we use that sign all the time—and then she spaced out. She sat there, gaping at nothing and signing that word made the world, word made gorillas and apples and all kinds of blarney."

Claire looked up from the keyboard where she'd been typing. *"What'd she say?"*

I shook my head. "Is Parker on his way? I think Sema's really sick. She's never signed this kind of nonsense before. At first I thought she was teasing, but then she signed something about Kamili's baby—" I shrugged as tears stung my eyes. "She needs help."

"Maybe"—Claire's eyes narrowed—"she wasn't talking nonsense."

For an instant I wondered if the entire world had slipped a gear, then I remembered I was conversing with Miss Mystical. "Claire, if you're going to tell me about the songs of the gorilla nation—"

"Not this time." She glanced at Fielding as if seeking support, then drew a deep breath. "I keep thinking about the shiny man. What if she's seeing some kind of a spirit guide? Animals can see more than we can, you know."

I shot her a glare that should have singed the fringes of her bangs. "I thought I told you not to talk to Sema about religion."

She lifted her hands in a *don't-shoot* pose. "I haven't said another word, I swear."

"Then please keep your opinions to yourself. And see if you can get Parker over here now. I'm really worried."

While Claire picked up the phone, Fielding leaned his elbow on the desk and rested his chin in his hand. "What'd she say about Kamili's baby?"

The question startled me. "What?"

"You said Sema said something about the baby."

"Yeah . . . so?"

"So what'd she say?"

I stared at him, amazed and irritated by his curiosity. "I don't remember exactly. Something about helping Kamili's baby."

"*She* wants to help? Or does she want you to help?"

"She sure didn't want *me* to help," I drawled, "because she wasn't talking to me at the time. She was talking to her imaginary friend."

Claire lifted her head. "The shiny man?"

My eyes drilled into her. "Yes. The wonderful shiny man who does everything right and loves everybody, including good gorillas. Obviously I don't love good gorillas, because if I did"—my voice clotted and threatened to break—"if I did, I wouldn't have let Sema get hurt."

Like blood out of a cut, silence spread from my chair and permeated the office. The three of us sat in the heavy quiet, and I suspected we were all thinking the same thing: Sema was an imaginative individual. Could she have invented an invisible caretaker because I failed to protect her?

If so . . . the implications were unbelievable. If true, I might be able to demonstrate that gorillas not only possessed nearly human mental and emotional faculties, but, like humans, they could also suffer from mental and emotional illnesses.

I took a deep breath and felt a dozen different emotions collide. I had stumbled across a scientific threshold undreamed of by other gorilla researchers, but my arrival at this place had not been without cost. Sema had been traumatized, wounded, and damaged. The nurturer in me wanted to heal her at all costs; the scientist in me wanted to explore her psychosis.

What should I do? My options were not entirely open—much would depend on Parker's analysis of Sema's physical condition. Much would depend on Sema herself. But in the end, everything depended on me.

I leaned my elbow on Fielding's desk and pondered my next course of action.

"I've been doing some reading," he said, wearing an intense but guarded expression. "Did you know there's an American artist who had to teach herself how to paint again after she suffered a stroke? The remarkable thing is that her new paintings are better than her older works. The article I read said she sold more pieces in the twelve months after her stroke than she did in her first twenty years as an artist."

I shook my head, unable to see his point. "She's selling now because people feel sorry for her."

"It's more than that, Glee. I found her Web page and looked at examples of her work. I'm no artist, but even I can see that her new paintings have a kind of haunting quality—it's really amazing. In fact," a blush burned his cheek, "the images remind me of an MRI scan. It's like you can see blood vessels and the pulse of life in her work."

"Are you saying that Sema should take up painting? She could, you know. Koko has painted pictures, and elephants have been producing artwork for years—"

"I'm not talking about painting. I was thinking maybe the stroke did something to Sema's brain—opened a window, so to speak. Maybe by damaging one region, the stroke has caused her to use another—you know the body compensates for loss. Perhaps this other part of the brain is fueling these unusual behaviors."

"Reminds me of that Jimmy Stewart movie," Claire quipped. "You know the one? Black-and-white, a classic. About the nice man who goes everywhere with this huge invisible rabbit—"

"Harvey," Fielding and I answered in unison.

"The rabbit wasn't real," I went on. "The Jimmy Stewart character was an alcoholic and crazy as a loon."

Claire's smile dissolved into a bewildered expression. "He *was?*"

I rubbed my temple, where the drummer from a mariachi band had begun to warm up on my nerve endings. "I don't disagree with you, Fielding. I think it's entirely possible the stroke is causing these hallucinations. I've read that if certain areas of the brain are stimulated, people can see, hear, and even smell things that aren't really there. I was going to read more about it on my lunch break."

We both flinched at the soft beep of the security

system. I looked over my shoulder, hoping to greet Dr. Parker.

But Ken Matthews strode into the office, his suit as neatly pressed as his smile. He nodded at us, then tucked his thumbs behind the loops of his red suspenders as he scanned the monitors over our heads. I automatically followed his gaze, looking at the other gorillas for the first time that morning. All seemed quiet in the habitat—Dakarai sat atop his favorite rock, surveying his kingdom, Mosi and Rafiki played in the grotto. Kamili sat in the smaller observation cave, invisible to all but Sema and the security camera.

"Good morning, everyone." Like an actor, he pitched his voice to reach the farthest corners of the room. "I came to check on our most talented gorilla. How is she doing?"

Civility forced me to swallow a sudden surge of bitterness. "She's not in the habitat; she's in the observation room . . . and we've sent for Dr. Parker."

Fielding shot me a warning glance, then stood. "It's probably nothing, but we heard crackles in her lungs this morning."

"Really? Is that serious?"

"It could be. We'll want to keep an eye on her."

"Can I see her?"

Fielding gestured toward the hall, so I stood too. "When I left her, she was getting ready to sleep. If she's not well, I don't want to disturb her."

Matthews exhaled as though I was taxing his patience, but Fielding nodded. "We'll be careful."

He led the way to the observation room with Matthews trailing in his wake. I should have let them go, but I didn't want Matthews to see or know anything about Sema that I didn't see or know first.

The zoo director grunted when he looked through the reinforced window. "I thought you said she was asleep."

"She was—or she should be." I insinuated my way between the two men and peered through the glass. Sema sat in her inner tube nest, her bear in her lap, but she wasn't sleeping. She was sitting erect, her hands flying as she signed . . . to whom?

I shifted to look at the opposite wall where the one-way mirror opened into the private cave. Sema could have been signing to Kamili . . . but she wasn't. At some point in the last two minutes, our heavily pregnant female had left the cave, probably to stretch her legs.

Behind me, Fielding cleared his throat. "Maybe she's signing to someone on TV. She does that sometimes, right?"

I looked toward the television, but the tape had finished and the screen had gone black. I shifted to look at Sema, whose hands were still moving.

Matthews moved close enough to nudge my right shoulder. I was strangling on the scent of Michael Kors for Men when he whispered, "What's she saying?"

I cleared my throat, not certain I wanted to translate. "Sema good gorilla. Sema hate water. Water cold. Water dark. Sema in water . . . with shiny man."

Matthews laughed. "Well, that's fine."

I pulled away and blinked at him. "Pardon?"

"Obviously, she's still able to talk. This is great. We can continue with our plans to conduct demonstrations. Our guests will be amazed."

I tapped the window as my thoughts sputtered. "You want her like . . . like *this*?"

"Like what? I want her to talk, and she's talking."

"But she's talking nonsense!"

"Who cares? Nobody expects a gorilla to make sense. They expect her to be *entertaining*."

My anger, successfully restrained just minutes ago, stretched its limbs, a caged animal about to break out and claw a path through this moron's brain. I might have struck Matthews with words if not with my fists, but with none too gentle a grip, Fielding pulled me away.

"We think, sir," he said, planting me behind him, "that Sema may have suffered a stroke due to oxygen deprivation. It's not like her to sign when no one's around."

Matthews snorted. "So she talks to herself. Who doesn't?"

"This is a different behavior," I insisted, stepping sideways to avoid Fielding's shoulder. "Sometimes she signs to her dolls or manipulates them as if they're signing to me. But look at her now! She's signing to nothing!"

Matthews leaned toward the window, his eyes narrowing, then he shrugged. "She's fine. Let's get her well and continue to have Parker keep an eye on her.

But as far as I'm concerned, the more she signs, the better. If she gets confused, we'll help her out and edit our translations."

He clapped a hand on Fielding's shoulder. "You and your team are doing good work here. Keep it up."

My eyes met Fielding's as he grimaced beneath Matthews's grip. Though something in me wanted Brad to knock the director's hand away, neither one of us were free to tell Matthews what we really thought of him. He had the power; we were the pawns. He cared for the business; we cared for the animals.

Like Dian Fossey, who once had to surrender a beloved gorilla youngster to a zoo in order to prevent an entire family from being slaughtered in defense of yet another baby, I had learned to make deals with the devil.

But I didn't have to like it.

30

Dr. Parker didn't arrive at the gorilla pavilion until after two; by that time Sema's temperature had risen a degree above normal and the crackles in her lungs were more pronounced. He prescribed antibiotics, which I mixed into a bowl of applesauce and fed her myself.

Claire left at four; Fielding lingered until five. The g's trooped into their rooms and settled down for the evening, though Dakarai seemed more restive than usual. I lingered in the office for two reasons—first, I wanted to keep an eye on Sema; second, I wanted to use the zoo's broadband Internet connection to search out more information about stroke and hallucination.

Several times I looked up from my research and felt Dakarai's dark gaze upon me. He sat in his room across the hall, his arms folded over his wide chest, his eyes intent. Who knew what he was thinking?

At eight o'clock, I turned off the computer, stretched, and rolled my chair away from the desk. The hallway had filled with the rumbling sounds of gorilla snoring, but as I took one last walk down the corridor to check on the g's, I realized two were still awake: Kamili and Dakarai.

I paused outside Kamili's room. According to Dr. Parker's calculation, she wasn't due to deliver for another ten days. Sema's comment, however, compounded with Dakarai's alertness, made me pause. Did the animals know something we didn't?

I opened the door to Kamili's room, then slowly sidled along the wall toward the chain-link gate separating her from Dakarai. If I were her, I'd certainly want him near.

The silverback grunted when he saw me open the gate, but he waited until I retreated before he advanced. He knuckle-walked to the opening between the two rooms, then sank to the floor and propped one arm on his bent knee, his attention fastened on Kamili.

From the hallway, I looked through the window and studied our pregnant female. Free-living gorillas usually gave birth at night and rarely needed assistance, but Sema's comment hovered at the edge of my mind.

Would Kamili need help with this birth?

The pregnant gorilla stirred in the straw, apparently unable to find a comfortable position. On a hunch, I went into the office and dialed Fielding's home number. He didn't answer, so I left a message on his machine: "Fielding—I think Kamili's in labor. If you want to witness the big event, you'd better hurry up and get here."

I crept back into the hall and peered through the wide window of Kamili's room. She grunted softly, her hands swishing through the straw as she paced along a wall. Dakarai watched her, a look of concern on his face. A sense of awe washed over me when I realized that these two were behaving almost exactly as they would in the wild—the male would give the female space at the same time he offered support and protection. The female would withdraw and . . . well, some things a female had to do alone.

I smiled at Kamili, then tiptoed down the hall to check on Sema. She slept in her nest, one hand half-covering her face. Good. She needed to rest.

I stopped in the office long enough to grab my ragged chair, then brought it into the hallway where I could watch in relative comfort. Kamili had begun to grunt softly, and the sounds increased their tempo as the moments passed.

Since coming in from the habitat, she had built three nests—one in the corner, one on a wire platform, one beneath the window. After sitting a few moments in each nest, she rose and moved to another, apparently unable to find one that suited her. At one point she looked at me with bewilderment in her eyes. I felt my heart contract in pity—this was her first pregnancy, and she hadn't witnessed Rafiki's birth two years earlier. If only she could communicate! I might have been able to explain childbirth and ease her fears.

Fielding came in at ten thirty and hurried toward me. "Do we need to call Parker?"

"Nothing's happened yet." I lifted a brow. "You got my message, I see."

He nodded. "I was at the movie."

"Oh? See something good?"

"It was all right, I guess. I would have enjoyed it more if my date had shown up."

The words stung, but I couldn't let my feelings show. I forced a smile. "Sorry you got stood up."

"My fault. I didn't call until nearly seven, and I asked her to meet me at the theater. Later I realized you never got my message."

My smile froze. "You called *me?*"

"I thought it might be nice for us to talk about something other than the g's. But that's okay—we can bond while we have this baby. We've got all night."

I turned back to the window as heat flooded my face. He had called me . . . to ask me out. And he wanted to talk about something other than gorillas?

The implication sent a wave of warmth through me. "I'm not going anywhere."

For the next two and a half hours we sat in the hall and talked about the zoo, previous pets, our dreams and hopes. I learned that Fielding had earned his undergraduate degree in zoology and his master's from the University of Missouri; he also confessed that he'd hoped to be a big-game hunter until he watched an actual hunt on television, then he realized he'd never be able to shoot one of those glorious beasts. I confided that I had wanted to be a mermaid and used to spend hours lolling in the waves near Nana's place, keeping my legs together as if they were encased in scales.

"After my parents died," I added, "I hated the beach. I haven't been swimming in the ocean since."

Shortly after 1:00 AM, Kamili moved to the corner nest, braced her back against the wall, and extended her legs on the floor. She grunted again, louder this time, then a flood of liquid, blood, and baby poured onto the straw. Fielding and I both stood, our adrenaline rushing, and watched in breathless wonder as Kamili plucked the infant from the wet straw and swiped at the tiny face.

My hand rose to my throat. "Would you look at that?"

Fielding flipped on the light switch to illuminate every corner of the room.

The two of us, gawkers in a building heavy with after-hours quiet, stood with our eyes glued to the sight beyond the window. After a long moment I put my hand to the glass. "Do we need to do anything?"

"Doesn't look like it."

His comment carried me back to the night of Sema's birth. We had been so inexperienced back then, so determined to follow our principles. I'd stepped into the night room of an animal I barely knew and broken every rule to pick up the abandoned baby; Fielding had clung to his conviction that rules should never be bent.

We had both changed a lot since that night.

Brad slipped his arm around my shoulder. "What are you thinking about?"

"Sema. And about how much you've changed."

He eased into a smile. "Really."

Kamili nestled the infant in the crook of her arm, then picked up a piece of the placenta and ate it. Though my stomach shriveled at the sight, I knew she was doing the right thing—most researchers believe the placenta possesses antibiotic properties that help both the mother and her offspring.

"This behavior," I pointed to Kamili nestling the baby against her breast, "is familiar because she's seen it. Aisha has been a good example."

When Kamili jostled the infant, Fielding and I both gasped when the baby opened its eyes—they were the clear blue of an African sky. They would change, of course, as the infant grew, but now they were bright and serene.

The baby stretched out its thin arms, flashed a glimpse of his or her pink-spotted palms, then shivered and rooted for a nipple. Kamili tenderly guided her offspring to nourishment, then settled back into the corner and closed her eyes, weary from a job well done.

"She's going to be a good mother," I whispered, not wanting to wake the sleepers around us. "And he"—I pointed to Dakarai—"what a father he'll make."

Dakarai had witnessed the birth without moving; now

he rose and knuckle-walked toward Kamili. Leaning over her, he stared at the suckling infant, then turned to look at Fielding and me as if to say, *that's really something, isn't it?*

Tears stung my eyes as I nodded in reply. Assured that all was well, Dakarai moved back to his doorway, where he settled with folded arms to watch over the newest addition to his family.

Fielding scratched at his jaw. "Do you think she had help?"

I looked around. "Who?"

"Kamili. Didn't Sema say the shiny man was going to help her?"

"I don't think I'd put too much stock in anything she says about the shiny man." I laughed softly, too overwhelmed by the miracle of birth to be ruffled by the reminder of Sema's psychosis. "I'm not like Nana; I don't see God's hand in every flower and bug. But after seeing this . . . I could almost be tempted to believe."

31

Despite having only two hours' sleep, the next morning I floated through the parking lot on a tide of euphoria. Dr. Parker didn't usually work on Saturday, but I wasn't surprised to see his Jeep outside the gorilla pavilion. I knew he'd want to visit Kamili and her infant as soon as possible. We still had to learn the new arrival's gender.

When I entered the building and saw him kneeling in

Sema's room, my euphoria shriveled into cold dread. I hurried forward and knelt beside him. Curled in her nest, Sema was laboring to breathe while an unmistakable trail of green mucus ran from her nostrils.

"We have a sick animal on our hands," Parker said, rising stiffly. He paused to brush straw from his knees, then scratched at his ear and looked at me. "I'm going to put her on an IV. None of the other animals could handle that without sedation, but I'm trusting you to keep her calm. I want you to get as many fluids into her as possible, and see if you can keep her eating. Oh— and no one comes into this room without a mask, and nothing from this room goes near Kamili, the new infant, or any of the other animals."

"Of course." As he picked up a clipboard, I took Sema's hand and held it against mine. "Good morning, girlie. How do you feel?"

Sema opened her eyes, grunted hoarsely, and let her head fall back to her blanket.

My heart contracted like a squeezed fist. "She's never acted like this before."

Parker looked up from his notes. "Amoxicillin ought to knock out the infection. We started that yesterday, right? How many pills did you give her?"

"I followed your directions—one every twelve hours. She's due for another dose now."

"Good. I'm going to give her an injection and concentrate on getting some fluids into her. Keep her comfortable and warm, let her play with her favorite toys if she's up to it, and let her sleep all she wants." He gave me a small smile as he slipped his pen into his shirt pocket. "I think she'll turn the corner in a couple of days. Unfortunately, some things tend to get worse before they get better."

As he left the room, I sank onto the floor and wondered how much worse Sema could become before Parker would really worry. A moment later, the vet returned with a syringe. Sema didn't even whimper when he gave her the injection.

"Good girl." He rubbed her shoulder briefly before standing. "I've always meant to tell you, Glee—I don't know anything about sign language, but the way you've domesticated this animal is amazing. I hope someday you earn the recognition you deserve."

I thanked him with a nod, but at that moment I couldn't have cared less about recognition. Sema was more than an animal to domesticate, more than a project to fulfill the requirements of my dissertation. She had become the family I lacked and the child who embodied all my hopes and dreams.

I helped Parker hang a bag of fluids, then stroked Sema's hand as he shaved a small section of her forearm. "This might sting a little," I told her, hoping she was lucid enough to understand. "But you'll be okay. And this medicine will help you feel better."

When her dark skin had been exposed, the vet tied a rubber tourniquet above the shaved site, then ripped the packing from an IV catheter. When a vein appeared in her arm, he swabbed the area with an alcohol pad, then pushed the needle into her arm.

I had to look away. I'd never been squeamish around medical procedures, but I'd never had to watch anyone work on someone I loved this much . . .

"All done." Parker gave me a wan smile as I turned to face him. The IV had been inserted into Sema's arm; the line ran from the catheter to the hanging bag. The vet gathered his supplies and said something about washing up and checking on the new baby again.

Sema stirred slightly when the doctor left the room, then pushed herself into a sitting position.

"Careful, sweetie. You need to stay in your nest for a while."

She looked at the catheter in her arm, then reached for the tubing.

"No, Sema, don't touch that. And be careful when you sign. For a little while, you need to be still."

She curled her lips into a hooting smile, then blinked. *Glee hungry?*

"I've already had my breakfast. Are *you* hungry? Would you like an apple?"

She held out her hand, giving me hope, but when I took an apple from my bag and rolled it into her palm, she dropped it into her nest.

"Would you like some juice?"

Sema swung her head.

"Would you like me to read you a story? Put a video on the TV? Maybe *Goldilocks and the Three Bears*?"

She lifted her chin. I was about to congratulate myself for sparking her interest when she began to sign: *Shiny man likes stories. Shiny man said God made gorillas bears water sun sky trees apples watermelon ... babies.*

Like a battery-operated toy running out of juice, she lowered her head and hands. I slipped my arm around her drooping shoulders. "That's enough talking, Sema. Why don't you sleep for a while? I'm going to do some work, but I'll stay with you."

I thought she would argue or demand a game of tickle—the old Sema would have—but she exhaled a rattling breath and curled up in her Care Bear comforter.

Leaning back against the cinder-block wall, I closed my eyes and wished I could believe in Nana's God or Sema's shiny man.

At that moment, I could have used a miracle worker.

I stayed with my beloved girl until her fever broke. I spent the night on a cot outside the observation room and woke every time I heard her stir, cough, or snort in her sleep. Several times I rose to get a wet cloth and wipe mucus from her face; my touch seemed to help her relax. Remembering that humans and gorillas are susceptible to the same germs, I scrubbed my hands with antibacterial soap until my knuckles were raw.

Fortunately, Sunday morning brought improvement. Though Sema's sinuses continued to drain, the mucus was clear and her temperature had returned to normal.

I think Fielding was as relieved as I was. "Parker must have given her one heck of an antibiotic," he said, his voice muffled through the antibacterial mask. "I'll call him and pass on the good report." The lines at the corners of his eyes deepened as he looked at me. "It's your day off. Why don't you go home and get some rest?"

"I'm fine."

"Really, Glee, you look like you haven't slept in two days. At least go home and take a shower."

I understood the concern behind the request, but I couldn't resist a defensive jab. "Are you saying I look a mess?"

"Something like that."

He chuckled, and at the sound of his laughter, Sema pushed herself into a sitting position. *Sema love apples!*

"She's hungry," I told him. "That's a relief."

"I'll tell Claire to bring her breakfast."

"And I think I will get out of here for a while—since I obviously need a break." I gave Fielding a playful punch in the arm, then walked over to hug my bright-eyed girl. "Claire's going to bring your bowl, okay? I'm going home to clean up."

Glee come again?

"I'll be back soon, I promise. We'll read a book—maybe even take a nap together, okay?"

Bye.

Trusting Fielding and Claire to care for my girl—a gesture I couldn't imagine making a few weeks ago—I pointed the car toward home. I drove south on Belcher, but instead of turning toward my house, I found myself heading toward the beach.

Twenty minutes later, I pulled into the parking lot of Posey's Pink Palace.

"Hello, Herman," I called to the parrot as I approached Nana's apartment.

"Hey, cutie!"

"Is Nana around?"

"Hey, cutie!"

I stepped into the office. An earnest young preacher proclaimed the gospel from a small television in the corner, reminding me that another Sunday had rolled around.

Like a bona fide tourist, I rang the bell.

My grandmother appeared a moment later, her arms laden with folded towels. "Glee! My goodness, are you all right? When you didn't come for dinner last night, we got a little worried. Rob called your house, but there was no answer—"

"Sema was sick. I spent the night at the zoo."

"I thought something might be wrong, so we prayed for you." Her blue eyes brimmed with compassion. "You poor dear, you must be exhausted. Come on back and have a cup of coffee while you tell me all about it."

At least *she* hadn't felt obliged to remind me I looked awful. Like an obedient puppy, I followed her behind the counter and into the kitchen where the air smelled of coffee, molasses cookies . . . and love.

As Nana moved toward the coffeemaker, I sank onto a stool and pushed my limp bangs away from my forehead. "Sema was really sick, Nana. I wasn't sure she was going to pull through, but her fever broke this morning."

Nana poured a mug of steaming coffee, then glanced

in my direction. "Is she out of the woods now?"

"She's better, but we're not sure of anything because her lungs were damaged during her accident. Dr. Parker, the zoo vet, will check on her later this morning."

"Oh, Glee."

"And that's only part of it—her body seems to be healing, but I'm afraid the accident affected her mind. An MRI scan revealed brain damage in several areas."

Nana set the mug before me, then sank onto the next stool. "I'm so sorry, hon. I know how much Sema means to you."

I felt my chin wobble. "It's . . . not as bad as it could have been. Sema can still talk, but every once in a while she talks nonsense. She's talking to people who aren't there, talking about things that make no sense."

Nana's forehead knit in puzzlement. "What sorts of things?"

"Nutty things—she has this new best friend she calls the 'shiny man.' Claire says Sema is like Jimmy Stewart in that old movie, *Harvey*. She seems to think Sema's babbling is cute, but her life's work isn't riding on this project."

A slightly perplexed expression settled over Nana's face, as if a thought had risen in her mind but not the courage to offer it. She turned toward the window over the sink, her eyes wide and abstracted.

I knew that look. "What?"

"Hmm?"

"What are you thinking?"

She smiled at me, her forehead wrinkling with an idea. "Have you considered that perhaps Sema really *is* seeing someone?"

I stared at her, speechless.

"I know it sounds nutty to someone like you," Nana went on, glancing down at her fingertips, "but animals can see things we can't. They are much more in tune with the created world."

Good grief, my grandmother was beginning to sound like Claire. "Nana"—I forced a laugh—"if you knew what she was saying, you'd know there's no way she could really be seeing someone. From what I can tell, she thinks this 'shiny man' was in the water with her, and she sees him at night when no one else is in the building. She says he tells her things."

Nana cocked her head as a thoughtful smile curved her mouth. "Many animals can hear subsonic sound waves the human ear can't pick up. And animals can see angels—the Bible says so."

"You think the 'shiny man' is an *angel?* That's . . . that's—"

"I know you think it's crazy." Glancing at her hands again, Nana laced her fingers. "But you have to admit a supernatural being might well appear as a shiny man. Perhaps you should give her the benefit of the doubt."

Somehow, I resisted the urge to lower my head and groan. Nana would never be a scientist. She was too religious, too old-fashioned. She would rather believe in angels and demons than in the simple scientific certainty that the accident had damaged Sema's brain and her perceptions.

"Open your mind to other possibilities, sweetheart." Nana bent to catch my eye. "Isn't that what a scientist is supposed to do?"

Unable to bear the sweetness in her smile, I covered my eyes with my hand and cleared my throat. "I need to get home."

Nana pulled away. "Is there anything I can do to help?"

Despite my frustration, I had to suppress a smile—if I'd told her Sema needed blood, she'd go down to Pinellas County donor services and roll up her sleeve.

"Thanks, but there's really nothing anyone can do. She's already on antibiotics and an IV drip. Now we just have to watch her and make sure she isn't exposed to any new infections."

Nana's eyes gleamed. "I can keep praying. I have some prayer partners who will pray for Sema, too."

For a second I thought she was kidding, but I couldn't see the slightest glimmer of amusement in her blue eyes. "Won't your friends think it's silly to pray . . . you know, for an animal?"

She squeezed my shoulder. "Sema is one of God's creatures, isn't she? Jesus said our heavenly Father cares about the sparrows . . . and about you, for you are worth more than many birds. Anything that affects your life concerns God, and I'm blessed to have friends who are concerned about the things that affect me. So we'll pray, honey. We'll ask God to continue to improve

Sema's health, for your sake as well as hers."

Her concern touched me, but I didn't believe her prayers would be any more effective than the magic beads sold in the zoo's safari souvenir shop.

I patted her hand. "Don't hug me too tightly, Nana. I'm afraid I smell like gorilla. Fielding told me to go home and clean up—how's that for a heartfelt compliment?"

She gave me a bright-eyed glance, full of shrewdness. "I like that young man. You should bring him next Saturday for dinner."

"He's a little too by-the-book for my tastes, but I think he's growing on me." I kissed her cheek and slipped off the stool. "Let me get to that shower before I stink up your kitchen."

"But you haven't finished your coffee!"

"I'll have to take a rain check. I'll call you later."

As I started the car and pulled out of the parking lot, I couldn't help but wonder why I'd felt compelled to visit Nana's place. Had I been searching for a safe place to vent? Or had I known that my grandmother would offer to pray, and that offer would meet some deep-seated and primitive need for reassurance?

I didn't believe in prayer, but at that point I was happy to accept reassurance any way I could get it.

Refreshed and showered, I returned to the zoo at noon and spent the entire afternoon playing with Sema. Dr. Parker confirmed that her fever had broken, the nasal discharge had lessened, and the sound of her breathing had improved. Her appetite returned along with her enthusiasm and playfulness.

Glee stinky nut! she chided me after I hid her juice box under a plastic hard hat from her toy box. *Glee stinky fat cat!*

Her enthusiastic rebound led me to consider the possibility that Sema had been suffering from some kind of infection ever since the accident. I jotted a note in my journal, intending to ask Dr. Parker if something—some form of meningitis, perhaps—could inflame particular areas of the brain and result in altered behavior. I would be thrilled to forego my study on possible mental illnesses in lowland gorillas if a biological agent could explain my girl's bizarre behaviors.

In a quiet moment, I told Sema all about the new addition. As simply as I could, I described how the baby girl was born, how Kamili cared for the infant, and how Dakarai watched everything from the doorway of his room. I laughed when I told her how earlier that morning Kamili had held her baby up to the window so Claire and I could have a look.

Baby name?

I shook my head. "Kamili's baby doesn't have a name yet. We're just calling her *baby*."

Sema reached into her toy box and pulled out an old gorilla doll, then held it to her breast. Pain squeezed my heart when Sema bent to press a kiss to her doll's forehead.

On the pretext of getting something from my bag, I stood. I was about to call out and tell Fielding the old

Sema had returned when from the corner of my eye I saw her turn. Curious, I shifted my position and watched as she looked into an empty corner of the room and belched softly, communicating *I'm here* and *all is well*. Sema had picked up the sound from the other g's.

So who was she talking to now?

Disappointment struck like a fist to my stomach. Regret rose in my throat, a lump so invasive I had to swallow in order to breathe.

Completely engrossed in whatever she thought she was seeing, Sema signed a flurry of words: *Sema feel fine, Sema not sick, Sema want gorilla visit play with baby. Shiny man like apples? Sema loves apples bears Glee. Sema loves Dakarai Aisha Kamili Rafiki Mosi. Sema hate water. Cold stinky water bad, shiny man in water.*

Fighting the sting of tears, I flipped a page in my journal and began to transcribe her disjointed words. If Sema's hallucinations were a symptom of mental illness or a by-product of stroke, I would need this data. As far as I knew, no one had done much work with gorilla neurology. A study of the effects of stroke on a gorilla brain might be invaluable to humans. It would certainly be unique.

I waited until she had finished carrying on her imaginary conversation, then closed my journal and lowered my lashes to hide the dismay in my eyes.

She tugged at my knee. When I looked up, her dark eyes searched my face. *Glee sad?*

I never could hide much from her.

"Glee is tired." I forced a smile as I signed the words. "Glee needs to sleep, and so do you. Good night, sweetie. I'll see you in the morning."

She tilted her head and smiled at me, then held up her arms in invitation. I gave her a hug and kissed her cheek, then slipped out of the room before she could hear my heart break.

32

Fielding had scheduled me for late arrival on Monday morning, so I didn't head to Thousand Oaks until just before nine o'clock. The sky hung over Pinellas County like a faultless curve of blue while honey-thick sunshine bathed the road. As the radio played the Beach Boys' "Help Me Rhonda," I tapped the steering wheel and wondered if Brad would repeat his invitation this weekend and take me out.

My thoughts skittered to an abrupt halt as I turned into the employees' entrance and spied a WSET news van beneath a hulking satellite transmitter. The vehicle was one of many in a long line idling outside the security gate. At the sight of so many newspeople, I felt my stomach sway—had something happened to Sema?

Of course not—Fielding would have called me. So all the fuss had to be directed at one of the other pavilions. Perhaps there'd been another accident or the zoo had received an exotic new animal. I'd probably know what was going on if I'd read my copy of the *Thousand Oaks Weekly Report*, but I didn't care much about anything outside the gorilla pavilion.

Drumming my nails against the steering wheel, I wished I'd turned on the television news while dressing. But after waking from a long and much-needed sleep, I'd been so anxious to check on Sema that I'd done little more than shower, brush my teeth, and slip into my uniform. I'd applied mascara and lipstick at a traffic light and brushed my hair at a railroad crossing.

I eased up on the brake as the line of vehicles advanced. *Something* had happened . . . something that translated into big-time news. The zoo had dozens of pavilions, each with its own staff and its own life-and-death dramas, so which of them had the power to attract this kind of attention?

I smiled as I remembered that one of the manatees was due to deliver her calf—Parker had mentioned the impending birth. A newborn manatee could have resulted in a call to the local media, and they'd show up in droves for footage of a new calf. Manatees weren't particularly photogenic or friendly, but people loved underdogs, and the endangered Florida sea cows certainly fit that description.

I rolled up to the thatched-roof shack, flashed my employee ID, and smiled at the security guard on duty. "Busy morning, Tom?"

He rolled his eyes. "I'll say. They started lining up at eight thirty, but Matthews said we couldn't let them in until nine."

"Everybody heading over to the manatee lagoon?"

"Nope. The press conference is outside your pavilion."

My stomach dropped. "The gorillas'?"

He laughed. "Where have you been? One of the gorillas had a baby over the weekend, and Matthews wants to tell the world about it."

"He's letting them in to see the baby?" My alarm flared into indignation. "Good grief, the man's crazy. You can't let a pack of reporters near a gorilla infant—"

"I wouldn't know about that, Miss Granger." Tom stepped back and politely waved me through. "Good luck finding a place to park."

The driver behind me honked, so I thanked Tom and pulled away.

The security guard wasn't kidding—cars and vans had already filled the parking lot around the gorilla exhibit. I parked on the grass at the far edge of the lot, then pulled my extra-large shoulder bag from the backseat. I had packed it with toys to stimulate Sema's curiosity—crayons, two new coloring books, a tray of watercolors, and an assortment of paintbrushes. Sema had always loved art, and Fielding's comments about the artist who'd suffered a stroke convinced me I should pick up some new enrichment supplies.

But at that moment my thoughts were focused on Kamili's baby.

A group of professionally dressed reporters and cameramen in shorts and T-shirts stood in a knot outside the staff entrance, most of them smoking as they waited.

"Miss," one woman called, breaking from the group. "You work here?"

I nodded.

"Can you tell us anything about the miracle gorilla?"

I waved her off. "I can tell you not to count on getting in to see the baby today. If you want an official comment, better wait for the zoo director."

The woman stopped, but tendrils of apprehension wound through my stomach as I fished my key card from my wallet. Miracle gorilla? Kamili's baby was wonderful, but there'd been nothing miraculous about the birth unless Matthews's press release had described it in mystical terms.

I quickened my step as other reporters approached.

"Excuse me, do you work here?"

"The talking gorilla—is she feeling better this morning?"

"Do you expect her to talk to an angel today?"

I halted in midstride as a chill climbed my spine. Time slowed as I turned to face the reporter who had asked the last question. "Excuse me—*what* did you say?"

A half dozen tape recorders and microphones materialized before my face.

"I said," the woman repeated, "do you expect the gorilla to hear from an angel today? Does he really talk to God?"

I pressed my lips into a straight line. I'd been stunned by this ambush, but I could feel my senses recovering, and anger led the front of the pack.

"You all had better get your story straight." I turned and zipped my ID card through the security lock, then left the reporters outside and stalked forward in search of Claire Hartwell.

"What did you tell them?"

Claire quaked under the heat of my gaze, a deep flush rising from her collar. "Nothing, I swear. I got here at five thirty, and I haven't been outside since bringing in the produce boxes. I haven't had a chance to tell anybody anything."

"They're asking about angels and God, Claire. You're the only one around here who uses those words with any frequency."

"I told you, I didn't say anything!"

"What's going on in here?"

I whirled at the sound of Fielding's voice. "That's what I'd like to know."

Fielding stepped into the kitchen, his eyes dark and serious. "What could Claire possibly have to do with that ruckus outside?"

"Don't you know?"

"Obviously not." He folded his arms. "Matthews called a press conference to announce our new gorilla. He's all excited about some name-the-baby contest that's going to be sponsored by Channel Nine and Rico's Pizza."

"That may be true," my voice went hoarse, "but that's not the only reason they're out there. They asked me about Sema when I came in—wanted to know if our

314

gorilla was going to talk to God or if she'd had any word from the angels."

Claire brought her hand to her mouth. "Oh, no."

I looked from her to Fielding. "Come on, admit it—someone said something to those reporters about Sema. How else would they know?"

"I didn't say anything." Claire's flush faded, staining her complexion with rosy blotches. "Last night I was at the library until ten; then I went home. I got up at five; I came here; I fed the g's and sprinkled the browse. While I was on the roof I saw a lot of traffic, but I didn't think anything of it. I sure didn't talk to any reporters."

"You don't owe us an explanation, Claire." Fielding focused on me. "Could *you* have said something to someone, Glee?"

"Are you serious?" I gaped at him, amazed he could even *think* I might leak information to the press. "If I had talked to a reporter, Sema's condition would be the last thing I'd want to discuss. Maybe *you* said something."

Fielding shook his head. "Not me. And I saw the press release Matthews faxed to the media outlets—it focused completely on Kamili and the baby. Besides, he wouldn't want to publicize that catastrophe with Sema. A half-drowned gorilla wouldn't be good for the zoo's image."

I sank into a chair, closed my eyes, and pinched the bridge of my nose. "This is insane."

Claire slid into a chair across from me. "Why don't

you go out and ask someone where the story came from? Someone's got to know something."

"The media are like flies." Fielding turned to face us. "They catch a whiff of something on the wind, then they gather where all the other flies are swarming. Sure, someone out there knows something, but I'd bet my last dollar most of them are here as part of the swarm. Someone leaked the story of Sema's accident."

"One of them asked me if she was feeling better," I said, thinking aloud. "So they knew she's been sick. The only people who know about Sema's illness are Matthews, Parker, the three of us . . . oh. And Nana."

I closed my eyes as the truth hit like a blow to the forehead. "I am so stupid."

Fielding lifted a brow. "You think your grandmother called the television station?"

"Worse. She called her prayer partners."

"Who—what—how many is that?"

"I have no idea, but I think it's a chain. She calls somebody, that person calls someone else. Nana said she was going to ask her friends to pray for me and Sema . . . and for all I know, her prayer chain reaches across the country. People in Alaska are probably talking about Sema right now."

Claire's eyes glowed. "Really?"

"That's sarcasm, Claire." Fielding turned back to me. "You told your grandmother about Sema's odd behavior?"

I nodded. "You know how Nana is—I open up like a book when she's around, but I never dreamed the things

I told her would be all over the county by morning."

Fielding exhaled loudly, then slipped his hands into his pockets. "If it makes you feel better, I'm sure Nana didn't intend to make trouble. These things happen. People talk."

I lifted my head as the cell phone on Fielding's belt began to chime. "Bet I know who that is."

Fielding's face told me he knew, too. He unsnapped the phone and held it to his ear. "Yes?"

He listened, murmured, "We'll meet you outside the pavilion," then punched the power off.

My eyes clung to his, analyzing his reaction. "Matthews?"

He nodded. "Reporters have been calling him all morning. They don't want to ask about the new baby; they want to see the talking gorilla. He's not thrilled."

"Surely he told them it's all a mistake."

"Yeah, and he'll tell them again at the press conference. But I've got to warn you, Glee"—his eyes darkened—"I don't think you're going to be able to stall Matthews much longer. The media interest in Sema is only going to reinforce his conviction that she needs to meet the public. Soon."

"But she's not completely recovered from her infection, and she's still not right—"

"He won't care. That mob outside may be annoying, but it's reinforcing what Matthews has said all along: Sema is a potential gold mine for Thousand Oaks. So you might as well formulate a plan where she can perform for the public *and* continue her work with you. I don't see how you can satisfy Matthews any other way."

I didn't answer, but winced as my nails sliced deep into my palm.

33

I moved through my routine like an automaton as my mind wrestled with unwieldy questions. What was I supposed to do? I didn't want Sema put on display, but I knew Fielding was right—Matthews wasn't going to budge. The director had gone through considerable trouble to bring Sema back to Thousand Oaks, and soon he'd figure she'd had enough time to recover from her accident. Then he'd demand that I present her to the public.

I dropped into my chair as a cold coil of regret unwound beneath my breastbone. I should have taken Sema and fled to Mexico. I should have accepted Rob's offer to lend me the money to buy her freedom. I should have appealed to gorilla supporters the world over, done anything to keep Sema out of this prison.

To think that my research, begun so early and with so much promise, should culminate in a hokey presentation for tourists who yearned for sights more suitable for the *National Enquirer* than a reputable scientific journal . . .

The mere thought sent a current of nausea rippling through my stomach.

I propped my head on my hand and shivered at the

chilly touch of my palm. Could I be coming down with something? I should grab a mask before I went in to see Sema when she woke from her mid-morning nap. And if—when—she had to appear before people, I should require everyone within ten feet to wear a mask as well. Maybe that simple annoyance would keep the crowds away. Fielding and Parker would support my request, and if Matthews complained, he'd come off like a man who didn't care about the health of his animals.

I pressed my hand to my forehead, vainly seeking signs of a fever. Before they let the reporters in to see the baby, I'd tape paper over the window in the door to Sema's room. I'd tell Matthews that if anyone asked about angels or spiritual gorillas, he should laugh off the query and move on to the next person. And when Sema had to appear before the public for the first time, I'd lead her down familiar conversational paths, ask pointed questions to which she'd have no trouble responding, and whisk her away if she showed any sign of spacing out.

I closed my eyes and tried to sort through my options. I suppose I'd known this moment would come—Thousand Oaks needed good publicity, and Matthews wanted the world to see the result of my labor. Attendance had never been all it could be; how could animals and campy souvenirs compete with the shows and screaming roller coasters at Busch Gardens? And newspaper reports of last month's tiger attack had cast a shadow over Matthews's administration; he had to be nervous about his image. The certifying body of the

AZA didn't blame animals for accidents; they usually attributed the cause to a lack of security or improper handling.

I tucked my hands under my arms, deciding that my cold fingers and warm face resulted from air-conditioning and irritation. I was mad at Matthews, who wanted Sema to dazzle the press and zoo visitors. If he could get city and state reporters buzzing about his amazing gorilla, perhaps they'd forget about the tiger mauling that poor girl.

And wasn't public recognition part of my goal? I had labored for years, loving Sema, teaching her, becoming mother and father and sister to her so she could establish my place in the research community. My intentions may have been nobler than Matthews's, but in the cold light of honesty, I had to admit I needed publicity too.

Nana had a knack—actually, an annoying tendency—to find "blessings" in every crisis. If she were sitting across from me, she'd say Sema's accident could be considered a blessing because it would give me time to figure out how to present my girl's accomplishments in a way more appealing to scholars than to the hoi polloi.

Even my eyes were sharp enough to spy a few silver flecks in this cloud—first, the news vehicles I'd seen outside bore county license plates, so perhaps we could confine this rumor to local news outlets. Second, Sema was feeling better, and she honestly loved people. She might enjoy an opportunity to show off before a live audience. Finally, by letting my girl talk to visitors, I might be able to expand her linguistic horizons even further than I'd anticipated. Thus far she'd been limited to the phrases and concepts I taught her. By introducing the thoughts of others—screened as much as possible—she would move beyond the things I could teach her. My control over the experiment's variables would vanish, but Sema would be exposed to a wealth of words.

And she'd always loved words.

I looked up at the monitors that displayed the g's in the outdoor habitat. Dakarai was sunning himself on a boulder with Rafiki in his lap. The stately silverback was running his fingers over the youngster's fur, probably searching for fleas or other insects.

The g's looked out for each other . . . and I would look out for Sema. I would write my dissertation on her progress to date; I would record any future observations and save them for my own reference. Sema might never be able to read *Green Eggs and Ham*, but she'd be able to go on *The Late Show with David Letterman* and ask the comedian if he wanted an apple. Wouldn't the end result be the same? From the beginning, I had set out to demonstrate that the gap between humans and gorillas was not only smaller than anyone had ever imagined, but it was bridgeable.

Not even Matthews's meddling could stop me from accomplishing that goal.

Movement on the monitor caught my eye. Mosi had stood and was shaking his fist, probably at a pack of reporters. The rabble had caught the scent of my extraordinary gorilla, and Matthews wouldn't want to keep them waiting. I might as well brace myself for Sema's first public appearance and do whatever was necessary to make sure our presentation was more scholastic than silly.

If I used the upcoming situation instead of letting Matthews use me, both Sema and I could come out ahead.

I drew in a deep breath, exhaled slowly, and glanced through the office doorway. Sema should be waking from her nap at any moment. I hoped she would wake in a mood to work.

When Matthews sauntered through the pavilion en route to his press conference, I didn't protest when he said it was nearly time to introduce Sema to the public. "After all, the girl's a hero," he said, slipping his thumbs beneath his suspenders like a bragging uncle. "From what I hear, she risked her life to save the little monkey. That story will warm the heart of anyone who hears it."

I bit the inside of my cheek, irritated by his use of the word *monkey*. "I think Sema would like to meet people when she's fully recovered from her illness," I said, hoping he'd realize I was behaving with more graciousness than usual. "But we'll have to set a few stipulations."

He halted in the hallway. "Such as?"

"Only a few reporters at a time, and they must wear antibacterial masks if they approach within ten feet of her. Sema is recovering from a serious infection, and you know how susceptible gorillas are."

Matthews cocked a brow. "Anything else?"

"Reporters may submit questions beforehand, but we can't have people yelling comments at her. They'd only confuse her, and then she might not be able to respond correctly." I gave him the sweetest smile at my disposal. "We don't want her to look flustered and silly, do we?"

"No." His voice was clipped. "We don't."

"And we'll need a couple of weeks to prepare her for the first presentation. We had to habituate Sema to the other gorillas; we'll need to prepare her for meeting the public too. Otherwise it would be a new and bizarre experience . . . and we don't need to frustrate a large, strong animal."

Matthews frowned. "We need to strike while the iron is hot, don't you think? Interest is high right now. We'll be lucky to get a pair of reporters from the *Farm Gazette* out here if we wait two weeks."

I shook my head. "The people asking about Sema today have heard rumors about a psychic gorilla." I forced a laugh. "Let's give those silly rumors time to die. We'll all be better off."

Matthews glanced at Fielding, who nodded in agreement.

"Well," the director slipped his hands into his trouser pockets, "I suppose the first thing we need to do is tell the crowd outside they can meet the talking gorilla, but not today. With any luck, they'll come back."

"And don't forget the main reason they're here,"

Fielding added. "Our pretty new arrival. Not every captive gorilla succeeds in caring for her infant, so Kamili deserves a lot of credit."

Matthews drew his lips into a tight smile. "Indeed she does." He gestured down the hall, where Claire had hung pink balloons over the windows of the room where Kamili had been sequestered with her infant. "After I announce the contest, I lead the photographers through this hall, right?"

"Yes sir. We'll give them five minutes for a few pictures through the window, then ask them to leave. And absolutely no one opens the door."

"Very good."

I blew out my cheeks in frustration when Matthews straightened his shoulders and strolled out to meet the press. Fielding followed, but stopped in the doorway, catching the door before it closed.

"You okay?" he asked, searching my eyes.

"I can't believe you're letting those people into the building."

"A few photographers, Glee, for five minutes. The baby will be safe behind a glass window."

"Still—"

"You're very protective, you know?" Fielding wagged his finger at me and grinned. "That's a fine quality. I like that about you."

He stepped through the doorway, leaving me frustrated and embarrassed. With all that was going on in our pavilion, why on earth was he thinking about my fine qualities?

34

By Friday morning, Sema's sniffling had completely cleared up, so I made a mental note to ask Fielding about moving her back to the exam room. I wasn't quite ready to reintroduce her to the habitat, but she missed the other animals, and in the night area she'd be able to watch them come and go. I also knew she'd love to see Kamili and the six-day-old infant, both of whom would remain indoors for several weeks.

After Sema had eaten her breakfast, I sat on the floor in front of her. "Sweetie," I signed, "would you like to visit the other gorillas again?"

Sema love gorillas. Sema love Rafiki.

"I know you do. And now that you're well, I think you can move back to your other room. Would you like that?"

Sema love gorillas fine. To emphasize her happiness, she held out her arms. I gave her a hug.

"I have another surprise for you." I pulled out of her embrace to look her in the eye. "Some people would like to talk to you and ask you some questions. Would you like that?"

Talk now?

"Not today, sweetie, maybe in a couple of weeks. They will be nice people, and they might want to take your picture. You'll be the prettiest gorilla girl they've ever met."

Sema camera people?

I shrugged. "Why not? I think I can find your camera."

One of Sema's favorite toys was a children's digital camera I'd picked up at Target. When I first gave it to her, she spent hours taking pictures of me, her toys, her play yard, and her bear.

The photographers might enjoy having *their* pictures snapped for a change.

Fielding leaned into the room and grinned at Sema. "Hey, kiddo. How are you feeling today?"

Fine. Sema camera Brad?

Fielding shook his head. "I don't have a clue what she just said."

I laughed. "She wants to take your picture. I told her that soon she'd be talking to people, and she could bring her camera."

"That'll be rich." He stepped into the room and slipped his hands into his pockets.

I studied him. "What's up? You didn't drop by just to chat."

"I could have."

"But you didn't."

"You're right, I didn't." He pulled one hand out of his pocket and rubbed the back of his neck. "I hate to upset your schedule, but Matthews's secretary called a minute ago. Seems there's a guy over at Busch Gardens who needs you, and Matthews promised he'd send you right over."

"He'd send *me?* Today?" I shook my head. "I'm not sure where he got the idea he can command my every move."

"Come on, Glee—he's our boss."

"Bosses are supposed to be reasonable."

"He was willing to be reasonable about the press conference, wasn't he?"

"Only because waiting worked to his advantage, too."

"Relax—it's a nice day and the drive shouldn't take more than thirty minutes. Besides, I was hoping we could hook up with the gorilla guy over there. He's a good man—his name's Vic Wilson."

A wry smile tugged at the corners of my mouth. "If you're so fired up to meet this guy, why don't *you* go?"

"I would, but Matthews has scheduled me to talk to some reporter who has questions about the baby name contest. After that I'm supposed to meet with a couple of the sponsors—I'll be lucky to be finished with all this busywork before the end of the day."

I sighed and looked at Sema, whose eyes kept shifting from me to Fielding. "I was hoping to get in some productive time with her today. She's feeling so much better."

"Go ahead, work if you want. You can go to Tampa during her nap and be back in plenty of time for dinner. In fact"—his eyes twinkled—"if you do this for me, I'll take you out for seafood. It's all-you-can-eat shrimp night at Crabby Bill's."

"Promises, promises," I grumbled, but as I reached for Sema's flash cards, a tingle of anticipation slipped through my veins. This unexpected trip to Tampa might be a pain in the neck, but dinner at Crabby Bill's would be a nice consolation prize.

I slid the first flash card off the deck and held it up. "Come on, Sema. Tell me what this word is so I can go for a drive."

Sema ride?

"Not today, sweetie. Maybe next time."

The drive to Tampa passed uneventfully, as did my approach to Busch Gardens. After examining my Thousand Oaks ID at the gate, the security guard gave me a parking pass and directions to the employee lot, sparing me from mingling with thousands of tourists more interested in log rides and G-forces than endangered wildlife.

I found the gorilla habitat tucked away in an area called the Myombe Reserve. After pressing the buzzer at the back entrance, I thrust my hand toward the khaki-clad employee who opened the door. "Hi. I'm Glee Granger from Thousand Oaks and I'm looking for Vic Wilson."

An uncertain expression filled the man's eyes, but he smiled and shook my hand. "I'm Vic."

I laughed. "That's certainly convenient. It's a pleasure to meet you."

"Likewise."

I hooked my purse over my shoulder as somewhere in the distance a roller coaster rumbled over a track. "Wow. It gets pretty loud here. Do your animals mind the noise?"

He tilted his head. "Not really. I think we all get used to it."

"Oh. That's good." I cleared my throat. Was the man ever going to step aside and invite me in?

His eyes narrowed. "I'm sorry—would you mind repeating your name again?"

"Glee. Glee Granger." I shrugged. "I know it's an odd name. My mother had eccentric tastes."

"That's all right." He leaned against the door frame, pointedly blocking the entrance. I didn't know what he could be thinking, but my patience had nearly evaporated.

"Hey." He snapped his fingers. "You guys just had a birth over there, didn't you?"

I gave him a polite smile. "Yes—a bouncing four-pound baby girl."

"How's that going?"

"Fine. Kamili set the infant on the floor yesterday for the first time, and we all heard the little one voice her displeasure. Kamili picked her up again, but it's a lesson she seems intent on teaching."

Wilson leaned against the door frame. "The little one will learn. They all do."

I waited, but he made no move to invite me into the building. This man was either the oddest zoo man I'd ever met or he'd completely forgotten about calling us.

I smiled and clutched the shoulder strap of my purse. "Mr. Wilson, I hate to seem rude, but how can we help you?"

He crossed his arms. "I'm not sure I understand what you mean. Do we need help?"

"I've heard you do."

His smile deepened. "We all need help of one kind or another, Ms. Granger. But what kind of help are you offering us?"

"You're Vic Wilson?"

"Yes."

"And you don't need me?"

He laughed. "I guess that all depends on what you're selling."

"I'm not selling anything!"

"That's a relief. If it's a job you're looking for, I suggest you check with the folks in the personnel office."

My brain whirled as I ran my hand through my hair, then shook my head. "Um . . . why don't we start over? I'm Glee Granger from Thousand Oaks Zoo in Clearwater. My boss, Ken Matthews, said you wanted to see me as soon as possible, so I drove all the way across the bay to see you. And now I'd really appreciate it if you could tell me why I'm here."

He stepped back and jerked his head toward the interior of the building. "Come on in; you seem safe enough."

I moved into the hallway and inhaled the familiar scents of gorillas and straw. Wilson moved down the hall, talking as he went. "Let me get you something to drink. We have all kinds of soda, coffee, water—"

I hurried to catch up. "Water's fine."

"Smart lady. The coffee's pretty sad, and we don't have much selection on the soda front."

I followed him into an office a lot like the one at Thousand Oaks, but equipped with better-quality furniture. The air smelled of cinnamon and citrus, as if someone had tucked an air freshener into a vent.

"I haven't spoken to Ken Matthews in months." Wilson pulled a bottle of water from a small fridge, handed it to me, then sank into a chair. He gestured to the seat opposite the desk. "You might as well relax while I do some checking. One of the other staffers might have called over there with a question. I can't imagine why they'd make you drive all the way over, though, when most anything could be handled with a simple phone call."

He glanced at his desk, then looked up, his eyes alight with realization. "You're Glee Granger."

"Right."

"The woman who taught sign language to a zoo gorilla and had to give her back."

I grimaced, then nodded as I screwed the top off the water bottle. "That'd be me."

He blew out a breath. "We read about it in the paper. Tough break for you."

I shrugged and brought the bottle to my lips. Even though Wilson seemed sympathetic, I didn't want to revisit a situation that couldn't be changed.

He was poring over a list of employee extensions when a gray-haired woman in baggy khakis thrust her head into the room. "Hey, Vic—turn on channel 9, quick. They've put that talking gorilla on TV."

My fingers tightened around the bottle in my hand. She couldn't be referring to Sema. PBS was probably replaying one of the *National Geographic* videos about Dr. Patterson and Koko.

"Channel 9?" I took pains to keep my voice light. "Is that a PBS station?" I asked, hoping the channels were different over here . . .

"It's the news channel." Wilson picked up a remote and clicked on the power. A television in the corner bloomed to life, and a moment later we were watching a windblown reporter. I recognized her—she'd been at the zoo the day Matthews announced our latest gorilla birth.

I tensed as the camera shifted to the employee parking lot behind the pavilion. Workers had erected a small canopy over a lectern decorated with the Thousand Oaks logo. Matthews stood behind the lectern, flanked by Fielding on one side and an unsmiling Claire on the other.

The camera focused on Sema. The end of my girl's leash lay in Claire's hand.

Wilson cleared his throat. "That one of your animals?"

I stared at my smiling girl, who seemed to be enjoying the attention. "That's my gorilla."

Wilson punched the remote, elevating the volume.

"This is Sema, our talking gorilla," Matthews told the crowd. "She's a wonderful example of all that can be accomplished through persistent and patient training. To demonstrate her abilities, we're going to allow you to ask a few questions. Sema will answer them with the help of our translator, Claire Hartwell."

I lunged for my cell phone.

35

Five minutes later, I dropped my phone back into my purse. Fielding didn't answer, of course, and neither did Matthews's secretary—every available zoo employee was probably standing in the crowd, their eyes glued to the unfolding spectacle.

I paced in front of Wilson's television, shivering with nervous energy as the camera moved from Matthews, who played the part of emcee like Bob Barker on speed, to Sema, who sat on her favorite stool and occasionally clapped in delight.

"They weren't supposed to do this." I glared at the television. "Sema is my project. That's why they sent me over here, you know. Matthews wanted to get rid of me."

"I know Ken Matthews." I glanced at Wilson, whose eyes had filled with an odd mingling of wariness and relief. "Worked with him on a project for the ASPCA."

"Really."

"He's a superb businessman, no doubt about it."

I waited for Wilson to continue, then lifted a brow. "What else?"

He shrugged. "Let's just say I was glad when our association ended. Matthews knows how to talk the talk, but I don't think he cares much for the animals. It's all *here*"—Wilson touched his forehead—"and not *here*." He pressed his hand to his heart.

I sank to the edge of a desk as the camera shifted to a

young woman holding a tape recorder. "We've heard," the beginnings of a smile curved her lips, "that this gorilla not only speaks, but she talks to God. Can you confirm that?"

Behind the lectern, Matthews laced his fingers together and leaned into the microphone. "I'm not privy to all aspects of the project, but Glee Granger, Sema's teacher, is an unbiased and dedicated scientist whose work concentrates on demonstrable data. While Sema has learned to understand and speak of several abstract concepts, I do not believe religion has been a particular focus of this study."

The woman waggled a finger at him. "If you'll excuse me, I'd really like to ask the gorilla's opinion."

Matthews's brows rose to his hairline. "You want—"

"With all due respect, Mr. Matthews, if the gorilla can express herself, I think she should be allowed to do so."

Matthews gripped the edges of the lectern. "Surely you can offer a more reasonable question."

"Surely you can humor me, Mr. Matthews. Let me ask. If she has no answer, I'll withdraw the question."

Despite my burning resentment, at that moment I almost felt sorry for Matthews. He'd been caught between his grandiose claims and the public's love of rumor, and he'd made certain I wouldn't be around to bail him out.

I crossed my arms and found myself hoping Sema would take this opportunity to wig out and talk to her shiny man. The sight of a 250-pound gorilla gazing into space and waving her hands might convince the reporters they'd been duped. Then they'd go away and leave us alone . . . but not before blasting Matthews in their reports. With a little luck, Matthews would be so humiliated he'd want to be rid of Sema altogether, so he'd let me take her back home where she belonged.

Matthews sighed into the microphone, screwed a smile onto his lined face, and gestured to Claire.

The blonde reporter walked to the microphone on a stand before the platform. I was relieved to see that the mike had been placed several feet away from Sema, because none of the reporters wore antibacterial masks—another promise broken.

"Hello, Sema." The woman spoke in an artificially bright voice. "Do you believe in God?"

Groaning, I buried my face in my hand. While human children exercised their fledgling powers of imaginative belief with stories of Santa Claus and tooth fairies, I'd never given Sema fictional explanations for things I'd have to truthfully explain later. If the word *believe* had entered a conversation, I would have automatically translated it as *think*.

Sema looked around the crowd for a moment—probably looking for me—then began to sign. I leaned forward, desperate to be the first to know exactly what my girl would tell the world.

Her hands flew, creating the signs we had adapted for gorilla language: *God made bees trees. God made gorillas bears. God loves Sema.*

Claire wore a tentative expression as she turned to

interpret for the crowd. "Sema says God made every-thing and he loves her."

The translation was close enough for this silly bit of theater, but I bit my lip as I struggled to make sense of the words. God made bees and trees? Sema liked trees and tolerated bees, but what had made her mention them? I understood why she combined bears and gorillas—they were her favorite things. But trees and bees . . .

The answer came like a thunderbolt: to Sema, *believe* sounded like *bees* and *leaves,* which grew on *trees*. She had displayed the same sort of homonymic word asso-ciation one morning when she stood in the habitat and swiped her thumbs across her forehead. I thought she was trying to tell me she had a headache until Claire laughed and pointed out that Sema was making the sign for *brows*. She wanted more *browse*.

The sight of another reporter at the mike stiffened my spine. "Mr. Matthews," he said, "may I ask why Glee Granger is not present?"

Matthews sent the man a bland smile. "Ms. Granger is working in the field, but she'll be available later if you have follow-up questions. You can reach her by calling Thousand Oaks."

Unable to bear the sight of Matthews's hypocritical mug, I closed my eyes.

My right foot alternated between pounding the gas and the brake as I drove back to Clearwater. I dodged slower drivers in traffic, yelled at more than one car with an out-of-state license plate, and once slammed my hand against the steering wheel so hard that I bruised the base of my thumb. Fury and regret burned within me, both emotions flamed by the realization that I'd walked blindly into Matthews's trap.

I should have known he'd want to hold a press conference while interest in the Thousand Oaks gorillas was at its peak. I should have realized his promises were worthless, and I should have suspected the trip to Tampa was nothing but a ruse. Vic Wilson, who'd proven to be a nice and sympathetic man, needed my input about as much as a bald man needs a comb.

My mind burned with the memory of Matthews's treachery as I whipped around a tanklike sedan oozing down Highway 60. After glibly explaining my absence at the press conference, he had allowed other reporters to question Sema. In giddy ignorance, they had treated her like some kind of gorilla fortune-teller, asking, "Will you have a baby?" and "Does the zoo need more animals?" One young man, probably a card-carrying member of PETA, had said, "Given your choice, Sema, wouldn't you rather be living free in the jungle?"

To the stupid questions, Sema grinned and gave stupid answers—she probably thought the reporters were playing a game. To the young man who asked if she'd rather live in the jungle, she simply signed *Sema loves Glee.*

One older woman had been sharper than the others and seemed to intuitively understand Sema's childlike nature. Instead of asking about wildlife conservation or the unknowable future, she had asked, "Sema, what do you want people to know about gorillas?"

Sema considered the question, then answered: *God made people animals. God loves people gorillas.*

Her answer made me want to shrivel up and disappear.

What had happened to my girl? At that moment Sema sounded like one of those TV preachers who recite platitudes while their tears carve gullies through their pancake makeup. When I got back to Thousand Oaks, I just might strangle Claire for teaching Sema the word *God*.

Why couldn't God stay in ancient history where he belonged? Until now, I'd managed to banish almost all thoughts of a deity from my life. Nana kept dropping God into our conversations, but I'd been blocking out her well-intentioned comments for so long they rippled over me without too much effect. Once I had believed in God and Santa and the Tooth Fairy, but I stopped believing in mythical powers when a riptide carried my swimming parents out to sea and drowned them.

The intuitive reporter hadn't been content to leave Sema's last comment alone. She had immediately blurted out a follow-up question: "Sema, where do gorillas go when they die?"

Sema looked pensive for a moment. *Sleep. Good-bye.*

"Do gorillas go to heaven? To be with God?"

The resulting silence was like the hush after a storm when nature catches her breath. Claire looked at Matthews, probably hoping he'd take advantage of the break and bring the event to a close, but the director seemed oblivious to everything but the mesmerized group of reporters.

Through the eye of the camera, I saw Sema look at Claire. *God make trees sky. God make home gorillas people.*

With a relieved smile, Claire faced the audience. "Sema says God will make a home for gorillas and people."

I grimaced at her translation. Sema signed *make,* but surely she meant that God had *made* a home for gorillas . . . but where would she have picked up that idea?

The reporter laughed softly. "One more question, if I may. Sema, how do you know so much about God?"

At that point, Ken Matthews had stepped up, tapped his watch, and declared that Sema needed to return to the habitat. If the reporters had further questions, they should call the zoo and ask for Glee Granger.

But as the reporters put their heads together and compared notes, the camera zoomed in on Sema and I read her answer to the woman's question: *I hear shiny man talk.*

36

Sema was sleeping in the observation room when I arrived back at the pavilion. Claire sat at her desk, and her usually pleasant expression wilted when I entered the office.

"Glee!"

"Yes, I'm back. And I have to know—what gave you

the right to participate in that disgraceful display? I thought you were a friend."

She gulped hard, her eyes welling with hurt. She might have tried to reply, but Fielding walked up behind me and spared her the necessity of mounting a defense.

"Don't blame Claire."

His voice wasn't much above a whisper, but the effect was as great as if he'd shouted in my ear.

Rounding to face him, I gave him a glare that should have frizzled his eyebrows. "Don't blame Claire? Then who was that interpreting for Sema on television? But Claire isn't alone in this—you were there, too, and you're the one who sent me to Tampa."

Fielding moved past me and dropped into his chair, then crossed his arms and pinned me with a look. "I was hoping you wouldn't hear about that before we could explain."

"Well, guess what? They have TV in Tampa, too."

He shook his head. "You may not believe this, but I didn't know what Matthews had in mind until ten minutes before the newspeople showed up. And since that guy at Busch Gardens needed to talk to you—"

I snorted. "Vic Wilson needed me, all right. The man didn't even recognize my name until after we'd been talking ten minutes."

Fielding's gaze dropped to his desk. "I'm sorry."

"When Matthews told you about this press conference, did you at least have the decency to protest?"

"Of course." His voice went soft. "I told him we

needed you to pull it off. But he knew Claire could interpret, and he had already faxed out announcements."

"So you went along with it."

"I didn't want to."

I let out a sharp laugh. "What could Matthews do, threaten to fire you?"

Fielding looked toward Claire, who peered woefully at us through tear-clotted lashes. "I don't want to talk about it anymore, Glee. What's done is done, and frankly, given the tone of that interview, I should think you'd be relieved you had nothing to do with it. I suggest we put this behind us and get back to work—I know I have plenty to do."

Without another word, he stood and left the office, turning toward the night cages. I watched through the windows until he stepped into Dakarai's room, grabbed a rake, and began to scoop up old straw.

Still seething, I turned to Claire. "I thought Fielding had more chutzpah. I thought he cared about the animals and he had spine enough to protect them. But if he'd cave just because Matthews threw his weight around—"

"Matthews didn't threaten to fire him." Claire lifted her chin, her eyes blazing above her pale cheeks. "Brad only agreed to go along because Matthews threatened to fire *you*."

I stepped back, stung. "He can't do that. We have an agreement."

"That's what Brad said, but Matthews said your

agreement didn't say anything about a transfer. So if Brad didn't cooperate, the director said he'd transfer you to the manatee exhibit."

Wave after wave of shock slapped at me. How could I have been so blind? If Matthews transferred me, I'd have no choice but to quit or file suit . . . and either option would take me away from Sema for weeks, if not forever.

I walked forward in the chill of shock, then sat at my desk and buried my face in my hands.

An hour later, I sat on the floor and tried to make sense of the morning. I had been wronged by Matthews and my coworkers, but Claire hadn't stopped sniffling since my return, and the man who was supposed to take me out for a seafood dinner behaved as though I didn't exist.

After several uncomfortable minutes in the office, I retreated to Sema's room. She, at least, would love me no matter what.

I sat in silence until she woke from her nap, then crawled over the straw to curl up beside her. "Hi there, sweetie." I pillowed my head on my bent arm and I met her gaze. "How are you feeling?"

Fine. Her hand dropped to my shoulder.

"I missed you this morning."

Glee want kiss?

"I'd love one."

I put my arm around Sema's neck, then leaned forward until her lips grazed my cheek. "Thanks, sweet girl. You always know how to make me feel better."

Glee sad?

"Not anymore." Determined not to let my troubles spill onto my best friend, I pushed myself upright. "You had a big morning. I saw you on TV."

Sema's eyes brightened. *Sema talked people. Much people.*

"I know. Were you scared?"

No camera.

I had to think a moment before I remembered. "That's right, I forgot your camera. Sorry, girlie. I didn't mean to forget. Did you have fun without the camera?"

Sema happy.

"That's good. What did you talk about?"

Gorillas. Bears. God bees.

I offered her a smile that felt fake. "I know you talked about gorillas and bears because you love them. But why did you talk about God?"

She tilted her head and looked away. I caught her arm, afraid I would lose her to another one of her odd trances. "Sema? Why did you talk about God?"

Because God is.

I waited for her to add another thought, but she reached toward her basket of toys and pulled out her View-Master.

Sighing, I hugged my knees and I watched her hold the View-Master up to the light. This morning's accomplishment no longer held her interest; she wanted to move on to other things. I ought to be able to move on, too . . . but how could I?

Fielding would disagree, but I was certain Matthews's media monstrosity had derailed my plans for a career in anthropological research. An animal of Sema's age and intellect should speak what she's been taught, but after hearing her this morning, anyone would assume I'd been sending her to Sunday school instead of enrichment sessions.

And the word would get out. Though Matthews had only invited local press people, a single report on a national news service would kill any chance of credibility I might attempt to claim. If the *National Enquirer* or the *Star* learned about the gorilla who believed in God, my future was destined for the toilet.

Only gullible people like Nana thought science and theology could exist in the same sphere. Those fields were oil and water, fire and ice. My instincts had been reinforced when I read that more than 90 percent of National Academy of Science members and 95 percent of its biologist members are proclaimed atheists or agnostics.

Those people were my peers—so how could I hope to impress them with a God-loving gorilla? I could publish a study on Sema's facility with language, her memory, her emotions, and her intellect. I could omit the material about her sudden interest in spiritual matters, but how could I present her to colleagues in a live demonstration? I could try to direct her conversation, but Sema had a mind of her own, and she could be as inflexible as a rock. Though our version of sign language was unique, it was close enough to Ameslan that anyone with a basic understanding of sign language would know if I misinterpreted Sema's words.

I propped my chin on my arms and felt a tear slide down my cheek. Sema clicked her View-Master, opened her mouth in a pink smile, then lowered her toy.

The View-Master rolled from her hands onto the straw as her smile disappeared. *Why cry?*

"Just feeling a little sad."

Why sad?

I shrugged. "It's hard to explain, sweetie. Sometimes people are sad when they plan something and those plans don't work out. Sometimes we are sad when it rains. And sometimes we are sad for no reason at all."

I spoke without thinking, letting my thoughts rattle out in elementary Sema-speak, and I had no idea if she would understand. But after a moment, she touched my knee to catch my attention.

Glee no sad. No cry. God loves Glee.

I covered my face with my hand and wept harder.

By one o'clock, the office phone was ringing as regularly as a heartbeat. Claire answered a couple of the calls, discovered reporters on the line, and took messages for me. After that, we left the answering machine to handle the phone for us.

Late that afternoon, after bringing in the gorillas and settling them in their night rooms, Fielding called a staff meeting. I sat at my desk and ran my hands up and down my arms. The day was warm, but a chill occupied this room.

"Grab a pencil and paper," he said, nodding at me. "I'm going to let the phone machine play. If a message is for you, jot it down."

I reached for a pencil. I didn't particularly want to talk to anyone who called as a result of Matthews's fiasco, but stalling a few reporters wouldn't be a problem.

The first five reporters wanted one-on-one interviews with Sema. "Absolutely not," I told Fielding, avoiding his eyes as I jotted down a number. "I won't risk exposing her to some infection. Plus, there's the liability issue. If she decides to tug on someone's arm and pops it out of joint—"

"Fine." The line of Fielding's mouth tightened. "Call those people tonight, will you, and tell them interviews are against zoo policy. They can interview *you,* but not Sema."

"I don't want to talk to them."

"Then don't. But Matthews said you would."

I drew a ragged breath as impotent anger tightened my lungs. I hated this, but I would have to follow through. If I didn't, Matthews would say I was being uncooperative . . . and he could transfer me to another area.

The next caller identified himself as Dr. Justin Marchland of the Natural Wildlife Society. Even through the cheap speaker of the answering machine, his voice resonated pleasantly. "Ms. Granger, I'm assuming you had nothing to do with that ludicrous performance this morning—your absence spoke volumes. If you are interested in continuing your work with

346

serious researchers, please give me a call. My colleagues and I would be interested in meeting with you. You can reach me at 202-555-1232."

My pulse quickened as I jotted down the number.

Fielding leaned back in his chair, looking impressed. "Natural Wildlife? They don't call just anybody."

I scribbled Marchland's name beside the number. "I can't imagine how they heard about me, but I'm glad they did." I checked my watch. Five thirty in Florida and in Washington, DC, but I could leave a message at Marchland's office.

"Excuse me," I said, standing. "You guys can take care of the other callers, can't you?"

For an instant I thought Fielding would object out of sheer obstinacy, but he nodded.

Leaving my coworkers to listen to the rest of the messages, I slipped into the kitchen and dialed Marchland's number on my cell phone. I fully expected to hear a robotic voice on the end of the line, but after two rings a resonant baritone said hello.

"Um . . . this is Glee Granger, returning a call from Dr. Marchland."

Silence followed my announcement, then an abrupt bark of laughter. "Ms. Granger! Are you ready to strangle the zoo director down there?"

Sensing the company of a kindred spirit, I allowed myself to chuckle in response. "You'd be correct if you suspected he isn't number one on my list of favorite people."

"I'm not surprised. I didn't see the press conference,

but I read an account of it in the afternoon wire reports. My colleagues and I did a little checking around, and we've decided to ask if you would like to continue your research in a more suitable environment."

I pressed my hand to my chest and drew a deep breath. "You're kidding. If you're kidding—"

"Ms. Granger, we never joke about situations like yours. We're quite serious."

"Dr. Marchland, you can't imagine how good it is to hear this! I've had so many struggles since being forced to return Sema to the zoo—"

"I know—my assistant found several stories online this afternoon. We did a little digging in the AZA files to discover the family history of your gorilla, so we learned that you had recently lost legal custody of the animal. We also read about her accident—a terrible tragedy that could have been avoided. I'm assuming, of course, that you'd like to continue working outside the zoo?"

"Of course! But I can't afford to purchase Sema outright, and I haven't the time to create and manage a foundation—"

"You won't need to take the time, Ms. Granger, because our foundation would be happy to step in. The Society has funds available for researchers in your situation, and we're vitally interested in work involving the higher primates. Let me consult with my colleagues and we'll see if we can clear a date to meet with you. We'll fly you to Washington and together we'll come up with a workable solution."

I stared wordlessly at the phone, my heart pounding.

"Ms. Granger? Is that acceptable?"

"Of course, that'd be incredible! I'd be thrilled to come. But I should warn you—our director is determined to have Sema conduct daily demonstrations for visitors. He sees her as a prime attraction, so it won't be easy to convince him to sell her."

"I think we'll persuade him to be cooperative," Marchland said, his voice warm and confident. "Most zoo directors can be convinced to be flexible—and we can use the press to help us accomplish our goal. If we can convince a few reporters that Sema's progress would be hindered by forced exchanges with a curious public, I'm sure your director will agree to do what's best for the gorilla."

"That'd be wonderful. By all means, let's talk."

"We are eager to meet with you. I'll have my assistant call you later this week to arrange your trip."

"Thank you. I'll look forward to it."

"By the way"—his tone lowered—"one of my colleagues expressed concern about some of the sentiments communicated by your gorilla at the press conference. We assumed the integrity of her knowledge base has been contaminated by unavoidable influences."

I sighed. "It's been hard to maintain a controlled environment at the zoo. Yes, she's been taught words and concepts outside my goals, and she's been a little bewildered. Her injury has only added to the confusion."

"I'd love to hear details."

I wiped my damp palm on my slacks. "Sema is fine,

absolutely fine, but we have determined that she suffered a stroke during her accident. Since then she's been suffering hallucinations that leave her confused and cause her to sign nonsensical words and phrases. But we are certain she will make a full recovery."

"Perhaps our doctors can be of help. Even if these episodes continue, her reactions could be useful to medical researchers . . . as long as her communication skills aren't affected."

"Her sign language skills are completely intact. She speaks as much as she ever did."

"Wonderful. Expect a call from my assistant Monday, then. We'll set up a date for a meeting and discuss what we need to do. We want you to devote your full attention to your gorilla language project."

"Thank you, sir."

I lowered the phone to its cradle, then sat in the silence of the deserted kitchen. How quickly things could change! Something in me wanted to run into the hall and hug the first anthropoid I met, but I knew I'd have to restrain myself. I would need to keep this development to myself. If Matthews knew the Natural Wildlife Society wanted to buy the zoo's star gorilla, he'd try to find a way to stop them.

Wrapped in a comforting bunting of hope, I rubbed my hands over my arms and shivered in anticipation. Sema and I would soon be out of here. All I had to do was wait, keep my mouth shut, and make sure Sema remained healthy.

Ken Matthews had enlisted my coworkers and my

gorilla to commit an act of sheer betrayal, but a posse of knights on white horses had come to my aid. With the help of Dr. Justin Marchland and the Natural Wildlife Society, I would not only continue my work, but I would restore it to a place of scientific integrity.

37

According to the schedule, Fielding was supposed to have Saturday off, but his 4-Runner sat outside the pavilion when I pulled into the employee parking lot at nine. I first thought he had come in to see if he could discover why the Natural Wildlife Society wanted to talk to me . . . then I realized Claire's car wasn't in its usual spot. Fielding must have come to handle the breakfast shift.

I couldn't help feeling a small tug of guilt. Fielding should have asked me to come in early and handle breakfast 'n browse. On the other hand, after yesterday's fiasco he had to know I wasn't feeling like a team player. He never even mentioned our date for all-you-can-eat shrimp night at Crabby Bill's.

I got out of the car, tossed my keys into my purse, and headed toward the building. No matter what happened today, I would take it in stride. Dr. Justin Marchland and the NWS had taken up my cause, and they had international clout. Matthews would crumble like a leaf if they decided to apply pressure.

Sema was happily munching on a bunch of broccoli when I peeked into her room and tapped on the glass.

"Hey, sweetie," I called. "See you in a minute, okay?"

She gave me a broccoli-studded smile, then picked up a cherry tomato and tossed it into her mouth. Grinning, I walked to the office and dropped my purse into a desk drawer.

I looked up as the door creaked and Fielding came in. He nodded. "Morning."

"Thought you were off today."

"I was, but Claire's not feeling well." He walked to his desk, dropped a clipboard to the desktop, then rapped on it with his knuckle. "Hey—maybe it's time we moved Sema back into the exam room. She's well now, and being near the other g's will help her readjust—"

"I'd like to wait awhile." *Until I hear from Dr. March-land and the NWS.*

"Really? Because Sema seems to miss the others."

I'd had the same thought less than twenty-four hours before, but I shook my head. "We've lost a lot of ground, and I'd like at least a week to take her through some intensive review sessions. The other animals would only distract her."

"But you work during the day. She wouldn't be distracted if she couldn't see them."

"If Sema's in the night area, she thinks about the other animals no matter where they are. Besides, you know how fascinated she is with Kamili and the baby, and they're still spending their days indoors." I forced a smile. "By the way, have we decided on a name yet?"

Fielding grunted. "The sponsors went through the

entries and picked Jamila—Swahili for 'beautiful.' They're going to announce the winner and present the prize tomorrow. That's something we need to talk about."

A sense of unease crept into my mood like a wisp of smoke. "Why do we need to talk about a stupid contest?"

"Because the contest means another press conference. Matthews is having a big one in the amphitheater tomorrow. He wants to announce the baby's name, hand out the prize, and let the photographers snap pictures of the winner with a guy from Channel 9 and the manager from Rico's Pizza."

The tension left my shoulders. "Sounds like fun."

"That's not all—he wants to bring Sema out again. He's having a bunch of kids come in to talk to her. He thinks she will respond better to kids because they won't be asking weird questions."

"And when did he tell you this?"

"Last night, after hours. He said his office got so many calls yesterday that we need another presentation. This time we'll have national media present—and you, of course. He wants you to interpret"—he flushed—"and do whatever you must to make sure her answers are appropriate."

"What does that mean, Fielding?"

He looked at me for a second, then broke eye contact, his gaze drifting off to safer territory. "He didn't come right out and say this, but I assume he wants you to ignore the goofy stuff. Make sure Sema's answers could be quoted on the front page."

I clenched my hand and struggled to maintain my self-control. Matthews had been smart not to come down and deliver this news in person. If he'd been standing in the room, I might have hurt him. How was I supposed to filter Sema's words when surely there would be people who could interpret Ameslan themselves? We'd be exposed in no time!

Fielding pushed away from his desk. "So—what do we need to do? Will Sema be okay?"

"It isn't right, Fielding."

"So what do you want me to do, scream at the director? Ken Matthews is a respected zookeeper. The community loves him; the mayor adores him. Shoot, the governor has tentatively agreed to come and say something tomorrow."

I snorted. "I'll bet Matthews didn't invite representatives from the gorilla conservation movement, Natural Wildlife, or PETA."

"No, but he did invite people who can make a whole lotta noise." Fielding stood and walked around the desk, then his hand closed around my arm in a surprisingly gentle grip. "Look, Glee, I know this goes against your grain. But every job has aspects you have to muddle through. This is our muddle."

"I don't want to muddle through anything. It's not fair to Sema. People twist her words—"

"That's the reporters' problem. She'll be okay. She seemed to enjoy the other event, right? Let's get her through tomorrow, then work on getting her settled with the other g's. We'll get through this, Glee. I promise."

I looked up, torn between wanting to believe him and wanting to run to the safety of the Natural Wildlife Society. Perhaps we could endure this without experiencing another media disaster. If I could put all this nonsense behind us, I could look to the future with hope.

I swallowed hard. "When's the grand event?"

"Tomorrow morning, eleven o'clock. Matthews wants to bring in all his celebrities when the zoo's closed to the public."

Distracted by my thoughts, I nodded. Marchland and his people wouldn't like Sema being used in this way, but a national press conference might spur them to faster action. With a little luck and some outside help, Sema and I could be out of here in a couple of weeks.

I glanced at Fielding, wanting to tell him about Marchland's proposal, but I didn't dare trust him with the news. Old-fashioned loyalty to the boss might lead him to spill my secret, and I couldn't let my adversary know he was about to be ambushed.

I drew a deep breath. "You'll be there tomorrow, right?"

He nodded. "I'm supposed to announce the baby's name. By the way, did you reach that guy from Natural Wildlife?"

I hated lying, but knew I had to offer a half-truth.

"I talked to him."

"What did he want?"

Keenly aware of Fielding's scrutiny, I shrugged. "He heard about Sema on the news wires. I think he wanted to make sure she wasn't being exploited."

Though the wariness in his eyes froze into a blue as cold as a block of ice, his mouth curved in a nonchalant smile. "Oh."

"And by the way"—I glanced at the floor, unable to meet his gaze—"I guess I should thank you for saving my job. I hate what you had to do, but I appreciate that you kept Matthews from transferring me away from the g's."

He chuckled. "You know, when you're not flashing your claws, you can be a really decent human being."

We both flinched when an electronic beep broke the stillness. Someone had entered through the employees' door, and I couldn't imagine who had come in—

Claire stumbled through the office doorway and tossed a tabloid newspaper on my desk. "Here," she said, swiping at her red nose with a tissue. "You won't believe the headline."

"Put a mask on," Fielding told her.

I murmured in agreement, but my eyes focused on the caption beneath a photo of Sema and Claire. *Talking Gorilla Says World Will End Soon!*

My jaw dropped. "Good grief! Sema said nothing like that!"

"She did say something about God making a new world," Claire said, sniffling again. "I think that's what they meant."

Fielding moved closer to read over my shoulder as

Claire headed toward the cabinet where we kept the antibacterial masks. "That's not all," she said, sliding the drawer open. "Did you see *The Tonight Show* last night?"

I shook my head.

"Leno asked the audience if they'd heard about the Florida gorilla who believes in God. Then he said she was going to court to have the teaching of evolution banned from schools. She was insulted by the idea that man developed from monkeys."

I turned to look at Fielding. "Are you *sure* we have to do this tomorrow?"

"Glee—don't even ask." Though his voice held a warning note, his eyes told me he'd cancel if he could.

"Your problem," I lowered the newspaper, "is you're too much of a team player. Sometimes the crew needs to mutiny."

"Not tomorrow, we don't. We're going to go over there, congratulate the boy who submitted the winning baby name, let the photographers snap pictures of the kid holding his prize check and free pizza. Then we're going to let a couple of children talk to Sema. That's it. Short and sweet."

"If you say so." I closed my eyes, visualizing the area Sema and I would have to cover on our way to the amphitheater. "That pavilion has a little backstage area, right?"

"Yes—you'll be able to walk Sema over there while the zoo's closed. Take her over early; get her relaxed."

"The action begins at eleven?"

"That's what I heard. The governor's chopper is supposed to land on the lawn at 10:58. He'll run down, welcome the guests, shake a few hands. Then he'll hand it off to Matthews for the introduction of a few more VIPs. Then we're supposed to talk about Kamili's baby and invite people to visit the gorilla exhibit often to watch the little girl grow up."

"How nice. And thoughtful of Matthews to give us so much notice."

When Fielding turned away, I regretted my sarcasm. Though something in me wanted to use him for a scapegoat, I couldn't hold him responsible for the actions of the businessman who employed us.

"Okay." I dropped the tabloid into the trash and smiled at Fielding and Claire. "I'm going to come in early tomorrow and feed Sema, then walk her over to the staging area. I want to prepare her for the people, the helicopter, and any other foolishness we might encounter."

Fielding turned toward Claire, who had collapsed at her desk. "You need to go back to bed, kiddo. I'll cover for you today and tomorrow and stick around in case Glee needs a hand."

I was about to tell him I wouldn't need any help, but the contrite look on his face made me hesitate.

A reluctant smile tugged at my mouth. "Thanks. That'd be nice."

38

Nana's kitchen smelled of tomato sauce and oregano when I entered through the office. She was standing at the sink, her hands encased in yellow rubber gloves, so I dropped my hand on her shoulder and kissed her cheek.

"Sorry." I laughed as she turned, wide-eyed. "I let myself in."

"Glee! I'd hug you, honey, but my hands are all wet."

"I can fix that."

I pulled a dish towel from the drawer. She took it with a smile that lingered on me, more warming than the waning sun outside. "It's good to see you, sweetheart. We've missed you."

I leaned against the counter. "I've missed being here."

She tossed the towel onto her shoulder, pulled off the gloves, then dried her damp hands. "Rob's coming tonight too. Cheri has something else to do, so I hope you don't mind that I invited a fourth."

I pulled a peeled carrot from the veggie tray and bit off the end. "Since when have I minded having a stray or two at the table?"

Her gentle laugh rippled through the air. "That's what I hoped you'd say. Now"—she frowned as she studied the dishes on the island—"I think I've taken care of everything. There's a cheesecake in the fridge, a loaf of bread in the oven, the veggie tray, the spaghetti, the sauce . . ."

I swallowed the last of the carrot. "No salad?"

"You think we need one?"

"Not really. But most people have a salad with spaghetti."

She shook her head. "We're doing veggies instead. Sometimes I get so tired of salads I could scream. After all, you feed Sema a lot more than lettuce, don't you?"

"Sure." I picked up another carrot, then whisked my hand away as she threatened to administer a playful slap.

"Save some for the guests. Oh—speaking of Sema, how is she?"

"Considering that she's a tabloid star and the butt of jokes on late-night television, she's great."

Nana's pleasant expression withered to an anxious look. "I heard; Brad told me about everything. I'm so sorry."

I nearly choked on my carrot. "*Brad* told you? When did you speak to him?"

"When I called to invite him to dinner, of course. He said you were furious with him, so I told him not to worry; you've never been able to hold a grudge for long."

"Fielding's coming here? For dinner?"

"Well, of course." Her sparkling blue eyes sank into nets of wrinkles as she smiled. "I knew you wouldn't mind. I also know you like him."

Surprise held my tongue hostage, but anger leaped to its rescue. "He's a weasel."

Her brows lifted. "I thought he was a charming young man."

"He's only charming when he wants to be. The rest of the time he's . . . well, he's too loyal."

"And all this time I thought loyalty was an admirable character trait."

"Not when he's being loyal to a jerk. He's more devoted to Ken Matthews than to me or Sema, and we're the ones who suffer for his devotion. But I think things are about to change, because—"

I halted in midsentence, realizing that Fielding could walk through the doorway at any moment. I wanted to tell Nana about my call from the Natural Wildlife Society, but I couldn't tell her anything until the matter had been settled. She might let something slip at dinner . . . or she might activate her infamous telephone chain and have them pray for my success. The way my luck had been running, Channel 9 would call to ask about my affiliation with Natural Wildlife before my head hit the pillow tonight.

Nana pulled a pot holder from a hook near the oven, then glanced at me over her shoulder. "Go on, hon. I'm listening."

"It's nothing."

She opened the oven door and pulled out a beautiful loaf of bread. "I think you and Brad will be fine. There's nothing like good food and good conversation to smooth out the bumps in a friendship."

Easy for her to say; she'd never had to work with Fielding. I picked up the veggie tray. "Want me to take this into the dining room?"

She glanced around, then nodded. "Good idea. Rob

and Brad should be arriving at any moment."

I wanted to see my brother, because I hadn't talked to him in weeks. If not for that, I might have set the tray on the table, slipped through the French doors, and gone home.

An hour later, Nana, Rob, Fielding, and I leaned on Nana's table and groaned for mercy. Our hostess had plied us with extra helpings of spaghetti, thick slices of creamy cheesecake, and spoonfuls of cherry topping. Between the entrée and dessert we had helped ourselves to steaming portions of home-baked bread and creamy butter . . . and veggies, of course.

I have never been able to understand why I feel more virtuous after pigging out if I've managed to stuff a few carrot sticks into my bulging belly.

None of us could speak after eating so much, but the sound of Christian radio flowed into the space our silence had made: "For the animals of the forest are his," a woman sang, "and he owns the cattle on a thousand hills. Every bird of the mountains and all the animals of the field belong to the Lord, whoa-whoa."

The first to catch his breath, Fielding pressed his palms to the edge of the table. "Thank you, Miss Irene, but if I swallow another bite, you're going to have to roll me out of here."

Rob grinned at him from across the table—and I realized my brother liked Fielding, too. "Want more coffee?" Rob asked. "I don't know how she does it, but Nana's is the best."

Nana waved away the praise, then pushed away from the table. "You all sit and relax while I get the other coffeepot. No, Brad, leave the dishes. They'll keep."

I waited until she had shouldered her way through the swinging door, then I stood and gathered up the dirty plates. Nana wouldn't have minded if I left them, but I wanted a change of scene.

She was waiting for me. As I lowered the dirty dishes into the sink, she gave me a sly smile. "That wasn't so bad, was it?"

I knew what she meant. "Dinner was okay," I admitted, "but Fielding was on his best behavior."

"You were, too." Nana picked up the spare coffeepot. "And I appreciate it. Bring that tray of after-dinner mints, will you, dear?"

By the time I returned to the dining room, the conversation had shifted—not surprising, really, considering who remained at the table. Rob was talking about the trend toward bestowing full legal rights upon animals while Fielding disagreed.

I took my seat and passed the tray of mints. "Why not give Sema legal rights?" I asked, meeting Fielding's gaze. "You know she thinks, feels, and remembers. She is completely self-conscious. She feels guilt and joy. And if you believe the tabloids, she holds daily conversations with the Almighty."

Fielding shook his head. "I love animals, Glee, but they're not human. If you start granting legal rights to creatures, where are you going to draw the line? I can see why you might want to protect apes and chimpanzees, even dogs. But what about roaches?"

Nana screwed up her face. "Please, let's not talk about vermin at the table."

"All right," Rob said, "let's say we grant certain legal rights to mammals. That would protect whales, dolphins, apes, dogs, cats, elephants—"

"And rats," Fielding pointed out. "Disease-carrying vermin—excuse me, Miss Irene—that infest slums and bite babies. You want to make it a crime to spread rat poison? Should we send a poor father to jail because he killed one of the mice infesting his apartment?"

In tandem, the men turned to Nana. "What do you think?" Rob asked.

Fielding nodded. "I'd be interested in hearing your opinion."

My grandmother's mouth quirked with humor. "I'm sure you all can imagine what I think."

I certainly could, but Fielding hadn't heard her positions a thousand times.

"Please," his forehead furrowed, "I'd like to know."

Nana looked at her coffee mug. "While I know God cares deeply about animals, Scripture also tells us he regards humans as the pinnacle of creation, for we alone were formed in his image. Yet animals are linked to mankind like the sun is linked to the earth. When man obeys God, animals thrive. When man's heart is evil, animals suffer. God is in the business of redeeming men one individual at a time, and one day he will redeem the animals and the earth. That time is coming, perhaps sooner than we realize. The animals know this

. . . even if men refuse to acknowledge the obvious."

I lowered my gaze, afraid I would look over and see Fielding staring openmouthed at my precious grandmother. When he spoke again in a perfectly reasonable tone, I lifted my head. Was he taking her seriously?

"How can you know," he asked, "that animals realize these things? They don't talk—well, most of them don't. They are aware of so few things that happen outside their limited worlds."

Nana's fingertip gently circled the rim of her mug. "I believe the Bible, and Scripture tells us all creatures are eagerly waiting for the day when God will reveal himself. The animals didn't sin, you see. But because God placed them under man's dominion, they have suffered and died along with us. Against its will, everything on earth was subjected to God's curse. God didn't institute death in the Garden of Eden; man did."

Fielding shook his head. "I'm sorry, but I've always had a hard time with that. People say God is good and perfect—how, then, could he create evil?"

"Evil is not a tangible creation." Nana's gentle smile assured me that she enjoyed this gentle sparring. "It is a consequence; it is the negation of good. Our Creator endowed us with a great gift—the freedom to obey God, who *is* goodness—or to reject God, which is sin."

Fielding nodded, thought working in his eyes. "And sin results . . . in evil."

"Yes." Nana focused on Fielding, an almost imperceptible note of pleading in her face. "Free will is a good thing, but it can result in bad decisions and dire consequences. For thousands of years men have paid dearly for their freedom of choice. Because they are so closely linked to us, the animals have paid dearly as well."

"They're still paying," I added, thinking of Matthews's desire to use Sema for the zoo's profit. "And they'll keep suffering until . . . well, until somebody rescues them."

I lifted my mug and gulped several swallows of coffee, alarmed lest someone read my eyes and discover my secret: Dr. Justin Marchland was going to be my savior; he was going to pull me and Sema out of Matthews's clutches.

Apparently oblivious to my sudden thirst, Nana continued. "One day, soon I hope, God is going to redeem the earth. Then the lion will lie down with the lamb, and the elephants and mountain gorillas will care for their young without fear of poachers. All those who love the Lord will worship him in heaven and on a new, redeemed earth. The Bible says every creature in heaven and on earth and under the earth and in the sea will sing, 'Blessing and honor and glory and power belong to the one sitting on the throne and to the Lamb forever and ever.'"

She sighed and rested her cheek on her hand. "I get misty-eyed just thinking about it."

Fielding glanced at Rob, then shifted his gaze to me. "I can see how you two came by your love of words," he said, smiling. "You learned from the master."

Rob grinned, but I lowered my head and pinched the

bridge of my nose. I was chagrined to think Fielding associated Nana's religious ramblings with my scientific conjectures, but he wasn't a researcher. He was a gorilla guy, pure and simple. At some times a wonderful gorilla guy, at other times maddening.

"Brad," Nana reached out to cover his hand with hers, "you're too bright to ignore the obvious. The next time you're with your animals or walking along the beach, look around and let creation speak to you. It *does* speak, you know. The mountains and seas, day and night, even the birds and beasts all speak of God in their songs, their cycles, their design. The ancient Greeks, who had gods for everything, realized an intelligent universal mind had to support all reality. They called this the *Logos*, and Scripture tells us that Jesus was the Logos clothed in flesh. He is the source of all knowledge; he is the One who spoke creation into existence."

I stared at Nana as words jostled and competed for space in my brain. "Logos . . . like *logo?*"

Nana smiled her congratulations. "In Greek, *logos* also means *word.*"

She kept talking, but my thoughts filtered back to the day I'd taught Sema the sign for *word.* She had zoned out after that lesson, signing *Word made world, word loves Sema word made gorillas people apples bears . . .* She said the shiny man—*an angel?*—had told her those things.

A four-letter word slipped from my lips before I realized I had spoken. I froze and closed my eyes as all conversation ceased. Nana didn't like vulgar language at her table, and in a minute she was going to scold me as if I were still thirteen . . . But I heard only the hollow rumble of the surf rolling over the beach beyond the French doors.

When I cautiously lifted an eyelid, I found Fielding, Nana, and Rob staring at me. "Sema," I said, hoping the name would explain my thoughtless reaction. "The other day I taught her the sign for *word*. She went a little loony after that, signing that *word* made the world and gorillas and . . . well, I thought she'd completely lost it."

"Oh, my." For a brief instant Nana's face seemed to open so I could look inside her mind and watch my words take hold. I saw astonishment followed by a quick flicker of awe; then absolute certainty settled over her features. "The Lord is using Sema to speak to you." Her voice vibrated with a faint tremor, as though a seismic emotion had rumbled through the depths of her soul.

"Nana?" Rob asked. "You okay?"

"Oh, yes." She rested her chin on her hand, a bemused smile on her lips. "How like God to use the things we hold dearest as instruments to teach us."

I had reached my limit; Nana was making about as much sense as Sema in one of her fugues. I pushed away from the table, my chair scraping across the chipped Mexican tiles. "Thanks, Nana, for the wonderful dinner." I blew her a kiss. "I've got to run—busy day ahead." I nodded at Rob and Fielding. "See you guys later."

I half-expected Nana to call me back as I stood and strode toward the kitchen to fetch my purse, but with glowing eyes she watched my retreat and smiled me out of the room.

A shrill ring shattered the stillness about ten minutes after I turned out the lamp. I peered through the darkness, fumbled for the phone, and managed to jam my index finger against the side of the nightstand.

I wasn't in the most cheerful of moods when I said hello.

"Glee?"

Fielding's voice, but why was he calling at this hour? "Has something happened to Sema?"

I heard him sigh. "She's fine—and the world doesn't revolve around that gorilla, you know."

His world didn't. I sat up and bent my knees under the covers, then glanced at the clock. Ten fifty-eight PM.

I laughed. "Don't tell me you have just now managed to escape Nana's."

"Not exactly. We all sat around and talked until about ten. I got home a few minutes ago."

I propped my arms on my knees. "So what's up?"

Silence rolled over the line; then he said, "We can't go on like this."

"Like what?"

"Like a teeter-totter. One minute we're friends, the next we're enemies, then we're more than friends. You're driving me crazy, Glee. I need to know where we stand."

I closed my eyes and exhaled a breath. Where *did* we stand? I'd been mad at Fielding about the press conference, but I knew I really couldn't blame him for that. Then I'd been ticked at the world, with only Fielding and Claire to bear the brunt of my frustration.

I gripped the phone more tightly. "Look, I'm sorry for how I've been acting. I was upset about Matthews."

"I understand that. But friends should be able to talk about things. Pouting doesn't make things easier."

"I wasn't pouting!"

"Yes, you were. And I'll admit it: I was too. Not a terribly mature way for either of us to handle the situation, but I didn't want to deal with the chip on your shoulder."

An angry answer leaped to the tip of my tongue, then I remembered Brad had lots of reasons to be frustrated with me. I'd been forced on him as surely as Thousand Oaks had been forced on me.

I stared into the darkness and smiled. "Truce?"

"Truce."

A moment of companionable silence followed, then Fielding caught a breath. "So, then"—he spoke slowly, as if carefully considering each word before pronouncing it—"are we going to be friends or something more?"

The question hammered at me. I would have liked to pursue a relationship with Fielding, but my life was about to take a drastic turn. Justin Marchland and the Natural Wildlife Society were going to free me and Sema from the zoo, which meant Brad and I would no longer be coworkers. My life would return to its ordinary course; my concentration would focus again on Sema alone. Under the auspices of the NWS, I would have to come up with a program that would help Sema overcome her brain injury and rid her intellectual framework of all destructive influences.

In the next few months, I would have to write a dissertation unlike any gorilla study ever published. I'd probably find it difficult to find the time to sleep, let alone *date*.

But I couldn't share these things with Fielding, not yet. So I tried to dodge the question.

"Did Nana put you up to this?" I slipped a teasing note into my voice. "She likes you, you know."

"I told you, she's a little too mature for me. Seriously, Glee, your grandmother didn't say anything about . . . us. I need to know where we stand, for me. I thought we were growing closer, but if you don't want that—"

"I like you, Fielding—Brad. I think you're great, and I will never be able to thank you enough for saving Sema's life. But I can't deal with a relationship right now. And I'm sorry about that."

Sorrier than you can know.

"Fine." His voice scraped like sandpaper against my ears. "I'll let you go, then. I shouldn't have called so late."

"It's all right. I'm just . . . Fielding?" I listened intently, but I could hear nothing on the other end of the line. He had hung up.

39

Sema was snoring like a piglet in the sun when I entered the pavilion early Sunday morning. I left her sleeping in the observation room and moved down the hall to check on the other g's. The first rays of the rising sun had awakened Dakarai, who peered down at me from his elevated night nest. All the other animals slept except Rafiki, who pig-grunted and tossed handfuls of straw in my direction when he saw me.

"Shh, little one," I whispered, signing to him through the glass. "Your breakfast is coming soon."

Our new mother and her baby made a sweet picture through the window of the corner room. The sleeping infant clung to Kamili's chest, her pale skin now only barely visible through the fuzzy black fur that had begun to cover her tiny frame.

"Jamila." I whispered her name. "You *are* beautiful."

I had to turn away as a sudden pang of melancholy brought tears to my eyes. Dr. Marchland and I hadn't even worked out the details of Sema's departure, but already I missed the other animals. Though I loved Sema desperately, I admired Dakarai's steadfast protectiveness, Rafiki's playfulness, and Kamili's loving care for her infant. I would worry about Mosi, wondering if and when he would be transferred to a family of his own, and how could I help but miss Aisha, the glorious matriarch of this group?

Each animal had become precious to me; each had

become an individual every bit as unique as Claire . . . and Fielding.

The idea that I might miss Fielding was so absurd I began to laugh, though I felt a long way from genuine humor. I was still chuckling when I went into the kitchen and flipped the light switch; I smiled when I pulled out the breakfast bowls and spread them over the table.

By the time I brought in the just-delivered produce boxes, though, my smile had faded. In the bright artificial light of the fluorescent bulbs overhead, I couldn't indulge in shadowy half-truths.

Truth was, I had enjoyed this job. Matthews was a pain in the rear, and Fielding had the power to elevate my blood pressure, but what woman couldn't use a few challenges in her life? Challenges force us to grow and think. The last four months had been difficult, but even the tragedy of Sema's accident had opened new horizons. Before coming here, I had worried that my project would not surpass the work of Penny Patterson and Koko . . . now my research would be uniquely valuable to medical researchers and anthropologists alike.

For the next half hour I divvied up vegetables and lettuce and fruit, stopping occasionally to wipe wetness from my eyes. When all the bowls had been filled, I delivered them to each gorilla's night room, greeting each of my friends with a verbal "good morning" and the corresponding sign. I didn't care if they noticed my signing . . . but what might happen if they did? If Sema and I stayed at Thousand Oaks, in time we might teach an entire gorilla group to communicate with human beings.

I made one more visit to the kitchen, picked up Sema's bowl, then carried it to the observation room. I set it in the straw next to her Care Bear nest, then sat next to her. When she did not awaken, I gently tapped her shoulder. "Hey, sweet girl. Got a hug for Glee?"

Slowly she opened her eyes, then smiled and stretched out her arms. I snuggled within them, resting my head on her smooth chest as if she were the mother and I the child. I closed my eyes, relishing the innocence of the moment, then remembered we had one more public duty to endure.

Reluctantly, I pulled out of her embrace. "I've brought you a good breakfast, sweetness. Eat up; then I have a surprise for you."

Give toy?

"No, not a toy. Something special, though. Something I think you'll enjoy."

To prevent her from continuing with questions, I lifted a bunch of green grapes and dangled them before her eyes. "Look at this, little girl. Your favorite."

Sema grinned. *All Sema's?*

"Unless you want to share with Glee."

She took the stalk, then daintily pulled off a grape and held it above my head.

"Is that one for me? Well, you *are* a sweet girl, aren't you?"

I took the fruit from her hand and nibbled at it, deliberately exaggerating the time it took to eat a

374

single grape so she could get the larger portion. As I popped the last bite into my mouth, she offered another grape.

"Thanks, sweet Sema."

Glee stinky nut.

I pretended horror. "Is that any way to talk to the nice woman who brought your breakfast? Eat up, now. We have a busy morning."

She ate her grapes, her celery, the patty of microwaved hamburger, and the watermelon. She drank her apple juice from the sippy cup, then tossed it to the floor.

While Sema knuckle-walked to her potty, I picked up her bowl and empty cup and returned them to the kitchen. While I rinsed the bowl, I heard the beep from the entrance door.

Fielding had arrived.

A moment later I felt the pressure of his eyes on my back. "Good morning," I called.

"Morning," he said.

I hesitated in the awkward silence, then smiled over my shoulder. "You didn't say what you guys and Nana talked about so late last night."

I heard the scrape of a chair across the linoleum. "Interesting stuff. You shouldn't have left so early."

"I wanted to get home . . . get some sleep." I waited for him to answer, but he didn't. "I hope Nana didn't drive you crazy with all her ideas."

"Not at all. Your grandmother's brilliant, by the way. She makes a lot of sense."

I turned in astonished silence.

Fielding lifted his chin. "What?"

"Don't tell me you bought into all her religious clap-trap."

He crossed his arms. "I don't think you should ridicule things you don't understand. Has your grand-mother ever mocked your beliefs?"

"What beliefs? I'm not religious."

"No, you're scientific—and you seem to think science requires a bias against religion."

I turned back to the sink. "I don't want to argue. I get a boatload of Bible every time I visit Nana, and that's more than enough."

"Fine." Disapproval filled his voice, but I ignored him and dried Sema's bowl. How had Nana managed to penetrate his thick skull?

His chair squeaked as he shifted position. "Are you ready for the press conference?"

"Yes. I'm going to walk Sema over in a little while, and I'll tell her what to expect on the way. If I tell her too soon, she'll drive me crazy with questions."

"What if"—I heard reluctance in his voice—"what if she has another of her episodes?"

"If she does, I'll just call a halt to the session and say she hasn't been herself lately. I refuse to give those reporters another chance to humiliate us, and I'm not going to lie for Matthews. If I misinterpret her signs, someone out there will know."

Fielding cleared his throat. "She'll be okay, though—don't you think?"

"She's rested and in a good mood. I think she'll be fine."

I dried my hands on a paper towel, then glanced at my watch. Eight thirty, so Sema and I had a couple of hours to kill before we strolled over to the amphitheater.

"I'm going to let her watch a movie." I tossed the wet towel into the trash can. "Something she likes, maybe a comedy."

Fielding's brow rose. "What's her favorite?"

"*Charlotte's Web*—though lately she's been partial to *Dumbo*. I think she has a soft spot for elephants."

Fielding shifted his long legs, clearing the path to the door. "Enjoy the show."

After ninety minutes of flying elephants and swirling animated colors, I turned off the DVD player and pasted on a bright smile. "Do you remember I promised you a surprise?"

Hurry, hurry surprise.

"All right. Do you feel like a walk outside on this beautiful morning?"

In answer, Sema rushed to the door, then pulled her leash and collar from a hook.

Guilt surged through my veins as I adjusted the collar around her neck. Nature had designed gorillas for life outdoors, and except for the brief walk to the other press conference, Sema hadn't been outside in over two weeks. No wonder she was anxious to feel the sun on her face!

Hurry hurry visit outside.

I laughed and slipped the loop of the leash around my wrist. "Let's go, then. We're going to do something fun this morning, but first we have to go read in another room. I'll bring some of your favorite books, okay?"

I pulled some picture books from her basket, dropped them into a canvas bag, then slung the bag over my shoulder. Sema stood at the door, her right hand on the knob, her left hand signing *hurry hurry hurry*.

"You are a silly girl."

We moved into the hall, where Fielding waited to release the other g's into the habitat. He saluted Sema as we walked past. "Break a leg, kiddo."

Brad stinky nut.

"You got that right, sweetie."

As soon as we moved from the exit and into the sun, Sema straightened and walked bipedally, slipping her hand into mine. The gesture caught me by surprise—as eager as she was, I had expected her to practically pull me down the path. But perhaps this excursion frightened her—after all, the last time she ventured into the depths of the zoo, she'd been drowning.

We strolled beneath the sprawling limbs of a live oak, lacy with golden spring leaves. The asphalt path baked in a golden sunshine that hinted of a warmer afternoon to come.

On Sunday mornings, when the only individuals stirring were khaki-clothed employees and animals, Thousand Oaks seemed a welcoming place. Whenever Sema saw something interesting, she stopped on the path and sank to a squatting position as her hands flew in various questions.

Her curiosity didn't surprise me. Though she had glimpsed all sorts of situations through television and travel in my car, she had never seen so many wheeled refreshment stands, souvenir kiosks, and symbols. A sign stood at each intersection along our path, and cartoon images of animals adorned each wooden marker. Sema wanted to know about every species.

She pointed to a picture of a pink flamingo. *Lipstick bird?*

I laughed. "He is the color of lipstick, isn't he? And he has long legs. He's called—" I hesitated, not knowing the sign for *flamingo*. "Well, we'll find the sign later."

She pointed to a picture of a wombat, one of the most popular animals in the Australian Outback exhibit. *Fur pig?*

"Um, I think that's a . . ." I paused to think of a sign, then combined a *W* with the sign for *pig,* hand beneath the chin with flapping fingers. "Wombat." Any marsupial expert would chastise me for implying that wombats and pigs were related, but Sema had made the connection, not me.

The wind picked up, sending a wave of oak leaves toward us with a sound like scattering seashells. I glanced at the sky, knowing that spring winds often brought sudden showers. A cloud bank had risen behind the crest of the oak behind us, and the air had become thick and damp.

"Come on, sweetie, we need to move on. Remember my surprise? We're almost there."

Glee give toy?

"Not a toy, my girl, something else. I'll explain after we look at a few books."

Obediently, Sema took my outstretched hand. We continued our steady walk along the path that led to the amphitheater where local high-school bands played on Saturday afternoons and the community college chorale sang on summer nights. How many guests would the amphitheater hold, two hundred? Since Matthews had insisted on this location, he must be expecting a crowd.

I looked around. In the distance, a custodian pushed a wheeled garbage can toward one of the brick restrooms while a hungry seagull hovered above the man's head, probably hoping for a scrap. The custodian hadn't noticed us, and I didn't want to attract his attention. Better to get Sema calmly situated backstage before anyone else began to mill about.

Aware of the passing time, I tugged on Sema's arm, urging her forward. She walked slowly, rocking on her hips, her head swiveling to check out sights and sounds she'd never had an opportunity to investigate. A flock of sparrows moved as one over our heads, then looped back to settle on the branches of an oak ahead of us.

"Look there." I pointed toward the birds. "All those little friends have come to say hello."

Without warning, the stillness of the setting shivered into bits, the echoes of a siren scattering the sparrows. Sema's fingers tightened around mine as I looked around. What was this, a fire drill?

I searched the sky and saw no signs of smoke, but the wail continued, lancing the silence, drilling straight into my head. "Come on, Sema." I tugged her toward the amphitheater. "We need to hurry."

She jerked her hand from mine. Amazed at this unexpected display of rebellion, I turned, a rebuke on my tongue, and saw the white tiger crouching beside an overturned garbage can no more than twenty feet away. The cat lay flat against the asphalt, his hindquarters twitching, his golden eyes focused on us. Sema uttered no sound at all, but the rank odor of fear rose from her glands and invaded my nostrils.

What should we do? Some rational part of my brain, the small portion not occupied with immediate panic, told me to face the creature and wave my arms in an effort to make myself look bigger and more intimidating, but who could listen to reason when faced with a man-eater? Instinct screamed *run!*, but I couldn't run. I had to think of Sema, whose African cousins occasionally faced leopards. According to gorilla researchers, *sometimes* the gorilla won the encounter—

But tigers were four times heavier and stronger than leopards, and Sema had not been reared in the wild. Neither did she like cats, not even Nana's tabby.

"Sema." I struggled to push words past the lump of ice in my throat. "Sweetie, don't move."

The wind pushed at my hair, bringing with it the sound of cars on the highway. Hard to believe civilization and salvation lay a few feet away and we were standing in one of the nation's most cosmopolitan areas—

The tiger's whiskers quivered with the ghost of a growl. The low sound scraped across my nerves, but as long as he didn't charge, we might be able to escape.

I glanced toward the restroom, where the custodian had disappeared. If I screamed, he would come running. He carried a radio; all the maintenance crew did, and he would call for help. In the worst-case scenario, I might have to wrestle with the tiger, but if I screamed loud enough, the animal might run away.

"Sema," I strengthened my voice and slipped the loop of her leash from my wrist, "see the big tree ahead of us? I want you to run to the tree. Run as fast as you can, okay? Climb up in the tree and don't come down until you see Brad."

I wasn't sure she understood until she released my hand. I looked down, grateful that my words had taken hold, but Sema only lifted her arms and pulled the bent fingers of both hands across her face. In a barely comprehendible flash, I realized she was signing *tiger*. But this wasn't the cuddly tiger of her Winnie the Pooh book; this one could kill us.

I ignored her sign. "Ready to run, Sema? Okay—*go!*"

The tiger charged at the sound of my shout. I pushed at Sema's shoulder, thinking she would run to the tree while I waved my arms and drew the cat's attention, but Sema, my brave girl, ran straight toward the beast.

I froze as terror lodged in my throat, making it impossible to utter another cry. The heavy air filled with the shrill sounds of screams and snarls as the tiger took Sema down. My sweet girl exhibited traits I'd never seen in her, flashing her canines as she roared. The powerful stink of fear blew over me as the two combatants rolled on the thin grass, teeth flashing, claws ripping, blood flowing.

The world had shrunk to a black-and-white blur when I heard sharp sounds, one shot followed by another. The tiger roared again, then collapsed. Sema rose unsteadily to a standing position, looked at me, then folded gently at the knees and toppled backward.

Both animals lay on the grass beside the path. The tiger's side rose and fell in one last shudder. Sema lay flat, her eyes wide, her gaze focused on the spreading limbs of the treetop canopy overhead.

"Sema!" I sank to the ground and frantically ran my hands over her torso. Had she been shot, too? My palm came away wet and red when I brushed her chest; spurts of blood pumped from a gash on her neck. She might have wounds on her back as well, but I didn't want to move her until help arrived.

"Help!" I couldn't seem to draw in enough air to push a shout out of my throat. "Could someone please help me?"

From somewhere to my right a pair of men ran forward, but I dared not take my eyes off Sema for more than an instant. Her hands rose as though she wanted to say something, but I shook my head.

"Be still, Sema, until help comes. Someone will be

here in a minute. You know how I've always taught you to be patient?" My voice cracked. "You need to be patient now."

Love shone in her eyes as her face settled into lines of contentment. Such emotions are difficult for humans to falsify; I now believe it is impossible for animals to lie about love.

Her hands rose again. *Sema go.*

"Sure, sweetie, we're going home in a few days. We'll be back in the trailer before you know it, and I'm going to take care of you until you feel better. We'll be able to read and play and watch movies—"

Shiny man say . . . her hands faltered . . . *Sema go now.*

"No, Sema, not now. Don't do this. You don't have to go anywhere. You stay with me. Stay here, so I can take care of you. Don't you even think about leaving, girlie, because Brad's going to help me take care of you, and I know you like Brad. Together we're going to make sure nothing like this ever happens again—"

Sema happy. Sema love.

Her head rolled to one side as the silvery spark of recognition slipped from her eyes. Emptiness rushed in to fill her face, and I didn't need a doctor to tell me her heart had stopped.

Swallowing the sob that rose in my throat, I pulled her closer, pillowing her head in my lap. In that moment I understood the mystifying behavior of elephants and gorillas that lose loved ones—I wanted to pound on her chest, slap the dullness from her eyes, do anything I could to catch the spirit of life and force it back into her body.

But it had gone. I sat on the grass, numb to everything, as color ran out of the world and the clouds began to weep.

40

In his book *The Year of the Gorilla*, George Schaller warned that scientists frown on the tendency to interpret the actions of animals in anthropomorphic terms, or to read human feelings into the behavior of creatures. "But animals frequently do resemble man in their emotional and instinctive behavior," he wrote, "although, unlike man, they are perhaps not consciously aware of their own thought processes."

My gorilla language project ended with Sema's death four months ago, but I am now convinced she knew exactly what she was doing when she communicated in sign language, when she challenged the tiger, and even when she talked to visitors I could not see.

At the beginning of this record, I predicted that my conclusions would not be widely accepted in the scientific community. Yet approval from my peers doesn't matter so much to me now—I know what I know.

In the days immediately following Sema's death, however, I didn't know what to think or believe.

Instead of attending Matthews's press conference that Sunday morning, I submitted my resignation to Thousand Oaks and went home to change out of my bloody uniform. When I couldn't bear the sight of Sema's trailer and play yard, I called to reserve a room at Posey's Pink Palace.

Nana met me at the reception desk and opened her arms. I melted into them and wept as she walked me to a guest room.

"I wanted to take care of her body," I managed to whisper as she led me down the hall.

"Why didn't you?"

"Because she belongs to the zoo . . . and they have an arrangement with a crematory."

"You can do something later, then. We'll talk about it tomorrow."

We didn't discuss Sema, though, until nearly a week had passed. I spent the intervening days staring out the window or watching mindless television. I wept through idiotic comedies and snickered at weepy chick flicks. After tasting genuine grief, make-believe emotion seemed . . . tawdry.

When I wasn't weeping or watching TV, I sat in the streaming shower and wondered how to live without my girl. My life had lost its focus; my goals had evaporated in an instant. I couldn't bear to think of beginning again with another gorilla; the thought of reentering the Thousand Oaks gorilla pavilion made me physically ill.

In my periods of reflection, my thoughts drifted to odd moments and snatches of conversations past. I remembered Nana smiling as she said, "How like God to use the things we hold dearest as instruments to teach us" and Sema insisting that the shiny man had said the Word made the world.

Later, the shiny man had told her it was time to go.

As I sat on the beach and pondered these things, comprehension seeped through my sorrow. Sema had told me about the shiny man only minutes after she gave her life to save mine . . . and in that brief interval she did not act out of delusion or dementia. The same love and reason that propelled her to sacrifice herself also fueled her desire to tell me about her supernatural visitor.

Sema happy. Sema love.

She was . . . both.

Sema had been either solidly irrational or solidly sound in her last days and I, who knew her like no one else, had to admit that what had seemed impossible wasn't impossible at all. Like any child, she could tease and dodge responsibility, but when it came to things that mattered, Sema had always been honest with me.

I dredged this admission from a place beyond logic and reason, then held it up to the light and found it flawless.

On Saturday afternoon I left my room and walked toward the Gulf, stopping a few feet from the line where the breaking waves purled on the sand. At the edge of the horizon, the sun leaned toward Texas, bidding Florida farewell in a splash of reds and golds.

I sat on the beach and felt dampness seep through my jeans and chill my skin. Gooseflesh pebbled my arms, but I didn't care. For the first time in my life, I wanted to look at a sunset through the eyes of someone who believed in a power far beyond science.

A wry smile twisted my mouth as I gloried in the colorful display. Until a few days ago, my focus had been on trying to bridge the gap between humans and animals. How ironic that an animal could be used to bridge the gap between me and God.

Sometimes, I think, when our minds have been hardened with misconceptions, God has to impress his lessons on our hearts.

"I thought you might need this." Nana dropped a soft green afghan around my shoulders, then crossed her legs and sank to the sand beside me.

Fresh tears sprang to my eyes when she slipped her arm around my shoulders.

"It's okay to cry," Nana said, misunderstanding the source of my tears. "Pain assures us our hearts are sensitive."

"I never realized," I hiccuped a sob, "that God cared so much about beauty."

A tiny flicker of surprise widened her eyes; then joy, swiftly tempered, curved the corners of her mouth. "Of course he does. Why else would he make so many splendid creatures?"

"Look at that." I gestured toward the water. "The sun sets every day, 365 days a year. Scientifically a sunset is no big deal. But each one is different; each is gorgeous. Why does he do that?"

Nana studied the horizon, her features suffused with joy. "Perhaps it's because he's a God who longs to communicate with his creation. He splashes the sky with

388

different colors every night because he wants us to look up and ask, 'Who did that?' He has yearned for you to know him, Glee, since before you were born."

I lifted the corner of the afghan and swiped wetness from my cheeks. "I believe, Nana."

She nodded. "I know."

"Because of Sema. The things she said."

"I thought as much."

We fell silent as a pair of tourists, pale skinned and straw hatted, walked behind us on the beach. When they had passed, Nana squeezed my arm. "I've always had a feeling the Spirit of God would use Sema to draw you to the truth. Your love for animals is a gift from him, and all his gifts have a purpose."

I looked away and focused my attention on a ship moving along the horizon. "All of them?"

"Of course. People find it easy enough to blame God when things go bad. Why is it hard to give him credit for his gifts and the beauty of his creation?"

"I suppose I took the earth for granted." I struggled to keep my voice steady. "I wanted to believe you, Nana, but I couldn't understand why he allowed so many terrible things. I still don't understand."

Her brow wrinkled as something moved in her eyes. "The truth, Glee, is that God is the sovereign master of the created universe. Everything—good, bad, even indifferent—happens according to his will. If I didn't believe that, I'd have given up long ago."

I hugged my knees, then pillowed my chin on my folded arms. "When Mom and Dad died, you had your religion to comfort you. I had nothing but questions."

"Don't you think I had questions, too?"

She nodded when I lifted a brow.

"Oh, yes, I had lots of questions. I lost the best daughter a woman could ever want and a son-in-law I loved dearly. I wept for them, and I wept for you and Rob. Yes, I had God, but I had questions too."

She turned her face to the sea, where the setting sun gilded her perfect profile. "But God was big enough to handle my questions and my doubts. Yes, the loss hurt, but Jesus knows about pain. God knows about loss—he created this perfect world for us to enjoy and filled it with nourishing plants, amazing animals, and innocent humans. Adam and Eve walked with God and talked with God . . . I think they laughed with him, too. Then Adam ruined everything by choosing to follow his own inclination rather than obeying the Creator's law. His action spoiled the Garden of God and resulted in a curse on the earth, but God promised he would redeem his captive children . . . and his creation. He did that by sending his Son, a second Adam, who passed the tests of temptation and endured the penalty for our disobedience."

I raked my hands through my hair. "I still don't think God's fair."

"Well, of course he's not." Laughter lined her voice. "If God were fair, none of us would have any hope at all. We don't deserve his notice; we don't deserve his mercy. They are gifts."

"But what about Sema? She was so special, so unique

and innocent. Why would God let her die?"

"I can't presume to understand all God's intentions; he's far bigger than I." Her smile softened. "But perhaps he accepted her life because he knew her willing sacrifice would touch the deepest part of your heart. She did what no one else could . . . because you haven't let anyone else get close to you in a long, long time."

I had worried about Sema's lack of freedom . . . while stubborn blindness held me captive.

As the truth of Nana's words turned and twisted inside me, I caught a glimpse of her own pain. How many times had she gently talked to me about God, left Christian music playing on the radio, and tantalized my senses with delicious breakfasts in the hope I'd get out of bed and join her at church? She had yearned to draw me to God, and in the end, she had prayed that Sema could do what she could not.

I dropped my head onto her shoulder. "Thank you, Nana."

"Whatever for?"

"For never giving up."

She didn't answer but patted my arm. Insects whirred in the tall grasses behind us while the wind whispered of the coming night.

"Do you think," I asked, "I'll see Sema in heaven?"

She laughed with the sound of tears in her voice. "Have a little faith, sweetheart." She patted my shoulder again. "The Lord has promised that heaven will be a place of joy and perfection. Why would he withhold something from you if it will bring you joy and reflect his glory? He wants your joy to be full."

"Why would he," I sputtered, lifting my head, "after all the grief I've given him?"

"I think the Lord has a special love for hard cases." A smile trembled over her lips. "He loved the prodigal; he loved the wandering lamb; he even loves—what did Sema call you?—*stinky nuts*."

At the sound of pebbly tire noises from the parking lot, Nana excused herself and went inside.

For a long while I sat on the beach watching the sun dip below the horizon. Fielding's voice finally broke the silence. "I thought I'd find you here."

I looked up, surprised to see him . . . and glad he'd come. "Did Nana invite you for dinner?"

He squatted on the sand next to me. "I didn't come for dinner. I came to give you this." He pulled a folded sheet of paper from his shirt pocket and handed it to me. For a moment I assumed he was delivering my final paycheck; then I recognized the paper.

My resignation.

"I didn't hand it in, Glee. I told Matthews you were taking some vacation time."

I snorted softly. "Bet he was relieved to hear that."

"I also told him you were the foremost gorilla expert in Florida and he'd be a fool to let you get away. So he's offering you a raise . . . and the opportunity to teach sign language to Jamila. You'll have to work with her at the pavilion until she's weaned, but after that, he's already agreed you can take her to your place."

Surprise siphoned the blood from my head, leaving

me dizzy. "Would you mind repeating that? I don't think you said what I heard you say—"

"You heard me . . . and I meant every word."

"Hang on a minute, will you? I need to think."

I closed my eyes to digest this latest bit of surprising news. Matthews would allow me to take Jamila away from the zoo? The man must be worried that I was planning a lawsuit. Otherwise he'd never allow me to take a thriving infant away from her natal group.

But how could I take Jamila away from her mother? More than most people, I knew how strongly the g's bonded to one another. Sema had adored every member of her gorilla family, so to take Jamila away from Dakarai and Kamili and Rafiki would be nothing short of cruel.

"I have a better idea." I opened my eyes and met Brad's gaze. "Why don't I investigate an entirely new area? Yes, I'd love to work with Jamila, but I want to keep her in the group. Let me work with her a few hours a day; let me document how much cultural transference occurs when she tries to speak to the others in sign. I'll set up procedures so you and Claire can use a few basic signs for all the g's . . . ." I grinned as my thoughts raced. "The other day I read about work being done at the Louisville Zoo. They call it *targeting,* and they've been able to teach even the older gorillas how to respond to given words. 'Show me your arm,' they'll say, and the animals respond by holding out an arm. The practice helps tremendously with vet care."

Brad laughed. "Whatever you say, Glee. I'd love to

teach Dakarai how to brush his teeth."

I made a face. "That'll be the day."

"Oh—before I forget, there's this." He fished another slip of paper from his pocket.

I found myself staring at a picture of a padded executive chair. "What in the world?"

"I promised I'd get you a decent chair—this one came in last week. Apparently the requisition got held up in Matthews's office, but it's all settled now. The chair is in front of your desk. All it needs is you."

I bit my lip. "Fielding?"

"Yeah?"

"Do you need me, too?"

He caught my chin and turned my face to meet his. "I can't imagine the pavilion without you, Glee Granger. But the decision has to be yours."

He pressed a kiss to my forehead, then stood and gestured toward the motel. "I'm going up to give Mr. Mugs and Charlie a hard time. You think about Matthews's offer and let me know. I'll wait for your answer."

He walked away. I sat on the sand, blank, amazed, and shaken, as the stars seeped through the dusky satin of the sky. When the sun came around again, I would enjoy the gift of a new day. I would also begin a new life . . . and perhaps I could salvage elements of my old one. I had, after all, a few friendships worth saving, and I knew more than any woman ought to know about gorillas.

I huddled in Nana's afghan, relishing its warmth as the air chilled and the breeze quickened. Why not go back to Thousand Oaks and enjoy being a gorilla girl? Apparently Sema's death had shaken Matthews, too. If he would guarantee that I could decide what was best for Jamila throughout her lifetime, we might be able to work together.

Fielding would support me. So would Claire.

Kamili knew and trusted me. She would allow me to teach her infant daughter. And while I worked through the two years before Jamila's weaning, I would be able to develop my friendships with the pavilion's primate population—Dakarai, Mosi, Aisha, Rafiki, and Kamili would miss me if I stayed away too long.

And Jamila, being female, would be disposed to communicate. I could begin teaching her almost immediately. We already had a room stocked with picture books and educational toys.

First, I'd teach her the sign for *more. Do you want more oatmeal? Ask for* more. *Do you want more juice? Sign* more. *Yes, the watermelon is delicious. And you can have* more *if you ask with the sign.*

In time I'd teach Jamila the sign for *God;* over the years I'd pay special attention to how she used it.

I would definitely not teach her *stinky nut* . . . unless, of course, she wanted to use it to describe Fielding.

I pressed my hands to my cheeks and realized I was crying only when my fingertips encountered wetness. "Oh, Sema," I whispered, "thank you."

After pushing myself off the sand, I wrapped the afghan more closely about my shoulders and walked toward the light shining from Nana's French doors.

Acknowledgments

I would be remiss if I did not thank the novelists collectively known as ChiLibris for allowing me to pester them with assorted questions as I percolated a few ideas. Randy Alcorn, as a theologian, and James Scott Bell, as a lawyer, received more than their fair share of pestering and answered my questions with patience and wisdom. Gentlemen, I am grateful.

Thanks also go to Susan, Celene, Heidi, Diana, Deb, and Theressa for reading a rough draft.

The true story of Tina the elephant's death came not from a *Natural Wildlife* video but from *Elephant Memories*, by Cynthia Moss.

The story of Jabari the gorilla is true, but the timeline was adjusted to fit this story. The real Jabari escaped from the Dallas Zoo in March 2004. He attacked three people before being shot and killed by police. As of this writing, no one knows how he escaped.

For more information on Koko, the *real* talking gorilla, visit www.gorilla.org. Dr. Penny Patterson and her associates with the Gorilla Foundation are currently raising funds for a gorilla preserve in Maui, Hawaii.

Another wonderful Web site is www.gorilla-haven.org. The authors of this site have kept up with nearly every gorilla in captivity, and their reports make fascinating reading. Finally, www.howletts.net features live Web cams trained on their gorillas—wonderful to watch!

And—while all the references cited below provided information, inspiration, or food for thought, their presence in this list does not imply my unequivocal endorsement. If you are interested in the issues raised in this novel, however, you may find them interesting reading.

A Conversation with Koko, Video Nature Library, Visty/Brennan Productions and Thirteen/WNET, 1999.

Randy Alcorn, *Heaven*. Wheaton, IL: Tyndale House, 2004. (Highly recommended!)

Allen and Linda Anderson, *God's Messengers*. Novato, CA: New World Library, 2003.

Benjamin Beck, Tara S. Stoinski, Michael Hutchins, Terry L. Maple, Bryan Norton, Andrew Rowan, Elizabeth Stevens, and Arnold Arluke, eds., *Great Apes and Humans: The Ethics of Coexistence*. Washington, DC: Smithsonian Institution Press, 2001.

Sharon Begley, "Cultures of Animals May Provide Insights into Human Behavior," *The Wall Street Journal*, May 7, 2004, B1.

Dian Fossey, *Gorillas in the Mist*. Boston: Houghton Mifflin Company, 1983.

Tim Friend, *Animal Talk*. New York: Free Press, 2004.

Gorilla, National Geographic Video, 1981, National Geographic Society.

Gary Kowalski, *The Souls of Animals*. Walpole, NH: Stillpoint Publishing, 1991.

Bill Marvel, "Jabari Was Enigma, Much Like His Escape," *The Dallas Morning News*, April 6, 2004, online edition.

Sy Montgomery, *Walking with the Great Apes*. New York: Houghton Mifflin Company, 1991.

Cynthia Moss, *Elephant Memories*. Chicago: University of Chicago Press, 2000.

John Piper, *The Pleasures of God*. Portland, OR: Multnomah, 1991.

Dawn Prince-Hughes, *Gorillas Among Us: A Primate Ethnographer's Book of Days*. Tucson: The University of Arizona Press, 2001.

George B. Schaller, *Gorilla: Struggle for Survival in the Virungas*. New York: Aperture Foundation, 1989.

George B. Schaller, *The Year of the Gorilla*. New York: Ballantine Books, 1964.

Barbet Schroeder, producer, *Koko: A Talking Gorilla*, Home Vision Entertainment, 1977.

Matthew Scully, *Dominion: The Power of Man, the Suffering of Animals, and the Call to Mercy*. New York: St. Martins Griffin, 2002.

Niki Behrikis Shanahan, *There Is Eternal Life for Animals*. Tyngsborough, MA: Pete Publishing, 2002.

Kelly Stewart, *Gorillas: National History and Conservation*. Stillwater, MN: Voyageur Press, 2003.

Center Point Publishing
600 Brooks Road ● PO Box 1
Thorndike ME 04986-0001 USA

(207) 568-3717

US & Canada:
1 800 929-9108